1. 75

Toby had seen Sarah offer a consoling hand to the *kinder*, but he hadn't expected her to treat him with the same familiarity.

"I know how difficult that is," she said.

Did she? Or, he wondered, was she referring to what made her eyes dim? He was curious what it was Sarah wanted to do when she seemed so content living in the new Amish community. The longing for roots among Plain folk gripped him, but he pushed it aside.

"You're like the *kinder*. If there's something you don't want to do, you need a goal to convince yourself to do it."

"What is this goal you've got in mind?"

"If the *doktor*'s opinion says your ankle can handle the exertion, I'll ask Mr. Summerhays to arrange for you to spend a day at his stables in Saratoga." She grinned. "Enough of a challenge for you, cowboy?"

His efforts to keep a wall between them had been futile. She was able to see within him to know what he'd prize.

He was getting in too deep with her but, for once, he didn't retreat. He was le   n as he healed, so why not enjoy a chal   smile—until then?

D0554962

Jo Ann Brown has always loved stories with happily-ever-after endings. A former military officer, she is thrilled to have the chance to write stories about people falling in love. She is also a photographer and travels with her husband of more than thirty years to places where she can snap pictures. They have three children and live in Florida. Drop her a note at joannbrownbooks.com.

Carrie Lighte lives in Massachusetts next door to a Mennonite farming family, and she frequently spots deer, foxes, fisher cats, coyotes and turkeys in her backyard. Having enjoyed traveling to several Amish communities in the eastern United States, she looks forward to visiting settlements in the western states and in Canada. When she's not reading, writing or researching, Carrie likes to hike, kayak, bake and play word games.

JO ANN BROWN

The Amish Christmas Cowboy

&

CARRIE LIGHTE

An Amish Holiday Wedding

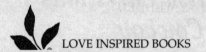 LOVE INSPIRED BOOKS

Recycling programs for this product may not exist in your area.

ISBN-13: 978-1-335-22979-3

The Amish Christmas Cowboy and An Amish Holiday Wedding

Copyright © 2019 by Harlequin Books S.A.

The Amish Christmas Cowboy
First published in 2018. This edition published in 2019.
Copyright © 2018 by Jo Ann Ferguson

An Amish Holiday Wedding
First published in 2018. This edition published in 2019.
Copyright © 2018 by Carrie Lighte

www.Harlequin.com

Printed in U.S.A.

CONTENTS

THE AMISH CHRISTMAS COWBOY

Jo Ann Brown

For Melissa Endlich.
Thank you for making me feel so welcome
in the Love Inspired family.

And the multitude of them that believed were of one heart and of one soul: neither said any of them that ought of the things which he possessed was his own; but they had all things common.
—*Acts* 4:32

Chapter One

Harmony Creek Hollow, New York

"Guess what, Sarah?"

The last thing Sarah Kuhns wanted to do was play a guessing game with Natalie Summerhays, the oldest of the four *kinder* in the house where Sarah worked as the nanny. At ten, Natalie was poised partway between being a *kind* and standing on the precipice of becoming a teenager.

"What?" Sarah asked as she wondered why anyone with small *kinder* would build a house with columns within a youngster's reach from the bannister on the staircase curving above the elegant entry's marble floors. She'd talked four-year-old Mia into letting Sarah pluck her off one fluted column. Ethan, who at five years old considered himself invulnerable, wasn't willing to give up his attempt to touch the ceiling twenty feet above the floor.

God, grant me patience, she prayed as she did often while watching the Summerhays *kinder*. *Please let this be the last time I have to save these little ones from their antics. At least for today...*

Motioning with her hands, she called to Ethan again, *"Komm, kind."*

His head jerked around, and he grinned as the *kinder* often did when she spoke to them in *Deitsch*. For some reason, they found the words she used at home funny. She had no idea why.

Ethan's blond hair fell into his blue eyes, and he reached to push it aside. With a yelp, he began to slide down the column.

Sarah leaned over the bannister, praying it wouldn't collapse or her glasses wouldn't slip off and crash to the floor. She caught the little boy's shirt as he dropped past her. He shrieked, and she wrapped her fingers in the fabric. With a big jerk that resonated through her shoulders, she flipped him across the rail and into her arms. The motion knocked her from her feet, and she sat hard on a step.

Her heart hammered against her ribs as she held the little boy close. He shook, and she cuddled him to her. Maybe he understood how he could have been hurt.

Then she realized he was laughing! He thought the whole thing had been fun. When he squirmed to get out of her hold, she tightened it.

She felt sorry for the four *kinder* who always were looking for ways to be noticed. Their parents were busy—Mr. Summerhays with his businesses and his racehorses and Mrs. Summerhays redoing her wardrobe and the house every two to three months—and they paid little attention to their kids. Even when one or more acted outrageously, the mischief seldom registered with their busy parents.

Carrying Ethan down the stairs while leading Mia by

the hand, Sarah said, "You told me you wouldn't climb the columns again."

"We didn't climb them," Mia said with the aplomb of a four-year-old attorney arguing a legal loophole in a courtroom. "We got on them up there."

Sarah resisted rolling her eyes as she put Ethan on his feet. The youngsters nitpicked everything. In the nine months since she'd taken the job as nanny, she'd learned to be specific when setting parameters for them. Apparently, she hadn't been specific enough.

How her friends in the Harmony Creek Spinsters' Club would laugh when she told them about this! They were getting together that evening to attend the second annual Berry-fest Dinner to benefit the local volunteer fire department. She wondered if her friends had guessed that she told them less than a quarter of the "adventures" her charges got into each day. She tried to head the *kinder* off before they were hurt, but didn't want to hover over them. Being overprotective wasn't *gut* for anyone. She knew that too well.

"Sarah!" Natalie stamped her foot. "Did you hear me?"

"Just a minute." Frowning at the younger *kinder*, she ordered, "No more getting on the columns anywhere."

"From floor to ceiling?" asked Ethan.

"And everywhere in between. No getting on the columns. Understood?"

Ethan and Mia glanced at each other, then nodded.

"Sarah!" Natalie crossed her arms over her bright red T-shirt. "Sarah, are you listening?"

Watching the two little ones skipping across the fancy rug that cost more than the farm where she lived with her two brothers, Sarah sighed. She faced the impatient ten-year-old who'd inherited her *mamm's* glistening black hair and gray eyes. Someday, Natalie would be a beauty like her *mamm*, but with her lips compressed, she looked like the *kind* she was.

"I'm listening." Sarah smoothed her black apron that had gotten bunched against her dark green dress when she'd kept Ethan from falling. For a moment, she wondered what Alexander, the fourth Summerhays youngster, was up to. She would check once she listened to Natalie. Checking her *kapp* was in place, she asked, "What's up, Natalie?"

"Did someone order a cowboy?"

Stunned, she stared at the girl. "Why would you ask me that?"

"Because there are cowboys on the porch."

She struggled not to frown. The *kinder* had played plenty of pranks on her when she first began working for Mr. and Mrs. Summerhays. Childish practical jokes like a whoopee cushion beneath her and spiders in her glass. She'd laughed along with them, until they'd stopped. Or she'd thought they had.

When she'd been offered the job, she'd seen it as a gift from God. It provided her with an open window into *Englisch* lives, allowing her to learn what she'd need to know if she decided to move away from the Harmony Creek settlement. Her stomach clenched. She didn't want to leave her brothers or the *wunderbaar* friends she'd made since they moved to northern New York last year, but being baptized meant surrendering her dream of helping others.

That dream had been born the day she went to visit her *daed* in the hospital after a serious barn accident. He'd lost his right arm, and she guessed he might have given up if it hadn't been for the nurses and physical therapists who'd believed in him. Watching them, she'd decided she wanted to learn to do such work, but that would be impossible if she became a full member of the Amish church. However, a job like a volunteer EMT might be allowed.

"Natalie," she began.

"There are cowboys out there!" insisted the girl. "If you don't believe me, look for yourself."

Sarah took a quick glance at the top of the wide door to make sure someone hadn't rigged a bucket of water on it. The fancy door was hinged in the middle, and she kept a close eye on the other side…just in case. The August heat battered her like an open oven door.

"See?" demanded Natalie.

Lowering her gaze from the door's top, Sarah gasped when she saw who stood on the wide porch.

A cowboy!

A real live cowboy!

She stared in disbelief at his wide-brimmed straw hat that looked as if it'd been plucked out of one of her brother Menno's Zane Grey novels. Though the day was warm, he wore a long-sleeved light green shirt and denims. His black Western boots had scuffed toes. Sun-streaked brown hair fell forward into the bluest eyes she'd ever seen, bluer than a cloudless summer sky.

"Ma'am, is this Ian Summerhays's place?" asked another cowboy, who tipped his black hat as he came up the steps. He was older, old enough to be her *daed*, and his slow drawl came, she guessed, right out of the heart of Texas.

"*Ja*… Yes, it is." She couldn't pull her gaze from the younger man, who gaped at her in outright astonishment.

Hadn't he seen a plain woman before? If he hadn't, he should still have known it wasn't polite to stare.

Then, realizing she was doing the same, she cut her eyes to the older man and asked, "Are you looking for Mr. Summerhays?"

"Is he around?"

"He's in his office." She didn't add how rare that was. He spent most days at the stables in Saratoga, about an hour's drive south.

"Can you let him know we've got a delivery for him?" The older man gestured toward a large truck with a massive horse trailer behind it.

South Texas Stables was written on the side of the trailer in fading red letters. Through the narrow windows, motions revealed animals were inside. She was relieved to hear the sound of an air-conditioning unit coming on, knowing the animals would be more comfortable than she was in her bed on a hot summer night when the air was still.

"Of course." She turned to Natalie. "Please go and let your *daed* know there's a delivery."

The little girl glanced at the men on the porch and, for a moment, Sarah thought she would protest.

Natalie grinned. "I told you there were cowboys out here."

"You did." Bending, Sarah said, "Mrs. Beebe said she was going to have a treat for you this afternoon." The cook knew the youngsters were always ready for a snack. "You can check with her if it's ready after you let your *daed* know someone wants to talk with him."

"Okay, I get it. You want to talk to the cowboy by yourself. Don't let him sweep you onto his horse and ride off with you into the sunset." She giggled before running inside.

Sarah hoped neither man had heard the girl. Those

hopes were dashed when she aimed a furtive look in the younger man's direction and saw his frown. His light brown brows were lowered like storm clouds over his bright blue eyes. Intense emotion filled them, but she didn't know why he was distressed.

After Natalie had rushed away to her *daed's* office in the left wing of the house, Sarah looked at the men, unsure what to say next. She wished Mrs. Summerhays were there, but the *kinder's mamm* was in Europe, buying items in antiques shops in Paris and Rome and Vienna to create her new vision for the house. Should Sarah ask the two men in? No, three men. Another guy with a cowboy hat walked around the trailer. Leaning against it, the dark-haired man lit a cigarette, startling her. Mr. Summerhays didn't like anyone smoking near the house or stables.

Her face must have revealed that, because the older man snapped an order at the third cowboy. With a grimace, he dropped the cigarette and ground it out with the toe of his boot.

"Sorry, ma'am," said the older man. "Ned forgets his manners sometimes." He aimed a frown at the man by the trailer.

Wanting to put an end to the uncomfortable conversation, Sarah asked, "Was Mr. Summerhays expecting you?"

"We're a day early, but I warned him we might be. By the way, I'm J.J. Rafferty, and that talkative guy there—" he pointed at the younger man who hadn't said a word "—is Toby Christner. Toby, show the lady that you can talk."

"Nice to meet you," the handsome cowboy said. His baritone voice would have been pleasant on the ear if he'd put inflection in it.

"I'm Sarah Kuhns," she answered.

J.J. nodded toward her, then looked past her.

Sarah turned to see Natalie standing behind her. "Did you talk to your *daed*?"

The girl nodded. "He'll be out in a few minutes. He's finishing a call."

"We'll catch up on a few things," J.J. said, "while we're waiting." He walked toward the truck, motioning for Ned to follow him.

The dark-haired man winked at her before going with J.J.

Toby remained where he was. So did his frown. What was bothering him? Was he upset Mr. Summerhays hadn't dropped everything to greet them when they arrived? If they'd done business with her boss, they should have known how busy he was. So busy he seldom came home before ten, long after the *kinder* were tucked into bed. He was gone at dawn to the stables in Saratoga or to New York City, where he did something there with the stock market.

Sarah wished she could think of something to say to the tall man who didn't seem in a hurry to join the others. She'd gotten comfortable talking with *Englischers* since she started working as a nanny. Something about the man's posture told her engaging him in small talk would be futile. She was curious how many horses were being delivered to the stables, but held her tongue.

J.J. and Ned returned to the porch after a few minutes. If they'd come to the house she shared with her two brothers deep in the hollow with Harmony Creek at its center, she'd know what to do. She would have brought them into the kitchen and asked them to sit at the table while she served iced tea and chilled pie.

Should she do the same here? She couldn't invite them into the kitchen. Mrs. Summerhays had her guests brought to the room she called the library, though there weren't any books in it. Sarah wished the housekeeper were here, but it was Mrs. Hancock's day off. Mrs. Beebe, the cook, had her hands full with getting meals ready while the kitchen was being renovated…again. It was the third time in two years Mrs. Summerhays had decided it needed a complete updating.

Knowing she must not leave the men standing on the porch in the heat, she said, "Please *komm* inside where you can wait for Mr. Summerhays."

Toby cleared his throat. "I can—"

"Come along, both of you," said J.J. "I don't want to unload the horses until Summerhays checks them to make sure they meet his satisfaction. We had a tough enough time getting the bay into the trailer the first time. He'll be more resolute not to go in again."

"But—"

"No sense standing out in the heat. Any chance you might have something cool to drink, young lady?"

"I'm sure there's something. I can check."

"Much obliged." J.J. motioned for her to go ahead of him, then followed her into the large entry along with Toby and Ned. As J.J. took his hat off, he gave a low whistle. "Mighty fine spread here."

She hadn't heard anyone talk like him before but guessed he was complimenting the house. She had a lot to learn about *Englischers*. Finding out about *Englisch* ways was going to be a bigger task than she'd guessed.

"I'll find out what's on ice in the kitchen." She shouldn't leave them in the entry, but she wasn't sure where to take them. Mrs. Beebe would know what to do, because the cook had been working at the house since the family moved in.

"Whatever you've got will be great," J.J. said.

She smiled in return, then spun and hurried toward the kitchen. She glanced back. Her gaze was caught by the younger man, who regarded her with the same expressionless look.

How odd! At that moment, she would have given a penny to know his thoughts. Maybe even two.

The last person Toby Christner had expected would answer the door was an Amish woman. If someone had warned him ahead of time, he would have thought it was a joke. She wasn't any more out of place in the fancy house than the house itself was among the other simple farms they'd seen along the road toward the Vermont border. Stone pillars by the road were set next to a fancy sign announcing Summerhays Stables, which lay beyond them. The whole setup matched the prestige Ian Summerhays was garnering with his excellent racehorses, including the three his boss had brought from Texas, where Toby had been working with them for a year.

He glanced at the young Amish woman, who was rushing away as if she couldn't wait to be done with them. Not that he blamed her. Ned Branigan hadn't stopped trying to get her attention. Toby wanted to tell his coworker his sly wiles wouldn't work on an Amish woman, but Ned would have ignored him.

Sarah wasn't tall. In fact, when he'd moved closer to her to go inside, she'd taken a step back so she didn't have to tilt her head to look at him. She had bright red hair beneath her *kapp*. Her gold-rimmed glasses hadn't been able to hide the surprise in her mahogany-brown eyes when she'd seen him on the porch.

Toby let his boss and Ned lead the way into the magnificent house. It was grander than the house on J.J.'s spread, and larger than what everyone called the Hacienda. That long, low house didn't have pristine marble floors glistening like mirrors and columns as formal as the ones he'd seen in a casino in Las Vegas when they'd made a delivery out to the desert about six months ago. A staircase curved up to an open gallery on the second story. On either side of the front door, rooms were two steps below the entry's marble floor. Furniture that looked like it belonged in a mansion was arranged in each. None appeared comfortable.

A plain woman didn't fit in this setting. Neither did he.

"How long," J.J. asked, "will it take us to get to our next stop?"

"From what I saw on the map, I'd guess about three hours."

The two of them took turns driving and keeping track of their route, while Ned rode with the horses. Toby had been on map duty today because J.J. didn't trust a GPS to get them where they needed to go. Many of the farms where they delivered horses were far off the beaten path, making map programs useless.

J.J. frowned for only a second because Sarah reappeared. She carried a tray with a pitcher of lemonade and glasses. Behind her, like ribbons on the tail of a kite, were four youngsters. The oldest had been out on the porch, but there was a little girl and two boys, too. The quartet must be siblings, though the younger two were blond while the older ones had black hair. They couldn't be Sarah's because they wore bright colored shirts and sneakers with soles that lit each time they took a step. Yet, it was clear she was in charge of them.

"If you'll follow me…" Sarah motioned with her head toward her left.

"Let me help you with that big load," Ned said, stepping forward with a grin.

"I'm fine. *Danki.*"

"Nonsense. There's no reason for a pretty filly like you to tote such a load." Ned snatched the tray, and lemonade splattered out of the pitcher set in the center.

Dismay skittered across her face, but she turned to the kids, who'd skipped ahead of her into the big room, where they each grabbed a seat, the younger two wanting the same one. She convinced them to share as Ned put the tray on a low table. She turned and bumped into him. Without a word, she edged away.

Toby glanced at J.J. His boss was frowning. Ian Summerhays was an important client, and J.J. wouldn't want Ned's antics to cause problems. The plan when they left the ranch in Texas was for Ned to remain behind for a couple of weeks with the horses delivered to Summerhays. If J.J. changed his mind…

With a frown, Toby walked to a nearby sofa. If J.J. decided he couldn't trust Ned—and he had plenty of reasons not to, assuming half the things Ned bragged about were true—Toby would be stuck at the fancy stables. Not that he wouldn't have liked to spend more time getting the horses he'd worked with acclimated, but he'd hoped to use the time without Ned to ask J.J. about starting a small herd of his own. It would give him deeper roots on the ranch, something he'd never had while living with vagabond parents.

He hoped the rough seams on his denims wouldn't

snag the smooth lustrous material on the couch. He made sure his worn boots weren't anywhere near the expensive upholstery or the wood that looked as if it'd been white-washed. Everything about the house shouted the owners had spent a bundle on it.

They should have worried more about comfort, he thought as he sat. The chairs and sofas seemed too frag-ile and tiny for a full-grown man. His boss looked as if he perched on nursery furniture, because his knees rose to his chest level.

While Sarah served them lemonade, Ned kept trying to catch her eye. She stiffened each time he came close, but kept a smile in place as she told the youngsters they could have lemonade in the breakfast room.

Toby guessed she was their nanny. He thanked her when she handed him a glass that was frosted from the humidity, though the air-conditioning was keeping the house cool.

Ned moved too near to her when she offered him a glass. His broad hand closed over the glass and her hand. Her faint gasp brought Toby to his feet.

J.J. didn't stand as he fired a glance at Toby, a warn-ing to sit. At the same time, his boss asked, "Why don't you drink that while you check on the horses, Ned?"

"I—"

"Never hurts to check again."

Ned gave Sarah a broad smile but aimed a scowl at Toby as he strode out of the room.

J.J. motioned for Toby to remain sitting. Toby wasn't sure why. Did Sarah have any idea that Ned was going to be remaining at the farm while Toby and J.J. left to deliver the rest of the horses?

Wishing he had an excuse to leave the ornate room

where most of the surfaces seemed to be covered with gold leaf, Toby sipped the tart lemonade. Sarah still appeared uncomfortable, he realized, as J.J. smiled at her.

"May I ask you a personal question, young lady?" he asked.

Toby swallowed a silent moan. He recognized that grin. His boss was about to shake up what he considered a dull discussion. When J.J. looked at him, Toby guessed what his boss was about to ask. If he could think of a way—any way—to distract J.J., he would have. Stopping J.J. was about as easy as halting a charging bull with a piece of tissue paper.

"Of course." Sarah squared her shoulders, preparing herself for whatever J.J. had to say.

"Are you Amish?" J.J. asked.

"I am."

He chuckled and hooked a thumb toward Toby. "Like you. How do you say it, Toby? Like you, ain't so?"

"You're Amish?" A flush rushed up her cheeks, and he could tell Sarah wished the question would disappear.

Toby nodded as he waited for her to ask one of the next obvious questions. The ones he was always asked. If he was Amish, why was he traveling with J.J. and Ned delivering horses? Where did he live when he wasn't on the road? Was he related to—or knew—someone connected to her? He hated the questions as much as he hated the answers he'd devised to skirt the truth.

Almost fifteen years ago, when he'd first gone to work for J.J., he'd answered those questions. He'd explained traveling wasn't new to him. It was the life he'd always known. His parents had moved from one Amish settlement to another, seldom staying longer than six months, sometimes less than a week before heading somewhere new. They'd done that for as long as he could remember. He'd learned not to establish close relationships because soon he'd be leaving them behind. How could he have fun flirting with girls when he'd be going soon, breaking her heart as well as his own?

His life had changed after the family had arrived at a settlement in southern Texas. They'd stayed eight months. Toby had found work he loved: training horses at J.J.'s ranch. When his parents left, he'd stayed. The ranch was perfect for him. People and horses came and went. He didn't have to worry about being the only outsider.

When he'd shared honest answers, he'd gotten pity or, worse, someone wanting to help him. To accept assistance would mean obligations he didn't want. He'd created other answers. Not lies, but not the whole truth, either.

"Ja," he said, letting himself slip into *Deitsch* for a moment.

"If you're here on Sunday, you're welcome at our services," she replied in the same language before turning to J.J. and asking in English if he wanted more lemonade.

Toby was taken aback at her lack of curiosity. Why hadn't she posed the questions others had? Was she worried he'd have questions of his own? Was she hiding something like he was?

He'd never know if he left as soon as the horses were unloaded. Guilt clamped a heated claw around his throat. How could he leave her here with someone like Ned, who would see a plain woman as an easy target for his heartless flirtations? Should Toby suggest J.J. take Ned with him and let Toby stay instead?

You've lost your mind! The best thing he could do was get out of there as soon as possible. He needed to avoid the faintest possibility of a connection with Sarah, a lovely woman who intrigued him. Maybe it was too late. His determination to keep Ned from breaking her heart proved that. He didn't want to see her hurt as he'd been many times.

Chapter Two

Sarah had never been so relieved to see her boss as she was when Mr. Summerhays strode into the room. J.J. had been telling an endless tale about people she'd never met in places she'd never heard of. Her polite interruptions to offer lemonade hadn't stymied him. He would reply that he'd like more to drink; then once again, he'd relaunch into his story. He shared a multitude of events that were, in Sarah's opinion, barely related to one another. When he mentioned Toby by name, she was surprised to hear him say he was glad to have Toby with him because they could share the driving on long trips.

She wondered if J.J. found Ned overly pushy, too. Instantly, she was contrite. She shouldn't judge *Englisch* folks and their ways when she was considering becoming one of them.

"Thank you, Sarah," Mr. Summerhays said with his easy smile as he entered the room. To look at him, nobody would think he was a wealthy man. He dressed in beat-up clothes and always appeared to be in desperate need of a haircut. He was the complete opposite of his wife, who never emerged from their room without makeup, a perfect hairdo and clothing that had graced the pages of the fashion magazines she read.

Sarah nodded and rose. Thanking God for putting an end to the stilted conversation that felt as if every word had to be invented before she could speak it, she left the lemonade and extra glasses on the table.

As she reached the door, she spread out her arms to halt Ethan and Mia from racing in and interrupting their *daed*. She quickly realized they didn't want to see him, but the horses Natalie had told them were in the trailer.

Sarah's heart grew heavy at the thought that the *kinder* weren't interested in spending time with their *daed*, though they hadn't seen him for a week. How she wished she could have another few moments with her *daed*! He'd died before she and her two older brothers had moved to the Harmony Creek settlement. Unlike Menno and Benjamin, *Daed* had listened to her dreams of finding a way to help others. Her brothers dismissed them as silly, but *Daed* never had. When she'd suggested she take EMT training when they became volunteers at the Salem Fire Department, her brothers had reminded her that they were the heads of the household.

And they disapproved of the idea.

As one, they told her she must not mention it again and should focus on more appropriate duties. No Amish woman should be giving medical aid to strangers. It wasn't right.

Neither Benjamin nor Menno was being honest with her. They were worried she'd get hurt if she served as an EMT. Maybe their being overprotective wouldn't have bothered her if Wilbur Eash hadn't been the same. When Wilbur had first paid attention to her at youth group gatherings in Indiana, she'd been flattered such a *gut*-look-

ing and popular guy was interested in her. Before the
first time he took her home in his courting buggy, he'd
started insisting she heed him on matters big and small.
He, like her brothers, seemed to believe she wasn't capable of taking care of herself.

What would *Daed* have said? The same, or would he
have suggested she find out if Menno and Benjamin—
and Wilbur—were right in their assumption that she
needed to be protected from her dreams? *Daed* had always listened to *Mamm's* opinion until her death a few
years before his. Sarah had heard him say many times
Mamm's insight had often made him look at a problem
in another way.

She'd asked her friends if they knew of Amish women
taking EMT training. They hadn't but offered to write to
friends in other settlements. So far, no one had received
answers to their letters.

"We'll go ahead and get those horses unloaded," J.J.
said from the room behind her. "Toby, tell Ned to help
you."

"Can we watch?" Ethan asked as Toby hurried out
the front door.

"We'll be good," his little sister hurried to add.

Sarah didn't answer as she pushed her uneasy thoughts
aside and concentrated on her job. She loved these *kinder*,
but she had no illusions about what rascals they were.
Her predecessors hadn't stayed long, according to Mrs.
Hancock, because they couldn't handle the rambunctious
youngsters. With a laugh, Sarah had replied she'd been
quite the outrageous youngster herself, which, she acknowledged, was one reason her brothers looked askance
at every idea she had. Though she was twenty-seven, they
treated her as if she were as young as Mia. She wished

they'd give her the benefit of the doubt once in a while and realize she was a woman who yearned to help others.

Just as she needed to offer the Summerhays *kinder* a chance to show they could be *gut*. Giving the youngsters a stern look, she said, "I'll agree to take you outside to watch if you promise to stay with me every second, hold my hand and not get in the way. If Mr. Christner says you have to leave, you must."

Though the Amish didn't use titles, even when speaking of bishops and ministers, she wanted to impress on the *kinder* how vital it was to heed Toby's instructions while he put the horses in the paddock. Racehorses were high-strung, and she guessed he and Ned needed to keep their attention on the task.

"Can we come, too?" asked Alexander, who was going to be as tall as his *daed* and maybe broader across the shoulders. He was nine, but the top of his head was two inches higher than Sarah's.

She'd never figured out how these *kinder* learned what was going on when she hadn't seen them nearby. She suspected they put the decorative columns and other architectural elements in the house to *gut* use.

"Ja," she said, looking each youngster in the eyes. "You may come, but Ethan and Mia must hold my hands. Natalie, hold Mia's other one. Alexander, hold Ethan's. If anyone lets go, I'll bring you inside right away, and there'll be no going out until the horses are unloaded. Do you agree?"

The *kinder* shot wary glances at each other. When she repeated her question, they nodded.

Sarah took the younger two by the hands and watched to be certain Natalie and Alexander did as she'd requested. Leading them onto the porch, she paused as

Toby opened the trailer. She breathed a sigh of relief to see Ned sitting in the truck, going through a stack of paperwork. Tossing it aside, he stepped out of the truck and flashed her a wide smile.

She looked away and right at Toby, who stood with one foot on the bumper. Under his straw hat, a faint frown appeared again as his brows drew together. His eyes were concealed by the shadow from the hat's brim.

Realizing she should have spoken to him before she agreed to bring the *kinder* outside, she asked, "Is it a problem if we watch you unload the horses?"

"Not if you stay out of the way," he answered.

"I'll make sure."

His only reply was an arch of one eloquent eyebrow. She'd heard cowboys could be men of few words, but this one took being terse to ridiculous lengths.

Herding the *kinder* to the far side of the pair of linked paddocks in front of the main stable behind the house, she knew they'd have an excellent view of the proceedings. She'd vetoed Ethan's request to stand on a bench because it was too close to the gate. She wanted the youngsters as far as possible from the animals when they emerged from the trailer and had room to show their displeasure at being transported in close quarters. Sarah was grateful the Texans would be on their way soon. She hadn't expected to have a *gut*-looking Amish cowpoke come into her life.

A faint memory stirred, and she remembered a letter she'd read in *The Budget*, the newspaper printed for and written by scribes in plain communities, about new western settlements that had developed ways that differed from other communities. One in eastern Oklahoma had started using tractors in their fields, because a team of mules couldn't break the soil. The tractors had steel wheels with no tires and couldn't be used for anything but fieldwork, but it was a compromise the settlement had to agree upon if they wanted to remain on those farms.

Toby's settlement in Texas must have made similar concessions to the climate and the land. That could explain why he was allowed to drive the big truck, something that wouldn't have been allowed in most settlements.

The *kinder* began to cheer when Ned brought the first horse and Toby went into the paddock. She hushed them as the big black shied when it came off the ramp. She wasn't sure if her warning or Toby's scowl silenced them. Either way, none of the youngsters made a peep as Ned guided the horse into the first paddock, shoved the reins in Toby's hand and, leaving, closed the gate.

Toby began to give the sleek horse a quick examination. "I need to make sure, while the horse was in the trailer, he didn't injure himself without us noticing," he said, answering the question she'd been thinking but hadn't wanted to ask out loud.

She watched how Toby ran his hands along the horse, keeping it from shying away or rearing in fright. He kept his motions to a minimum, and if the horse began to tense, he soothed it with soft words.

Satisfied the horse was fine, Toby led him into the inner paddock and took off the lead rope. The horse galloped, happy to be out of the trailer and able to stretch out his legs.

"Pretty horse," Natalie said in a wistful tone. The girl was as obsessed with horses as her *daed*.

The second horse, also dark in color, took his arrival in stride. He pranced into the paddock, dragging Ned with him, and stood like a statue during the examination. When Toby turned him out in the other paddock, he walked in as if coming home.

"That was easy," Alexander said with a grin. "Too bad they aren't all like that."

Toby nodded but didn't smile in return. Maybe his lips grew a little less taut.

When Alexander looked at her with an expression that asked *What did I do wrong?* she smiled and said, "Mr. Christner needs to concentrate. I'm sure he'll be more ready to talk once he's done."

She *wasn't* sure of that or why she was making excuses, other than she didn't want Alexander to be hurt. The boy nodded, and she turned as the *kinder* did to watch the final horse being taken from the trailer.

Even she, who didn't know much about horses beyond the quiet buggy horse she drove, could tell the bay prancing around Ned was magnificent. Muscles rippled beneath the sheen of his coat, and his black mane and tail floated on the air with each movement.

As soon as the horse was brought into the first paddock, Toby began the same swift examination he'd done with the others. He was squatting, checking the horse's legs, when a gray barn cat flashed through the paddock. The horse started, whinnied, then reared in a panic.

Sarah tightened her grip on the younger *kinder's* hands and called to Natalie and Alexander to back away from the fence. The horrified youngsters froze as the bay's hooves pawed the air as if fighting off a giant invisible rival.

Mia screamed, "Look out, kitty!"

The little girl tore her hand out of Sarah's and lunged

toward the fence. Sarah grabbed Mia by the shoulders, tugging her back as the horse bucked toward them.

"Hold my hand and don't let go," Sarah ordered in not much more than a whisper. She didn't want her voice to upset the horse more, though she doubted it could be heard in the paddock over the thuds from the horse's hooves on the ground. "Nobody move. Nobody say a word."

She stared at the paddock, horrified. Toby tried to calm the horse. He kept the horse from bucking by guiding it away from the fence. The horse jerked forward. He stumbled after it, refusing to let go of the lead. He grimaced and stutter-stepped. Dropping to one knee, he pushed himself up again. Fast.

Not fast enough. The horse was spinning to strike out at him again. It yanked the lead away from him.

Releasing the *kinder's* hands, Sarah pushed aside the gate and ran into the paddock. Toby shouted as the Summerhays kids cried out in fear. Ned called a warning. She ignored them and tried to grab the rope, ducking so it didn't strike her.

She'd handled a frightened animal before. When a new buggy horse had been spooked by a passing truck, she'd known she needed to reassure the horse and show it there was nothing to fear.

Not looking at the horse directly, she kept talking as she evaded its flashing hooves. She was relieved when Toby grabbed the horse's halter. He stroked the shuddering animal but didn't say anything while she continued to murmur. The horse began to grow calmer.

When she thought it was safe, she asked, "Where do you want him?"

"The inner paddock with the others." Toby's voice was clipped.

Was he upset with her for stepping in? No time to ask. She walked the horse to the gate and into the paddock. Unsnapping the lead, she moved slowly to keep from scaring the horse again.

The moment Sarah closed the gate, Alexander called out, "That was cool, Sarah!"

"Quiet. There's no sense upsetting the horses more."

Not waiting to see if the kids would cooperate, she went to where Toby was leaning against a fence post.

"How badly are you hurt?" she asked.

Instead of answering her, he asked, "Is Bay Boy okay?"

"He's shivering," she said, glancing at the other paddock, "but he'll be okay."

"You've got a way with horses."

When she saw how he gritted his teeth on each word, she said, "You are hurt! Where?"

"I twisted my ankle. It'll be okay once I walk it off." He pushed himself away from the rail and took a step to prove it.

With a gasp, he sank to his left knee and grasped his right ankle.

She scanned the yard. Where was Ned? She didn't see him anywhere.

"Alexander," she shouted, "go inside and call 911. Right now!"

"I can call them from here." He pulled a cell phone out of his pocket.

"Quickly!"

Later, she'd remind Alexander he wasn't supposed to have his phone for another week. He'd gotten in trouble while prank calling his friends because he was bored. By mistake, he'd reached the private phone of the police chief in the village of Salem. She wondered how the boy had retrieved his phone. She'd asked Mr. Summerhays to put it in his wall safe. With a grimace, she guessed Alexander had watched his *daed* open it often enough that he'd learned the combination. She'd have to find another way to make him atone for bothering the police chief.

At that thought, she added, "Dial carefully."

He averted his eyes, a sure sign he knew a scolding would be coming his way once Toby was taken care of.

The call was made, and Alexander reported the rescue squad was on its way. He gave her the phone. Dropping it into a pocket under her black apron, she looked at Toby, who was trying not to show his pain.

Just as he hid every other emotion. What was he worried about revealing?

Everything, in Toby's estimation, had gone wrong since J.J. had pulled the truck into the Summerhays' long drive. The moment Toby had gone to the door and found an Amish woman there, he should have known this wasn't going to be like other deliveries they'd made on this trip from Texas. He hadn't guessed he'd be hurt by a horse he'd trained himself. A beginner's mistake. After years of working with horses and convincing them it was better to behave, he should have been prepared for every possible move Bay Boy could have made.

At the worst moment, as the cat decided to chase something right under Bay Boy's nose, Toby had let himself be distracted by Sarah and how the reflected sunlight off her gorgeous red hair seared his eyes. *Dummkopf*, he chided himself. He spent the past dozen years avoiding relationships, romantic or otherwise, and he'd been at Summerhays Stables less than two hours and already was thinking too much about her.

"Ned?" he managed to ask.

Sarah shrugged her slender shoulders. "I don't know where he went. *Komm* with me," she said in a tone that suggested he'd be wasting his time to protest. He guessed she used it often with the Summerhays kids. "You need to get your weight off that ankle before you hurt it worse."

He wasn't sure he could hurt it worse. Each time he took a breath, stabs of pain danced around his ankle, setting every nerve on fire.

"I'm fine right here." The idea of moving was horrifying.

"There's a bench on the other side of the fence. You can sit there until the EMTs arrive."

She didn't give him a chance to protest. Squatting, she moved beneath his right arm, which he draped over her shoulders. The top of her *kapp* just missed his chin. She put her arm around him. With a strength he hadn't expected, she assisted him to his feet. His face must have displayed his surprise.

"I've been wrangling four *kinder*, cowboy," she said in an easy copy of his boss's drawl. "One bumped-up cowboy is easy."

"I'm sure it is." He glanced at where the kids were watching, wide-eyed.

Why hadn't she sent them into the house? He didn't need an audience when he hopped along like a hobbled old man.

Pride is a sin. His *daed's* voice ran through his head. *Daed* had always been skilled at preaching the dangers of *hochmut*. Maybe if he'd been a bit less judgmental, the family could have settled somewhere instead of continuously moving to another district.

Sharp pain coursed up his leg and down to his toes. Had he broken something? He didn't think so. Was it *only* a sprain? Each movement was agonizing.

"It's not far," Sarah said.

To herself or to him? His weight must have been wearing on her slender shoulders, though she didn't make a peep of complaint.

A scent that was sweet and woodsy at the same time drifted from her hair. She was careful to help absorb each motion as she helped him from the paddock and out onto the grass.

"This is far enough," he said, panting as if he'd run across Texas.

"You're right." She hunkered down and let his arm slide off her shoulders.

"I'm sorry if I hurt you."

"I'm okay." She smiled, but her eyes were dim enough to confirm he was right. Her shoulders must be aching.

Toby was grateful when she waved the *kinder* aside and urged them to let him get some air. He thought they'd protest, but they turned as one when the distant sound of a siren resonated off the foothills, rising beyond the stable.

"They're coming!" the older boy—Toby couldn't recall his name through the curtain of pain—shouted.

The siren got louder moments before a square and boxy ambulance appeared around the side of J.J.'s trailer. The kids let out squeals of excitement, but Sarah hushed them. Had she guessed every sound reverberated through his throbbing ankle?

Two men jumped from the ambulance. Each one carried emergency supplies. Shouts came from the direction of the house, and Toby recognized his boss's anxious voice.

What a mess he'd made of this! The boy he'd once been would have offered a prayer to God to bring him fast healing, but he couldn't remember the last time he'd reached out to God. He didn't want to make that connection, either, remembering how his Heavenly Father seemed to stop listening to his prayers when *Daed* had moved them yet again before Toby had even finished unpacking the two boxes he took with him from one place to the next.

"Hi, Sarah!" said a dark-complexioned EMT who wore thick glasses. "What happened here?"

She explained and introduced Toby to the man she called George. The other EMT, a short balding man, was named Derek. They worked on the volunteer fire department with her brothers.

He didn't want to know that. Everything she said, everyone she introduced him to, every moment while depending on someone threatened to make a connection to the farm and the community beyond it. To say that would sound ungrateful. He needed to focus on getting on his feet again so he could help with their next delivery.

As they knelt beside him, the two EMTs began asking him question after question. *Ja*, he replied, his right ankle hurt. No, he hadn't heard a cracking sound when he stepped wrong. *Ja*, he'd stepped on it after feeling the first pain. No, it didn't radiate pain except when he'd hopped to where he sat.

"Let's get a look at it," George said with a practiced smile. "Sorry if this hurts."

That was an understatement. When George shifted Toby's right foot and began to slip off his boot, the world telescoped into a black void of anguish sparked with lightning.

"Stay with us, Toby," crooned Derek as he pushed up Toby's sleeve and grabbed an IV needle and tube. "Slow deep breaths. Draw the air in and hold it and let it out. Nice and slow." He kept repeating the words in a steady rhythm that was impossible not to follow.

The darkness receded, and the sunshine and the smells of animals and dirt rushed to awaken Toby's senses.

"Back with us?" George asked.

"I think so."

"Good. Breathe deeply. It'll keep you from getting light-headed." The EMT stuck the needle into Toby's left arm.

Though Toby didn't wince, he heard the kids groan in horror.

Sarah hushed them but gasped, "Oh, my!" when George rolled down Toby's sock with care.

Her reaction was a warning, but Toby was shocked to see how swollen his ankle was. Twice its usual size, it was turning as purple as an eggplant.

"What's happening here?" called J.J. as he reached the paddock with Mr. Summerhays in tow. Ned trailed after them like a half-forgotten pup. He must have gone inside to alert their boss to what had happened.

"A horse wanted to dance," Toby replied with grim humor, "but he didn't want me to lead."

"Is he hurt bad?" J.J. looked past him to the EMTs.

"We'll know when we get X-rays at the hospital," George said.

"Hospital?" Toby shook his head. "Bind it, and it'll be fine."

"I didn't realize you were a doctor, Mr. Christner."

The kids giggled on cue, and Sarah smiled at the EMT's jest. Yet, in her gaze, he could see her anxiety. He wanted to tell her not to worry about him, though he guessed he'd be wasting his breath. As much as she focused on the *kinder*, she might be the type to fret about every detail of every day.

The last kind of person he needed in his life.

If that was so, why did he keep thinking about how sweet it'd been to lean on her? She'd been strong and soft at the same time, a combination that teased him to learn more about her.

Toby shut his mouth before he could say something. Something that would make him embarrass himself more. He'd thought nothing could be worse than the pain in his ankle, but he'd been wrong. The only way to keep from saying the wrong thing again was to do what he always tried to do: say nothing.

Chapter Three

Hushing the *kinder*, Sarah moved aside to let the EMTs stabilize Toby's ankle. How useless she felt! If she'd had the training she yearned for, she could have helped him instead of having to wait for the rescue squad to arrive.

"Sarah?"

She looked at Mr. Summerhays, who crooked a finger to her. Telling the youngsters not to move or interrupt the EMTs, she went to where her boss stood by the paddock fence.

Without preamble, he said, "I want you to go to the hospital with him."

"Me? But why?" The words were out before she could halt them.

"Someone needs to go." He glanced at J.J.

Sarah understood what her boss didn't say. He wanted to get his business with the Texan taken care of as soon as possible. With the racing season underway at Saratoga, Mr. Summerhays made it a practice never to miss a single race of his horses or horses that might compete with his.

"Ned could go," she said.

"Ned?" When she looked past Mr. Summerhays toward the overbearing cowboy, he frowned. "We're going to need an extra hand to get the horses settled."

"The *kinder*... I mean, the children—"

He interrupted her. "Leave them with Mrs. Beebe. She can watch them for the rest of the afternoon."

"Okay." What else could she say? Mr. Summerhays was her boss, and he was the *kinder's daed*.

He held out a cell phone. "Use this to call for a ride when you're done at the hospital."

"I have a phone." She pulled out Alexander's.

"Oh." Mr. Summerhays looked puzzled for a moment, not recognizing his son's cell phone. "Well, good. I trust you to make sure he gets the best possible care. I'll call the hospital to let them know that I'm responsible for the bill."

"*Ja*, sir." Though husband and wife were too distracted with their pursuits to give their *kinder* the time and attention they craved, they were generous. "I'll call you—" She halted herself when he raised a single finger. "I meant, of course, I'll call the house when we're done at the hospital."

"I can go and get him," J.J. said as he came closer.

Mr. Summerhays waved aside his words. "Nonsense. There's no need for you to put yourself out. Sarah can handle it. She's had a lot of practice dealing with small crises like this."

Wondering if Toby would describe his injured ankle as a *small* crisis, Sarah nodded as the two men turned to go to the house. When Mr. Summerhays paused long enough to remind her the *kinder* should be left with Mrs. Beebe, Sarah nodded again. She was sure the cook was going to be annoyed. Mrs. Beebe had to prepare food for the household while the kitchen was being taken apart.

She would be relieved when it was redone with the finishes Mrs. Summerhays had chosen before she left for Europe, but the end of the project was still weeks away.

Sarah gathered the *kinder* and led them toward the house, though she would have preferred to stay and watch George and Derek work. Taking the youngsters up the ramp into the kitchen, she wasn't surprised when Mrs. Beebe, who was as thin as one of the columns, frowned.

"Now?" The gray-haired cook sighed as the *kinder* spread out in the huge kitchen, checking the many boxes stacked in every available space, blocking tall windows and cupboards waiting to be ripped out. "If they tip a cabinet on themselves, we'll need another ambulance."

"I'm sorry, but Mr. Summerhays—"

"Go and do what he asked." Mrs. Beebe waved her apron at Sarah. "I'll find something to keep them out of trouble."

Hoping the cook would do better than she had, Sarah rushed outside. She bumped into J.J., who was with Mr. Summerhays.

"Steady there," he said, putting his hands on her shoulders to keep her from falling. "Are you okay? You didn't get hurt, too, did you?"

Assuring him that she was fine, she hurried toward the paddock. She reached it as the two EMTs were raising the gurney with Toby strapped to it. Seeing his straw hat in the dust, she picked it up and carried it toward the ambulance.

Toby's face was in full view without his hat. She was startled to see, in spite of his face's strong lines and angles, a hint of boyishness that had been hidden before. Was pain forcing him to lower his guard a tiny bit?

"I appreciate your retrieving my hat," Toby said, holding out his hand for it. *"Danki."*

She didn't give it to him. "Let's wait until we're in the ambulance."

"We?" He started to sit up.

When Derek cautioned him to remain still, Toby leaned back against the pillow. He glared at her. She hoped he'd understand when she explained her boss—and his—had sent her with him. Maybe then he'd see she wasn't any happier about this situation than he was.

Her prayer from earlier echoed in her mind. *God, grant me patience. Please let this be the last time I have to save these little ones from their antics. At least for today...*

She needed to be more careful what she prayed for.

Toby tested his ankle, shifting it as he sat in a wheelchair in the emergency waiting room. He couldn't move the thick air-cast boot encasing his leg enough to do more than cause him pain. Had he groaned aloud? A woman stopped and asked if he needed a nurse. Thanking her, he shook his head.

He was glad when she kept going. Each person who passed by, and there were a lot, glanced his way and added to his self-consciousness.

Two hours ago, after a half-hour drive over pothole-ridden roads, he'd arrived at Glens Falls Hospital. Since then, he'd been subjected to X-rays, examinations and questions. He'd started to wonder if every member of the hospital staff had stopped in to see the useless man who couldn't control a horse he'd trained for the past year.

Every member of the hospital staff except a *doktor.*

Finally, a short man had walked in wearing a white

lab coat. He'd introduced himself as *Doktor* Garza before saying, "You did a real number on your ankle, Mr. Christner."

The words had stung like a rebuke. He'd let his attention wander, and he was paying the price.

"How long before I can work?" Toby had asked.

"You shouldn't put full weight on it for eight weeks."

"Eight *weeks*?"

Doktor Garza had sighed. "I know it's not what you wanted to hear, but to be honest, I haven't seen anyone sprain an ankle quite that bad in a long time. You're going to need to work with a physical therapist to strengthen the muscles so you don't injure them again. If you don't—"

A laugh from the cubicle where Sarah had gone with a nurse intruded into his thoughts about what *Doktor* Garza had said before leaving to check his next patient.

The desk was right behind where Toby now waited. He hadn't listened to their conversation, but he sat straighter when Sarah spoke.

"Oh, it's no worry," she said with another easy laugh. "I can make sure everything is taken care of. I'm used to dealing with recalcitrant kids, big and small."

The nurse chuckled, but Toby didn't.

Was Sarah referring to him? He wasn't going to be her problem. Once he returned to Summerhays Stables, he'd be on his way. The tenuous connection between him and the pretty redhead would be broken.

After he left there, what would he do?

Eight weeks!

Eight weeks of being unable to assist J.J. If his boss sent him back to Texas, he'd be as useless there. He couldn't ride, not with the inflated boot on his right foot. He couldn't take care of the animals, even the ones in the barns, because shoveling out a stall would be impossible on one leg.

Toby looked up when Sarah came around the side of the cubicle, carrying a white plastic bag. She gave him a taut smile.

"It'll be at least forty-five minutes before someone can get here," she said, taking a seat next to his wheelchair.

"Have you seen my boot? My regular boot."

She pointed to the white bag on the chair beside her. "It's in here with your instructions and prescriptions you'll need to get filled. Do you want to see?"

"No hurry. It sounds as if I won't be wearing my boot for a few days."

"Are you hungry?" she asked in the gentle tone he'd heard her use with the Summerhays kids.

He couldn't keep from thinking about how she'd told the nurse she was accustomed to taking care of stubborn *kinder*. Had she cast him in that role? "Not really."

"Thirsty?"

He sighed. She was determined to take care of him as if he were a Summerhays youngster. How could he fault her for lumping him in with the rambunctious *kinder*? He'd been rude to her from the first word he'd spoken, and she'd made every effort to be nice. He doubted he could have acted the same if their circumstances were reversed. It was long past time for him to show her a bit of gratitude. She'd ridden in the bumpy ambulance with him and waited two long hours in an uncomfortable chair while he was tended to.

"I'm a bit thirsty," he replied.

"Me, too. There's a snack shop. We've got plenty of time to get something before the car arrives."

When she stood, he almost apologized for his curt replies. She didn't give him a chance as she handed him the plastic bag and grasped the handles of the wheelchair.

Toby grimaced as he caught the plastic bag before it could slide off his lap. He'd thought sitting by the entrance door was the most humiliating thing he could experience, but being pushed along the hallway as if in the middle of a bizarre parade was worse. The scents of disinfectants and floor polish followed them.

Behind him, Sarah kept up a steady monologue. He didn't listen as they turned a corner. The slight jar sent pain surging through him.

When she steered the chair through a door as easily as he would have sent a well-trained horse into its stall, he saw a half-dozen colored tables. A pile of cafeteria trays was stacked to his right, and three people were pushing theirs along rails as they selected food and drinks. A woman with a hairnet and apron assisted them.

"What do you want?" Sarah asked.

"I'll have whatever you're having."

"I was going to have a cup of tea."

His nose wrinkled. "Make mine a cup of *kaffi*. Black."

Sarah left him by an empty table and went to get a tray. Carrying it to the far end of the rails, she spoke to the woman in the hairnet, took two blue cups and went to the cash register.

Realization dawned on him, and when she set a cup of fragrant *kaffi* in front of him, he said, "Before we leave, I need to talk to someone about paying for this."

"This?" She looked from his cup to hers in bafflement.

"No, the bill for the emergency room."

Reaching for a packet of sugar, she sprinkled it into the tea. "Don't worry. Mr. Summerhays is taking care of it."

"No!" He lowered his voice when heads turned toward them. "I mean, I'm grateful, but I pay my bills."

"You'll have to discuss that with Mr. Summerhays." Her voice was unruffled as she stirred her tea and then took a sip.

"I will. I don't like being beholden to anyone."

Sarah laughed as she had while talking with the nurse. "You say that as if I'm supposed to be surprised."

Lowering his gaze to his *kaffi*, Toby said, "Sorry. I know I'm prickly."

"As a blackberry bush."

"Danki." His lips twitched.

"It's okay. It's *gut* to see you can smile. I won't tell anyone and ruin your stern cowboy reputation."

"Stern? Is that what you think I am?" He looked at her in spite of himself.

She was staring into her cup. "I think it's what you want the world to believe you are. Or maybe you were going for forbidding or contrary. They look pretty much the same to me."

"How's that?"

"As if you sat on a porcupine." When she raised her eyes, they were twinkling with amusement.

"No, you can be certain that if I'd sat on a porcupine, folks would have heard me yelp from here to the Rio Grande." He wasn't sure if he should blame the pain arcing across his ankle or the drugs he'd been given to ease it for giving her such a playful retort.

When she laughed, her eyes widened when he didn't join in.

"Sorry," she said. "I know you're feeling lousy."

Seizing the excuse she'd offered him, he nodded.

They sipped in silence for several minutes. He was

amazed the quiet didn't seem to bother her as it had in that fancy room in the Summerhays house. She watched visitors and medical staff coming in and out. An odd expression darkened her eyes when a pair of EMTs wandered in to grab cups of *kaffi*. He thought about asking her if she knew the man and woman, but he kept his curiosity to himself.

Every question he asked, every answer she gave would add a layer to that connection he wanted to avoid.

"Finished?" she asked, coming to her feet.

He was surprised to see his cup was empty. He didn't recall drinking the *kaffi*. His mind wasn't working well.

She took the cup and threw it and her own into a trash can. Coming back, she reached to unlock the chair's brakes.

For a split second, he wondered when she'd set them in place. The sweet aroma of her shampoo drifted to him, and he was tossed back to the moment when she'd helped him in the paddock. Having her holding him close had been enough for him to forget how much his foot hurt. The memory swept over him, diminishing the pain faster than any drug could.

Had he lost his mind? Thinking such things threatened his promise never to get close to anyone again. He needed to be careful. He had to remember how his heart had hurt each time he'd had to leave *gut* friends behind, knowing he'd never see them again. To be honest, somewhere along the way, he'd lost the key to his padlocked heart. He told himself it was for the best. How did he know he wouldn't start acting like his parents, leaving without looking back?

Sarah straightened. "Are you okay? Maybe you should take another pain tablet so it's working by the time the car gets here."

"I'm fine."

"Gut." She bowed her head for a moment.

He thought her prayer would be silent, but she whispered, "God, *danki* for making sure Toby wasn't hurt worse. Please send him quick healing. You know his heart far better than I do, but I don't think he's a patient man."

Gnawing on his bottom lip, he remained silent. He pretended not to see her questioning glance in his direction. He didn't want to explain he and God had an arrangement that had worked most of his life. Toby wouldn't expect anything of God, and God wouldn't expect anything of him. Knowing that had eased Toby's sorrow each time his parents decided to move.

That was why a faint twinge deep in his heart astounded him. A twinge of longing? For what? To be close to God, who had given Toby a life of chaos and loss? He couldn't see a reason to reach out to his Heavenly Father. He'd learned to get by on his own.

"Would you like to pray with me?" Sarah asked.

"Not right now. We need to hurry. I don't want to delay J.J. more than I already have."

She sat facing him again. "Don't you remember? He's left."

"What?" This time he didn't care that his raised voice caught the attention of everyone in the snack room. "How do you know that?"

"I found out when I called for our ride home."

"When were you planning to tell me that little tidbit?"

"I told you while I was wheeling you here."

He started to argue that she hadn't, then recalled how pain had stripped his mind of everything. She had to be wrong. J.J. wouldn't go without him.

When he said as much, she shook her head. "I asked

for confirmation when I called, and I was told to tell you that he and Ned would—"

"Ned left, too? Who's going to help get the horses settled?"

She shrugged. "I don't know. That's all your boss said. They'll return in a couple of months to get you."

"A couple of months?" He closed his eyes as waves of pain flooded him, waves he'd tried to ignore. Opening his eyes, he met Sarah's. "What am I supposed to do until then?"

"Heal."

"Where?"

"I told you. Mr. Summerhays has taken care of everything. There's a guest room on the first floor near the kitchen. You can recover there."

He forced his frustration down. If he'd been thinking straight, he would have known J.J. couldn't stay while Toby went to the hospital. Their schedule was tight, and delaying one place meant upsetting many valuable customers they hoped would give them more work.

Was *this* the answer to his problem on how to protect Sarah from Ned's machinations? He hadn't guessed it'd be for him to have a sprained ankle and be as helpless as a *boppli*.

"I guess I don't have another choice." His voice sounded childish even to his ears. "I'm sorry, Sarah. I—"

"Never mind. We need to be out front for when the car gets here, so let's go," she said with something that sounded like disappointment.

Disappointment? With him?

If so, she would have to get used to that during the next eight weeks. He'd disappointed everyone in his life.

Including himself.

Chapter Four

The second annual Salem Volunteer Fire Department Berry-fest Dinner was well underway by the time Sarah arrived at the new fire station. Parked out front were the big fire engines and the ambulance that had taken Toby to the hospital earlier that day.

That day? To Sarah, it seemed impossible only a few hours had passed since Natalie had come to alert her that a cowboy was on the porch.

After a quiet drive home from the hospital in Mr. Summerhays's luxurious truck, Sarah had been relieved when, as they came into the house, her boss had offered to help get Toby, who was reeling from his pain medication, into the guest room on the main floor. She'd agreed to come early the next day so Mr. Summerhays could finish work he'd had to ignore that afternoon. When he asked her to arrange for Toby's physical therapist's first visit, she realized her boss had added the Texan to her list of responsibilities.

She looked forward to talking with a trained physical therapist, but she wasn't sure how Toby would feel about her involvement.

As she opened the door into the firehouse, she pushed that concern aside. She was attending the festive dinner with her friends, and she didn't want her mind mired in thoughts of the injured man.

Inside the new fire station, which had been dedicated the previous year, tables were set end to end in three rows. Folding chairs were occupied by neighbors who were enjoying barbecued chicken and salads before the volunteer firefighters served them generous slabs of berry pie. A kitchen could be seen beyond a wide pass-through window where urns held *kaffi* and rows of cups of lemonade and iced tea waited to be claimed. Faint strains of country music came from a speaker in one corner, but it was drowned out by the dozens of conversations in the open space.

A few months ago, heads would have turned when Sarah and her three best friends walked in. However, the residents of the small village had become accustomed to their new plain neighbors among them.

She wondered what the reaction would be if they learned Sarah's friends had jokingly named themselves the Harmony Creek Spinsters' Club. They were too old to belong to a youth group but weren't married, so they didn't fit in anywhere except with each other. As a group, they enjoyed shopping in the village or attending events like the Berry-fest Dinner.

"Where do you want to sit?" asked Annie Wagler, the more talkative of the Wagler twins. She and her sister, Leanna, were at least two inches shorter than Sarah. Their lustrous black hair glowed with a bluish sheen in the station's bright lights.

"Do you see four chairs together?" Sarah scanned the room, seeing many familiar faces. People she'd met in the village as well as those living in the new settlement along Harmony Creek.

"There." Miriam Hartz, a tall blonde, pointed to the right. "Two empty chairs facing two empty chairs."

"Perfect." Sarah led the way. When she sat facing the twins, she smiled as Miriam took the chair next to her.

She was delighted. She hadn't had a chance to talk to Miriam in the past couple of weeks because her friend was busy making preparations for the new school year, which would begin at the end of August. As the Amish school opened two weeks before the private school the Summerhays *kinder* went to, she was hoping to arrange for a visit. Her charges had so many questions about their plain neighbors, and it would be a *gut* way to introduce them to *kinder* their own ages.

"What a *wunderbaar* idea!" Miriam exclaimed when Sarah brought up the subject. "It'll help my scholars, too, by letting them meet younger *Englisch* neighbors. For the most part, their interactions have been with *Englisch* who work in the stores in Salem."

"When do you start school?"

"The last full week of this month."

"The same week as the Washington County fair?"

Miriam gave her a wry smile. "It was either that, or we'd be in session when it was time for next spring's planting. However, we'll be doing half days at the end of the first week, so the scholars and their families can go to the fair later in the day. The days count toward our total, and to be honest, the kids have too much summer on their minds to get much work done."

"Especially as they had to make up days in June and July."

With the disruption of moving into the new settlement

in Harmony Creek Hollow, many of the school-age *kinder* hadn't attended the minimum number of days required by the state, so a short session had been necessary. Miriam had held school in her home until the new building had been completed after the Fourth of July.

"I'm hoping they'll be eager to get back to work," Miriam replied, "instead of thinking about playing ball. Some would be happy to do that all day, every day."

The Summerhays kids didn't play ball other than in video games. A basketball court behind the house hadn't been used except for storage of supplies for the house renovation. Other than Natalie, who took every opportunity to be with the horses, the *kinder* preferred to stay indoors. Each time Sarah had insisted on them joining her for a walk, they complained as if being sent to the North Pole in the middle of winter, instead of enjoying the chance to pick fresh berries from the bushes along the road and edging the farm's fields.

"Sarah!"

She stiffened at her older brother's voice, which seemed to silence everyone else. She wondered if Menno's hearing was being damaged by their sawmill. He usually had sawdust clinging to his hair, but tonight it was neat.

Her brothers stopped by where she sat. Menno was short, only an inch or two taller than Sarah. Benjamin's head reached several inches higher than their older brother's. Both were built wide and thick like the stumps they left behind when they felled trees on the wood lot. Benjamin worked at the sawmill, but he'd spent most of his time for the past month planting apple trees.

"Why didn't you tell us you were coming tonight?"

asked Menno. "You could have come with us. I don't like the idea of you driving alone after dark."

Heat rose along Sarah's cheeks as eyes turned toward them. Why did her older brother, who was ten years older than she was, treat her as if she were Mia's age? Her brothers had always been protective of her, but since their move to the new settlement, they didn't seem to believe she could breathe without supervision.

"I came with my friends," she said, irritated that her brother's sharp voice had drawn attention to them. "We hired Hank Puente to bring us in his van." She couldn't keep from raising her chin in defiance. "I mentioned that to you at least twice in the past week."

Benjamin nodded with an apologetic smile, but Menno didn't crack his stern facade. For a long moment, her older brother stared at her. She met his gaze, refusing to let him daunt her. At last, he clapped Benjamin on the shoulder and walked away.

"Whew," Annie breathed. "Is it my imagination, or are your brothers keeping an eye on you more closely every day?"

"It's not your imagination."

Leanna reached across the table and patted Sarah's hand in silent consolation.

"That's ridiculous," Miriam said at the same time. "You're a grown woman, not a *boppli*."

With a smile she hoped conveyed her appreciation for her friends coming to her defense, Sarah said, "I've tried to tell them that, but they don't want to listen."

"But they're okay with you working for the Summerhays family?" Annie asked.

"They haven't said otherwise." She didn't add her brothers knew—as she did—how important her wages were while they worked to establish their sawmill as a viable business.

In the past few weeks, Benjamin and Menno had been discussing the pine trees in their steep fields. A Christmas tree farm is what Benjamin called it, and she guessed that they hoped to sell fresh trees as the holidays approached. Plain families wouldn't buy them, but *Englischers* might. However, until the harvest was in and the holiday season rolled around, the household depended on what she was paid each week. That her pay from Mr. Summerhays was always on time was a blessing she never took for granted.

"*Guten owed*, ladies," came a deep voice, silencing her thoughts.

A look over her shoulder wasn't necessary when Sarah saw the soft smile blossoming on Miriam's face. Even if Sarah hadn't recognized the voice as Eli Troyer's, her friend's expression announced how happy Miriam was to see the carpenter who lived at the far end of the hollow. The two had been walking out together for the past few weeks, a fact Sarah had guessed, though neither Miriam nor Eli had said a word.

Setting plates in front of them with a flourish worthy of the finest restaurant, Eli reminded them the dinner was all-you-can-eat.

Sarah chuckled when she looked at her plate heaped with chicken, french fries, and potato, macaroni and green salads. "I can't eat all this."

"Not if we want pie," added Annie with a laugh.

"You definitely want pie." Eli motioned toward the counter. "Help yourself to something to drink, too." He hurried away to serve more food.

"Miriam, how did you arrange for Eli to be our waiter?" Sarah asked with a wink to her friends.

Miriam's face grew as red as the filling in the slices of berry pie arranged on a nearby table, then she smiled. "I didn't, but I'm grateful for small favors."

"I wish more of those handsome firefighters would stop by," said Leanna.

Sarah put her arm around her friend as they went to get their choice of drinks from the counter. She didn't know what to say to Leanna, who was eager to get married since the man she'd fallen for wed someone else.

When she saw how Miriam glowed as Eli spoke to her, Sarah was sure this fall would be Miriam's last as a schoolteacher. Would she marry Eli before Christmas? Though such matters were kept quiet, the small size of the community settled along Harmony Creek made it impossible not to notice who was spending time together.

She wished Miriam every happiness, because Eli seemed like a *gut* man. She prayed the Wagler twins would find such *wunderbaar* matches, too. As for herself, she needed to sort out her future before she could commit the rest of her life to someone. She must not make the same mistake she had when opening her heart to Wilbur Eash and having him assume he could make every decision for her.

"So what trouble did your *kinder* get into today?" Annie asked after they'd shared a silent prayer of thanks for the food in front of them.

Sarah was relieved by Annie's question, which gave her an excuse to shove aside her uncomfortable thoughts. "The high point was when I had to get them off those tall columns in the entry." She stabbed a piece of green salad. "I don't know how you deal with a dozen, Miriam, when I'm on my toes with four."

"The *kinder* didn't get hurt, ain't so?" asked Miriam.

"No." She explained how she'd gotten to the two younger ones before they fell.

"I'm glad to hear that after Caleb mentioned the ambulance went out to the stables this afternoon."

Sarah nodded. Like her brothers, Miriam's brother, who was the founder of the new settlement along Harmony Creek, was a volunteer firefighter. They wore beepers to alert them about emergencies.

"Is everyone okay?" asked Leanna.

Again, Sarah nodded. "Horses were being delivered, and one was startled by a barn cat. When Toby tried to control it, he got hurt. We were worried his ankle was broken, which was why I had Alexander call 911."

"Toby? I think you may have mentioned the name before." Annie glanced at the others as she arched her brows.

Sarah ignored her teasing. "He delivered the three horses to Mr. Summerhays from Texas."

"A cowboy?" Annie asked with a chuckle.

Again Sarah acted as if she hadn't heard the silly question. "Toby was examining the horse when it spooked. He needed to go to the emergency room, but he's at the house now. He'll stay there while his sprain heals." She shook her head. "I'm not sure who's going to give me more trouble, the *kinder* or Toby."

"You'll be taking care of him?" Miriam asked.

"Mr. Summerhays wants me to oversee his physical therapy." She took a bite of the delicious macaroni salad, which tasted like the one served at the last church Sunday. She guessed an Amish volunteer had shared the recipe with the other firefighters. "It was such a bizarre accident. Watching Toby, it's obvious he's skilled with handling horses. If he hadn't been, Mr. Summerhays would have insisted on his grooms checking the horses. It's too bad he was hurt."

Expecting her friends to show sympathy for Toby's situation, Sarah was astonished when the others began laughing.

"What's funny?" she asked.

"You and your Amish cowboy." Annie put her hand to her lips as she giggled again.

"He's not *my* cowboy."

"Not yet."

Turning to Leanna, Sarah said, "Maybe you can talk sense into your twin. She's not listening to me."

"Annie doesn't listen to anyone." With a warm smile for her sister, Leanna added, "This time I've got to agree with her. You seem pretty taken with this cowboy. You've known him for a few hours, and you've talked more about him this evening than anything else."

"I—"

"Don't deny it, Sarah!" Annie winked at her twin and Miriam. "Isn't it true?"

Sarah waited while they laughed again, then, smiling, asked her friends about what they were busy with. Miriam had school plans, and Leanna had recently purchased some goats and hoped to sell their milk and homemade soap at the farmers market in the center of the village.

When the topic didn't shift again to Toby, she was grateful. It wasn't easy to keep the man out of her thoughts. Several times, she found her mind wandering to him and had to focus on the conversation. It'd been a stressful day, and she was thankful God had put her in a place where she'd been able to help.

Eli came to the table, and Sarah was surprised to see

she'd eaten the rest of her meal without tasting a bite, including the pie. Hearing the others commenting on how *wunderbaar* the dessert had been, Sarah wished she'd taken notice of it.

She felt a pang of something she didn't want to examine when she saw how Eli smiled at Miriam at the same time his young nephew gave her a hug. She was happy the three were becoming a family. Why the pang? Maybe she was more like Leanna than she wanted to admit. No, that was silly. Sarah didn't need another man telling her what to do in an unnecessary attempt to shield her from her own choices.

In spite of herself, her eyes cut to where her brothers waited to deliver food to the tables. Her brothers laughed and chatted with plain and *Englisch* firefighters. She frowned when she saw Benjamin say something to two women in T-shirts and jeans that were identical to what the other *Englischer* volunteers wore. He seemed okay with those women being firefighters, but he had agreed with Menno that Sarah must not take EMT training.

There must be something she could do to persuade them she deserved the same respect.

God, please help me discover what.

"Is he *ever* going to wake up?" asked one young voice.

Another answered, "Don't know."

"If he doesn't, how are we going to find out if he's a real cowboy?"

"Don't know."

Toby realized the childish voices weren't part of the dream—no, the nightmare—holding him in its grip. Pushing his way out of a collage of disconnected images, he paid no attention to the conversation. How thin were the walls of the motel J.J. had found for them?

Opening his eyes, he realized he wasn't in a rented room. Instead of a pair of beds with worn headboards and a TV set on a narrow chest, Toby stared at a white-and-gold canopy. Wide dark slats supported it, and more of the fancy fabric was draped around each post supporting the top. Sunlight streamed across floors that glistened as if lit from within. On the other side of the bed was…

He shifted to look in the opposite direction. Pain slashed across his ankle and exploded in his head. A groan escaped his clamped lips.

"Is he dying?" asked the first childlike voice.

"Don't know."

"Should we get Sarah?"

Before the second voice could repeat the same words, Toby raised his head. More agony pierced him, but he gritted his teeth and stared along the bed.

Two small forms were silhouetted against the light. Sunshine glistened off their pale hair.

The younger Summerhays kids! What were they doing sitting on his bed? He must be dreaming.

He shifted. More excruciating pain. No, he wasn't asleep.

"Why are you here?" he asked in a raspy voice he didn't recognize.

"Are you a real cowboy?" asked the little boy. "Where's your six-shooter?"

"I don't carry a gun."

"How do you fight off train robbers and cattle rustlers?"

What were the kids' names? Maybe he could remember if his head didn't pound like a sprinter's pulse. "I don't work with cattle. I train horses."

"How about horse rustlers?" asked the little boy.

"No!" cried the little girl. "Don't say that!"

Toby winced at her shrill voice. He was about to ask her to whisper, but the two youngsters began to argue. Each word was a separate blow against his skull.

The door opened, letting in more light and revealing that the *kinder* were dressed in pajamas with cartoon characters flitting across them.

Risking more pain—and getting it—Toby turned his head again. His breath caught when he realized who stood in the doorway, holding a tray.

Sunlight was filtered by Sarah's *kapp* but shone on her red hair. It accented the curves of her high cheekbones and the outline of her lips that were drawn in a frown. Her brown eyes were focused on her two younger charges.

"Shoo." Her voice was soft enough not to resonate across his aching head, and she put the tray on a white chest of drawers without making a sound.

"You told us that we could talk to him," protested the little boy.

Why couldn't he remember their names? He was sure he'd heard them…was it only yesterday?

"Ethan, you know I meant *after* Toby was awake. After he had his breakfast."

Ethan… That was the little boy's name. What was the girl's?

As if he'd asked aloud, Sarah said, "Mia, you need to put your breakfast dishes in the dishwasher."

The *kind* pouted. "But Mrs. Beebe—"

"Has her chores to do. Putting away your dishes is *your* chore."

When Sarah lifted the youngsters, first one and then the other, off his bed, the slight motion exacerbated the invisible feet marching across his skull. He was grateful she hadn't had them clamber down, which would have made the mattress shake more.

He kept his eyes closed as the sounds of the *kinder* leaving the room ricocheted through his head. A single set of footfalls, so light he guessed Sarah was walking on tiptoe, came across the room. He heard a faint scrape as she picked up the tray and brought it toward the bed.

"Do you need help to sit?" she asked.

He imagined her slender arm sliding beneath him and her warm breath caressing his cheek as it had when she helped him in the paddock. Another groan slipped past his lips.

Distress entered her voice. "Are you okay?"

"I've been better." Putting his hands against the firm mattress, he pushed himself up to lean against the headboard.

"Your meds are here with your breakfast."

"I don't need—"

"The *doktor* insisted you take them for at least three days."

He met her eyes, half expecting her to look away. She didn't as she leaned forward to put the tray on its short legs on either side of his lap. When she straightened, she held his gaze.

"Okay," he said, knowing he was being foolish. She wanted to help him get better.

That was all he should be thinking about. Getting well and getting to work. Spending time with pretty Sarah risked messing with his mind and his plans. He couldn't start thinking, as he had last night before he fell asleep, how it would be interesting to get to know her better.

"I'm sorry Ethan and Mia disturbed you. I told them not to come in until after you'd had breakfast, but I guess they thought I'd said after *they* had breakfast."

"Or their curiosity wouldn't let them wait."

"Curiosity? About what?"

He looked at the tray she'd brought. It held enough food for half a bunkhouse. "They want to know if I'm a real cowboy."

"I'm sure you set them straight."

"I didn't have time. You came to my rescue." He reached for the bowl of oatmeal.

"I'll speak with them again."

"*Gut.* The *doktor* told me to rest for a few days. I'd appreciate it if you kept the kids away."

Her shoulders became more rigid. "I'll do my best."

"From what I saw when we were unloading the horses, they don't listen to you."

"Are you saying it's the *kinder's* fault you're hurt?"

"No, of course I don't blame them for what happened."

"But you blame someone. Me?"

"No, that's not what I meant, either."

"Then what *do* you mean?"

He faltered. He couldn't be honest with her about his concerns of having Ned hanging around and bothering her. In addition, the fact that Toby had allowed himself to be distracted by Sarah was on his shoulders, not hers.

When he didn't answer, she said in a crisp tone, "You should rest while you can." She walked to the door. "Your physical therapist will be here later."

"Sarah?" he called.

Either she didn't hear him or she didn't want to let the conversation continue, because she kept walking. The door closed behind her, leaving him alone with his breakfast, his swollen ankle and the wish he could go back to sleep so he could start the day again.

Chapter Five

The middle-aged man who arrived at the Summerhays house an hour later introduced himself as Howard Abbott when he walked into Toby's room after the briefest knock. He looked as fit as any man working in the saddle at J.J.'s ranch but was dressed in khaki shorts and a black T-shirt. His sneakers were orange with bright yellow swirls and green soles. He carried a box that was big enough to fit Mia in and have room left. As he set it on the floor, Toby heard a clang, though the man had carried it as if it were empty.

"I'm here to do the physical therapy ordered by your doctor," Howard said with a practiced smile that hinted most of his clients weren't pleased to see him.

Toby was. The sooner he could get on his feet, the sooner he could finish training the three horses and find a way to meet J.J. and Ned. No doubt with a plain community nearby, there were *Englischers* who drove Amish to distant places. He'd hire one. He'd already spent too much time at Summerhays Stables.

And with Sarah Kuhns.

He should be grateful Mr. Summerhays was paying

for his medical care and for Sarah making sure he was fed, but gratitude meant connections to others. Those obligations he had to avoid. He'd been miserable amid his parents' drama, so he knew getting close to people might seem like a *gut* idea, but it led to misery. The years since he'd gone to work on J.J.'s ranch had been the calmest of his life. His time at the Summerhays house would be brief, and he didn't want to have regrets tugging at his heart when he left.

"So tell me what happened," Howard said as he moved elegant fragile-looking chairs aside to open a space on the fancy gold, white and dark red rug. With a flick of his wrist, he spread a bright blue mat into place before setting a single chair on it.

Toby gave him an abridged explanation. When the physical therapist nodded at various times, Toby guessed Howard had gone through his hospital records. Howard pulled a computer pad out of his big bag and made notes while he asked questions about the level of Toby's pain, when he'd last taken pain medication and where his ankle hurt most.

The door opened as Toby was pointing to the top of his right ankle.

Sarah stepped in. "Howard, I'm sorry I'm late." She pushed a vagrant red-gold strand beneath her *kapp*.

Howard laughed. "Mia or Ethan?"

"Mia this time." Sarah chuckled, her whole face glowing as stress fell away. "She claims as long as she keeps one hand on the top rail, she's still on the fence and not in the corral."

The physical therapist shook his head with another laugh. "I don't know how you keep up with those kids."

"I don't. That's why I'm late. Have you begun?"

Toby noticed how careful she was not to glance in his direction. He needed to apologize for what he'd said earlier. Or what he hadn't said. Not that it mattered, because, despite his denials, he'd given her the impression he blamed her for his accident.

He didn't, and he had to persuade her of that. He didn't want to leave unpaid obligations behind him, and he owed Sarah a huge debt for helping him.

"We're just getting started," Howard said before putting the tablet back in his bag. "Let's get to work. First thing, Toby, is to get you up, so swing your legs over the side of the bed." He chuckled. "This will be easier if we don't have 'help' from the kids."

"You know them?" Toby asked as he pushed himself to the edge of the bed. He wanted their attention on his question instead of him.

"Too well." Howard drew the chair closer to the bed and motioned toward it. "I worked with both boys and Natalie about a year and a half ago. Two broken wrists and a broken leg when they discovered they couldn't fly. Mia was the only one who didn't break something, though she got pretty badly bruised. I don't think they'll try again." He glanced toward Sarah. "You weren't here then, were you?"

"No, that was three nannies before me."

"They tried to fly?" Toby asked, raising his arms as Howard put a wide elastic band around Toby's back.

With an ease Toby envied, the physical therapist used the strap as a way to balance them as he drew Toby up onto his left leg. The motion, though he didn't do much to help, left him light-headed.

"Breathe slowly," Howard said. "You've been sitting

a long time, so you've got to get used to standing again. The pain meds can make you dizzy, too."

"I didn't take one this morning."

The physical therapist frowned as he lowered Toby back to the bed. "You need to take them as the doctor told you for at least three days. If the pain gets ahead of you, it's harder to get it under control again. Don't try to muscle through it. Sarah?"

She stepped forward with the pain pills and a glass of water. Howard lowered Toby to the bed, then stepped aside to let her hand Toby the pills and the glass.

He tried to catch her eyes, but she edged away. Swallowing the pills with a hearty gulp of water, he sighed when Howard stepped forward to take the glass. Sarah wasn't going to make it easy for him to apologize.

Again, Howard helped him stand. When Toby swayed, the physical therapist said, "Breathe in and out, deep and slow. In through your nose, out through your mouth."

Toby listened to Howard's calm voice and followed his instructions. The darkness nibbling at the corner of his vision eased and the room no longer threatened to telescope into nothing. Leaning on the other man's shoulder, he hopped to the chair on the mat.

The urge to thank God for Howard's help surprised him. He hadn't felt that impulse in years. Glancing at where Sarah was setting the glass on a table, he wondered if hearing her heartfelt prayers had gotten him thinking about how long it'd been since he'd reached out to God.

No, that was another connection he didn't want to make.

Toby worked on the exercises Howard had given him as the physical therapist talked with Sarah. Toby didn't expect the motions to be so simple or so painful. A roller he needed to move with his foot made his whole right leg ache as if he'd worked for hours. He concentrated on doing the task, barely listening to Howard answer Sarah's questions about why he'd decided on that exercise and what its purpose was. They spoke with medical jargon he couldn't understand. He was astonished Sarah—as a plain woman—was familiar with the words.

He stopped paying attention to them after Howard asked him to pretend to write the letters of the alphabet with his toes. It was agonizing. His ankle spasmed, and he halted the motion as Howard had told him to do if the pain got worse.

"Sarah, will you please hold his shoulders to keep him from looking at his foot?" asked the physical therapist. "I don't want him to get out of alignment in an attempt to do this exercise."

She moved to stand behind the chair. When her fingers settled on his shoulders, he fought not to react. He didn't want her to think he was flinching because he found her touch bothersome. The light brush of her fingertips sent something more powerful—and more pleasurable—than the pain from his ankle coursing through him.

When Howard told Toby to begin again and start "drawing" the letters, the physical therapist was interrupted by a ringing cell phone. He glanced at it, then excused himself.

Just the opportunity Toby had been waiting for. As soon as the other man stepped out of the room, Toby looked at Sarah. "I need to tell you I'm sorry."

"Now isn't the time for anything but going through these exercises," she said in a crisp tone that contrasted with the easy *gut* humor she'd shown Howard.

"I can apologize at the same time."

"You don't have anything to apologize for."

"No?"

"Not to me."

He frowned with pain as the movement tugged at the abused muscles along his ankle. He was about to retort when Howard returned.

"You're all the way to *Q*, I see," the physical therapist said. "Well done, Toby, but you can stop. We don't want to overstrain your ankle. Do the exercises again this afternoon." He looked past Toby. "Sarah, will you be here to help?"

"Ja."

Toby couldn't tell what she was feeling because there was no overt emotion in the single word.

"Good," Howard said. "Any questions before we get you back in bed, Toby?"

"How soon can I go outdoors?" The words burst from him before he had a chance to think.

Before Howard had arrived, Toby had been staring out the window, wishing he was working with Bay Boy and the other two horses, Dominion and Lou. He wanted to be certain they were being properly exercised, because he didn't want to have to start their specialized training from the beginning again. It would add weeks to the process.

"Outdoors?" Howard seemed surprised by the question. He paused, rubbing his chin. "You sprained your ankle yesterday, right?"

Toby nodded. He didn't want to chance his voice revealing how much pain he was in.

"You can go anywhere," the physical therapist said, "as long as you have someone with you. Have you used crutches before?"

Again, he nodded. "I broke a couple of toes a few years ago, and I had to be on them for about three weeks."

"You'll be on them longer this time, but you'll be done with them sooner if you do your exercises."

"Sarah will make sure I do them." Toby wasn't sure if he or Sarah was more shocked at his comment. Just because Howard had asked her to check on him didn't mean she'd be responsible for his physical therapy every day.

His shoulders stiffened, and she drew her hands away. As before, he couldn't guess what she was thinking without turning around and looking.

Howard chuckled. "Sounds like you've been volunteered, Sarah."

"Mr. Summerhays asked me to help him."

"Okay, so I'll need to go over a few things with you. However, first…"

Reversing the process of getting him out of bed, Howard steered Toby onto it.

"I don't want you on crutches for more than a few minutes at a time until you're accustomed to them again," the physical therapist ordered. "A single misstep could do more damage to your ankle. You've twisted it badly. An additional injury could cause permanent harm."

"I get that."

"Then I hope you also understand you're going to have to baby your ankle except when you're doing your exercises. It needs time to heal. If you don't give it time, it's going to make you sorry." A smile eased his grim expression. "That's not a threat, by the way. It's a fact."

"I know."

He didn't have time to say more before Howard gathered his equipment and, with Sarah, left the room.

Toby's fingers curled into fists of frustration on the

bed. He had been in this bedroom for a single day and already it felt like a pretty prison as everyone could come and go...except him. He leaned his head against the pillows propped behind him and glared at the ceiling. Never had he imagined eight weeks could feel like an eternity.

"I appreciate your help and the attention you paid today," Howard said while Sarah walked with him to the front door.

"I appreciate you answering my questions."

"Glad to explain. Most people don't care about the details as long as they know they're going to get better. I want you to know I wasn't asking you to help Toby with his physical therapy. Just to remind him in case his meds make him forget. The wheelchair Mr. Summerhays ordered is on the porch. You've had your hands full before, but now..."

He didn't finish.

He didn't have to.

Sarah understood what he meant. She was responsible for Toby's physical therapy in addition to taking care of four boisterous *kinder*. What would Mr. Summerhays have said if she'd told him she couldn't take on another task? Mrs. Hancock, the housekeeper, hadn't been pleased having to agree to take an hour away from her regular duties twice each day to keep track of the youngsters so Sarah could help Toby. If Mr. Summerhays had asked the housekeeper instead...

He wouldn't have done that. Her boss had interviewed Sarah extensively before she was hired. He'd quizzed her about health care and first aid. She'd assumed he'd been interested about the *kinder's* safety, but he must have remembered her enthusiastic responses. That was the sole reason she could imagine for why he'd put her in charge of making sure Toby improved. As with everything her boss did, it was a simple solution...for him.

"You'd make a good physical therapist because you're gentle but steady with the patient." Howard pulled a business card out of his case and held it out to her. "Here's the admissions office information for the school I attended."

She shook her head. "*Danki*, but it isn't our way to go to college."

"Where did you learn enough to ask those questions, then?"

"Reading books."

He arched a graying brow. "I'm impressed, Sarah."

"Learning is simple when it's a subject that interests me." She smiled, wanting to put him at ease again. To halt herself before she blurted out her dream of becoming an EMT, she went on, "Don't ask me about long division."

"No worries. I hated that myself, though I find that I'm using it more often than I'd guessed when it comes to computing various stresses for my patients."

She gave an emoted groan, and he chuckled.

Telling her he'd be back tomorrow afternoon, he left. She didn't even have a moment to savor the idea of taking classes to learn more about medical care.

An angry shriek came from upstairs, and she took the steps two at a time. She couldn't imagine what the *kinder* might be doing now, but she guessed she needed to put a halt to it right away.

Sarah knocked on Toby's door as she balanced the tray Mrs. Beebe had made for his lunch. She took the muffled answer as an invitation to enter.

Opening the door, she faltered as she was about to

enter. Toby must have fallen asleep after his exertions, because his sun-streaked hair was tousled and his eyes were now barely open. Gone, for a moment, was the aloof man who seemed to care more about horses than people. Was that an honest expression of gratitude on his face, a hint at the real man he hid behind curt comments and cool stares?

His face hardened. The gentler man, the one who wouldn't be looking for someone to fault for what had happened to him, had vanished.

"Hungry?" she asked in a cheerful tone that sounded fake to her. "Want something to eat?"

"I'd rather have it as a picnic."

"What?"

"Howard said I could go outside as long as someone went with me."

"True."

"Will you? I'd like to check the horses we delivered to make sure they're doing okay."

She was astonished at how his expression altered again, and candid entreaty appeared on his guarded face. She shouldn't have been surprised. A man who spent his whole day outdoors must be going stir-crazy stuck inside.

"I'll get the wheelchair." When he grimaced and started to protest he could manage on crutches, she said, "No chair, no going outside."

He scowled. "I'm not one of your kids."

"No, they would have figured out the only way to get what they want is to cooperate." She chuckled. "Or devised a way to distract me long enough for them to sneak outside."

"Is that what you think I should do? Distract you?"

She looked away. Didn't he know how much he beguiled her every time she was near him? The thought of putting her arm around his sturdy back again while she assisted him into the chair made her knees rubbery.

"Eat, and I'll get the chair." She'd use any excuse to get out of the room before she couldn't control her unsteady legs.

By the time Sarah returned with the wheelchair, Toby had eaten half of the roast-beef sandwich and finished the potato salad. She was relieved when he asked her to hold the chair steady; then, grasping its arms, he swung himself into it. Was he aware of the sensations that rushed between them, too?

The chair moved along the smooth floors as she wheeled him through the kitchen. Mrs. Beebe looked up from her work with a smile. On the other side of the vast room, two workmen were unpacking the new cabinets, which appeared to be a lot like the ones in place, only a few shades lighter.

"Are they replacing the cabinets?" asked Toby.

"Ja."

"They look pretty much the same."

"I know." She'd taken the job at the Summerhays house, in part, to help her learn more about *Englischers*, but she was more confused than the day she'd started.

A workman held the door open for them, and Sarah pushed the chair outdoors. Toby drew in a deep breath. She smiled, knowing he felt as if he'd escaped a closed box. Neither of her brothers liked being inside, either, preferring to work at their sawmill or in the fields or among the trees they planned to sell for Christmas.

If he was surprised the house had a ramp, Toby didn't say anything. Had he guessed the ramp had been built to allow renovation supplies to be moved more easily into the house? Or—and she suspected this was the truth—he was so eager to get out to where he could see the horses he didn't notice anything else.

The ground was rough, but Toby didn't complain each time the wheelchair pitched or halted. When Mick, a stableman, rushed to help, Sarah let him push the chair. Toby peppered the man with question after question until Mick glanced at Sarah and shrugged.

Knowing her patient wouldn't rest until he got the answers he needed, Sarah had Mick push the chair close to the paddock fence. She went around to the gate and inside. With Mick's help, she got a halter on the big horse and a lead rope hooked to him in less than ten minutes.

"Howdy, Bay Boy," called Toby.

The horse's ears pricked, and his head swung toward the fence. Sarah had to skip several times to keep up with him. Putting his head over the fence, he tried to reach Toby, a familiar voice and scent among the strange ones.

When Toby patted Bay Boy's nose, the horse nickered.

"He misses you, too," Sarah said.

At her voice, Bay Boy turned to her. She put out her hand for him to sniff, and she smiled when his chin whiskers tickled her skin.

"He seems to have taken a liking to you." Toby was smiling at her as if the horse's opinion mattered more to him than any human's. Most likely that was true.

She stroked the horse's face. "He's a *gut* boy. Mick says he's settling in well."

"I'm happy to hear that." His grin widened, amazing her. "Or are you telling me if a horse can settle in to new circumstances, I should be able to?"

"If the horseshoe fits—"

"Got it!" He stretched forward to touch the horse again.

Moving aside to give the two room, she listened as he spoke to Bay Boy as if the big stallion could comprehend every word. When Mick brought the other two horses, Toby greeted them, too. Her "patient" looked more relaxed than she'd ever seen him. Maybe now that he was reassured the horses were okay, he'd focus on his recovery.

Then he'd leave, and she wouldn't find herself paying too much attention to a plain man. That attraction could be another thing to come between her and her dreams of studying medicine. That must never happen.

Chapter Six

Sarah stood at the bottom of the porch steps. She made sure she could jump forward, but wouldn't step on the flowers blooming in front of the porch. Flowers that weren't poisonous to horses. Any bush or plant that might harm the valuable animals had been banished from the farm.

At the top of the steps, Toby was rising from the wheelchair he despised. Not that he'd complained, but his upper lip had a tendency to curl whenever the chair was mentioned.

She was surprised at his reaction. She'd thought, when she'd first brought him the wheelchair, he'd be pleased. It allowed him to get around the house and outdoors, though no farther than the porch or the ramp, because he couldn't maneuver alone across the uneven ground.

Without asking, she rushed up the steps and lifted the crutches lying by the wheelchair. She handed them to him, and he gave her a silent nod.

The door opened. Childish voices poured out onto the porch.

Sarah prepared to step between Toby and the youngsters. In their excitement, they might bowl him over or even knock him off the porch.

"Stay where you are," a stern voice ordered.

Beyond the screen door, Mrs. Hancock stood. As always, she wore a prim gray suit. The skirt's hem was as long as Sarah's dress. Her black hair was swept in a French twist, and she wore two pairs of glasses on glittering chains around her neck. An expensive watch peeked out from beneath her unadorned cuffs. It was a gift from Mrs. Summerhays after her previous trip to Europe.

Mrs. Hancock was not much taller than Sarah, but her aura of authority gave a first impression she had the stature of a giantess. Her family had lived in Salem since the village's founding in the late eighteenth century.

She frowned as she held back the two younger *kinder*, who were eager to come outside. Was she upset at the *kinder* or at Sarah, who was working with Toby? Either way, Sarah knew the housekeeper wasn't happy.

Toby looked over his shoulder and waved. The youngsters grinned as if they hadn't seen him in months instead of having breakfast with him that morning. When they called to him, he motioned for them to join them on the porch.

"Are you sure?" Sarah asked.

"I'd rather have them in my way than someone else's."

She smiled at how he'd phrased that so Mrs. Hancock's fragile feelings weren't hurt. Sarah called, "*Komm* out."

The *kinder* exploded from the house, swinging the screen door behind them.

"Whoa! No slamming the door." Sarah rushed to catch it in the *kinder's* wake.

Ethan and Mia glanced at each other as if finding it difficult to believe either of them could have been at fault.

When Sarah motioned for them to follow her down the steps, they complied.

She led them in the center of the walk. Putting a finger to her lips, she said, "We need to be quiet so Toby can concentrate on what he learned this morning."

The *kinder* had been busy with swimming lessons while Toby had his session with Howard. The physical therapist had to put a halt to the practice on the stairs because Toby wanted to keep going until he was proficient. Only the warning that every additional trip without a break to rest his ankle could do more damage to it had stopped Toby from trying "just one more time."

Making sure the youngsters wouldn't be in the way if Toby fell, Sarah signaled for Toby to start but halted him as he started to lower his left foot.

"That's wrong," she said.

"I made sure I've got my crutches under me before I moved." Impatience rippled through his protest.

"You can't lead with your foot. Remember? You put the crutches on each step before going down. Howard said that's important, so you keep your balance and don't tumble. He said you need to remember that until you can begin to put weight on your right foot." Sarah kept her tone light and wished Toby wouldn't act as if it were a life-and-death matter. "It shouldn't be hard to remember, ain't so?"

"Maybe not for you."

She refused to be drawn into an argument, so she said in her gentlest tone, "Lead with the *gut* foot going up, and then let the bad one swing through going down."

"Cuz good things go up and bad ones go down," said Mia and Ethan at the same time before Ethan added, "See? I remembered from when I broke my leg."

"So you did." She smiled at the *kinder*.

She had to keep her focus on Toby but knew how much mischief Ethan and Mia could get into as soon as her back was turned. Natalie and Alexander were having swimming lessons in the pool behind the house, and the teenager teaching them couldn't keep an eye on them as well as watch the younger *kinder*.

So she was grateful Toby was willing to have an audience while he did his afternoon exercises. After he worked on the steps, Sarah instructed Toby to write the alphabet with his right foot. Ethan and Mia copied him. They giggled when Mia made the letter *S* backward. The little girl started again and wore a proud grin when she did the letter correctly the second time.

Natalie stuck her head, which was wrapped in a colored beach towel, past the door. "Your turn now!"

"We want to help Toby," Mia argued. "I went swimming this morning."

"You know Mom wants us to be able to swim when we go to Aruba in January."

With a sigh that suggested she was sacrificing the most precious thing in the world, Mia shuffled after her brother.

The screen door slammed in their wake, and Toby glanced at Sarah.

She shrugged. "What's the point of reminding them not to slam the door *again* when they won't hear it?"

"It seems like they didn't hear it the first time."

"They did, but sometimes it takes a long time for an idea to go from the ears to the brain when those ears belong to someone six years old or younger." She smiled. "You've got to be patient."

"I'm not sure I could be."

"Why not? You're patient with your horses, aren't you?"

"That's different."

"How? You're teaching a horse to behave as you want. I'm doing the same with the *kinder*. In either case, we have to keep them safe as we teach them to behave without breaking their spirits."

He relaxed against his crutches and grinned. "I didn't realize our work had so much in common."

"It's strange, ain't so?" She moved to the walk and looked at him. "I'm ready when you are."

Sweat glistened on Toby's forehead by the time he went down the steps and then returned to his chair. She poured a glass of water from the pitcher she'd brought out with them.

Handing him the glass, she said, "You did it."

"*Ja*, but I should be doing better than this by now."

Sarah gave Toby the stern look that worked best with the Summerhays *kinder*. He ignored it and instead glowered at his right foot.

"It's only been two days," she said, hoping being reasonable would help.

It didn't.

"Two days of doing these exercises again and again. What have I gotten for it? I still can't put my weight on my right ankle."

"Two whole days?" She gave him an expression of feigned shock. He wanted a pity party. At least, that was the term Alexander had used when he complained about how Toby wouldn't do anything but grouse last night during supper.

She'd guessed that Toby would appreciate coming out to the small breakfast room where the *kinder* had their meals. Not only would he get practice with his crutches, but he'd have an excuse to leave his room.

She couldn't have been more mistaken. Toby hadn't said more than a couple of words. Though she guessed his meds were making it difficult for him to think, he could have taken Mia's and Alexander's hands when they bowed their heads to say grace.

"I thought you'd have more sympathy for me," he grumbled.

"I've got plenty of sympathy for you, but not as much as you have for yourself. Maybe you'd rather be a race-horse," she fired back. "With an injury like this, the kind thing would be to put the horse down."

"I see what you're doing."

"Getting you to stop feeling sorry for yourself."

"With reverse psychology. It may work with the kids, but it won't work with me."

She gave a terse laugh. "I guess it won't, though I don't know what you're talking about. I guess you'd rather be a horse so you could be put out of your misery. And put the rest of us out of your misery, too."

"Okay, I'll put a positive spin on it, if that's what you want."

She sat on the other chair and faced him, wondering if all Amish men were *dikk-keppich*. As stubborn as a pair of mules. Her brothers were hardheaded when they wanted to get their way, as they had been that morning when they cut her off in the middle of her explanation of how she was helping with Toby's physical therapy so they could remind her they'd forbidden her to study medical matters.

Frustration threatened to overwhelm her. Why had Menno and Benjamin jumped to the conclusion her story was aimed at making them change their minds? It hadn't been her intention, and she was annoyed they thought she was trying to find a way around their edict. If they suspected she was considering leaving the community... No, she didn't want to think about that. Better to focus on Toby and his sense of futility than her own.

"What positive spin could there be?" he asked, and she realized she'd been lost too long in thought.

"When you're training a horse, you don't expect it to be able to master everything you need it to learn in two days, ain't so?"

"I'm not a horse."

Irritated, she snapped, "No, you're acting more like a donkey!"

Toby watched Sarah's eyes widen as her face paled before turning as red as her hair. She hadn't meant to call him a donkey. Not that he could fault her. He knew he was being unreasonable, but he was tired of doing simple exercises that didn't bring perceivable improvement.

When she started to apologize, he waved her words away. "You don't need to ask forgiveness for the truth. I have been acting like a stubborn old donkey, braying and kicking." He gave her a wry grin. "Well, maybe not kicking. I'm not used to doing nothing and still being exhausted."

"Are you tired now?" she asked.

Ja, he wanted to shout. He was tired of being an invalid. He was tired of being dependent on others for things he'd done without thinking a week ago. Most of all, he was tired of being inside unless Sarah had the time to take him out to the porch.

He looked at the stairs to the yard. Three steps

shouldn't be a barrier between him and the stables. But without someone to help him, the stables might as well be on the far side of the moon.

When Sarah put gentle fingers on his arm, he was shocked. He'd seen her offer a consoling hand to the *kinder*, but he hadn't expected her to treat him with the same familiarity. Or for his heartbeat to erupt into high gear at the light pressure of her warm skin against him.

"I'm sorry nothing is turning out as you'd hoped," she said. "I know how difficult that is."

Did she? Had she been thwarted in doing the simplest things as he was? Or, he wondered, was she referring to what made her eyes dim? He was curious what it was Sarah wanted to do when she seemed so content living in the new community with friends she would have for the rest of her life. The longing for roots among plain folk gripped him, but he pushed it aside with disgust. He had his home at J.J.'s ranch. Even the thought of moving somewhere could lead to the nomad life he'd had with his parents.

He aimed his glower at the wheelchair. "Do you know what I hate most? That chair, because if I want to go anywhere beyond the house, I need someone to push me."

"You don't like others pushing you around?"

He gave her a scowl in response to her smile, then felt horrible when her twinkling eyes grew dull. "I'm sorry, Sarah. You're trying to lift my spirits, and I'm acting as if I want you to be as miserable as I am."

"If that's not what you want, then what is?"

"I want to be able to work." He leaned toward her. "I suspect you'd be as impatient as I am if our situations were reversed."

"You're wrong."

"You rush about, chasing the *kinder* and taking care of them. If—"

"You didn't let me finish. If our situations were reversed, I'd be more impatient than you are."

A laugh bubbled inside him for the first time since... He couldn't remember the last time he'd laughed, and he wasn't going to today. Laughter was another invisible thread weaving people together, which was why he'd avoided it.

Pushing the laughter into the dark place deep in his heart where it'd been locked away, he saw she was waiting for his reaction. *Sever any chance of connection*, ordered the quiet, but annoying, voice that had first sounded in his mind after his *daed* had come home and insisted they prepare to move, right after twelve-year-old Toby had asked the cutest eleven-year-old girl in his school to sit with him during recess the next day. They never had that chance to sit together. In fact, he never saw her again.

That leave-taking had been the one to persuade him—at last—that he'd be a fool to make friends again. He counted the men who worked for J.J. as acquaintances. Most didn't stay long but went looking for other work, or whatever they wanted for their lives.

Sarah sat straighter, drawing his eyes to her. "You're like the Summerhays kids. If there's something you don't want to do, you need a goal to convince yourself to do it."

"What I need to do is be able to walk."

She laughed, shocking him. He hadn't guessed she'd be the type to find humor in someone else's pain.

Stop it! She wasn't laughing at him. Because he didn't want to be beholden to her wasn't her fault.

Making sure his voice didn't reveal the tumult inside him, he asked, "Okay, what is this goal you've got in mind?"

"Something you'd enjoy and what might make your stay here feel as if it's been worthwhile."

A kiss? He tried to smother that thought, but it popped into his head as he admired how her brown eyes glowed behind her gold-rimmed glasses.

"Aren't you curious what I've got in mind?" she asked.

"What?"

"If before the racing season ends at Saratoga next month, in the *doktor's* opinion—not yours—your ankle can handle the exertion, I'll ask Mr. Summerhays to arrange for you to spend a day at his stables there." She grinned as she asked, "How's that for a goal? Enough of a challenge for you, cowboy?"

He was astonished how she'd discovered the exact carrot to hold out as incentive for him to work even harder. His efforts to keep a wall between them had been futile. She was able to see within him to know what he'd prize.

Happiness flowed through him, as gentle and inviting as her smile when he replied, "I'm not a cowboy. I'm a groom. A horse trainer."

"So?"

"So this horse trainer is going to accept your goal. You'll see. I'll make it happen."

"I hope you do."

As she put her fingers on his forearm again and gave it a kind squeeze, he realized she meant what she'd said.

He was getting in too deep with her and the Summerhays family, but, for once, he didn't retreat. He was leaving as soon as he healed. They knew that, so why not enjoy a challenge—and her sweet smile and enticing touch—until then?

Chapter Seven

It wasn't right to be proud of being able to lean at the same time on his crutches and on the top rail of the fence around the pasture where Bay Boy had been turned out while his stall was being cleaned. But Toby was. With the crutches holding him, he folded his arms on the fence and stood as if his ankle had never been hurt.

At last, he was where he belonged. No longer a complete invalid.

He watched the big horse's gait with a practiced eye. Bay Boy showed no sign of favoring one leg as he'd seemed to on the trailer during the ride from Texas. Had the horse been faking an injury, or had it been so minor it had healed?

Without getting closer to the horse, he wouldn't be able to tell. The *doktor* and Howard had instructed him—and Sarah—that Toby must stay away from horses and view them from the far side of the fence until he could walk without crutches. The sight of the metal crutches might spook Bay Boy again.

Toby had to admit the precaution made sense, but he didn't have to like it. After more than a week and a half of doing exercises and spending too much of his time doing little more than sitting, he was itching to work with Bay Boy.

"Whatcha doing?" asked Natalie as she trotted to where he stood.

She wore bright pink shorts with polka dots and a garish orange shirt with a stylized cat on it. Her hair looked as if it hadn't been brushed, and neither her sneakers nor her socks matched.

"Watching Bay Boy. Does Sarah know you're out here?" He'd seen the girl wandering into the stables earlier but had figured she'd found something else to do by now. The grooms had mentioned there were two litters of kittens hiding in the hay stored behind the main building. If Natalie had been looking for them, she must have given up.

Natalie shrugged. "Sarah didn't get here early enough. If she wants me, she knows where to find me. She knows I love horses."

He translated that to mean Natalie had slipped out of the house before Sarah had arrived for the day. He waited for the irritation he expected to feel when realizing that he should keep an eye on the girl until Sarah came looking for her. It didn't buzz through him, and he was surprised to discover he was curious why the girl had sought him out.

Natalie scrambled to the top of the rail fence with an ease he had to envy. At times, it seemed as if it'd been someone else, instead of him, who used to be able to scale fences with ease. His hands could recall the firm, rough strength of a wooden rail beneath them as he vaulted over.

He grinned. Maybe Sarah was right. In some ways, he didn't act older than the kids who needed a goal to work hard. He should have laughed along with her when she'd said that. As he imagined laughing with her, seeing her eyes crinkle, he knew he'd been a fool to resist the impulse when they'd been sitting together on the porch last week. It was better in the long run that he hadn't, but letting the moment go past felt like a loss.

"He's special, ain't so?" Natalie asked.

He smiled at the phrase she'd learned from Sarah. "I think he could be."

"Bay Boy is strong." Her gaze followed the powerful horse galloping around the pasture. "Have you been working with him long?"

"About a year and a half, though I started training him when he wasn't much more than a foal."

"Did you start him off with a halter or a lead?"

He looked at the young girl beside him. She spoke with the authority and knowledge of a seasoned groom. "A lead."

"That's good."

"*Ja*, I agree. But why do you think so?"

Not taking her gaze from the horse, she said, "A lead lets the horse see you at the same time you're teaching it to listen to your commands." She leaned forward to rest her elbows on her knees, shifting to keep her balance on the top rail. "Horses don't like surprises. If you want them to trust you, you can't surprise them."

"That's true." He waited, wanting to gauge if she knew what she was talking about or just repeating what she'd heard in the barn.

"Bay Boy is special," she said again.

"Why do you think that?"

"He's well built, and he eats like a teenager." She

grinned. "Daddy said so on the phone." Her smile vanished as she looked at the horse.

Guessing she wasn't supposed to be eavesdropping on her *daed's* calls, Toby replied, "Eating well is important, ain't so?"

She smiled again. "Running is hard, and if he doesn't eat a lot, he can't run fast. He's calm." She glanced toward his bandaged ankle. "Getting scared by a cat doesn't count."

"No, it doesn't."

"He's going to be the best." The girl continued to list the reasons Bay Boy would make a great racer.

He listened, impressed with her insight, though he shouldn't have been surprised. The few times he'd seen Summerhays since his arrival, Natalie's *daed* seldom spoke of anything other than the horses in his stables and his hopes for them. *Kinder* soaked up everything they heard…even things adults didn't realize they'd overheard.

"*Ach*, here you are!" came Sarah's voice from behind them.

Natalie jumped from the fence, her smile vanishing. The girl nodded but didn't hide a rebellious expression when Sarah reminded her she should have let someone in the house know where she was going.

"I know," Natalie said.

"*Gut.* Now hurry inside. Your French tutor is waiting for you."

The girl muttered, *"Je déteste parler français!"* Her words were understandable to Toby, who knew no French but could read her body language. Her distaste for her lessons was as clear as if she'd shouted it. She stamped toward the house.

He turned to Sarah and couldn't help smiling when

he saw how the morning sunshine glowed off her downy cheeks. As always, that single strand of bright red hair refused to stay pinned beneath her *kapp*, and it edged her cheek to accent its gentle curve.

"How many times do you have to repeat the same thing before they listen?" asked Toby as Sarah pushed the vagrant hair into place.

"I'll let you know when I find out." She sighed. "It's not easy to scold them when they're doing what kids do."

"Did you say she's learning French? During the summer? Did she fall behind in her work during school?"

"No, Natalie is very smart. All four *kinder* have regular lessons. Language, swimming, dance, gymnastics, art classes."

"When do they have time to play?"

She grimaced. "On rare occasions, and when they do, they don't seem to know how to play the games our *kinder* do. They tend to go looking for trouble inside instead of finding a game to enjoy outside. They're learning foreign languages and how to swim, but not how to play."

"That's sad."

"I've been teaching them tag and a few other outdoors games." She walked to the fence and looked at Bay Boy and the other horses that had been let out with him. "Ah, now I see what lured Natalie out here. She loves everything about horses."

"Does Summerhays realize how much she knows?"

"I don't think anyone can be unaware of it. Natalie breathes and sleeps and dreams and talks endlessly about horses." Her smile faded as the girl's had, and for a moment, Sarah seemed as wistful as Natalie had while talking about Bay Boy. "I wish…"

"You wish what?"

Her battle with herself was visible on her face. She wanted to say something but was unsure if she should.

He halted himself from telling her she could trust him, that he wouldn't repeat what she said. Doing so would create another strand connecting them together. He had to figure out a way to pull apart the ones in place, not make more.

If she was aware of his struggle, there was no sign of it in her voice as she replied, "The *kinder* are eager to spend more time with their parents, but Mr. and Mrs. Summerhays are busy with other aspects of their lives. They don't offer their *kinder* much other than a nice home and plenty to eat, nice clothes to wear and educational experiences. You haven't been upstairs, but Natalie must have close to a hundred plastic and porcelain horses on shelves in her room. The other kids have as many toys, and there are enough books for a public library. They've got everything they need, just not what they want."

"So what are you going to do about it?"

Sarah closed her mouth that had gaped at Toby's forthright question. What was *she* going to do about the youngsters' longing to spend more time with their parents? From what she'd learned from Natalie, Ian and Jessica Summerhays had concentrated on their own lives for as long as the *kind* could remember. At first, Natalie as Jessica's daughter and Alexander as Ian's son had believed their parents would pay more attention to them after they were married. Nothing changed, though, even when Ethan and Mia were born. The girl said she and her siblings had hoped a move from New York City to Washington County two years ago would mean their *daed* wouldn't have to work endless hours and their *mamm* would spend more time with them.

Again, nothing changed. In fact, their *daed* was frequently gone overnight to New York City for business meetings, and their *mamm* seemed to come home only long enough to unpack and repack for her next trip.

Sarah had no doubts the parents loved their *kinder*, because they'd asked many questions during her job interview, and Mr. Summerhays had insisted on a background check. Each time either parent traveled, they brought home *wunderbaar* gifts for the *kinder*. They never seemed to comprehend that what their kids wanted most was time with them.

"Well?" he prompted when she didn't answer. "You're here for a reason, aren't you?"

"Ja." She'd applied for the job to help her brothers pay the bills while they made their sawmill, Christmas tree business and their few fertile fields profitable.

That wasn't what Toby meant. God must have brought her to this family for a reason. Could it have been to help the *kinder* by assisting their parents to see how much they were missing in not spending time with the mischievous quartet? The kids had done everything they could, being so outrageous she couldn't imagine what they'd do next, in an effort to get their parents to notice them.

Leaning her elbows on the fence, she said, "I've got to think about how to approach Mr. and Mrs. Summerhays."

"With the truth is the best way. They've pretty much handed their responsibility for their *kinder* to you and the others working in the house."

"I realize that." She wished her brothers would be a bit more like Ian and Jessica Summerhays, instead of judging everything she said and did as if she were as untrustworthy as a toddler. "However, I don't want to upset them so much they'll get angry. If I get fired, I won't be able to help further."

He gave her a wry grin. "You won't get fired. From what I've heard, the *kinder* have chased away every other nanny before you. One didn't stay a full day. Until you came along, the longest stint of any nanny was less than a month. Short of rustling Mr. Summerhays's favorite horses, I can't imagine anything you could do that would get you fired."

Sarah had to admit he was right. Within hours of her first day at the house, she'd realized her main job was to keep the *kinder's* parents from worrying about their offspring. But it still didn't feel right to speak about Mr. and Mrs. Summerhays when they weren't there to defend themselves.

When she told him that, his shoulders relaxed from their taut lines. "To be honest, I wasn't sure how you'd take my advice."

"I want to help this family."

"I know. They are like your family at this point."

"They are." She turned to head into the house, then paused. "We're having church this Sunday. Would you like to *komm*?"

"I don't have a way to get there."

"Of course you do. I'll come by. It's not more than about a ten-minute drive from my house." She chuckled. "Not that I drive often, because it's quicker if I cut through the woods and the fields between our farm and the stables."

She was sure he was going to say no, so she was amazed when he replied, "I'll go with you."

"*Gut.* Our services start at eight, so I'll be here about

a half hour before." She faced him. "I'm glad you'll be joining us."

"As I'm going to be here another month, it'll be nice to meet your neighbors."

"Our *Leit* is welcoming."

"As you've been with an injured man who's added to your responsibilities."

"I haven't minded." She looked forward to talking with him.

"I see how much you love taking care of these *kinder*. Anyone who spends more than a few seconds in this house can see how important this job is to you. That's why I half expected you to tell me to mind my business."

"I wouldn't do that."

"No, I suppose you wouldn't, but, Sarah, I want *you* to know I wouldn't suggest anything to endanger your job. I know how important it is to you."

She stiffened, biting her tongue. Toby couldn't mean his words the way she was hearing them. She didn't want to believe he was being overprotective like her brothers and as Wilbur had. Toby wasn't telling her what to do. He was being honest as he tried to help her make the best decision.

Right?

She wished she could be sure about that, but she wasn't going to make the same mistake again and let another man think she needed his help to keep her from making mistakes.

Chapter Eight

When Sarah drew her family's black buggy to a stop along the curved driveway in front of the Summerhays house, she wasn't astonished to see Toby sitting on the bottom porch step. She wondered how long he'd been waiting there and how long it'd taken him to maneuver down the stairs. A faint sheen of sweat on his forehead warned he hadn't been sitting there for more than a few minutes.

Nobody would be awake in the house before eight on a Sunday morning. It was the one day Mr. Summerhays slept late, and the *kinder* knew to be quiet until he woke. She'd seen motions in the stables, but those had been slow and she guessed whoever was tending to the horses wished he was still in bed.

Climbing out of the buggy, she watched Toby push himself up and rest his weight on the crutches. His dark coat had buttons. It must have belonged to Mr. Summerhays. With it, he wore a simple white shirt and his jeans and boots.

Lifting a folded *mutze* coat and vest out of the buggy, she handed them to Toby. "These should fit."

"Danki." He shed his coat. The vest and the coat were a bit taut across the chest, but he was able to close them with the hooks and eyes. When she held out a black felt hat, he asked, "Where did you get these?"

"They belong to my brother Benjamin. He's the taller of my brothers, so I figured there was a chance the clothes might fit you. Neither of them will be attending church this morning. They've got two cows in labor, and one had a tough time with her last calf. Or so they were told when they bought her."

Taking his other borrowed coat, she draped it over a chair on the porch. She turned toward him and pressed a hand over her heart as she tried not to gasp.

Toby was settling the hat, which was a bit small, on his head. It completed his transformation. Gone was the *Englisch*-looking horse trainer, and in his place was an Amish man. The black clothing contrasted with the streaks of gold in his hair falling along the standing collar of the coat, emphasizing the paler color as well as the shadowed crags of his face.

She was glad her face didn't display her shock. Or at least he didn't seem to notice as he made his way on his crutches toward the buggy.

"Nice horse," he said as he paused by the horse that was the same black as the buggy. "Slim, but with strong legs."

"Charmer came with us from Indiana."

"Charmer?"

"It was part of the much longer name Charmer had before he was retired from training to become a racehorse." She stroked the horse's nose. "That way, we didn't have to teach him another name." She smiled at the big horse. "Charmer is a charming guy. Somehow, he can smell an apple a mile away and, as soon as he knows it's nearby, he always manages to get his teeth on it. Not by stealing it or begging. Just by looking adoring and pitiful at the same time so you can't help but give him the apple."

"Sort of like Mia, who finds a way to get her hands on the last cookie."

She shook her head. "No, more like Alexander. Mia is young, so she's not as aware of what she's doing as her big brother is. Be careful if either he or Natalie start complimenting you. They're sure to ask for a favor afterward."

"So it's not just me they see as an easy mark?"

"*Ach!* I didn't realize they'd tried something with you."

"Last night they began to talk about how *gut* the ice cream is at the shop in the village. Wouldn't it be a shame, they pondered at length, if someone as kind and generous as I am didn't have the opportunity to try it before I left Salem?"

"That sounds like their usual style. Did you give in?"

"No, though I helped them raid the refrigerator to find pie from supper."

When she laughed, she listened for him to join in. He didn't. She'd never heard him laugh, though he smiled more each passing day.

Instead, he reached to climb into the passenger side of the buggy. "*Gut* foot first." He smiled.

When his eyes sparkled like stars admiring themselves in a deep pond, every bit of oxygen seemed to vanish from her lungs. She was aware of his strong arm draped across her shoulders and his lean leg pressed against her skirt. They'd been close many times during his physical therapy sessions, but standing within the arc of his arm now seemed so intimate.

He lifted himself into the buggy, and she handed him

his crutches without looking at him. Hurrying around the buggy to get in herself, she took the reins.

The clatter of driveway gravel against the metal wheels was loud. Once they reached the paved road, the horseshoes and the wheels combined to make a resonant sound that followed them toward the road leading into the hollow. She steered the buggy around a large pothole. Though Charmer would have skirted it, he didn't always keep the buggy behind him in mind.

Beside her, Toby was silent as he scanned the fields and the foothills rising to the Green Mountains to the east. The lush foliage layered the hillsides in every possible shade of green. She wondered how the view compared with Texas's hill country, but she didn't want to intrude into his thoughts.

Each time new questions filled her head, she realized how little she knew about Toby Christner. Somehow, he straddled the two worlds, Amish and *Englisch*, in a way she hadn't managed. She wanted to ask him how he did it, but to voice her curiosity might disclose her uncertainty about remaining Amish. She couldn't speak of that to anyone, because she didn't want her brothers discovering she was thinking of becoming *Englisch*.

He brushed sweat away from his temple. "If it's hot this early in the day…"

"It's going to be another scorcher." She smiled in his direction. "Of course, you must have a lot of days like this in southern Texas."

"That doesn't mean I like them." He lifted off the black hat and ran his fingers along the inner band. "Today isn't the day for a wool hat."

"Do you wear straw ones to services in Texas?"

He shook his head. "No, but it would be a *gut* idea."

"Maybe you should mention it to your bishop."

"He dragged his feet for a long time when the *Leit* voted to use solar panels for their local businesses. He's a fine man but doesn't like change." He looked away. "Not that I've gone to services much. Whose house are we going to?"

His question warned her he didn't want to talk about why he hadn't joined others on a church Sunday.

"The Bowmans," she replied. "David is a widower with two school-age boys. Their *grossmammi* takes care of the boys and the house. Here we are."

She pulled into the driveway leading to a well-cared-for white farmhouse. The barn behind it was smaller than on the other farms they'd passed, but it was sufficient for the ever-increasing flock of sheep David was raising. Wide grassy pastures led to foothills behind the house. Though the farm had the same number of acres as her family's farm, it appeared much larger because the hills around her home were covered with trees.

"There are a bunch of different buggies here." He pointed to where a half-dozen buggies were parked beneath a large maple.

"We've come to this new settlement from various districts and states. It was voted during the discussions on our new *Ordnung* that we'll use gray buggies like the ones from Lancaster County in Pennsylvania."

"But yours is black."

"We're from Indiana. The changeover won't start until after the harvest is finished."

"So every family can contribute something to pay for new buggies?"

She wasn't surprised he understood. Helping one another in a community was common among the plain people. "*Ja.* These other buggies will be sold or remade into vehicles we can use. Some may become open buggies. The Troyers' Delaware buggy will become our bench wagon to take supplies from house to house for church Sundays."

"How far along are you on your *Ordnung*?"

"We've discussed most issues. Buggies and clothing were first and the simplest. Last week, when we met, the focus was on what equipment can be used on the farms. Having diesel engines to power milk tanks was approved at that meeting, but we need to have more discussion about skid steers to move bales of hay or other heavy items."

He shifted his right leg with care. "I never thought about how many details there can be in an *Ordnung*."

"I don't think we realized how long it would take, but we're making progress. We hope to have it in place before communion Sunday in October so we can ordain our first leaders."

She didn't add more because her neighbors waved and called greetings. She saw the interest in everyone's eyes and knew they were eager to meet Toby. The Wagler twins stood to one side. Sarah realized Toby wouldn't be the only one fielding plenty of questions.

Toby was welcomed by the district's men as if he were a longtime member of the community. Nobody asked questions about where he lived or what he was doing in Harmony Creek Hollow. Instead, they were curious to learn how his ankle was healing and how the horses he'd brought with him were faring.

For a moment, he was leery. What had the Amish grapevine along Harmony Creek shared about him?

That he was stubborn? That he was from Texas? That his *daed's* assumption he knew more than anyone else had disrupted every district they'd lived in? Recalling how Sarah had said the people in the Harmony Creek settlement came from many districts, was it possible someone living here had once been in a community he and his family had joined temporarily?

He calmed himself. Nobody spoke of the past. The men were talking about the harvest. One mentioned the dearth of canning jars and how his wife had sent him to the next town to purchase some, which brought questions about where the jars had been found. Everyone who had a garden was now reaping the results of a summer taking care of the plants.

As the men gathered to go into the barn for the service to begin, Toby found himself in the middle. He worried about slowing others but managed to keep up with the elderly man in front of him.

The benches, set so the men would face the women during the service, were familiar and welcoming. He'd gotten out of the habit of attending services in Texas, and he'd forgotten the warmth of worshipping with others. In astonishment, he realized everyone in the barn, the men sitting on the backless benches and the women and *kinder* coming in to take their seats, were newcomers. Every other service he'd ever attended had been filled with people who'd been born, raised, and would die in that district.

No wonder nobody asked about his past. Everyone along Harmony Creek was interested in the present and the future they planned to build together.

Through the service, led by the bishop from a more established settlement thirty miles to the north, Toby had to struggle to keep his gaze from Sarah, who sat across from him. She was keeping a toddler entertained with a handkerchief that she'd tied to look like a bunny or a cat. The *kind's mamm* sat beside her, holding what looked to be a new *boppli*.

Sarah drew his eyes again and again. She looked somber as she listened to the sermons, but an aura of joy surrounded her as she cradled the toddler, who'd fallen asleep, in her arms. Being with *kinder* made her as happy as he was when he spent time with horses. They were blessed to have found jobs that gave them satisfaction.

He couldn't help noticing, though, how several other men glanced in her direction. He guessed, when she was ready to marry, she'd have her choice among her bachelor neighbors. Instead of a *gut* feeling of knowing someone who'd done so much for him would have a great future, his stomach knotted at the thought.

Had he lost his mind? *He* wasn't going to bind his life to someone who could tear him away from what he wanted to do and where he wanted to be. Maybe Sarah would settle in Harmony Creek Hollow for the rest of her life, but maybe not. She and her brothers had moved from Indiana. That was the way it had started with his parents. They'd lived their whole youths in one district, but then once they'd moved a single time, it seemed they had never hesitated to do so again. Would Sarah be the same?

He tried to focus on the sermon, because the bishop was an inspired speaker, but his thoughts kept creeping toward Sarah. When the service was finished, he watched when she went to speak with three other young women on their way to the house to bring food for the shared meal.

Again, Toby was made to feel welcome by the men, who were interested in the techniques he used to train horses. Nobody pressured him about his past or his future, and the subject again turned to the harvest and the volunteer work many of the younger men did with the local first responders. He found it fascinating, but his eyes cut too often to Sarah. If the others took note, they said nothing.

As soon as the women and *kinder* had eaten and the dishes were cleared away, she walked toward him. He thought she was ready to leave, until he realized she wasn't alone. The woman walking beside Sarah had midnight-black hair and dark brown eyes.

Sarah introduced him to Mercy Bamberger, who wore an identical *kapp* to hers, before adding, "Mercy is attending the class for this fall's baptism."

"Ja." She spoke as if trying out each word. "I grew up a Mennonite, and I'm learning what I need to in order to join this community."

"We can speak in *Englisch,*" he said.

"No, no," she urged, continuing haltingly in *Deitsch.* "I need practice. My kids speak it better than I do, and they laugh at my mistakes. Nothing like *kinder* to keep you from suffering from *hochmut.*"

Sarah laughed. "That's a lesson I learn anew every day when I'm with the Summerhays *kinder.* Just when I think I've convinced them to do something the right way, they show me that they can figure out more ways to *not* do it."

"I'd like to pick your brain, Sarah, for ideas to keep *kinder* entertained," Mercy replied, "once my summer camp is running."

"A summer camp?" he asked.

"We plan to open next summer. It's for city kids to have a week or two in the country."

"I've heard of such programs, but I didn't think the Amish would run one."

"With the bishop's permission, we're opening it on a trial basis next summer." She glanced at Sarah before adding, "That's why I wanted to talk to you, Toby. We're going to need gentle horses willing to be ridden by inexperienced riders."

He nodded. "Your riders will be nervous, so your horses must remain calm."

"Would you be willing to look at a few horses I may buy for the camp?" She glanced at his crutches. "If it's too much, feel free to say so. Jeremiah is so busy with getting in the harvest I hesitate to ask him. However, I want to get the horses moved soon so they're accustomed to us before the first *kind* arrives."

"Where are the horses?"

"At a farm in West Hebron. It's on the other side of Salem. About ten miles from here." She turned to Sarah. "What is the name of the van driver you use?"

"Did you sell your car?" she asked.

Mercy nodded. "A couple of days ago." She smiled in Toby's direction. "I don't miss not having electricity, but I miss having a car and jumping into it whenever I need to go somewhere."

"Jeremiah says you're getting much better driving a horse." Sarah gave her a warm smile.

"At least I'm driving the horse instead of the other way around."

"There's a phone in the barn. I can call Hank and see if he's available to drive us to West Hebron tomorrow."

When Sarah excused herself, Toby continued talking with Mercy about the camp. Each word she spoke amazed him more, because he couldn't imagine his bishop in

Texas allowing anyone in his districts to open a camp for *Englisch kinder* who lived in big cities.

Sarah returned before he could ask more. "Tomorrow won't work. Hank has appointments all day."

Mercy's smile wobbled. "I'll just wait until after school starts. *Danki*, Toby, for being willing to join us."

"Let me ask Mr. Summerhays if we can use his truck," Sarah said. "It's got plenty of room." She faltered. "It'll depend on having someone able to drive us."

"I can drive," he said.

Sarah frowned. "You sprained your right ankle. Don't you need your right foot to drive?"

"If it's an automatic—"

"It is."

"Then I can use my left foot." He grinned. "I've had to do that sometimes when working in the fields."

Mercy looked from Sarah to him. "Aren't you Amish, Toby?"

"I was raised that way, but I haven't made decisions about the future yet." He clamped his lips closed. He'd said too much.

Far too much, he realized, when he watched Sarah's eyes widen.

Sarah silenced the questions she wanted to ask. Why was Toby sitting on the fence as she was, trying to decide which side to jump to? He could continue to do the work he loved with training horses if he was baptized, though he'd be proscribed from driving. That alone wouldn't cause him to hesitate, would it? There must be another reason.

Toby kept so much to himself. He talked about horses, but his past was lost in a haze that was impossible to penetrate. Several times, she'd noticed him halt himself from speaking. He was a private man, and she respected that.

Somehow, she kept her curiosity to herself while they made arrangements to go to West Hebron the next day. When she got in the big red truck with Mercy and Toby the next day, she let the other two talk about the horses Mercy was interested in buying. If she opened her mouth, her questions might tumble out.

Sarah was grateful when they reached the farm nestled between two hills covered with pine trees. Unlike the ones Benjamin had begun trimming in preparation for customers in a few months, these trees were tall and unsuitable for what *Englischers* sought for holiday decorating. The red outbuildings and the bright blue house were as tidy as an Amish farm. Clothing hung from the line, dancing in the light breeze, but unlike plain laundry, the clothes were decorated with a variety of patterns, buttons and zippers.

Toby stopped the truck and released the breath he'd been holding for the past five minutes while he'd driven the big truck along a twisting dirt road that seemed to be built of rocks and potholes. She didn't blame him. They'd been bounced about, and she guessed he hadn't been sure if, sitting at an odd angle to let himself drive with his left foot, he'd be able to control the big vehicle if it were tossed too far to one side or the other.

"Now I know what cream feels like in an ice-cream maker." Sarah settled her *kapp* in place as they got out of the truck.

"Spun about." Mercy smiled. "I'm glad you were driving, Toby, and not me. Thank the *gut* Lord, Mr. Fleetwood has offered to deliver the horses if I decide to buy."

A trio of small white dogs rushed toward them, barking an enthusiastic welcome. They halted and regarded Toby. A low growl came from one.

"They're leery of your crutches," said a man stepping out into the sunlight. He slapped a dark blue baseball cap on his bald head. "Frank Fleetwood. You are?" He offered his hand, his white mustache tilting with his smile.

Toby shook it as Mercy introduced him and Sarah to Mr. Fleetwood. The man's hands were ingrained with black.

As if they'd asked, the old man said, "I had a blacksmith shop for forty years, but I retired earlier this year. Still getting the last of the soot out of my skin. I heard you Amish folks have a new smith coming to join you."

Sarah exchanged a glance with Mercy before saying, "I hadn't heard that, but I hope you're right. It can take several days for us to track down a farrier and get him out to replace a shoe."

"Hearing you say that makes me want to heat my old forge again, but the wife wouldn't appreciate that. She wants to travel more to see the grandkids in Georgia and Missouri, so I've hung up my tools." He shot Toby a wink. "If the rumors are true, let your new smith know I'm looking to sell my tools, so he's welcome to come and check them out."

"You should mention that to Jeremiah, Mercy," Toby said as they walked toward the pasture where a half-dozen horses grazed.

Sarah understood what he wasn't saying. He didn't want to be obliged to pass along the information…in case J.J. arrived sooner than planned.

When they reached the gate, Toby motioned for Sarah to come inside with him. "Help me here?"

"How?" she asked while Mr. Fleetwood went to lead the first horse, a dark brown gelding, toward them.

"Let me use you as a crutch for a moment."

She looked puzzled but nodded.

Leaving his crutches to lean against the rail, he put his hand on her shoulder. He hopped on his left foot and, with her to steady him, maneuvered himself so he was facing the horse, which the older man brought to stand near them.

She nodded again when Toby told her to copy his motions. She squatted when he did, each breath she took flavored with the mixed scents of horse and man, an aroma that would always remind her of this handsome man.

He slanted toward the horse, talking to it, and each motion brushed his muscular arm or leg against her. Focusing on what he was doing would have helped, but she couldn't stop from thinking about his inadvertent touch. He seemed oblivious, concentrating on his task. Why couldn't she be more like that?

Toby ran his hands along the horse's leg and frowned. "You need to have a vet look at this leg. It's swollen."

"Is that a problem?" asked Mercy.

He glanced at her. "It can be, or it can be something minor. It's important to make sure. I don't want you to get a horse you can't depend on." He patted the gelding and stood with Sarah's help. "I don't know, though, the last time I've seen a calmer horse. He should be *gut* with your city kids who aren't used to being around live animals. If he let me check his tender leg when he doesn't know me, he's not going to be bothered by someone who doesn't know how to sit in a saddle."

"He'll be good," Frank added, "if you want to do trail rides. He doesn't mind work, but he doesn't have much initiative. So don't make him the lead horse, and he'll do great." He grinned as he scratched the horse's nose. "Isn't that so, Cocoa?"

The horse bobbed its head as if it understood what the old man was saying.

Toby examined three more horses. One, though not young, shied away from his touch. That wouldn't do for a horse ridden by different *kinder* each week.

Mercy and Mr. Fleetwood agreed she'd buy Cocoa, after the vet checked him, and two other horses. While they discussed when the horses would be delivered to Mercy's farm, Sarah handed Toby his other crutch.

"*Danki* for helping Mercy get the best possible horses for her camp," she said when they went to the truck to wait for Mercy.

"I like to help." He smiled at her, sending a trill of joyful music through her. "As you do."

Mercy interjected as she joined them, "You're two of a kind. I'm glad you were willing to give me your opinion today."

Toby smiled, but it wasn't a steady smile. Sarah understood, because Mercy's words pleased and disconcerted her. How alike were she and Toby? Really?

He made no secret of how eager he was to be gone from Harmony Creek Hollow and how he was straddling the fence between a plain life and an *Englisch* one; yet he hadn't made a decision where his future was. She was the same, though she'd miss her family and friends in the new settlement if she jumped the fence.

She guessed there was one major difference. More and more, she envisioned her future with Toby in it. Did he see her in his?

Chapter Nine

"**R**eady to go?" called Natalie as she bustled across the yard the next morning, herding her younger siblings toward the red truck.

Sarah stood by the passenger door while Cecil, a groom, sat behind the wheel.

"Can we stop for ice cream at the soda shop?" asked Alexander.

"Ice cream! Ice cream! Ice cream!" The youngest two grabbed each other's hands and began to dance about in a circle.

"Whoa!" At Toby's shout, the *kinder* froze and stared in astonishment. "Why do you expect Sarah to answer you when you aren't listening?"

His question startled the foursome into silence. Turning so the *kinder* couldn't see his playful wink, he walked to where she stood.

"Welcome to the chaos," she said with a chuckle.

"Looks as if you're going somewhere."

"To get haircuts for the *kinder*." She arched a brow. "I'm sure they can fit you in, if you'd like."

He touched his hair that now reached the bottom of his collar. "It looks bad?"

She was glad Ethan let out a shout at that moment. It kept her from having to devise a way to avoid answering Toby's question. The truth was he looked handsome with his hair curling along his nape. Going to separate the boys who were arguing whether chocolate or chocolate-chip ice cream was better gave her time to compose herself.

"*Komm* with us," she said as she motioned for the kids to climb into the back seat of the large pickup. "It'll give you a chance to see something other than this farm."

When he nodded, her heart did jumping jacks. She shouldn't be reacting so to a man who would be leaving soon, but today she wasn't going to worry. She was going to be grateful to have another adult along with her to deal with the *kinder*. She tried to convince herself that was the only reason she was happy he was joining them.

But she—and her eager heart—knew it wasn't the truth.

Veronica's Shearly Beloved Salon was one of two beauty shops along Main Street in Salem. The name came, Sarah informed Toby as they got out of the truck, from the fact that Veronica's husband was the pastor at the community church around the corner on West Broadway, and Veronica did the hair of many brides he married. The beauty salon was located in half of what had once been a grocery store, so it had high metal ceilings and, along one wall, the original shelves now held beauty products instead of canned vegetables and mayonnaise. Four chairs were set in front of a long mirror on the opposite wall, and sinks and dryers were arranged farther back.

Toby followed the Summerhays kids into the shop. It

was, he was relieved to discover, only a pair of steps up from the sidewalk. His nose wrinkled. The odors of hair spray and permanent-wave solution filled each breath.

Every head turned as they entered. Two beauticians were talking by the front desk, three more were cleaning and a manicurist sat with an elderly female client at a small table half hidden by an artificial palm. At first, he thought the women were focused on the *kinder*; then he realized they were staring at him. Maybe, despite Sarah's offer, they didn't usually cut men's hair in the shop.

One beautician by the desk came to greet them. It was Veronica, and she wore her pure white hair in a bun resembling the one visible through Sarah's *kapp*. She bade the other women to come and collect the *kinder*. As they went to have their hair washed and Sarah followed, Veronica smiled at him.

"Are you here for a haircut, too?" she asked.

He nodded.

"Don't worry…"

"Toby," he supplied.

"Don't worry, Toby. You aren't a stranger in a strange land here. We do everyone's hair." She walked to the nearest chair. "Sit here. Do you need help getting into the chair?"

Shaking his head, he sat. He handed Veronica his crutches and leaned forward while she hooked a cape around his neck. When she asked where he was from, he told her.

"Texas?" she asked with a smile he saw reflected in the mirror. "You go for big hair down there."

He smiled, appreciating how she hadn't mentioned how he'd hobbled across the salon like a bird with a broken wing. "They say everything is bigger in Texas."

"Do you want something new or a trim?"

"A trim."

Sarah, who had come to stand between his chair and the one next to it where Mia now perched on a booster seat, bit her lower lip. Was she trying to keep from asking why he no longer wore the bowl cut he must have had as a *kind*? He didn't mind telling her he'd started having his hair cut in the *Englisch* style once he began working on J.J.'s ranch. It had helped make the other ranch hands forget he'd been raised Amish. He wasn't ashamed of his background. He just didn't want to have to answer the same awkward questions each time someone new was hired.

That was why he'd changed his look, ain't so?

He was shocked by an uncertainty he hadn't expected. *Was* he embarrassed that his past was different from the other ranch hands? No, he was grateful to have been raised plain. So why did he work hard to be like the rest of the world instead of separate from it?

Veronica said, saving him from more of the tough questions he didn't want to answer, "I've seen other Amish guys around the village, so I know how you wear your hair. I can cut it that way if you prefer."

"I'm not part of the Harmony Creek community."

"Oh, I assumed… That is, you're with Sarah, so I… Never mind." She kept her face averted as she reached for a pair of scissors on the narrow counter beneath the mirror.

Veronica thought he and Sarah were together? He couldn't ignore how his pulse quickened whenever he saw Sarah, but linking their names unsettled him. It was as if a thick vine wrapped around him, slowly tightening.

Natalie rushed over. "Can I have a blue streak in

my hair?" She held up a magazine with a picture of a woman in her twenties who had blond hair except for a coil pinned behind her ear. It was as bright a blue as a roofing tarp.

"Why would you want to do that?" Sarah asked.

He was curious, too, why the little girl would want to do such a thing. Natalie's black hair would have to be bleached before the dye was applied.

"All the girls at school said they were going to do that this summer, and…"

She smiled. "Your *mamm* will be home before school starts. If she says it's okay, then I'll bring you back to have it done."

Natalie nodded. Maybe the girl had learned whining wasn't the way to persuade Sarah to change her mind. Or perhaps she really didn't want to dye her hair and was glad for an excuse not to.

Mia tugged on Sarah's apron. "If Natalie gets a blue streak, can I?"

"That's up to your *mamm*," Sarah replied in the same serene voice.

Alexander jammed his hands into his jean pockets as he walked to a chair on the other side of Toby. "She doesn't care what we do as long as we stay off the furniture." Bitterness tainted the boy's words.

Toby put a hand on the boy's shoulder. "*Mamms* and furniture." He captured the boy's gaze so Alexander couldn't miss how Toby rolled his eyes. "They don't understand a guy needs to put up his feet and chill now and then, ain't so?"

The boy cracked a smile, then chuckled. "You get yelled at about furniture, too?"

"Every guy has been told the same thing since Eve

warned Cain and Abel to keep their feet off the sheepskin. Always the same things." Seeing how the *kinder* were listening with unusual intensity, he knew he couldn't stop now. He hoped the other adults understood he wanted to ease the boy's unhappiness. "We're always being told not to put our feet on the furniture. Wipe them off before we come in. Wash your hands and your neck. Don't forget to clean behind your ears. Do you think they go to school to learn how to nag at a guy?"

Alexander giggled along with the other *kinder*.

Behind Toby, Veronica laughed. "I like that one about Eve scolding her boys. I'll have to share it with my hubby. I can just hear him using it in a sermon some Sunday."

Her words seemed to be an invitation for each person in the salon to try to be silly. Even the old woman having her nails done pitched in with an absurd comment.

Toby let Veronica clip his hair while he listened. When he looked at the mirror, he saw Sarah regarding him with a smile. He gave her a wink, and color blossomed on her face. She turned away, and his smile broadened. He hadn't expected to have so much fun getting his hair cut.

By the time the buggy pulled into the farm lane and parked by the house she shared with her two brothers, Sarah's ears had been battered by dozens of questions from the *kinder*. They were beside themselves with curiosity about the trip she'd told them would include visits to two farms. If Toby, who sat beside her in the buggy's front seat, wondered where they were going, he didn't ask.

Maybe because he couldn't have gotten a word in edgewise. His repeated attempts to remind the *kinder* they needed to give Sarah a chance to answer one question before they asked another had been ignored.

She knew the big white farmhouse looked shabby next to the elegant house where the Summerhays family lived, but it now felt like home. The flowers she'd planted beside the front porch steps were flourishing, and the vegetable garden was lush with vegetables. She spent every Saturday and most evenings canning them so she and her brothers would have delicious vegetables in the depths of winter.

"Here we are." She shouted to be heard above the roar of the sawmill on the hill beyond the barn.

"What's that noise?" Natalie asked as she helped Mia and Ethan out of the buggy. All four *kinder* wore denim shorts and T-shirts along with sneakers.

"My brothers are sawing lumber."

"Why?" Mia put her hands over her ears. "It's loud."

"They're cutting lumber so people can use the wood to build things. Like buildings or furniture."

"Like wood?" asked the little girl.

"Lumber is wood." She smiled, astonished how much these *kinder* who'd been raised in the city needed to learn about country life, though they'd lived on the fancy estate for two years.

She had to wait until she could speak with Mr. Summerhays, but she hoped the *kinder's daed* would agree to letting them play with Amish *kinder*. It was important the kids get to know each other as individuals, not as plain or *Englisch*.

"So you grow wood here?" Mia was having a difficult time figuring it out.

"We have a wood lot." She smiled. "And, of course, a Christmas tree farm."

"Christmas tree farm?" Now it was Ethan's turn to

look puzzled. "Don't Christmas trees come from the store?"

"*Real* trees are grown just like all the other plants God created for our world." She took the little boy's hand and held her other one out to Mia. "These aren't the artificial ones made out of plastic."

"We have a pink tree and a white one." Natalie grimaced. "Neither of them grew on a farm."

"We have plain old green ones. Would you like to see them?"

The four *kinder* nodded, even Alexander, who sometimes liked to pretend he wasn't interested in what his siblings were.

Sarah kept the pace slow enough so Toby could keep up with them. With the trees set into a hillside, the path rose steadily. Years of dragging cut trees had worn a gentle path between the rows.

The shriek of the saw ruined the quiet among the trees. Each time it halted, there was a moment of silence, and then the birds seemed to find their voices again. As the *kinder* looked around in awe at the trimmed Scotch pine and fir trees, their eyes seemed to get bigger and bigger.

Toby came to stand beside Sarah as she urged the youngsters to wander among the trees. When he added a warning to be careful and not damage them, she chuckled.

"I don't know what they could do to damage a Christmas tree," she said.

"Mrs. Hancock mentioned yesterday how, while you were helping me with my physical therapy, she found the boys fishing in their *daed's* tropical fish tank by tying strings onto chopsticks. After hearing that, I'm assuming they can always find something to create havoc."

Again, she laughed. "You're right."

Mia ran to them. "Why are there branches on the ground? Are the trees broken?"

Hearing the dismay in the *kind's* voice, Sarah knelt so she could look the little one in the eyes. "No, they aren't broken. We call those boughs."

"Like 'deck the halls with boughs of holly,'" said Ethan.

Mia bristled at her brother's superior tone. "These aren't holly! They're Christmas trees! What do we do with these?"

"Alexander, will you get the bags I put on the rear platform of the buggy? Let's gather the boughs, and I'll take you to visit someone who will know what to do with them."

Though the *kinder* tried to get her to explain further—and Toby asked a couple of times what she planned—Sarah would only say that they'd be happy they'd collected the boughs. She went to help the smaller two carry the boughs to where Toby held large plastic bags open.

He proved to be an excellent manager. He kept the four *kinder* running to collect the boughs that Benjamin had clipped off the trees before they arrived. The bags at the back of the buggy quickly filled.

As he teased the youngsters, making them laugh, Sarah felt her heart melt in the warmth of his smile. He was so *gut* with them, bringing out a silliness she'd never realized was there. He was luring her to be as zany, and it was *wunderbaar* to toss aside her worries about the future and revel in the day they were sharing.

Natalie held boughs to her face. "This smells cool."

"Hmm…" Toby bent to take a sniff. "To me, it smells

warm. Like a fire in a fireplace. Like the scent of gingerbread."

"I meant cool as in…as in really…" She looked at Sarah for help.

"As in fabulous?" Sarah asked.

"*That's* what I meant."

Toby dropped the boughs into a bag. "I agree. The scent is cool and warm at the same time." He glanced down when Mia tugged on his shirt. "Do you have something to add, munchkin?"

"You're goofy," she announced with the certainty of a four-year-old.

"Me?"

At his feigned shock, Sarah couldn't keep from laughing. The *kinder* joined in, but not Toby. He smiled.

She told herself she should be satisfied with seeing an honest smile on his face instead of the strained, false one he'd worn when he first arrived. She couldn't help wondering what his laugh sounded like. Would it resonate as his voice did?

Lord, You know the state of Toby's heart. He has allowed a bit of joy to enter it. Please help him keep it open for more happiness to sweep in.

What could she do to help? Getting an idea, she smiled and gathered the *kinder* near.

"Shall we pick out a tree now for you at Christmas?" she asked.

The excited youngsters cheered. Before they could scatter, she reminded them it was a decision they needed to make together.

For the next fifteen minutes, they wandered among the rows of trees. Once or twice, she thought the *kinder* might agree on one, but then another caught their eyes.

She had to veto some because even the high ceilings in their house wouldn't accommodate such a towering tree.

"I like this tree." Ethan pointed to one not much taller than he was.

"Don't you think we should let it have a chance to grow a couple more years?" Sarah asked.

"If we get a bigger tree, then what if Daddy isn't home to put the star on top? *I* can put a star on top of this one."

Pretending she hadn't heard Toby's sharp intake of breath, Sarah knelt in front of the little boy. She blinked away her tears before they could escape and upset the *kind* more. Not just Ethan, but his siblings, who also looked ready to cry.

"Don't you like having a bigger tree better, Ethan?" she asked as she cupped his elbows to make a connection between them.

He nodded, his lips beginning to quiver. "It needs a star on top."

"I'll talk to your *daed* about the star."

"Daddy is busy."

"*Ja*, I know. We're months away from Christmas. We can figure something out between now and when the tree arrives at your house."

He wiped his nose against his sleeve. "Okay."

When she urged Ethan to join his siblings, who were discussing the merits of a nearby tree as if it were the most important decision ever made, she waited until he was out of earshot before she released the sigh that weighed on her heart.

Behind her, Toby said, "You surprised me, Sarah."

"How so?" She faced him.

"You're always working for those kids to challenge

themselves. I thought you'd offer to help him put the star on the tree himself."

"I would have if he was worried about the star." She lowered her voice as she stepped closer to him. "What he really wants is time with his *daed*." Looking at the youngsters encircling a pretty Scotch pine, she added, "Just as Alexander was when he complained about his *mamm* being more worried about the furniture. *Danki* for drawing him out of his bad mood then."

"He was feeling sorry for himself."

"No, he wasn't. He isn't wrong, you know." She sighed. "His *mamm* spends a lot of time worrying about the furniture. I'm not sure why she changes it all the time. Whatever the reason, it keeps her away so often, and the *kinder* miss her. Those four *kinder* want someone—anyone—to pay attention to them."

"You said they want their parents' attention."

She put a hand on his arm to stop him from following the *kinder* up the hill. When he turned toward her, she said, "Of course they want their parents' attention first and foremost, but they'd be happy to have anyone's. That's why I try to take them places where they can be pampered a bit, like getting their hair cut or to the ice-cream shop."

"Have you mentioned this to them?"

"The *kinder*?"

He shook his head. "No, their parents."

"No."

"Why not?"

She clasped her hands behind her so he couldn't see how they tightened at the futility of the situation. "I don't want them to think I'm sticking my nose in where it doesn't belong. I'm their nanny, not a family member."

"Don't tell the *kinder* that. They treat you like a beloved *aenti*."

"Maybe, but an *aenti* isn't a *mamm*."

"Are you arguing for telling your bosses the truth or against it?" He gave her a taut smile. "As I've told you before, they're not going to fire you. Why would they when they've had so much trouble finding a nanny who will stay?"

"You're looking at this logically, and logic might not have anything to do with their reaction. If they do fire me, then the *kinder* will have nobody other than a parade of other caretakers."

"As they did before you were hired?"

"*Ja.*"

She must choose the time to confront them, so they would listen. How she wished Toby understood! He wasn't going to remain in Harmony Creek Hollow to see the consequences, so she had to trust her instincts.

Could she trust her instincts right now when her heart begged to be given to him?

Chapter Ten

Toby recognized the name on the mailbox as Sarah turned the buggy into the lane leading to a farm set on a broad lawn. Wagler was the surname of her twin friends. He wondered which one they were visiting after collecting the pine boughs. Or would both women be there?

He thought about what he'd witnessed after church when Sarah and her three *gut* friends laughed and chatted together with an ease that suggested they'd known each other their whole lives. However, he'd discovered that they'd met only a few months ago.

Was it possible for him to build strong friendships as Sarah had? He'd avoided them, even while working on J.J.'s ranch. Maybe he should consider lowering his guard and explore the possibilities of developing more than work relationships. Friendships and—he glanced toward Sarah, who was focused on driving along the twisting lane—perhaps something more.

Then what? demanded the voice that always warned him away from making rash decisions.

He wanted to retort to the voice but had never won an argument with it in the past. The one time he'd refused to heed it when he was twelve ended with his heart being broken into uncountable pieces. Once burned, twice the fool to try again.

To ignore his thoughts, Toby looked at the farm ahead of them. It looked like the others they'd passed on their way along the twisting road into the hollow. There was a rambling white house, recently painted because it glistened in the sunshine. A broad yard was edged by flowerbeds and a vegetable garden. Every row seemed to be exploding with vegetables waiting to be picked.

Behind the house were three barns, a chicken coop and what looked like a rabbit hutch. A pen was filled with goats in every combination of white, black and brown. One barn was much larger than the others, and he guessed it held the farm's milking parlor. The rumble from the smallest outbuilding told him the Waglers had a diesel generator to run their milking lines and the air compressors that powered other equipment.

Toby listened to the excited *kinder* behind them as Sarah slowed the buggy beside the house. The youngsters scurried out as soon as the wheels stopped moving, but halted when Sarah asked them to wait in case he needed help.

He could get out of the buggy on his own but didn't gainsay her, knowing she was using him as an excuse to keep the youngsters from scattering like windblown leaves.

Alexander stepped up, flexed his muscles with a big grin and offered to help Toby. With one hand on the boy's scrawny shoulder, Toby made sure he didn't put too much weight on Alexander.

Doing so made it more awkward to get out than on his own. He grimaced as he shifted his balance onto his right side while trying not to knock the boy over. Gripping the edge of the windshield, he nodded his thanks to Alexander, who was grinning as if he'd been the greatest help imaginable.

"*Danki*, Alexander," Sarah added, stepping toward them and steering the boy away without appearing to do so.

"Why are we here?" asked Natalie.

"You'll see."

"Why won't you tell us?" Ethan stuck out his bottom lip.

Sarah smiled and tapped it, making the boy grin and his siblings giggle. No wonder Sarah was so *gut* with Bay Boy. She'd shown the horse the same patience she exhibited with four impatient *kinder*. Not that she was passive. Quite to the contrary, because he'd seen her eyes filled with heated sparks, but she knew how to pick her battles and when.

When she hadn't said anything to him on the short trip from her brothers' farm, Toby was sure something was bothering her. He thought through their conversation among her family's Christmas trees. She'd been distressed by how Summerhays and his wife paid too little attention to their *kinder*, but she'd been ready to speak her mind on that subject.

So what was bothering her now?

You.

Again, the small voice in his mind startled him. He'd heard it as clearly as he could the birds chirping overhead and, for once, it wasn't warning him away from becoming too close to someone. Instead, it was telling him the reason why there might be a wall between him and Sarah.

Maybe it was for the best. Every day he lingered was

another drawing him into the community in the hollow. Each moment he spent with Sarah enticed him to look forward to the next time they could be together. In spite of his determination, his life was being linked to hers and her neighbors.

That would change once J.J.'s trailer pulled into the long driveway of Summerhays Stables.

A door to the house opened, and a petite brunette walked toward them. He wasn't sure which twin she was until Sarah greeted her.

"Leanna, in case you don't remember, this is Toby Christner." Sarah smiled.

"Nice to see you again, Toby." The brunette who was shorter than Sarah turned to the *kinder*. "Now, let me see if I can match the right name to the right person." She pointed to each *kind* and spoke his or her name.

"How do you know I'm Mia?" asked the littler girl.

"Because Sarah told me you loved animals, and I can see how eager you are to meet my goats." Leanna held out her hand.

Without hesitation, Mia grasped it. The two led the way toward the pen where the goats rushed forward as Leanna approached. The little girl didn't falter when the animals, which must have seemed huge to her, crowded around the fence. A pure white kid jumped onto a plastic box so it could look at Mia.

"Will it bite?" the little girl asked.

"Any animal with teeth can bite." Leanna's voice was calm. "Snowball is a *gut* little girl and likes to have her head scratched between her horn buds."

Mia reached through the fence and touched the kid on the head. When her hand was butted, she giggled before scratching Snowball. She grinned at her siblings as more young kids pushed forward to get attention.

When Leanna opened the gate, Mia was the first to follow her into the pen.

"She's brave," Toby said.

"*Ja*, she is." Sarah's smile softened. "She adores animals, but it's more than that." She gestured toward where the *kinder* were now encircled by the goats. "They're hungry for love."

"The goats?"

"No, the *kinder*." She faced him. For a moment, sunshine glinted off her glasses, hiding the expression in her eyes. "They've been left behind too often."

"You're worried they're going to be hurt when I go back to Texas."

"*Ja.*"

He wanted to ask how she would feel when he left, but he'd hurt his ankle, not his head, so he didn't have an excuse to ask a stupid question. Better to focus, as she was, on the youngsters.

"If you want," he said, "I'll wait here."

Shock filled her eyes. "No, that's not what I want. I don't know what I want." She grimaced. "Don't change what you're doing. The *kinder* will be upset when you go, but won't it be better to give them nice memories of your times together to enjoy when they think about you after you've left?"

Without giving him a chance to answer, she pointed at the buggy and asked him to bring a bag of pine boughs to the goats' enclosure. She lifted two bags off and walked toward the gate.

He sighed as she strode away. Nice memories of times together? Maybe that would be sufficient for the *kinder*, but he doubted it would be enough for him. Was it possible he'd been wrong? Could it be that time spent building a relationship had nothing to do with the pain of breaking that connection with someone? He wasn't sure any longer.

The pine boughs were a huge success for the goats who ate them as fast as the *kinder* could take them out of the bag. Sarah stood between Mia and Natalie as they hand-fed the goats. Leanna kept an eye on the boys and made sure no animal got too aggressive.

Sarah giggled when the goats tried to climb one another for the treat. If Mia made sure Snowball got more than her share, nobody said anything. Each Summerhays *kind* seemed to have a favorite or two among the small herd.

There were complaints from both the *kinder* and the kids when the bag was empty. Leanna was adamant that too much of a *gut* thing was bad for goats.

"How can fresh greens be bad for them when they eat tin cans?" asked Alexander, digging out a final bough from the bag.

"They don't eat cans," Leanna said as she rolled the plastic bag and held it too high for the goats to reach. "They will eat the paper stuck to the outside of cans, but not the metal itself. That's a *narrisch* story."

"What?"

"A crazy story," Sarah explained. "*Narrisch* means crazy. Or you can say someone is *ab in kopp*."

"*Kopp* means head, ain't so?" asked Ethan.

Sarah nodded. "I didn't realize you knew that."

"I want to learn to speak Amish so I can play with the kids in the hollow." He grimaced. "Not these kids, but the others."

"I know what you mean." She brushed dirt from an overeager goat's hooves off his back. "I didn't realize you knew the *kinder* here."

"I don't. Not yet." He turned to where Toby was leaning on the fence, his arms folded on the top. "Toby said we could have fun with them and go sledding after it snows."

"Did he?" She wondered when Toby had mentioned such things to them. Probably while they were collecting the boughs. Once she had a chance to speak to Mr. Summerhays, she wanted to introduce her charges to the local plain *kinder*. She had some ideas of how to do that, but she must make sure their *daed* approved.

As Ethan babbled about finding the biggest hill and riding on the fastest sled, she extracted the four youngsters from the herd. The goats stepped aside reluctantly. The *kinder* went out, telling Toby about everything they'd done, though he'd witnessed each minute. They skipped to the buggy to bring the other bags of pine boughs to the barn.

When Leanna closed the gate, she paused and looked at the goats feasting on the pine needles that had fallen on the ground.

Sarah waited beside her friend as the *kinder* followed Toby to the buggy. She couldn't keep from smiling. There was something so endearing about the strong but injured man listening to four youngsters vying to get his attention and asking his opinion. It would have been wiser to keep distance between him and the *kinder*—and her— but it was impossible.

"Be careful," Leanna said in not much more than a whisper as she latched the gate. "Don't get your hopes up, Sarah."

"My hopes up? On what?"

"On persuading Toby to stay here in our settlement."

"I'm not trying to convince him to stay in Harmony Creek Hollow." *I don't know if I want to stay.*

Leanna patted the head of a goat that butted her through the fence, looking for another treat. "It looks like you are. I'm not the only one who thinks so."

"Annie—"

"It's not just us. Lyndon asked me about you and Toby and your plans. Several people mentioned it to him after you arranged for Toby to check out the horses Mercy wants for her camp."

Lyndon was older than the twins. He lived nearby with his family, including his son, who was a *kind* Sarah had in mind for Alexander to play with. Now she wondered what the reaction would be if she asked.

"Your brother shouldn't listen to gossip or repeat it." Sarah struggled to swallow her dismay.

If her brothers heard such rumors and believed them, what would they do? They seemed determined to prevent her from making mistakes. They could insist she avoid Toby, though she had no idea how she would while working at the house where he lived.

Don't borrow trouble, her common sense warned her.

Leanna put kind fingers on Sarah's arm, and Sarah knew her thoughts had seeped out to be displayed on her face. "Don't worry, Sarah. Lyndon didn't speak about it to anyone but me. He wanted to know if it was true you and Toby were walking out together, because he planned to squelch the rumor if it wasn't."

"So you told him it wasn't so."

"I told him the truth. I didn't know if you were trying

to convince Toby to stay or not." She wiped her hands on her apron.

"Toby has made it clear right from the beginning that as soon as his boss returns, he'll go home to Texas."

"Things change."

"Not that much. Toby loves his life in Texas."

"How much do you love your life in Harmony Creek Hollow?" Leanna looked away as she asked, "Would you leave here to go with him?"

"I've never given that idea the slightest thought." Whether she stayed plain or became *Englisch*, she intended to remain close to her family. Her brothers might want nothing to do with her, but she couldn't imagine walking away from them forever.

Leanna smiled. "I'm glad to hear that. You've become a dear friend, Sarah, and I wouldn't want you to leave the Harmony Creek Spinsters' Club."

A gasp came from behind her. Sarah whirled to see Toby standing there. How much of their conversation had he heard?

"Harmony Creek Spinsters' Club?" he repeated as his eyes widened. "Did I hear you right?"

"It's a joke." She hoped her face wasn't turning red, but the familiar heat warned her that her skin was becoming the same shade as her hair. "It's a name we older unmarried women gave ourselves when we decided to do more things together. We didn't want to call ourselves the 'Older Girls Club' because that sounds worse."

"But Harmony Creek *Spinsters'* Club?" He started to add more, but his words dissolved into a laugh that burst from deep within him.

She couldn't help but stare. There was such candid and unabashed joy in his eyes and his stance as he leaned on his crutches. The Summerhays *kinder* rushed over to discover what was behind his unexpected laughter.

Then she began to laugh, too. She hadn't imagined Toby's laughter, once freed, would be so infectious. When Leanna and the youngsters joined in, the goats began to bleat as if they wanted to be part of the merriment.

"Everyone tell Leanna *danki* for letting us visit her and her goats," Sarah said when she could talk again.

The chorus of responses included Toby's much deeper voice.

"*Komm* anytime," Leanna said. "I can always use helpers to feed the goats."

"Now," Sarah added to curtail pleas to stay longer, "we need to get home for lunch, lessons and—" she turned to Toby and said with a mock frown and a stern tone "— physical therapy."

The *kinder* and Toby gave emoted groans but went to the buggy. Sarah gave her friend a quick hug before following. They waved goodbye to Leanna as Sarah drove them toward the road that followed the sinuous Harmony Creek.

Again, the conversation in the back seat was nonstop until the youngsters scrambled out in front of the Summerhays house. They rushed up the porch steps, and Sarah reminded them they needed to wash first.

Toby followed her as she unhitched Charmer and put him to graze.

"I owe you an apology," he said.

"For laughing at our club's name?" Her grin ruined her attempt to sound serious.

"No, for mentioning about the kids going sledding with the other *kinder* without saying anything to you first. I don't know if I've stepped on your toes."

"You haven't. I've been thinking about ways to get

the Summerhays *kinder* and the plain ones together to play when they're not in school. There aren't a lot of *Englisch kinder* nearby, and they need to have friends beyond each other."

"The *kinder* will be excited to have you act as a conduit for them to meet others their own ages among the *Leit*."

"I grew up with a group of five other girls who were with me from diapers to school and beyond. We did everything together, learning to cook and do farm chores and take care of the smaller ones. We helped each other in school and, when we were old enough, we attended singings and other youth gatherings together. I know how important those friendships have been to me."

"Do you still hear from them?" he asked as they walked toward the kitchen door.

"*Ja*. We have a circle letter that was started when the first of us moved away. Now we live in three states and five districts."

"You've got a miniature version of *The Budget*, ain't so?"

She laughed at the comparison. "The circle letter keeps us up-to-date on what the rest of the family is doing. Between the six of us cousins, we connect to two hundred people."

"You and your friends are cousins?"

"*Ja*. My *daed* had seven brothers and six sisters."

"And your *mamm*?"

"Was an only *kind*." She laughed at the memory of *Mamm* telling how much trouble she had learning all her future in-laws' names.

"As I was."

She stopped to pick up an early hazelnut that had fallen in the yard. Its husk tried to stick to her fingers, but she rolled it along her palm. "I can't imagine that." She tossed the nut into the bushes for a squirrel to find. "Or maybe I can because it's just Benjamin, Menno and me now. I miss the rest of the family. Do you miss yours?"

"Not really. After our first move, we never lived near family again."

"My brothers may be overbearing at times, but they're family." She paused as they reached the back door. "I'm sorry you missed out on having a chance to get to know your extended family."

"I am, too." His eyes widened. "Usually when people say things like that, I shrug it off. However, you're right. After seeing what the Summerhays kids share, it makes me wish I could have had that, too."

"You can have it now. Either with the kids, who think of you as a big brother, or in our community."

"You know I'm only staying until I get the *doktor's* okay to work, ain't so?"

"Of course, but why not enjoy what's here while you do?" She wasn't sure if she'd have another chance to share these thoughts with him. Having the *kinder* with them most of the day, it wasn't simple to discuss serious issues. "Natalie loves talking about horses with you."

"Ja."

"Alexander and Ethan need a man to talk to. I can help the girls with things unique to girls, but with the boys, it's not as easy." She smiled. "You were a boy. You know how they think and feel. Would you—while you're here recovering—be that person they can turn to?"

"I'll have to think about it. Being a mentor to a *kind* is a big responsibility, Sarah."

"The biggest, but from what I've seen of you, you aren't a man who avoids responsibility. If you were, you wouldn't be miserable waiting to get back on a horse and continue training those three horses you brought from Texas."

"And spending a day at the stables in Saratoga."

Her smile returned. "Don't worry. I haven't forgotten. If you get the okay from the *doktor*, I'll talk to Mr. Summerhays about taking you there."

"In the meantime, I'll come up with ways to spend more time with the boys."

"Danki," she said.

His gaze swept her face and held her eyes. His eyes narrowed ever so slightly as his fingers curved along her cheek. Startled by her powerful reaction to his questing touch, she recoiled. He lifted his hand away, but she edged toward him again.

He murmured her name. Or she thought he did. Her heart was thumping too hard for her to hear anything as his fingers cupped her chin. As he tilted her face toward his, she held her breath, wondering if his kiss would be as sweet as she hoped.

When his lips brushed her cheek, she bit her lower lip to keep her sigh of disappointment from escaping. She blinked as he opened the door to release the cacophony of four *kinder* talking at once. His *"danki"* remained behind when he entered, leaving her outside alone.

She turned away and wrapped her arms around herself, cold though the day remained hot and humid. How *narrisch* she'd been to think he'd kiss her! He'd been honest from the beginning. He couldn't wait to leave for his life with its few obligations. He knew how he wanted his life to go. She'd been *dumm* to think anything—or anyone—could change that.

Especially Sarah Kuhns.

Chapter Eleven

Sarah's brothers were quiet the next evening during supper. Instead of discussing, as they usually did, their day at the sawmill and what they would do the next morning, Menno and Benjamin were as silent as the clock she'd forgotten to wind before she left for the Summerhays house. They spoke only when they asked for food to be passed. As always, the evening meal was smaller than the midday meal. She'd prepared a casserole with ham leftover from earlier in the week along with cheese and pasta. A salad with vegetables she'd picked an hour ago in the garden and the bread she'd baked yesterday shared the table with pickles and apple butter and a bowl of chowchow.

Each attempt she made at starting a conversation failed while her brothers ate. Even when she asked how much longer it would take to fill the corncrib, they shrugged at the same time. That startled her because any other night, they would have given her a lecture about how, as a woman, she didn't need to worry about the crops and that she should focus her concerns on her garden and the house.

She tightened her grip on her fork before setting it on

her plate. Miriam and the Wagler twins didn't have to endure such reprimands. Their families treated them like vital members, not a fragile piece of china that needed to be guarded from encountering the realities of life on a farm.

When they had first moved to the hollow along Harmony Creek, she'd assumed her brothers' reluctance to be honest with her was because of their fears they couldn't make the farm a success. They'd set up the sawmill, tilled the fields and planted apple trees. It would take three years before the trees bore fruit, but in the meantime, Menno and Benjamin could build their other businesses.

However, her brothers were determined to farm. It'd been three generations since the Kuhns family had depended on fields for their livelihood. What once had been their farm in Indiana had been sold acre by acre until only a single one remained. The men had worked in the RV factories or in shops owned by *Englischers*.

Their first harvest was about to get underway, and they were concerned about the amount of corn they expected to get from the few arable fields attached to their farm. The old corncrib had been emptied and swept out. Slats to prevent animals from getting in had been replaced. She guessed the corn, when stripped from the stalks, would fill about half of it.

"More biscuits?" she asked, holding up the plate.

Benjamin took two and mumbled a "*danki*," but Menno didn't glance in her direction.

Her brothers couldn't look less alike. Menno had hair as dark as a bear's. In fact, his friends in Indiana had called him Big Brother Bear before he was baptized. Benjamin's hair had red highlights but was otherwise a plain brown. Both men had work-worn hands with layers of calluses from the long hours they'd spent at the sawmill or in the fields. Though neither brother would admit it, she guessed they'd discovered they didn't like farming as much as they'd hoped. As soon as they could make a go with the sawmill, she suspected the fields would be rented to a neighbor. Most likely to David Bowman, because she'd heard her brothers discuss having sheep near their house.

After a second silent prayer of thanks when their dessert of chocolate cake with maple frosting was gone, Sarah began to clear the table. She set the dishes in the sink and ran hot water. The dish detergent spit air, and she knew she needed to add another bottle to her shopping list for the next time she went into Salem to grocery shop with her friends. She turned to write it on the whiteboard hanging on the refrigerator.

"Sit for a minute," Menno said before she could return to the sink. "We need to talk."

"About what?" she asked as she wiped her hands on the dish towel. Hanging it on the oven door's handle, she walked to the table.

Her brothers exchanged glances but remained silent while she pulled out her chair and sat.

She was tempted to tell them they'd explained everything to her with that single shared look. How many times had she seen it since *Daed* died and her brothers took his place as head of their household? More times than she cared to count.

Each time, she saw those expressions before they were ready to announce something she wasn't going to like. They hadn't liked the idea of her working out as a nanny. They weren't sure she should spend so much time with her friends in the Harmony Creek Spinsters' Club. *Ach*, she was grateful she hadn't mentioned that name in front of them!

Worst of all was the look they aimed at each other—and at her—when she'd talked about becoming an EMT. They'd acted as if she'd announced she wanted to run off and join a Broadway show. Her brothers had refused to discuss it, even Benjamin, who could be more reasonable. They were so certain of their decision that they seemed to believe she was the one who couldn't see the truth.

Sarah folded her hands on her lap and waited to discover what her brothers had to say.

As always, Menno, as the oldest, took the lead. "Our sawmill is doing better with each passing week. We're gaining more customers. Many are our neighbors, who are fixing farmhouses in the hollow, but others are *Englischers* who wish to have custom work done for their homes or businesses."

"That's *gut*," she said with a sincere smile. "You've worked hard to establish the sawmill as the go-to place for fresh lumber."

"Go-to?" asked Benjamin.

"Something the Summerhays *kinder* say. It means—"

Menno interrupted her. "We know what it means. I didn't know you did."

"I hear the same things you do."

"I'm sure you hear more at that *Englisch* house."

She frowned. "Why are you acting distressed about my job? I've been there since the end of last year. You've been grateful for my wages and how I have time to take care of this house as well as be a nanny for the *kinder*."

"Things change." Menno raised his chin as if daring her to contest his statement.

"I agree." She wasn't going to quarrel with her brothers.

Benjamin surprised her when he said, "Get to the point, Menno." He usually went along with whatever their older brother did.

When Menno refused to meet her eyes, she could contain her curiosity no longer. "*Ja*, Menno," she said, "please say what you want to talk to me about. I'd like to get the dishes done in time to do mending before bed."

Menno drew in a deep breath, then said in a rush, "James Streicher is interested in meeting you."

She searched her mind. Three families had moved into the settlement along Harmony Creek in the past month, but she couldn't recall anyone by that name. There had been a tall, thin man she didn't recognize at the last church Sunday services. Was he James Streicher?

"I don't think I know him," she said.

Her brothers looked at each other again before turning to her.

Benjamin answered this time. "We met him yesterday. He's sharing a house with the Frey family while he builds his own place next door."

"Next door to the Freys?" She thought the Troyers lived there.

"No, next door to us." He pointed to the east.

"There's another farm between us and the Freys?"

"Not a farm. Just a couple of acres on the other side of the creek, but James doesn't need much space. He's a blacksmith. The last *Englisch* smith closed his forge a year or so ago. There's a real need for a blacksmith in the area."

She thought of Frank and the rumor he'd heard about a blacksmith coming to Harmony Creek. "It sounds as if James has seen a *gut* opportunity in our new settlement."

"James's got a *gut* head on his shoulders." That was

the finest compliment Menno could give. He had no use for emotion, only common sense and hard work.

Which made Sarah wonder why he didn't offer her more respect. She worked hard every day at the Summerhays house while making a home for her brothers. When they had to stay late at the sawmill or while doing other chores around the farm, she never once complained. She kept their meals ready for them whenever they wanted to eat.

"He's come from Milverton in Ontario," Menno added. "In Canada."

Not wanting to tell him she knew geography, too, she replied in the same steady tone, "I don't think I've ever met anyone from those districts." She smiled at her brothers, wondering why they were making such a big deal about a new neighbor. "I'll make sure I greet James after our next church service and welcome him to our settlement."

"Make sure you talk to him," Menno said. "It'll be better if you do before he brings you home from the singing."

Sarah sat straighter, her eyes widening. She must have heard her brother wrong. He expected her to accept an invitation for a ride home with a stranger from a youth event that she hadn't planned to attend?

Impossible.

As she started to say that, Menno waved her to silence. "You didn't hear me wrong, Sarah. James will be bringing you home from the singing."

"You told him I'd let him do that? Without mentioning it to me first?"

"You've been running around with your friends long enough, Sarah. Benjamin and I agree it's time for you to marry. As your brothers, we want to see you settled."

"Whether or not I'm happy to be settled with someone I've never met is irrelevant, ain't so?"

"We don't want you to be miserable," Benjamin said, shooting a frantic look at their older brother.

"But," Menno continued, as if they'd practiced the conversation—and she wouldn't have been shocked to learn that they had, "if you're going to argue you need to fall in love first, you know many marriages have been successful though the couple weren't in love when they married."

"I didn't realize either of you was an expert on either love or marriage."

Sarah should have wanted to take back the words as soon as she spoke them because she saw how Benjamin cringed, but she was too angry. She'd heard whispers about Benjamin and a young woman walking out together in Indiana, but even if it'd been true, the young woman had married someone else.

Was her brother the victim of a broken heart? Had he waited too long as Leanna had to share the truth with the one he loved?

Her sympathy for Benjamin was swept aside when Menno stood and pointed at her. "You will agree to this, little sister. We know it's time for you to be done with your work as a nanny and for you to start a family of your own. James has seen you, and he's willing to walk out with you in spite of your bizarre ideas."

"Like learning to help others as an EMT?" She rose, too, though she knew she was throwing oil on the fire of her brother's fury.

"He knows—as I do…I mean, as *we* do—that a plain woman's place is taking care of her family, not *Englisch* ones."

"But—"

"I won't argue about it. Our minds are made up." Menno whirled on his heel and stamped away.

She looked at Benjamin. Again, he wouldn't meet her eyes as he stood and followed their older brother into the front room.

Frustration sent her toward the back door. This time, her well-meaning brothers had gone way too far. She grabbed her bonnet off the peg and tied it beneath her chin. Going out, she prayed a walk would give her enough time to cool down.

She wondered if it was possible to walk that long.

Toby was standing by the pasture fence and watching Bay Boy go through his exercises with Mick, the most skilled groom at Summerhays Stables. Bay Boy wasn't as skittish with the other man as he'd been when Mick first started working with him. The horse was confused why Toby remained on the other side of the fence.

"Don't let him turn so slowly!" Toby called. "He needs to lean into the turn if he's going to keep up with the field."

Mick motioned he'd heard as he continued to work with the horse.

"He's stubborn, isn't he?" Natalie asked as she came to stand beside Toby.

He stared at the *kind* in astonishment. There wasn't an inch of her not covered with mud. Had she been rolling in puddles?

As if he'd asked aloud, she said, "We've been building a castle behind the house."

"Where they've been taking down the trees?"

Ethan bounded to join them. "It's the best, Toby! You

need to come and see our castle." The boy and the other two who appeared on his heels were as filthy as Natalie.

"It looks as if you've been having a *gut* time," Toby said with a laugh. Odd how easily laughter came now that he no longer tried to dam it inside him.

He listened as they told him how they'd dug around the disturbed ground and how Alexander had the big idea to link the holes to form a moat. When they finished their tale, he sent them off to the stable to wash off before going into the house. He doubted Mrs. Hancock would appreciate four mud-covered youngsters on the fancy floors and carpets.

When they scurried away, Toby turned to watch Bay Boy finish his session. His eyes focused on a familiar form that appeared from among the trees at the far side of the pasture. Sarah was coming across the meadow. He waved to her and smiled when she changed direction to come toward where he stood.

His smile faded as she strode past him and inside the house. She hadn't acknowledged him.

Turning, he hobbled into the smaller living room with its large fieldstone fireplace and beamed ceiling. He ignored the fancy overstuffed furniture and elegant wooden tables, his gaze focused on Sarah. He was amazed she didn't pound her feet right through the floor. He jammed the crutches under his arms and moved so he was in her path as she turned to storm across the room.

She stared at him. "What are you doing, Toby?"

"Trying to make sure you don't wear out your shoes with pacing."

"Leave me alone." She pushed around him and kept going as if the answer to whatever she sought was ahead of her.

"If you wanted to be alone, then why are you here?"

She halted midstep and blinked several times without speaking. At last, she said, "I'm not sure."

"About why you're here?"

"That and everything else." She began walking again. "I was headed out for a walk in the woods, then I ended up here." She gestured toward the door. "The woods aren't too wide between this house and my brothers' farm."

"Sit down, Sarah. I can't keep up with you."

She sank into the closest chair.

He pulled another closer to where she sat. Resting his crutches against his chair, he slanted toward her, his clasped hands between his knees.

"Danki," he said.

"For what?"

"For not making me chase you in order to find out what's going on." He appraised the tight lines he'd never seen in her face before. Emotion exploded through him. Anger, he was shocked to discover. He'd been angry plenty of times, but not like this. It was a cold anger ready to be detonated at whomever had caused her to pull inside herself like an armadillo curled into an armored ball. "What's wrong?"

She didn't answer him right away. Instead, she stared at her hands in her lap. Her knuckles were colorless, warning she was clenching her hands to the point they must hurt.

He reached across the space between them and put his hand over hers. He wanted to pry her fingers apart as he banished whatever was upsetting her, but he forced himself to do nothing but gently stroke her soft skin.

"What's wrong?" he asked again in a whisper. "Will you tell me?"

Raising her eyes, she met his gaze. He could see the flood of tears she was holding in by sheer will. "My brothers."

"What about them?"

"They're playing matchmaker."

"For each other?"

A reluctant smile tipped her lips for the length of a single heartbeat. "If they were doing that, I wouldn't be upset. They're matchmaking for me."

He arched his brows. "Brothers setting up their sisters with fellows is a pretty common occurrence."

"You don't understand. They've matched me with James Streicher, a man I've never met."

"He's a newcomer to the settlement?"

"So new he doesn't have a home of his own yet."

"So they knew him when you lived in Indiana?"

She shook her head again. "He's from Canada. They met him for the first time yesterday."

"They want you to marry him after they've met him a single time?"

He hadn't had a chance to speak with her brothers yet, but if they had half as much integrity as Sarah, they must be honest, *gut* men. Making such a snap judgment about a stranger made no sense.

"That's what they said." She wrung her hands together again in her lap. "After being so overprotective of me that they make it hard for me to breathe, now they're ready to hand me off to someone I've never met."

"Are you going to do as they ask?"

Her head whipped up. "Menno is the head of our household. It behooves me to do as he asks."

"Behooves?" He was rewarded by her faint, swift smile, but it faded again. "That sounds like the Sarah Kuhns you don't want to be. The one who wouldn't help the kids because she's worried about her job."

"I don't want to be that person."

"I know that. You'd rather be the Sarah Kuhns who lets everyone know how she feels. The one who longs for something she doesn't know she can have if she's Amish."

Her eyes grew so round that he could see white around her deep brown irises. "I've never said anything about that."

"No, you haven't, but you've said a lot about making sure the Summerhays *kinder* have the lives they want."

"I have?"

"About them having time with their parents and asking me to help with the boys. You're trying to give them plenty of experiences so they can learn and do things they may not be able to imagine now." He took her hands and folded them between his. "You don't want them to feel smothered as you do by your brothers' *gut* intentions."

She sighed as she stood. "*Smothered* is the exact word."

He pushed himself to his feet, too. "So what are you going to do about it?" he asked as he had when they spoke of the *kinder's* longing to spend time with their parents.

Unlike that time, she didn't square her shoulders and give him a strong, assertive answer. Instead, she hung her head and whispered, "I don't know."

He could have no sooner stopped his arms from enfolding her to him than he could have stopped the sun from rising the next morning. As he drew her against his chest, she pressed her face to his heart. He wondered if she could hear how it was breaking.

For her, because she was torn between her hopes for the future and what her brothers had planned for her?

Or was it shattering for himself as he realized he would never have another chance to hold this woman who fit so perfectly in his arms?

Chapter Twelve

On the next Sunday morning, a humid day where breathing was so hard Toby could have believed he was underwater, he found it hard to accept that two weeks had passed since the last time he'd sat on the front steps and watched for a buggy. It meant he'd completed nearly half of his banishment to Summerhays Stables.

Banishment? It didn't feel like that any longer. He was able to go to the stables, though he had to remain on the sidelines so the crutches didn't spook the horses. Even so, he could watch as the three horses they'd brought from Texas, along with the others, were exercised. He spent time talking with the stablemen about the horses and their idiosyncrasies. He learned training for Summerhays's horses began at these stables, and only the horses that achieved a certain competency were taken to the stables in Saratoga for further training.

In addition to his physical therapy, he spent time with the Summerhays *kinder*. He watched them take their swimming lessons while he put his foot in the hot tub, letting the jets work on loosening the muscles. He enjoyed talking with Natalie, who knew more about horses than most grown-ups, including people he'd worked with on J.J.'s ranch. He and Natalie had developed an easy rapport. She tried to stump him with questions and, so far, he'd been able to answer each one. The other kids would join them, but none was as horse-crazy as Natalie.

Then there was Sarah. Each morning as he opened his eyes, his first thought was how blessed he was to spend time with her. He hadn't had an excuse to hold her again as he had the evening she'd wandered from her home to the pasture out by the stable, seeking an answer to her dilemma. He doubted he'd done anything to help her make that decision simpler, but the memory of her, warm and soft, in his arms warned him his attempts to be standoffish with everyone until J.J. and Ned returned had been futile. He couldn't wait each day to see Sarah. Even last Sunday when there had been no church service, she'd come by to take him to visit with her neighbors.

They hadn't stopped at her family's farm, and she hadn't introduced him to her brothers. Toby didn't know if they wanted nothing to do with him or she was avoiding what might be an uncomfortable meeting. Though she hadn't said, he sensed she feared if her brothers discovered how much time she was spending with him, Menno and Benjamin would become more insistent she marry the new blacksmith.

He looked at his bound right ankle. The worst of the swelling had vanished, leaving a variety of colors from a plum purple to a banana yellow laced across his foot and on his shin. Gone, too, was the devastating pain of the first weeks. Each motion threatened to bring it back, but he'd learned to avoid movements that sent a jagged shard slicing along his leg.

Sarah had helped him get to this point. He must not do anything to make the situation worse for her.

Though he'd tried several times in the past three days to turn their conversations to her brothers' matchmaking, she'd refused to speak of it. He wasn't sure if that was a *gut* thing or bad. One fact was irrefutable. She was going to remain in the Harmony Creek settlement, and he was heading to Texas as soon as J.J. got back.

A gray-topped buggy drove up the long drive toward the house. Toby came to his feet. Sarah had been quite clear her family wouldn't be trading their black Indiana buggy for a Lancaster County style one until after the harvest was in.

Who…?

The buggy stopped, and a short man with a thick brown beard stepped out. He reminded Toby of someone, but Toby wasn't sure whom.

"I'm Lyndon Wagler," said the man. "My sisters, Annie and Leanna, are friends with Sarah. When she mentioned you'd need a ride to the service, I volunteered."

"Danki," he said, glad he had to concentrate on getting himself and his crutches into the cramped buggy.

That way, neither Lyndon nor his wife and *kinder* could get a glimpse of his expression. Before he'd been able to control his face, he knew his disappointment must have been visible on it. Why hadn't Sarah mentioned to him that she was sending someone to collect him for the service?

His stomach ached as if Bay Boy had driven a hoof into it. Could she have gone on her date with the newcomer and taken such a liking to the man she wanted to avoid complications by being seen with Toby? She hadn't said when she was seeing James. Had Toby been wrong to assume it would be after the youth singing tonight? No, he realized. She had arranged for someone to get him so she didn't have to bring him home when she was supposed to ride with James tonight.

Everything made sense.

And everything made his stomach threaten to erupt.

Making sure he was wearing an innocuous smile as he sat in the front next to Lyndon, Toby turned to say, *"Gute mariye."*

Lyndon's wife, who introduced herself as Rhoda, smiled before cautioning her young son and daughter to stop trying to peer out the rear of the buggy. Chuckling, Lyndon added that too often they had to halt the buggy to collect hats or bonnets that had fallen off the *kinder's* heads when they tried to see everything they passed.

Toby appreciated the Waglers' easy acceptance of him as they drove to the Troyers' house at the end of the hollow. When they pulled to a stop before a big farmhouse that looked as if it'd had recent repairs to its roof, he wondered how many different homes he'd entered on church Sundays. He'd lost count years ago. At least on this church Sunday, many of the faces were familiar from when he'd worshipped with these people two weeks ago.

While Rhoda took her *kinder* and went to stand with the women, Toby and Lyndon joined the other men waiting to enter the house with the beginning of the service. Which one was James?

It was easy to pick out Sarah's brothers. The family resemblance was strong between the siblings. They must be a decade older than she was. Neither wore a beard, showing they hadn't married, which was surprising.

Maybe, like him, they hadn't felt at home in one place and didn't want to put down roots and make connections until they found that place where they intended to stay. No, that didn't make sense. As far as he knew, Sarah had lived in only one community near Goshen, Indiana, before moving to Harmony Creek. Unless her brothers had jumped from district to district as his parents had, they came to the hollow from northern Indiana, as well.

As if he called to them, the Kuhns brothers edged toward him through the gathering of men. Lyndon gave him a bolstering smile before going to talk to a tall man Toby knew was Caleb Hartz, the man who'd gathered the families together for the new settlement.

"I'm Menno Kuhns," said the man with the darker hair. "This is my brother, Benjamin."

"*Gut* to meet you. I'm—"

"We know who you are. Toby Christner, the Amish cowboy who's living with the Summerhays family out on the main road."

"I work with horses, not cows." He tapped one crutch with the other. "Though right now, I'm not doing much of either."

His attempt at levity was wasted. The Kuhns brothers continued to scowl at him as if he were a snake they'd found in the henhouse.

"You're from Texas, we hear." Benjamin spoke but kept glancing at his brother.

Toby was curious why. *"Ja."*

"You're here for only a short time?"

He hit one crutch with the other. "I'm here until I can get rid of these."

"Looks as if you're doing pretty *gut* now."

Toby felt his feigned smile wither, and he struggled to keep it in place. Even if Sarah hadn't confided in him about her brothers' plans to match her with someone she didn't know, he would have been able to gauge what the real meaning was behind the interrogation. The Kuhns brothers wanted to make sure he remembered he wasn't staying long in Harmony Creek Hollow.

Why didn't they just come out and ask how long he was staying? He didn't appreciate their sly attempts to ferret out information he would have given them without a second thought. Did they think he would tell them a bold-faced lie? What sort of man did they think he was?

He flinched at the thought. Had the tales of his *daed's* troublemaking reached the brothers? His *daed* had believed he knew more than any minister or bishop, and he never hesitated to give his opinion, whether welcome or not. That outspokenness had vexed many people who hadn't liked the idea of a newcomer trying to change their ways. Corneal Christner had never learned, making the same mistakes as he moved his family from one district to another, always looking for those who would agree with his outrageous opinions.

Toby didn't remember living in northern Indiana, but families in one settlement had friends and family members in others, so rumors—both true and exaggerated—were shared along the Amish grapevine. Letters and gossip exchanged by neighbors moved more swiftly than the news printed in *The Budget.*

"I've been told it'll be a couple more weeks," he said coolly, "before I can head out of here."

The two men exchanged another glance before Benjamin said, "Sarah knows, ain't so?"

"She was there when I got the *gut* news. Your sister has been a blessing. She helps with my physical therapy. She has a real gift for helping those in need." He shouldn't have said the last, but he didn't like how the

Kuhns brothers acted as if she couldn't form a single worthwhile thought on her own.

"Ja," Menno said in his grim tone. "She'll make a *gut mamm*, tending to scraped knees and other childish injuries. Anyone can see that."

"That's true."

"Soon enough, she'll be settled here," Menno added, reminding Toby of how his *daed* had made his comments in a tone that suggested no sane person would argue with them.

The rebellion and irritation inside him were familiar. How many times had Toby heard his *daed* say such things and then watched as others reacted? Too many to count. Each time, Toby had wanted to shout that his *daed* spoke for himself alone. There were those who deemed the son should suffer for the sins of his sire, but they seemed to forget that God had promised in the Old Testament to make sons suffer if their *daeds* hated God. Corneal Christner didn't hate God. He insisted that others share his ideas of how to worship Him and live in His service.

The Kuhns brothers walked away without another word. That told Toby—in no uncertain terms—even if he had two legs that worked as they were supposed to, he wouldn't be welcome if he went to see Sarah at her house. Her brothers didn't want her spending time with him.

If he pushed the issue, he feared Sarah would be the one to suffer. As he and his *mamm* had suffered, time and again, for his *daed's* insistence that he knew more than others. After seeing his *mamm's* grief each time they'd prepared to move again, he knew he couldn't be the cause of Sarah suffering the same sorrow.

James Streicher gave Sarah a faint smile as he held out a stack of plates covered with cupcake and cookie crumbs. The food had vanished during a break in the youth group's singing. She put the three plates she held on the others and thanked him. When he said he was glad to help, those were the first words he'd spoken to her. She waited for him to add something, but he turned on his heel and walked away.

Was he shy? If so, why had he agreed to her brothers' suggestion that he escort her home from the evening's events? Maybe he'd been too timid to ask her himself.

Her eyes were caught by an uneven motion by the door, and her heart leaped to attention. Her joy deflated when she realized it wasn't Toby, but a teen boy who'd broken his leg when he fell asleep and toppled off a wagon.

She'd hoped Toby would remain for the singing but guessed he'd left with the Waglers. Each church Sunday, Lyndon got his family home in time for him to do barn chores, so he would have left earlier in order to get Toby to Summerhays Stables.

She sighed when she saw the teens streaming out of the barn. They'd be pairing up for rides home in open courting buggies. It seemed like a lifetime ago she'd hoped Wilbur would ask her to go with him. Before she got to know him well, he'd seemed lighthearted compared to her brothers. How wrong she'd been!

When she couldn't remain behind in the barn any longer, she went outside. Most of the buggies had left. The few who weren't courting were clumped in groups of three or more to share the walk home along the dark, twisting road. Each group had at least one flashlight with them. *Englisch* drivers often sped or raced on the road, so it was vital to have something to show them pedestrians were there.

James stood by his buggy. Even in the fresh air, the odor of smoke and heated metal drifted from him. He helped her into the buggy, and she gave him a grateful smile. She wasn't sure if he saw it in the dim light from the Troyers' front porch. She waited for him to say something, but he was silent other than giving his horse the command to go.

He didn't speak while they drove along the road, taking care to avoid walkers.

Unable to endure the strained silence any longer, she said, "I appreciate you giving me a ride home."

"You live right next door to me, so it makes sense."

She smiled again, glad he'd given her more than a single-word reply. To keep the conversation going, she asked, "Do you like our new settlement?"

"I've been here only a few days, so I can't have an opinion yet. So far, so *gut*." There was a hesitation, then he asked as if realizing he needed to say more, "How about you? Do you like living along Harmony Creek?"

"I'm looking forward to seeing fall, because the *Englischers* I've spoken with tell me these hills and mountains are glorious when the trees begin to take on their autumn colors."

"Are you with the *Englisch* often?"

"I'm working as a nanny for an *Englisch* family out on the road to Rupert."

"That is *gut*. I'm sure your brothers appreciate your help when they have to focus on getting the sawmill going."

James drew in the buggy near one of the few *Englisch* homes along the road. The gaslight on top of an antique lamppost washed over them, allowing her to see his face.

She averted hers because she wasn't sure what her expression might reveal.

"May I ask you a question?" he asked.

"Certainly." She forced herself to look from her folded hands to the man beside her.

"This whole me taking you home was your brothers' idea, ain't so?"

"They think it'd be a *gut* idea if we got to know each other better."

He smiled, shocking her because until then he'd been as serious as a sinner confessing before the *Leit*. "That's a nice way of saying I'm right. You're a nice person, Sarah."

"*Danki.* You've been kind to me, too."

"Kindness and attraction isn't the same thing."

"No."

A long sigh swept out of him. "I'm glad you agree, Sarah. I wouldn't want you to get the wrong impression."

"That you're desperate for a wife?"

"*Ja.*" His smile returned. "As you're desperate for a husband."

"Is that what you think?" She halted herself from asking if others thought that way, too.

"Not at all, but your brothers suggested you were."

"They said that?" Sarah bit her lower lip to keep her annoyed words from escaping. She hadn't imagined her brothers would say such a thing to a stranger.

"If it makes you feel better, Sarah, I never believed a popular woman like you was desperate for a husband."

"*Danki.*" She meant that sincerely. "And *danki* for being so nice about this."

"I've got older siblings, too, who think they know more than I do." He sighed. "I wouldn't say *ja* if someone asked me if I left Milverton because I was tired of their interference in my life, because one is supposed to speak well of one's family, but…"

"But?"

"I wouldn't want to lie, either, and say that person was wrong."

She relaxed, letting her shoulders ease from their stiff stance. "My brothers mean well, and I know they love me."

"As my older siblings do me. One saved me when I was little from falling into the farm pond and drowning. However, once I was old enough to swim and look both ways along the road, they didn't believe anything had changed."

Sarah laughed, something she'd doubted she'd do while with him tonight. "Maybe your older siblings and mine are the same people. They act the same."

He chuckled with a rasp she guessed came from his hours in his smoky smithy. "That would explain a lot, ain't so?"

"I'm sorry Menno and Benjamin welcomed you to Harmony Creek Hollow like this."

"Don't be. I'm glad to have a chance to talk with you. I could use insight about the settlement." He laughed again. "From someone who isn't focused on having me marry his sister."

"Ask whatever you want."

Sarah was able to answer most of his questions about where to shop for groceries and how to advertise his services. Several of the men with businesses had hung flyers at the hardware store in Salem and found work that way. Word of mouth had taken over from there, and many of their *Englisch* neighbors looked for help from the plain artisans. When she mentioned Mr. Fleetwood was interested in selling his blacksmithing tools, James was thrilled to hear that.

"I'm going to have to thank your brothers," he said with a grin, "for insisting on me taking you home tonight. You've been a great help."

"Feel free to ask anyone for help. We're learning the best ways to live here. Any questions you've got, we've had at one time or another."

"That's *gut* to hear. Look, Sarah, I know your brothers are worried about someone named Toby. They mentioned several times they were unhappy about you getting involved with a drifter." He frowned. "Though, I have to say, from what I can see, you've got a *gut* head on your shoulders."

"Toby works at the same place I do. He was injured, so my boss asked me to help him with his physical therapy." The words were bitter on her lips, but they were the truth. Her foolish heart begged her to give it to him, but Toby had been honest with her from the beginning. He couldn't wait to leave for Texas.

"Maybe so, but your brothers are determined to keep you from walking out with him. And I don't have time for their matchmaking. I assume you don't, either."

"You're right."

"Here's what we can do. We'll talk to each other when we encounter each other, whether at Sunday services or during the week. That's what *gut* neighbors do anyhow."

"True."

"Being seen together should encourage your brothers—and anyone else interested—that we're aware of each other. Maybe more. We can leave that to their imaginations. In the meantime, your brothers will back off, and I can focus on getting my business going. Is that okay with you?"

"I wouldn't want to lie."

"I'm not asking you to. I'm asking you to let others make assumptions."

It made sense. She could count James as a friend, but until her heart came to its senses, it wouldn't be willing to be offered to anyone except Toby. As that wasn't going to happen, she needed time to figure out what she'd do after he left. No doubt, Menno and Benjamin would redouble their efforts to find her a husband. She had to have a plan in place before their *gut* intentions ruined her life.

"Okay," she said.

"Danki." He raised the reins to tell the horse to drive toward her road a few yards away.

She halted him and got out of the buggy. There was no reason for him to come to the house. Walking up the lane herself would add to the supposition she and James were trying to keep their relationship a secret.

God, danki for having James be so honest with me. Please help my brothers understand their love for me doesn't have to be so overpowering.

Sarah turned to watch James drive away, the metal wheels on his open buggy catching the moonlight. A few minutes later, she smiled as she climbed the stairs to head to bed. Benjamin and Menno were grinning as if they'd won a great victory.

It was a temporary diversion. Eventually they'd take notice, especially if James found someone he wanted to court. For now, she'd appreciate the reprieve. It was a precious gift. She hoped God would soon show her what she should do once Toby left.

The thought sent tears flooding into her eyes. She was grateful he was healing well, but she had no idea how she was going to tell him goodbye.

Chapter Thirteen

"Mr. Summerhays, may I come in?"

Sarah peeked around the corner of her boss's office. When he smiled and motioned for her to enter, she saw he had a phone pressed to his ear.

She tiptoed into the room. Arranged on the dark green wallpaper above the dark wood panels was a collection of photographs of Mr. Summerhays's prize-winning horses. Two horses had been immortalized in oil paintings.

As soon as Mr. Summerhays was done with his call, he pointed to a chair in front of his large desk. "What can I do for you, Sarah? The children are doing well and behaving for you, aren't they?"

Sitting, she wondered what he would say if she spoke from the heart, pleading with him to discover the answer for himself. She'd grasp on to any excuse for him to spend time with his *kinder*, but he would beg off, saying he had important work to do as he had the few times she'd tried to broach the subject.

Toby was correct. If she didn't say something blunt, neither parent was going to see the mistakes they were making by being focused on things other than their youngsters.

Now wasn't the time to mention that. Not if she wanted Mr. Summerhays to agree to a favor.

"I'm here to talk about Toby," she said.

"Who?"

"Toby Christner. The man who injured his ankle and is staying here until J.J. Rafferty comes for him."

Mr. Summerhays's face remained blank.

"Toby is," she said, trying another tack, "the horse trainer who was hurt when unloading Bay Boy."

"Ah! I know whom you're talking about now. What about him? Is he having trouble getting better?"

She silenced her sigh. Mr. Summerhays was focused on his horses and his work in New York City. Nothing else, not even his family.

"No, sir," she said. "He's doing well. In fact, his physical therapist says he's improving faster than expected. That's why I'm here. He's anxious to get back to work."

"That's excellent news. I knew I could depend on you, Sarah, to make sure he was taken care of."

Amazed he recalled he'd asked her to assist Toby, she said, "I'm glad to help. I must admit I told him that he'd get a prize if he met his physical therapy goal." Realizing how that sounded, she hurried to add, "Would you be willing to let him spend a day at the stables near Saratoga if his *doktor* gives him permission to do so? He's interested in seeing your stables there."

Mr. Summerhays frowned. "It's the middle of racing season. I don't have time to babysit someone."

"You wouldn't be babysitting him, sir. You only need to have someone take him there and bring him home at day's end. Toby gets around fine now."

He drummed his fingers on his desk, then looked at his cell phone as it buzzed. His brows lowered. "I'll make sure he gets a tour."

"One other thing? May I cancel the lessons for the *kinder*—the children—tomorrow and take them on a special trip in the buggy?"

"Yes, yes." He waved her out of his office.

Before she had stood, he was talking into his phone. She hurried out, happy Mr. Summerhays had agreed to her requests, but sad he considered taking the call more important than finding out where she planned to take his *kinder*.

Soon, she promised herself. Soon, she'd do as she and Toby had discussed. She would speak to Mr. Summerhays about spending time with the youngsters. She wished she knew how to initiate that topic.

A hint of fall banished the humidity the next morning. Sarah guessed it would return, but, for now, she was going to enjoy the pleasant day. The Summerhays *kinder* should enjoy the treat she had for them. As for Toby...

She wasn't sure what he'd make of the surprise she had planned for the youngsters today. He'd seemed astonished when she asked him to join them for a drive along the road into Harmony Creek Hollow. To be honest, she'd been amazed when he agreed to come.

Charmer stepped along the road, as delighted as Sarah was at the cooler weather. The *kinder* were enjoying the ride and discussing where they might be going.

She didn't realize she was humming until Toby asked, "What tune is that?"

"My happy song," she replied with a smile.

"I'm guessing your date on Sunday night went well."

"It wasn't a date." She wagged a playful finger at him. "You've spent too much time with *Englischers*."

"Enough to know a plain man taking a young woman home from a youth event, Sarah, is like an *Englischer* asking her to a movie. Lots of darkness and whispering."

She arched a brow at him. "*Ach*, I didn't realize you were an expert."

"I'm not, but you're avoiding answering my question. Just tell me it isn't my business."

"It *isn't* your business, but I'll tell you my date went as I'd hoped it would. James was nice."

"But?"

"You're nosy, you know!"

"As nosy as your brothers?"

Sarah laughed without a hint of humor. "Nowhere near. I told them enough to be honest and keep them from planning another date for us right away." Folding her arms in front of her, she asked, "How was your evening?"

"Not as noteworthy as yours, I'm sure."

Gnawing on her lower lip, she turned away before he could see how his teasing hurt. It'd been barely a day, but she was tired of walking the fine line between truth and lies.

Toby became serious. "Sarah, I'm sorry. I was kidding."

"I know, but I don't like having to watch everything I say or do when I'm home. Not to be honest with my brothers bothers me. They think they're succeeding as matchmakers when I know they're not."

"I thought you said…" Abrupt understanding filled his eyes.

Dismay threatened to strangle her. She and James had agreed to keep their true feelings a secret from everyone else so her brothers didn't push them together all the time. And she had just blurted out the truth to Toby!

"I need you to forget what I just said, Toby."

"About you and James? It's forgotten. As far as your brothers, you haven't lied to them. You're letting them jump to their own conclusions."

"I know, but under other circumstances I would have corrected them because that's what a loving sister should do."

"Sarah, you *are* a loving sister. If you hadn't been, you wouldn't have agreed when they asked you to let James bring you home. If your brothers fail to see that, then they aren't looking at the situation with clear heads and fair eyes. I'm sorry if I upset you."

He grabbed the reins in front of her hands and pulled the buggy onto the grassy shoulder to the right as a car sped past them. "They drive way too fast along this road."

Sarah calmed the *kinder*, using the time to compose herself, too. She hadn't expected Toby to take the reins as her brothers used to do when she was younger. Being annoyed with him was silly.

Making sure her voice was even, she said, "We've alerted the sheriff, but the patrols can't be here all the time."

Mia leaned over the seat. "Will we be there soon, Sarah?"

"Where?" she asked as she winked at Toby, who struggled to keep a straight face.

"Where we're going!"

"We're there."

The buggy rolled to a stop near the new school building the settlement had opened about six weeks before.

Turning in her seat, Sarah said, "I know you're on

summer vacation for another couple of weeks, but would you like to see where your Amish neighbors go to school?"

"Here?" Ethan was eager to start kindergarten and anything about school thrilled him.

"Ja."

"Me, too?" Mia asked. With another year to wait until she went to school, she expected to be left out.

"You, too." Sarah tapped her nose and was rewarded with a grin. "Now, remember you are guests here. You need to use your best manners."

Alexander grimaced. "Aren't they schoolkids like us?"

"They are, but Miriam expects everyone to behave in her school. You know Miriam, and you know she's a nice person. Why don't you ask me your questions about an Amish school so you don't disrupt the class? Anyone got questions?" She smiled at Toby. He knew, as she did, the Summerhays kids *always* had a lot of questions.

"Why have they started school already?" Alexander asked. "We don't go back for two weeks."

"Amish schools need to begin the school year early so they can start their summer vacations in mid-May. That way, the scholars can help their families put in their crops. Maybe the school will go a bit longer here, because the fields won't be ready quite as early, but they'll be done with school by the end of May."

"What's a scholar?" asked Mia.

"A scholar is someone in school."

"Oh, like the ten o'clock scholar in Mia's *Mother Goose* book," Natalie said.

"Exactly."

"How many grades are there?"

"Eight. First grade through eighth grade, as you have at your school."

"We've got kindergarten, too," Ethan said.

Sarah almost laughed when Toby glanced back to give the little boy a wink, which made Ethan stick out his narrow chest with pride. "That's true. Once our scholars have finished eighth grade, they're done with formal education. After that, they may spend time with someone who will teach them a skill like woodworking or running a shop."

"So no high school?" asked Natalie.

"No. We feel it's important to learn a usable skill during those years."

That gave the *kinder* something to think about as they got out of the buggy. Sarah checked they were neat before she led them toward the school.

The new building looked like other plain schools, both outside and in. When Sarah opened the door, walking in as Miriam had asked, she saw the desks the dozen *kinder* used were in rows on the gray linoleum floor. The youngest scholars sat at the front and those in their last year of school had the privilege of having their desks closest to the door, so they could be the first outside for recess and at the end of the day. She recalled how grown-up she'd felt when, at fourteen, she reached the eighth grade and was ready to put school behind her. It'd been an honor, vied for by the oldest students, to clean the erasers and wash the blackboard. These scholars looked so young now.

Miriam stood at her desk on the raised platform in front of a wall covered with blackboard paint. A whiteboard was set on an easel beside her desk, and simple math problems were displayed on it.

"Scholars, our guests have arrived," she said as she

walked past the desks toward the door. "Let me greet them, and then we'll introduce everyone."

The tall teacher welcomed Sarah and Toby and the *kinder* to the school. The Summerhays kids grinned when Miriam said how much the scholars were looking forward to playing softball with them during recess.

"First, we have work to do." Miriam called out three names, and two boys and a girl stood.

They were each close to the age of the Summerhays *kinder*. The newcomers looked at Sarah, who nodded, amazed at how shy her usually raucous charges were.

"What about me?" asked Mia. "I'm not old enough for school."

"Mia, *komm* with me." Miriam held out her hand. "I've got a special seat for you."

Soon the *Englisch kinder* were sitting with their plain counterparts and working together on the lessons assigned for the day. Mia sat in the front row with the smallest scholars. She grinned as she bent her head over a workbook and pointed to a picture of a rabbit before she began to color it. As eager as she was to attend school with her older sister and brothers, coming to the one-room schoolhouse was an extra special treat for her.

Sarah smiled as Miriam paused beside her. Keeping her voice low so they didn't disturb the scholars, Sarah said, "*Danki* for letting them come here, Miriam. They're having a *wunderbaar* time. Learning about the lives of their plain neighbors is going to make them comfortable with them."

"Some of the scholars' parents have expressed concern about the Summerhays family offering an invitation in return."

"I understand."

174 *The Amish Christmas Cowboy*

"Gut." Miriam seemed about to add more but went to a student who had a question for her.

In her wake, Sarah's smile vanished. She should have guessed a few of the plain parents wouldn't want their *kinder* spending time at an *Englisch* house where they'd see toys and gadgets that could lure a young person away from an Amish life. Did people think that of her, too? That she was considering leaving because of fancy electronic devices?

She sighed. If she did jump the fence, it would be because of what the *Englisch* world would allow her to do for others, not what enticements it offered to her. Nobody would understand that, either. She prayed her brothers would change their minds, but that was as likely as snow falling on a hot August morning.

Toby stood to one side as the kids ran and squealed during a short afternoon break, tossing leaves into the air and at each other. Most were chattering about the upcoming fair. He knew none of them had gone before, because there hadn't been a settlement last year.

"You look as if you'd like to play with them," said Sarah as she joined him to watch the scholars.

"Why not? They're having a great time, and I always enjoyed recess."

"Did you go to school in Texas? Are their schools similar to ours?"

He shrugged. "I don't know. I was too old for school by the time we moved there. I'm not sure how many schools I went to, though I know one year it was six different ones."

"In one year?"

He nodded.

"I've never heard of anyone who moved six times in one year."

"Now you have."

She blinked when she heard the regret in his voice. He was glad he'd kept the bitterness hidden.

Maybe not well enough, because she said, "I've been curious why your family moved so often."

Toby didn't answer right away. He'd been asked about that as many times as they'd relocated from one district to another. Learning ways to avoid answering had become a habit, but he wanted to be honest with Sarah.

Drawing her closer to the tree so they were less likely to be overheard, he said, "The answer is simple. My *daed* is a man who's sure he knows everything. Well, if not everything, then more than anyone he's talking to."

"Uh-oh." Her eyes widened, and compassion filled them.

"*Ja*, uh-oh describes it. Not many people like being told they are wrong by someone who never doubts his opinions. *Daed* didn't care if the person he was speaking to was *Englisch* or plain or ordained or not. He felt others needed to accept his point of view without question."

"That wouldn't have worked here where everyone is working together to build our *Ordnung*. No one's voice should be louder than anyone else's."

"I agree, but *Daed* wouldn't. If the person he'd cornered didn't agree with him, he tried to browbeat the person into accepting he was right. People got tired of trying to avoid him or being stuck listening to him, so *Daed* would decide it was a waste of time to try to enlighten the others. That's what he always called it. Enlightening the foolish."

"He never saw his mistakes?"

"Never. We would move to a new district, and I'd have such high hopes. This time wouldn't be the same." He sighed. "I know *Mamm* felt that way, too, though she didn't complain—not once—when *Daed* would come home and announce we were leaving for another place where he hoped to find like-minded folks."

"You mean, people who agreed with him."

"That's what he's been looking for." He sighed. "I've tried to forgive him for dragging us from place to place."

"It must have been hard for a *kind* to understand."

"It was. That's why when I found work at J.J.'s ranch I refused to leave with them. I've lost count of how many times they've moved since then."

"You've found the home you've wanted." Her eyes didn't meet his, so he couldn't guess what she was thinking. "No wonder you're so eager for your boss to get you home." She flashed him a feeble smile before going to where her friend was calling the scholars in at recess's end.

Toby didn't move to follow. His gut warned him he'd made a big mistake, but he couldn't guess what it was. Sarah wouldn't judge him for failing to forgive his *daed*, would she? He thought of how many times she'd forgiven her brothers and sighed. He might be able to leave Harmony Creek Hollow without breaking any ties, because it felt as if, with a handful of kind words, she'd severed everything between them.

Chapter Fourteen

The *kinder* sat in the middle seat of Hank Puente's van, except for Ethan, who'd claimed the front seat. The little boy was chattering about the things he planned to do at the county fairgrounds, though he had no idea what would be there. Ethan had asked Sarah a slew of questions during breakfast, and to many she'd had to reply she didn't know. She'd never been to the fairgrounds, either.

Hank, the *Englisch* driver, listened as if everything the *kind* said was of the utmost importance. Sarah guessed he'd heard it many times before from youngsters who were excited about attending the fair.

Mia was half-asleep with her head on Sarah's lap. The little girl had been so wound up last night she hadn't slept well. Smoothing the *kind's* hair toward her braids, Sarah noticed Alexander's head was bobbing, too. She hoped fatigue wouldn't end up making them leave the grounds earlier than she'd planned.

She wished to celebrate the excellent news Toby had received yesterday. His *doktor* was pleased with how Toby's ankle was healing. Though the *doktor* wanted him to continue with physical therapy for another two weeks,

Toby now could walk with a cane rather than crutches as long as his ankle wasn't too painful.

She hoped he wouldn't put too much stress on the muscles by leaving his crutches in Salem, so he had to rely only on the cane. Natalie had assured her after checking the particulars on the county fair's website that it would be possible to rent a wheelchair at a booth near the parking lot. The obstacle would be to persuade Toby to use it.

He would acquiesce, she knew. He'd do anything to leave for Texas when J.J. got back to Summerhays Stables. Toby's explanation of his childhood instability and how he'd found what he wanted at the ranch in Texas had made many things clear.

One thing most of all: Toby wouldn't stay any longer than necessary.

Nothing she did could change that, not even if she offered him her heart.

Ethan's cheer from the front seat startled Sarah out of her unwelcome reverie. It also woke his younger sister and announced they'd reached the fairgrounds. The flat open fields were about half a mile from the forested edge of a cliff that dropped to the Hudson River and the village of Schuylerville. Buildings, many of them long, low barns with open sides, were painted white and set in neat rows on either side of a pedestrian road. Smaller booths and rides covered with bulbs trying to outglow the sunshine were close to the road leading to the parking area.

The fairgrounds teemed with people there to enjoy the games, rides and exhibits. Through the van's open windows came the scents of onions and peppers cooking on grills.

She stretched forward to hand Hank the passes Mr. Summerhays had given her before they left. Her boss hadn't said where he obtained them, but she guessed they'd come from someone in the horse-training community.

"There's one for you, too, Hank," she said, "if you want to stay."

"Thanks, but I've got a bunch of other folks waiting to be brought here." He held one ticket over his shoulder.

She shook her head. "Keep it and let someone use it."

"Thanks." He leaned his elbow on the window and greeted the teenage boy selling tickets. "Two adults and four kids. I'm dropping them off."

"Sure thing, Hank." The boy waved as the van drove past him.

Even with their seat belts on, the Summerhays *kinder* twisted in their seats, trying to see everything from the midway to the animal barns as Hank drove toward the parking lot beyond the last row of buildings. The van bounced hard into chuckholes that were invisible in the long, matted grass.

They stopped by one end of the parked cars. Hank got out and slid the side door open while Sarah helped Mia with her seat belt. By the time the little girl was ready to step out, her siblings were waiting for her. Sarah jumped out and swung Mia to the ground.

No one spoke as Toby lowered himself from the van with the help of his cane. He winced when he put weight on his right ankle but steadied himself as he shifted his balance to his left side.

Alexander jumped forward to shut the door once Toby moved away. He slapped the side of the van and waved to Hank, who'd climbed back in.

Making sure the *kinder* were watching out for the many vehicles, Sarah herded them toward the first row of buildings. The pens inside held a variety of farm animals. Pigs were displayed right in front of them in the nearest building, while pens at the other end of the building held goats. Sounds of cows, chickens and sheep came from other open-sided buildings. Among them, the youngsters who'd entered the animals for judging were feeding and tending them.

"Those are the cleanest pigs I've ever seen," Sarah said as the *kinder* paused to admire a huge pig in the outermost pen.

"The judges want to see every inch of them," a boy replied as he scrubbed his entry with soapy water and a brush. "They've got to look their best." He chuckled. "And smell their best."

Once they were past the road filled with a steady stream of cars and trucks headed for the parking lot, Sarah let the *kinder* walk in front of them. She asked Toby how he was doing with the cane.

"The uneven ground is more of a challenge than I'd anticipated," he replied.

"If you want to sit—"

"No, the *doktor* said it was important to exercise my ankle now that it's healed enough to put stress on it."

"Not too much stress. The muscles need time to heal."

"Okay, *Doktorfraa* Kuhns."

She smiled, because that was what he'd expect her to do. Wallowing in her grief that within a couple of weeks he'd be leaving would ruin the day the *kinder* had looked forward to.

What gut *will it do, Lord? I'm at fault for not listening to Toby from the beginning when he was honest with me. I know You have a plan for each of us, and, though*

I wish it, Your plan doesn't seem to have Toby and me being together. Please help me accept that.

It was for the best, she told herself. Until she knew whether she was going to remain in the settlement, she couldn't make any other plans.

"What do you want to do first?" she asked in order to escape her thoughts.

All four answered at once.

Raising her hands, she waited for them to stop. "Okay, let's try that again. Natalie, what do you want to do first?"

"It's almost nine. Let's go watch them judge the sheep."

Alexander crowed, "You want to see Nick!"

As his sister turned the color of the strawberries on her shirt, Sarah said, "Now, enough teasing. You all like Nick and will hope he does well."

"Nick?" asked Toby.

"He attends their private school that's halfway between Salem and Cambridge. He's in Natalie's class. They live about five miles north of the stables, and their *mamm* has been taking the Summerhays *kinder* to school for as long as I've worked there." She lowered her voice. "I've tried to arrange time for him and Alexander to play this summer, but either one or the other of them is busy every minute of every day."

"That's a shame. The *kinder* enjoy picking on each other, ain't so?"

"It's because they love each other so much. They wouldn't tease each other as they do otherwise."

"Or you."

Warmth swept through her as they neared the judging area. "When I first began taking care of them, I didn't see their pranks as anything except troublemaking. They were angry at being handed off again. Now, when they tease me, they have twinkles in their eyes."

"There's Nick," shouted Ethan, his voice carrying over everyone else's.

The boy leading a sheep with circular horns into the open area glanced toward them and grinned. Natalie hunched into herself, so Sarah put a bolstering arm around her shoulders.

"Don't distract him, Ethan," Toby said. "Nick needs to concentrate on showing off his entry to the judges."

The little boy nodded but clung to the fence. He was fascinated by the parade of sheep with girls and boys. Most of the kids were preteen or younger.

"I love sheep," Ethan announced to nobody in particular.

"Do you think your boss will agree when his younger son asks to raise sheep?" asked Toby.

"By the time we leave the fair, Ethan will have changed his mind a dozen times and set his heart on several other animals for pets."

"Kids that age are fickle."

"They are."

"It's a *gut* thing we outgrow that, ain't so?" he asked in a husky whisper that teased her cheek beyond her bonnet.

Warmth squeezed her heart, though his words could be a warning of his intentions not to be diverted from the life he'd built for himself in Texas. The rough edge of his voice offered an invitation she longed to accept. It would lead to worse heartache, but why not let her heart delight in this moment?

She remained next to Toby throughout the judging. They cheered when Nick was awarded second place and received a bright red ribbon. The blue ribbon went to the girl standing beside him. When they shook hands, the crowd cheered louder.

"I think there's fried dough waiting for us to sample it," Toby said, grinning.

"Don't get too far ahead," Sarah called as the kids took off as if rocket-propelled.

"We'll catch them at the fried-dough stand."

"If something else doesn't grab their attention on the way."

Toby wasn't surprised Sarah's joke of warning was proved true. By the time the *kinder* finished sampling fried dough, burgers and three flavors of ice cream, they were eager to visit the midway and the rides.

While Sarah went to the booth to buy tickets for them, he listened to the youngsters debate which ride they'd go on first.

Mia, Ethan and Natalie agreed it should be the merry-go-round. Toby guessed the thrilling rides seemed too scary for the younger *kinder*, and Natalie was fascinated by anything with horses, real or wooden.

"The carousel?" scoffed Alexander. "It's for little kids. I want to go on the snap-the-whip. Why can't we go on that first?"

"Want to ride the horsies first." Mia propped her fists on her hips and glowered at her older brother.

"We'll be trying a bunch of the rides," said Sarah when she rejoined them. "Let's start with the carousel, and then we'll decide which ride will be next."

Alexander glowered for a second but was grinning again by the time they reached the merry-go-round. As Sarah handed tickets to the man running it, she looked at Toby, "Do you think you can handle these horses, cowboy?"

"I'm not—" He laughed. "I guess I prefer to be called a cowboy instead of 'horse-boy' as Alexander suggested."

"Trust you to say something like that, Alexander." She ruffled the boy's hair, and he chuckled, his annoyance forgotten.

Toby lifted Mia onto a bright pink horse. When she giggled and grabbed the reins as if she could make the horse go right then, he turned to watch Ethan scramble onto a gold horse next to Mia's. Natalie chose a white horse, while Alexander climbed on an alligator. It was the only non-horse on the merry-go-round, but Toby wasn't surprised the boy had found it. Alexander was resolved to go his own way in life, no matter how strange it might be.

"Shall we ride in the shell?" asked Sarah. "It's the ladylike thing to do."

He appreciated how she pretended, so he wouldn't have to worry about his ankle while getting on and off a painted horse.

She selected the double seat behind where the *kinder* were perched, so she could keep an eye on them. It was painted bright pink and yellow.

He bent his head so he didn't bang it on the edge of the shell, which resembled the froth off a wave. Dropping beside her, he grimaced.

"You *are* doing better, you know," she said.

"I'd like to be doing *gut*."

"You will be. Last week, you were on crutches. Now you've got a cane."

He did not want to admit he wished he had his crutches because his right ankle ached on every step. If he complained, he guessed Sarah would cut their day short. He didn't want that.

The ride began moving, and Sarah bumped against him. She edged away, and he wished she hadn't. How easily he could have curled his fingers around her shoulder! To do so would be announcing a commitment he couldn't offer her, not if he intended to hold on to the life he'd built on J.J.'s ranch.

Was that the life he wanted?

He couldn't recall the last time he'd felt so content. *Content* was a word he used to despise, but no longer. He wasn't obligating himself to anything but enjoying the moment with Sarah and four outrageous *Englisch kinder.*

Danki, God, for this day and these people.

The prayer startled Toby. Not that he'd prayed, but that speaking to God seemed wondrously familiar. He'd missed it more than he'd realized.

Listening to Sarah hum the simple melody coming from the center of the carousel, he found himself doing the same. He wasn't sure what the name of the tune was, but he thought it might go along with a nursery rhyme. Ahead of them, the *kinder* were laughing as the horses and alligator rose and fell.

"Summerhays is foolish to miss this," he said.

"I agree."

"Why can't he see how much his kids want to spend time with him and his wife?" He answered his question before she could. "Maybe they'd know if they spent more time with their *kinder.*"

"Mia used to disappear, and I'd have to find her because she needed to eat. I would search but had to give up because her sister and brothers needed me. Then I discovered she hides in her *mamm's* closet." Sarah sighed.

"The other three vie for their *daed's* time, but days go by without them seeing him."

"We've got to be halfway to his stables in Saratoga."

"We are."

"It didn't take half an hour for us to get here, so why can't he get home to spend time with his family?"

"I don't know. I've worked for the man for nine months, and I don't know much about him or his wife. Other than when they hired me, I haven't spoken with either of them for more than an hour or two total."

Toby hid his astonishment and said nothing until the ride slowed to a stop. He got out of the seat while Sarah helped the littler ones from their horses.

Mia grabbed his hand as they walked down the steps at the exit. Looking at him, she said, "That was fun, ain't so?"

"Ja," he said, glad he could speak from the heart. "And the right speed for a man with a cane."

That made the *kinder* giggle, but his heart focused on the music of Sarah's laugh. It soared through him, as free and beautiful as an eagle's flight.

As the *kinder* surrounded her, each one asking to go on a different ride, he stepped aside and smiled. Now he couldn't be alone with Sarah, but he was going to find a way to do so. They didn't have much time before he had to leave. He wanted to take advantage of every second.

Toby tried not to think of how many eyes were watching his slow progress among the picnic tables. Sarah followed him, and he guessed her hands were outstretched to catch him if he started to wobble. In front of him, Alexander was walking backward, prepared to keep Toby from falling onto his nose.

"Slow and steady wins the race," Alexander said in tempo with the bump of the cane and Toby's footsteps.

"Do you believe that?" Toby grinned at the boy. "I can't believe your *daed* does."

"You aren't a racehorse." Alexander chuckled. "By the way, it's Sarah who says that, not my father." A cloud passed across the boy's face for a moment as he mentioned his *daed*. In its wake, Alexander avoided looking at him.

As soon as Toby was sitting at a wooden table, Ethan held out a plastic cup of lemonade to him. Taking the sticky cup, which warned that Ethan's attempts not to splash the lemonade hadn't been successful, Toby thanked him. He guided the *kind* to where he could sit so more didn't spill.

Taking a sip of the lemonade, Toby listened to Sarah chat with the youngsters. He thought of how she'd said Summerhays had spent less time talking to her about his *kinder* than he had to Toby about Bay Boy and the other horses at the stables in Salem. How could that be? Summerhays must be able to see how much his *kinder* wanted to spend time with him. Toby had noticed that shortly after he'd arrived at the stables.

People could train themselves to ignore what they didn't want to see. His *daed* had been an expert at that, refusing to believe he was making the same mistakes.

Toby wasn't done with his lemonade when Sarah handed a strip of tickets to Natalie. The *kinder* rushed off to get in line to ride the nearby miniature train.

"I thought you'd like to sit a little bit longer," she said to him as she folded her arms on the table.

"*Danki*. A few minutes more, and I should be able to

walk the length of the midway so they can ride on the snap-the-whip."

"We'll see about that." She straightened. "Listen to me. I sound like my brothers, always worrying too much. The kids are big enough for that ride."

"Your brothers do worry a lot about you."

"All the time." She shook her head and turned toward where fire trucks and other emergency vehicles were parked so the fair-goers could examine them. "Too much. They don't believe a plain woman should be involved as a first responder."

"And you want to?"

"Ja."

"You want to be a firefighter?"

She shook her head. "I want to train as an EMT. I know it's ridiculous, but it's something I feel God is drawing me toward."

"It's not ridiculous." He shouldn't have been surprised. She'd been interested in his physical therapy and had asked questions every session. She clearly had plenty of medical knowledge already.

"Benjamin and Menno think so. They've forbidden me from taking the training." Resentment slipped into her voice. "They said it isn't an appropriate thing for a plain woman to do."

"I've lived in plenty of plain communities, and many of them had plain women working with the volunteer ambulance services. In two, plain women served as fire-fighters."

Hope brightened her face. "I should tell them." The hope seeped away as she added, "Why? They won't listen to me. They don't believe Amish women do such things."

Shock pierced him. "So are you considering leaving the Amish?"

She nodded.

"Is that why you're working as a nanny? To learn more about *Englischers*?"

"It started out as an opportunity to do that, but now I do it because I love the *kinder*."

"If your brothers agreed to let you take the EMT training, would you stay on the Amish side of the fence?"

"They won't let me. End of story."

"Do you want my opinion?"

"Ja." The corners of her lips tilted. "Though I suspect you're going to give it to me, whether I want it or not."

"If you didn't want to hear it, I'd keep it to myself. As you do, here it goes. My opinion is Sarah Kuhns can do anything she puts her mind to. You need to figure out with God's help what that is."

Sarah blinked the sudden tears in her eyes. Toby couldn't guess how *wunderbaar* his words were as they fell like a healing rain on her heart. Someone believed she was capable of following her dreams. Even if she decided to remain among the Amish, this moment would stay with her the rest of her life.

She replayed his words in her mind through the rest of the day. They visited the exhibits and ate junk food before playing games and standing in ever-longer lines for more rides. Though the *kinder* were exhausted by the time Hank returned after dark to take them home, she was sure they had enjoyed every part of the fair.

Letting the youngsters stretch out on the seats, Sarah sat in the rear with Toby. His broad fingers swallowed her smaller hand, and tingles rolled in waves up her arm.

She gazed at him, though he was no more than a silhouette in the darkness.

When he drew her toward him, she stared at his lips that were visible in the light of a passing car. They tilted in a smile, and she couldn't halt her eyes from following the firm line of his nose. In his warm eyes, sparks of heat teased her closer. He caressed her cheek, eliciting a melody from deep in her heart. As his mouth lowered, she closed her eyes in sweet anticipation. His strong arms enveloped her at the moment his lips found hers. Everything she'd imagined—and so much more—was in that kiss.

She savored it more because it might be the only one they'd ever share.

He lifted his mouth away, and she leaned her cheek on his shoulder. For one special moment, she was going to forget the past and not think about the future and savor being close to the man she knew she'd love the rest of her life, whether they were together or not.

Chapter Fifteen

"Sarah?"

"Sarah?"

Hearing her name called a second time—or was it more times than that?—Sarah pulled herself out of the delicious memory of the moment from four days ago when Toby had drawn her into his arms and kissed her while coming home from the fair. She wondered if he would have taken advantage of the shadows among the berry bushes today and kissed her again.

Toby wasn't with them. He'd left at dawn to visit the stables near Saratoga today. His *doktor* had given him permission to spend the day there as long as he did his exercises and put his leg up if his ankle swelled. She hoped Toby was having an amazing time, talking with other trainers and seeing the horses.

"Sarah, are you listening?" asked Alexander as he came around a black raspberry bush.

"She's off in dreamland," Ethan answered.

The *kinder* laughed.

Natalie said through her giggles, "Sarah, your brain has fled your head."

"Sorry." She gave them a smile. "I was lost in thought. Have you picked a lot of berries?"

The *kinder* dumped the contents of their small pails of black raspberries into her larger bucket. The plop of every juicy berry made her mouth water.

"How many more do we need to get?" asked Natalie.

Hefting the bucket, she said, "I'd say we're there. Mrs. Beebe said we needed about six cups of berries for the cobbler she's going to make for your dessert."

The youngsters' cheers sent a flock of small birds fleeing into the sky.

Sarah took their pails along with hers and grabbed Mia's hand as they walked through the field beyond the pastures. She smiled when Natalie took Ethan's hand without being instructed. Perhaps the older *kinder* were beginning to understand the joy of helping each other.

"How will Mrs. Beebe cook our berries?" asked Ethan, always eager for the details.

"She'll wash them and mix them with sugar. Next, she'll make the cobbler with flour and more sugar and butter. After putting the cobbler on top of the berries, she'll bake it in the oven. You'll want to eat every bite of your supper so you can have dessert tonight."

"What are we having?"

She struggled to keep her lips from twitching. "Liver."

Fervent shouts of "No!" and "You're kidding!" made her laugh. The *kinder* knew then she was teasing them. The joking continued as they walked across the road to the drive leading to their home.

Mrs. Beebe greeted them warmly in the partially finished kitchen. A huge new gas stove sat in the middle of the floor, waiting to be swapped with the slightly smaller one that couldn't be more than a year or two old. Somehow, the cook continued to make meals for the family and the staff while new cabinets were hung and counters set into place.

"She's back," Mrs. Beebe murmured to Sarah while taking the buckets.

"She?"

"Her ladyship."

Baffled, Sarah started to ask another question.

As if on cue, a delicate voice called from the front hall. "I'm home! Where is everyone?"

Sarah gasped, realizing the cook had been referring to Mrs. Summerhays. The sound was lost beneath excited shrieks from the *kinder*. They raced toward the front of the house.

"Like I said, her ladyship's home," Mrs. Beebe said in response to Sarah's unspoken question. "She got here about a half hour after you and the children left." Stirring a pot on the stove, she smiled. "You'd better get in there and make sure they don't run roughshod over her."

Sarah nodded and hurried out of the kitchen. She'd spoken with Mrs. Summerhays fewer than a half-dozen times in the months she'd been working at the house, because even when the woman was home, she was busy elsewhere.

When she went into the entry, Sarah watched the *kinder* greet their *mamm*. Mrs. Summerhays was willowy. Every motion was so light it seemed to float like a branch on a gentle breeze. She reminded Sarah of a ballerina in one of Mia's storybooks. As if at any moment, she could rise to the tips of her toes and waft about to music.

As always, Mrs. Summerhays was dressed in an elegant style that matched the grandeur of her home. Her ivory coat had the sheen of silk. The fancy purse she carried, though Mrs. Beebe had reported Mrs. Summerhays had been home for an hour, was the exact same black as her stilettos. Each heel was no wider than a pencil, but Mrs. Summerhays didn't wobble. She wore those shoes as she did everything, with a confidence of knowing she looked stylish.

Sarah watched as Mrs. Summerhays hugged her *kinder*. She held each briefly, keeping them from putting their cheeks against her coat. No doubt, she didn't want to chance staining the elegant fabric.

Tears welled in Sarah's eyes. What would Mrs. Summerhays say if Sarah told her how much she was missing out on? Each enthusiastic dirty-faced hug and kiss Sarah received from the *kinder* was precious, because she knew how difficult it'd been for them—at first—to open up to her.

"Look at how you've grown," their *mamm* exclaimed. "Mrs. Beebe must be feeding you bean sprouts, because you're sprouting."

The *kinder* grinned. Those expressions faltered when Mrs. Summerhays stepped away, but the youngsters dutifully cheered when she announced she'd brought them gifts from Europe and put them in Mia's room. She encouraged them to check out what she'd bought them. For a moment, the *kinder* hesitated, and Sarah knew they didn't want to leave their *mamm* when they'd just said hello.

"Go! Go!" Mrs. Summerhays made dismissive waves toward the stairs. "I need to go out, but I should be back before you go to bed."

Natalie halted. "Mom, we picked black raspberries and Mrs. Beebe's gonna make cobbler."

"You've been busy." She laughed. "Enjoy the fruits of your labors."

The *kinder* glanced at one another, puzzled, but scurried away when their *mamm* urged them to look at their gifts upstairs. Mrs. Summerhays's enthusiasm must have rubbed off on them, because the youngsters chattered with excitement, their high-pitched voices reverberating off every corner of the high ceilings.

Mrs. Summerhays smiled at Sarah. "From what Ian tells me, you've been keeping them under control, Sarah. You're just what they need."

What they need is their mamm *and* daed.

Sarah halted the words before they escaped. Instead, she smiled and replied, "They've been looking forward to you arriving home before school starts."

"I can't believe Mia is heading off to school full-time, too."

"Mia won't be attending school until next year."

"Oh." Mrs. Summerhays looked nonplussed; then she composed her face into a smile again. "I meant Ethan. He's going to school this year, isn't he?"

"Yes, he is, and he's excited. He'll be glad you're here for his first day of school."

"I *hope* I will." She took a step toward the front door. "I'll know more after this evening's meeting with other owners' spouses. Do check on the children. By the way, I left a gift for you in Mia's room."

Then she was gone, the door closing behind her.

Sarah stared, speechless. She'd delayed too long in finding a way to speak to Mr. and Mrs. Summerhays about spending more time with their *kinder*. It was time to rectify that.

Tomorrow.

For now, she must go and see how the *kinder* fared.

As she climbed the stairs, she noticed how a peculiar

hush had settled on the house. The youngsters' exuberant voices were silent. She passed Mrs. Hancock in the upper hallway and sighed when the housekeeper shook her head sadly and hurried to the first floor.

Sarah paused. Would Mrs. Hancock help her find the best way to approach their boss to discuss what the *kinder* longed for?

That discussion was for later. Now…

She paused by the doorway of Mia's room. It was a big space with its white-and-pink-striped wallpaper. The room shared a bath with Natalie's bedroom that was decorated in everything horse.

Near the wide window, the *kinder* sat among scraps of the paper that had wrapped their gifts. The gifts themselves were stacked on Mia's bed. Sarah saw clothing and toys as well as a half-dozen books. Even the books about horses were piled with the others. As she watched, Natalie stood and sighed as she put a ceramic horse that could have been modeled after Bay Boy on the bed before wandering to the window seat and climbing on it so she could see out as she hugged Ethan, whose lower lip was quivering.

Sarah kept her sigh silent. *Lord, You brought me to this family. Please show me how I can help them become a true family like my brothers and I used to be.*

A new wave of sorrow rushed over her. Not so many years ago, Benjamin and Menno had made her feel important to them as Natalie did with the younger two. They hadn't acted as if she were an unwanted burden they couldn't wait to be done with. She missed that time.

"What a generous *mamm* you have!" she said as she entered the room.

If the *kinder* suspected she was pretending to be excited about the gifts, they gave her no sign. She could tell, however, the *kinder* were faking their excitement, too. The clothing was lovely and the perfect size. The toys and books had been chosen well.

She knew they would have traded every gift for a chance to spend just a minute more with their *mamm*.

It had been an unbelievable day. The aromas of hay, leather, horses and hard work filled every breath Toby drew from when he'd arrived just after dawn. Those odors made him homesick for the stables on J.J.'s ranch. He'd spent hours in and around them every day, except Sundays. Although on Sunday evenings, he was often found working with the horses.

Instead of savoring the chance to be among people who shared his obsession with training horses and the creatures themselves, he kept losing himself in thoughts of Sarah and their kiss. He grinned each time he thought about it. If the other trainers and grooms thought he was a grinning fool, he didn't care.

He'd looked for an opportunity to hold her again, but none had arisen. The one time he thought he might steal another kiss, the *kinder* had come looking for her. That he'd seen disappointment in her eyes before she turned to the youngsters had suggested she regretted the lost opportunity as much as he did.

Toby felt his grin grow wider and wider as he clumped along with his cane in Summerhays's wake at the day's end. The stable's owner had offered him a ride back to the house while on his way to Salem. Summerhays was leaving earlier than usual because he had a meeting to attend.

Horses poked their heads out of their stalls to discover who was making the strange sounds. Though Toby doubted he was the first one to walk with a cane in front of the stable doors, he'd gotten the horses' attention.

He paused and admired a sleek gray who moved along the pasture fence with the grace of a cloud in a bright blue sky. "Aren't you a handsome fellow!"

"You've got a good eye, Christner," Summerhays said. "He's my best. He's been entered in two races and came in first in one and second in the other. He'll be three next year, so I'm going to see that he gets high-visibility races."

Toby was pleased the man continued to discuss his favorite topic as they went to a white truck, which was bigger than the red one Toby had driven to Fleetwood's farm with Sarah and Mercy. When Summerhays asked his opinion on the horses he'd seen, Toby replied honestly. He could tell, as they drove north, Summerhays didn't appreciate all his comments.

Too bad. Toby knew the dangers of misrepresenting a horse and what it was able to do. Mishandling a young horse could mean it never would reach its potential. Thoughtless training might ruin a horse. He'd tried to retrain such horses, but too often they were beyond saving.

"That's an interesting take on the horse," Summerhays said when they discussed the horses at the stables near Harmony Creek Hollow. "You seem to know a lot about my horses after such a short time."

"I had an inside expert share information on the animals in your stables."

"Who?"

"Natalie."

Summerhays, shocked, looked at Toby. Cutting his eyes back to the road, he asked, "My daughter?"

"*Ja.* She knows more about horses and their training than a lot of adults I've worked with."

"You don't say," Mr. Summerhays drawled, pride sifting into his voice. "When do you think Bay Boy will be ready to come down to Saratoga for training?"

"I'd say you could start him here next month. He may be the finest horse I've trained," Toby replied, then smiled. "Natalie agrees."

The older man looked startled, then grinned. "You may be right about her knowing more than many equine experts. So you've done all you can with him?"

"I've worked with Mick and Cecil and showed them how best to work with Bay Boy," he replied, realizing that Summerhays might be proud of Natalie, but all his thoughts were on his horses. "They know how he hates being in the trailer so much that he refuses to run at his top speed for several days afterward." He glanced at the older man. "You're going to have to keep that in mind. It's not a normal situation, but he's not a normal horse. He knows his mind and thinks he's the boss. Once I let him think I believed it, too, he's been much more cooperative."

Mr. Summerhays nodded. "That makes sense."

"Why are you asking me? You've got experienced grooms and trainers at your stables."

"Too often they give me the answers they think I want to hear, not the truth." He chuckled. "You've heard that, haven't you?"

"Sir?"

"I'm sure Sarah clued you in." Not waiting for a response, he said, "She's one of a kind, Toby."

"Yes, sir."

"That sounds like an answer you give when you don't want to be honest."

Astonished, Toby said, "No, I was agreeing. She *is* one of a kind." He'd never meet another woman like her, no matter how far and wide he searched. But his life was in Texas, and hers was… Abrupt shame pierced him. Too late, he realized he shouldn't have kissed her. No matter how incredible it'd been, it had been a mistake, suggesting a promise he couldn't keep.

"Without her help," Summerhays said, interrupting his appalling thoughts, "I doubt you would have gotten on your feet as quickly."

"True," he answered, holding on to the conversation as a way to keep from thinking about the mess he'd made. "She isn't hesitant to say what is the right thing to do and make sure you do it."

"My kids have given her a lot of practice, no doubt."

Toby knew the horseman's words were the perfect opening for him to share Sarah's concerns about how the *kinder* needed more time with their parents. He almost said something but halted. Sarah had asked him to let her handle it, and he needed to do that. He wouldn't be like her brothers. Protective of her to the point that she was suffocating.

He wasn't thinking clearly at the moment as his emotions roiled through him like clouds in a thunderstorm.

Dropped off in front of the house a half hour later, Toby went inside after Summerhays had turned the truck around and headed toward Salem. Sarah stood in the entry. He didn't need to look at her face to know she was upset. The rigid angle of her shoulders and how her fingers were curling and uncurling by her sides warned him she was trying to calm her feelings before they burst out of her. Something or someone had upset her.

Who?

Had her thoughts followed the same path as his? Did she regret their kiss?

As if he'd asked those questions aloud, Sarah said, "I hoped to talk to you before you ran into the *kinder*. Their *mamm* arrived home this afternoon but spent less than five minutes with them before she had to leave for a meeting. They're having supper, and I don't think they've eaten a single bite."

Shocked, because Alexander could always be counted on to eat everything in front of him, Toby tried to imagine what the *kinder* were feeling. He couldn't. His parents had always kept him at the heart of their family. More than once, he'd heard his *daed* say they were moving to a place where life should be better for Toby. The constant search for a place where his *daed* would find kindred spirits had been aimed at the best life for all of them.

"That's sad," he said, unsure what she needed to hear.

"I plan to speak to Mrs. Summerhays tomorrow. I've been praying on this, Toby."

"I have been, too."

"You have? You seemed distant from God."

"He has never been distant from me. When I look in your eyes, I know He loves me. Otherwise, He wouldn't have given us this chance to be together. How can I not be grateful for His knowing my heart when I didn't?"

"I'm so happy for you," she said, hoping he meant his heart was filled with the same love that was within hers.

"I know you are. You've made me happy, Sarah, just as you have the *kinder*."

"*Ja*, they enjoy being with me, but I'm a poor substitute for their parents. The *kinder* want to be with their *daed* and *mamm*." Her gaze turned inward. "It's been three years since my *daed* died and more than a decade since my *mamm* did, and I would trade anything to have a few minutes more with them in this life."

"I know what you mean. When I stayed at J.J.'s, I had no idea how much I'd miss my folks."

"You should tell them that."

"I know, but I can't figure out how."

She grasped his arms. "Toby, you have to forgive your *daed* for the past. If you do that, you will find the words."

"I don't know if I can." How could he explain the years of hurt that had piled layer upon layer inside him?

"Pray. God will guide you. Please don't wait. If I'd waited to tell my parents how much I loved them…" She snapped her arms together across her chest and glowered. "Don't wait, Toby. Don't be like this family. I see them squandering their chance to be together."

Before he could reply, a phone rang in Summerhays's office. Toby waited in the foyer for Sarah to answer it and return. His arms ached to hold her close until she could push aside her sorrow.

"Toby?" Sarah's voice intruded into his thoughts. "The call is for you."

"For me?"

She nodded. "The man asked for Toby Christner."

He gave her what he hoped was a bolstering smile. "I'll be right back."

Sarah sat on the bottom step of the grand staircase and prayed for God to give her the right words at the right time—and soon!—to talk with the *kinder's* parents. *Open their hearts to hearing the truth so they can build a true relationship with the* kinder *who adore them.*

The sound of Toby's cane against the stone floor

brought her head up. God had blessed her by bringing this man into her life to remind her that what she said and did mattered. She was grateful for how well he'd healed…and how her heart had danced like stardust in the moonlight when he kissed her.

"That was J.J. He and Ned are on their way here," he said in an emotionless voice.

Her heart plummeted into her stomach. "When will they get here?"

"Early tomorrow."

His answer burned her like acid. "How long are they staying?"

"Long enough to pick me up."

Disbelief froze her heart. Somehow, she stood. "So you're leaving tomorrow?" Her words sounded as if they were coming through a long tunnel.

"Ja."

She waited for him to add something.

He didn't. Nor would he meet her gaze.

When she couldn't handle the silence, she said, "I understand." She wished it were the truth.

"You don't need to worry." He wore the same expression Ethan did when he hoped she'd overlook a jam he'd gotten into. "I'm done with our portion of training Bay Boy."

Her brows lowered. "What does the horse have to do with anything?"

"The plan was for one of us to stay and show Summerhays's men what training the horse was accustomed to. So I would have been here, even if I hadn't hurt my ankle. I wasn't going to leave Ned with a pretty woman like you."

"You weren't going to…" She couldn't get the words out.

"Trust me. I know Ned, and you don't."

"You could have warned me." She backed away. "But no, you thought I needed you to protect me."

"It's not that."

"No? Then what do you call making decisions for someone who can make her own decisions?"

"Like I said, I know Ned, and I didn't want you to get hurt."

Tears filled her eyes, but she blinked them away. Would he be like her brothers and see her honest emotions as a sign of weakness?

Taking a steadying breath, she asked, "Why weren't you honest later?"

"It wasn't an issue. Ned was gone, and I was stuck here."

Stuck?

Was that how he saw the time they'd spent together? Had she been nothing more to him than a way to keep from being bored while he was recovering? Worse, knowing he was leaving, he'd kissed her as if she were special to him. She'd shared her dreams with him and offered him her heart.

"I should go," she said. *Before I say something I may or may not regret.*

"Sarah—"

She didn't wait to hear more. He'd said enough to let her know she might have managed again to escape a life of being told what to do and having her decisions denounced as silly or useless. She should have been happy.

It took every bit of her strength to keep from crying while she hurried into the kitchen to check on the *kinder*. She would hold her tears in until later when she was out of the house and too far away for anyone to hear her weep.

Chapter Sixteen

Go to sleep.

Sarah ignored the *gut* advice in her head as she turned over her pillow, looking for a cooler surface that would help her fall asleep before sunrise. She needed to be at work before breakfast, because Mrs. Summerhays intended to travel with her husband to New York City first thing in the morning.

It had taken Sarah an hour to calm the *kinder* after she was sent to tell them that their *mamm* was leaving them again less than a day after she'd returned from Europe. If Mrs. Summerhays had seen their faces that displayed shock and hurt, would she have changed her mind?

Sarah was no longer certain.

Of anything.

On one hand, it was horrible to have someone you loved stifling your dreams at every turn. It was worse to have someone you loved leave you behind so that person could pursue his or her dreams.

As Mr. and Mrs. Summerhays were with their *kinder*.

As Toby was with her.

No, she didn't want to think about Toby. He personified both extremes, going to ridiculous lengths to protect her, though she knew he hadn't injured his ankle on purpose, and now planning to leave without a backward glance. He'd learned all about leaving from his parents.

This time, her tears refused to be kept in her eyes. They streamed down her cheeks, dampening the pillowcase. She tried to dash them away, but they kept falling.

Throwing aside the quilt on her bed, she sat and rubbed her wet cheeks. She rose and paced the small bedroom. She loved her room. The white maple furniture had been brought from Indiana, and the connection with what had been was important to her.

Such connections were what Toby fought at every turn. How could he believe the way to keep himself from being hurt was to hold everyone at a distance? He seemed to believe an endless parade of little hurts was better than a single powerful one.

Maybe he was right, because she'd been torturing herself with her uncertainty about what she should do with her life. Was it better to make a hasty decision and rip away any doubt like tearing a bandage off a healing wound?

She raised her eyes toward the ceiling. *Your will be done, Lord. I know You have a plan for Toby and me, and it isn't for us to be together. Help me come to accept Your will, but please heal his heart. He is too gut a man to be in such constant pain.*

She climbed into bed, knowing she'd poured out everything in her heart and the situation was in God's hands. As it always had been. Letting go eased the tension aching across her shoulders, so she was able to lie on her pillow.

Sleep refused to give her an escape from her thoughts

that went around and around as the carousel had at the fair. Was there something more she could have done to persuade Toby that fleeing from any relationship wouldn't lead him to where he wanted to be? Maybe he was too used to saying goodbye.

The room was stuffy, but it was too chilly to open the window. At least the summer heat had been banished for the night. Sarah closed her eyes and tried to keep her mind from drifting in a dozen directions.

It seemed minutes later, but it must have been a few hours because the moon had fallen to hide halfway behind the mountains along the western horizon. Its light crossed the foot of Sarah's bed as her eyes popped open at a horrifying sound.

Sirens!

Fire sirens!

She sat straight up in bed, then ran to her window. Throwing it open, she pressed her ear to the screen. The siren rose and fell again and again, each shriek sounding more frantic.

The siren on the top of the library building in Salem!

A flash of light reached under her bedroom door before vanishing toward the stairs. As she grabbed her robe, whipping it around her, she heard Benjamin urge Menno to hurry.

She opened her door so hard it slammed against the wall. Her brothers paused in astonishment as she burst from her room.

"Where is it?" she called.

Benjamin looked at the pager at his waist. It alerted him when there was an emergency. "The code says it's east of the village."

"Where?"

"Along the road to Rupert." He blanched as the beeper sounded again. "2127 Old Route 153. Isn't that—"

"Summerhays Stables!"

They shared a gasp of shock.

Menno grasped her shoulders. "Stay here, Sarah," he ordered. "You aren't trained, and you would just be in the way."

Her brothers ran down the stairs and out the door, slamming it behind them, before she could retort that she could have been a great help if he and Benjamin had let her become an EMT.

No matter! She wasn't going to wait. She'd stay out of the way, but she knew which bedrooms the *kinder* used and the best way to get to them. Surely the firefighters would appreciate such information.

Running into her room, she pulled on clothes and grabbed a flashlight out of the table by her bed. She ran down the stairs as soon as her shoes were tied. The door crashed closed behind her. As she ran toward the woods, she heard their buggy careening at top speed along the road. Other people and vehicles followed, but it would be quicker through the trees.

Her face was lashed by the branches and her legs scratched by the time she burst out of the woods. Ahead of her, the pastures were edged by white fences, which glowed in the moonlight. She saw no clouds of smoke rising from any building, but she didn't slow.

As she neared the house, she discovered the firefighters hadn't gotten there yet. She couldn't smell smoke. Had it been a false alarm? If so, why were the lights off in the house? Had everyone gone to bed?

Impossible! The *kinder* wouldn't return to their rooms quickly in the wake of such excitement.

She heard a muted buzz. Smoke alarms? Where was the smoke? Should she run out to the bunkhouse beyond the barn and alert the stablemen?

Someone reeled across the porch.

"Toby!" she cried.

Running to him, she gasped when she realized he had Mrs. Beebe draped across his shoulder. He eased the cook to the porch, then collapsed himself.

"The…others…" He hung his head for a moment.

"I'll get them."

"I'll help."

"No. I'll do it. Did you see where the fire is?"

He shook his head. "Stay out here. I'll…" He began to cough.

Knowing she couldn't waste time arguing that she was more capable than he was at that moment to help the family, she whirled and threw open the door. She focused her flashlight on the stairs.

No smoke, though the alarms shrieked. Thanking God, she ran upstairs and along the corridor leading to the *kinder's* rooms.

Mia was sprawled across her bed. Sarah couldn't wake her, so she slipped her arms under Mia. The *kind's* head lolled against her chest. Sarah pushed aside her panic. Rushing downstairs, she opened the front door. She placed the little girl on the porch beside Mrs. Beebe. The cook hadn't moved. Toby was on his knees, retching.

Hearing shrill sirens, Sarah prayed for the firefighters to get there as fast as possible. She didn't wait. She ran back into the house. Her head began to spin, and she had to clutch the banister as she came around the top. She saw motion at the far end of the hall where Mr. and

Mrs. Summerhays slept, but she continued toward the *kinder's* bedrooms.

She roused Natalie and sent the girl to wake Alexander. Her stomach rocked as dizziness tried to drive her to her knees, but she lurched into Ethan's room. Like his younger sister, he wouldn't rouse. She somehow lifted him and carried him toward the stairs. She felt sicker to her stomach with each step. Clamping her lips closed, she swallowed hard and ordered herself not to vomit. She checked to make sure Natalie and Alexander were behind her.

She wanted to urge them to hurry, but her lips refused to form the words. She waved for them to follow her. When they reached the first floor, Alexander started to sit on the bottom step, but Natalie jerked him to his feet. Putting her arm around him, she lurched toward Sarah.

"Help..." she choked.

Sarah kept Ethan balanced on her hip and put her other arm around his older brother. With Natalie's help, she was able to stumble out onto the porch. Flashing lights seemed to be everywhere around her. Mr. Summerhays was reeling toward the railing, dragging Mrs. Summerhays behind him.

She blinked, but her eyes wouldn't clear. Someone grabbed her elbow and pulled her forward. She wanted to protest that whoever it was needed to be careful. She didn't want to drop Ethan.

Mia! Where was Mia?

"The children are safe," said a kind voice. "You will be, too, once you get oxygen in and flush out the carbon monoxide."

Carbon monoxide?

The words echoed without meaning through her head.

A mask was pressed against her face. With every breath she took, everything became clearer.

She was sitting at the back of an ambulance. Inside, two people were smiling as one removed an oxygen mask from a form stretched out on a gurney. She peered through the dim light. The body was too long to belong to the *kinder*. From its height, she guessed it was Mrs. Summerhays. Sarah sent up a grateful prayer that the *kinder's mamm* was all right.

"Sarah, what are you doing here?" Menno's demanding voice sliced through the cobwebs in her mind but set off a headache that tightened like a heated band around her skull.

"Not now, Menno." The man's voice was familiar.

"George—"

"I said not now, and I meant it."

Sarah forced her eyes to focus on the two men standing in front of her. George, the EMT who had helped Toby, stood face-to-face with her older brother. There was nothing threatening in George's pose, but it also announced he wasn't going to change his mind.

Menno was called away. She didn't see by whom or why, but she was grateful to have to think only of breathing.

George squatted in front of her. "I don't know if you heard me tell you before, but everyone in the Summerhays family is safe."

"What about Toby and Mrs. Beebe?"

"They're going to be fine. Mrs. Beebe is doing the best. She was outside the longest, and she was beginning to recover by the time we got here."

She wanted to ask when she could go and check on the

others, but George told her to stay where she was until she got enough oxygen into her system.

The sun was rising over the mountains by the time Sarah felt steady on her feet. She thanked George for his help, then went toward the porch, where Mr. Summerhays was talking with the fire chief. Someone had given Mrs. Summerhays a bathrobe, and she held it closed around her as she listened to what the two men were discussing.

As Sarah walked up the steps, she was relieved to see the *kinder* with Toby. The youngsters ran to her. She hugged each one, unable to speak through the tears clogging her throat. Strong arms enclosed them, and she looked up to see Toby's drawn face.

"Danki," she whispered.

"If you hadn't come…" He cleared his throat. "You've got a way of always being where you're needed most, ain't so?"

She opened her mouth to answer but halted when she heard Fire Chief Pulaski say it would soon be safe to go in the house because the gas was switched off. They just had to wait while the central air cleared the rooms.

"The problem was your cook was using a stove without a vent—"

"It's being hooked up tomorrow," Mrs. Summerhays murmured.

"She was cooking a brisket overnight, and carbon monoxide built up beneath the pan. The vent would have sucked it out so it wouldn't have been a problem. If Mr. Christner and Miss Kuhns hadn't been here…"

Mr. Summerhays sighed. "I'll make sure it's working before the kitchen is used again. Next time, it could be a fire, which could destroy the whole house."

"Maybe you should worry less about your house and more about your *kinder*."

Everyone froze. Sarah did, too, when she realized those words had been hers. She pressed her hands over her mouth as every eye focused on her. Out of the faces looking at her, her gaze fixed upon Toby's. Instead of regarding her with shock and dismay, he gave her a nod.

Only he knew how she'd worried about the *kinder* missing their parents and longing for the chance to spend real time with them, not just being showered with gifts or having to make do with a quick conversation when most of the time their parents' minds were on something else. Was this the way God had provided to let her reach out to her bosses and find a way to open their eyes?

"What did you say, Sarah?" asked Mr. Summerhays in an icy tone she'd heard him use once before. That had been when he fired a groom who'd caused a horse to injure itself.

God, put Your words into my mouth so they might reach into the hearts of these parents.

"I said," she replied, "worrying about the house isn't as important as worrying about your *kinder*."

Both parents gasped, and firefighters standing nearby did, too. However, Mrs. Beebe patted her shoulder and Toby gave her a thumbs-up.

"Sarah—"

She interrupted Mr. Summerhays. If she didn't say what he needed to hear, then the *kinder* might never have a chance to have their parents in their lives. "It's not my place to tell you how to raise your family."

"That's the first thing you've been right about. I know your brain must be foggy with—"

"My brain is fine, but it wouldn't matter." She knew

she was risking his ire by not letting him finish again. If she lost her job, she needed to do the best she could for the *kinder*. "I'm speaking from the heart. I spend a lot of time with Natalie, Alexander, Ethan and Mia, and I know what's in *their* hearts.

"They're growing so fast, and you're missing it. Natalie wants to spend time with you, Mr. Summerhays. I don't know anyone who loves horses more than she does, and you'd be surprised how much she's learned from listening to you." Turning, she looked at Mrs. Summerhays, who somehow had managed to smooth her hair and look like the cover of a fashion magazine again. "Did you know Mia sneaks off to spend time in your closet because she wants to be with you? You love clothes, so she believes she can be closer to you by being near your clothes, too."

"I didn't know." Mrs. Summerhays looked dismayed. "I had no idea." Reaching out an awkward hand toward her youngest, she asked, "Do you really do that?"

"Yes, Mommy."

Tears filled gray eyes that were identical in *mamm* and daughter.

"The boys want to spend time with you," Sarah said, not sure how much time she had before Mr. Summerhays lost his temper. "They make mischief to get your attention. The more they have tried and failed to have you notice them, the more desperate they've become."

"I didn't know," Mrs. Summerhays said again. "Children?"

When she held out her arms, the quartet ran to her. They hugged her as Sarah knew they'd wanted to yesterday, and their *mamm* held them close, no longer acting as if her clothes were more valuable than her *kinder*. When she offered her hand to Mr. Summerhays, he didn't hesitate. He bent and waited for his *kinder* to look at him. Ethan was first. The little boy hesitated and glanced at Sarah. When she nodded with an encouraging smile, the *kind* threw himself into his *daed's* arms.

"God works in mysterious ways," Toby said from behind her. "A near tragedy may have opened their eyes to what they could have lost." Putting his hands on her shoulders, he turned her to face him. "They may find change difficult."

"That's why I'm here to help them for as long as they need me."

His eyebrows rose. "Does that mean you're giving up your dream of becoming an EMT?"

She shook her head. "No."

"Your brothers—"

"Don't you think it's time my brothers learned how serious I am about taking the training?" Stepping back, she added, "I do."

"Sarah, you don't have to do this right now." He moved in front of her.

"I think I do." So many things she yearned to tell him, about the state of her heart and how glad she was he'd been in her life, if only temporarily. She had to speak to Menno and Benjamin before her courage failed her.

She walked to where her brothers stood among other first responders. She watched their shocked faces when Chief Pulaski followed her.

"You and Christner made our job easy, Sarah," the chief said, smiling. "Not that I'm surprised. Benjamin and Menno always keep their heads during a fire. I guess good sense and bravery runs in your family. I know it's not your way to put one person above another, but you two are heroes in my book." The fire chief patted her on the shoulder before going to supervise his firefighters as they prepared to leave.

As soon as Chief Pulaski was out of earshot, Menno said, "Sarah, you shouldn't have come here."

"I had to."

"You could have been killed." Benjamin blinked on what looked like tears.

She put a consoling hand on his arm. "You need to know I've got the same yearning that you do to help others. I don't have to have your permission for EMT training, but I'd love to have your blessing."

Menno began, "You're our sister and—"

She didn't let him finish the lecture she'd heard too many times. It would lead to the same argument they'd had before. "You're my brothers, and I love you. I know you worry about me." She let a smile tilt her lips. "Too much sometimes, but you need to trust me to know what is right and wrong. Training to become an EMT won't lead to me planning to jump the fence or cutting my hair and dressing like an *Englischer*."

Benjamin flushed and lowered his eyes. Menno found something in the sky interesting. They avoided her gaze because they'd threatened to do those very things during their *rumspringa*.

Then Menno looked at her. "I've been afraid it would come to this since you took a job for these *Englischers*."

"A job that has allowed us the chance to pursue our dreams. You two have your sawmill because I was able to earn *gut* money as a nanny. I'm going to get the training I want." She took her brothers by the hand as if they were no older than Ethan and Mia. "I believe in you. Please believe in me. This is something I can do."

"But women—"

"I wouldn't be the first woman volunteering in the rescue squad in Salem."

"The first *plain* woman."

"As you were among the first plain firefighters. Someone has to be the first." She smiled. "I know you're worried, but give me a chance to prove to you I belong in the rescue squad as you belong in the fire department."

Benjamin cleared his throat, then said, "She has a point, Menno."

"We promised *Daed* we'd watch over her. Is this what he would have wanted?"

She wanted to shout *ja* but kept her lips clamped closed. Anything she said could make them close their minds again. At least, for the first time, they were being open about why they'd become so protective of her, to the point of breaking her heart.

"We may change our minds," Menno said, "but let's see how it goes."

She stood on tiptoe and kissed Benjamin on the cheek, and then did the same to Menno. When they turned as red as her hair when she was so demonstrative in front of their neighbors, she smiled.

"If you've got concerns," she said, "let me know, and we can discuss them…as *Daed* and *Mamm* used to do. We're a family, and we can't let something one of us does hurt the rest of us."

"When did she get so grown-up?" asked Benjamin as if she were no older than Mia.

Menno shrugged but gave her a rare smile.

Her brothers said they'd see her at home, then went to assist their fellow firefighters. She wanted to cheer her excitement but halted when her gaze locked with Toby's across the yard.

She had a chance at her dream of helping others, but it was a hollow victory when her heart's desire was leaving.

An hour later, with the sun warming the air, Toby rose from the rocker where he'd been sitting, his small bag packed and waiting beside him. He watched Sarah walk across the pasture toward the house. The Summerhays family had gone into Salem to have breakfast at the local diner, the trip to New York City postponed. They'd invited him, so he assumed they had offered to take Sarah with them, too. He'd declined, hoping to spend as much of the time left before J.J. and Ned arrived with her, but she'd gone home to change.

As she climbed the steps to the front porch, she said, "I need to say *danki* again, Toby."

"I heard George say you asked him about when the next EMT training class starts. I guess that means your brothers are okay with the idea."

"I couldn't have stood up to them if I hadn't known you, Toby Christner."

"I just told you about the women being EMTs in other settlements."

She shook her head hard enough to make her *kapp* bounce. "You did so much more. You helped me see what I do makes a difference."

"How could you have doubted that? Look what you've done for the Summerhays family!"

"No more than you did."

He caught her face between his hands and gazed into her eyes. How he wanted to lose himself in their sweet warmth, to swim in them and never worry about leaving again. That wasn't his family's way of doing things. They were leavers. Arrive, create a big to-do and then leave without cleaning up the mess.

"No," he whispered, trying to memorize every inch of her lovely face, "I mean, what you did before this morning. You made those *kinder* believe their dreams could come true." His voice grew husky as he whispered, "Even if you continued to believe yours couldn't."

"I never doubted that."

"You never believed those dreams should be put first. You were ready to stand aside and let everyone else's dreams—including mine—push yours aside. I'm sorry, Sarah. I don't know if I can ever be the man you need. A man who can set down roots. It's not the way Christners do things."

"You aren't your *daed* and *mamm*. You're you. Toby Christner."

"Who has been so careful not to let moss grow beneath his boots."

"You've stayed on J.J.'s ranch for years."

"I've worked for him for years, but as soon as the chance came to travel while delivering horses, I jumped at doing it."

"Of course you did, because you care so much for the horses you train. You were anxious for them to make a *gut* transition to their new homes."

Was she right? Could he be unlike his parents? If there was anyone in the whole world he was willing to change for, it'd be Sarah, but to try and fail would hurt her far more. That he was sure of.

The rumble of a big truck came from the long driveway. He prayed it was Summerhays, bringing the family home, but he recognized the powerful engine.

J.J.'s truck!

He lifted his bag.

Her face crumpled, and he realized she'd clung to the hope that he'd stay. He couldn't speak, because saying goodbye was impossible. Instead, he walked to the truck.

Sarah remained on the porch. He saw her flinch when he closed the passenger door. She waved half-heartedly when J.J. called a greeting before putting the truck into gear.

Toby's gut told him he was making the biggest mistake of his life, but he knew if he loved Sarah—and he did— he couldn't take the chance of subjecting her to the miserable life his *mamm* and he had endured. As the truck drove toward the road, like his *daed*, he didn't look back.

Chapter Seventeen

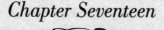

The week before Christmas, the large family room was redecorated in a style approved by the four Summerhays *kinder*. Unlike the flawless decorating magazine decor that once had seemed to shout "Stay out!" the room reflected—at last—the family who lived there. A huge sectional and chairs, looking well used, were arranged to offer a view of the enormous fieldstone fireplace with its crackling fire and the large flat-screen TV hung next to it. Books and video games were scattered over once pristine coffee tables. Photographs of the *kinder* were displayed throughout the room.

In one corner in front of a large bay window, a tree from the newly named Kuhns Family's Christmas Tree Farm held court. It was definitely not a designer tree, because it was covered with handmade ornaments and strings of popcorn and cranberries. Ornaments made of homemade dough were painted with food coloring. Others had been decorated with pasta or glitter. So much silver tinsel covered the tree it was almost impossible to see the greenery. Softly falling snow drifted past the window behind its branches.

From the ceiling, crepe paper in bright shades of red and blue were twisted and draped from each corner to the center of the room. Someone must have found an extra box of Christmas tinsel, because silver strands hung from the garlands to reflect the light from the pair of crystal chandeliers. A big sign hung over the fireplace where a nativity was displayed on the mantel. Both *congratulations* and *graduation* had been spelled wrong by the *kinder*, who'd wielded the bright orange and blue markers and still wore the colors on their hands.

A cut-glass bowl, filled with red punch being kept cold by rainbow sherbet, had been placed beside a sheet cake with the same words on top of it, but correctly spelled. The guests, *Englisch* and plain, mingled with a sense of familiarity and friendship that grew out of being neighbors and from working together in the Salem volunteer fire department.

Sarah hadn't expected Mr. and Mrs. Summerhays—or Ian and Jessica, as they'd asked her to call them in the wake of the near disaster—to throw a party for her upon her graduation from her EMT training. They'd insisted it was the least they could do for the woman who'd saved their family. Because Sarah suspected they meant more than when she and Toby had dragged the family members out of the house, she'd acquiesced.

The past three months had brought astounding changes to the Summerhays family and her own. Maybe because her brothers saw her training was as important to their fellow firefighters as to her. They treated her again as an equal in their household, making decisions with her. As for the Summerhays family, many trips had been cancelled so both parents remained at home more. Ian and

Jessica seemed amazed at how much they enjoyed their *kinder.*

Alternating between "thank you" and "*danki,*" Sarah let the guests know how much she appreciated them coming. She hugged her friends from the Harmony Creek Spinsters' Club and shared the evening with her fellow graduates from the EMT course. The Summerhays *kinder* raced about, playing with their plain neighbors. They'd become fast friends since; many of the parents in Harmony Creek Hollow had, with a bit of help from Miriam, changed their minds about the *kinder* playing together. Ian had invited the scholars to enjoy softball games in his unused pastures.

"Congratulations, Sarah," she heard yet again. This time from behind her.

Sarah started to turn and respond but couldn't utter a word as she stared into Toby's intense blue eyes. She couldn't mistake them for others. Glancing down, she saw he once again wore cowboy boots, a sure sign his ankle was healed. Snow was melting off the shoulders of his dark coat.

"You're here!" she whispered.

"I am," he replied, once again the terse man he'd been when they first met.

Tears rose into her eyes. They splashed along her face as the man who'd filled her dreams even before she met him stood in front of her.

"You're here for my graduation party?" Even saying the words out loud didn't make it seem possible that Toby had returned from Texas.

"For that and other things."

Her battered heart ached as hope died within it again. She'd heard Ian talking about a new horse he was expecting to be delivered. It must have been coming from J.J.'s ranch and, again, Toby had joined his boss in bringing it north. How soon would he be leaving again?

When his broad hand cupped her chin, she was shocked he'd be so brazen in public. It wasn't the Amish way to show open affection, even when a couple was walking out together.

Then again, Toby Christner was unlike any other Amish man she'd met.

"I had to see you again," he said, his voice as rough as his skin. "Our farewell felt wrong."

"And you want to get it right?" She hated her sarcasm, but she was mixed-up. She loved him. If he'd come back to say goodbye again, she wasn't sure her heart could bear it.

"There are a lot of things I need to get right." His thumb traced her cheekbone as he tilted her face so she looked into his eyes. They stood that way for a long minute, then he took her hand and led her out of the crowded room and into the entry hall.

Nobody followed them, and he didn't stop until they entered the fancy room where they'd first waited for Ian to arrive to talk with J.J. He released her hand but didn't move away from her.

As if there hadn't been a break in their conversation, he said, "Sarah, you know I've spent most of my life avoiding getting involved with people in order to keep from getting hurt. In doing that, I cut myself off from myself, too, to the point I forgot how to laugh until you gave me a reason to again." He gave her a wry grin. "Does that make sense? It did when I heard it in my head, but saying it out loud…"

"It makes complete sense." She laced her fingers together in front of her apron to keep from reaching out to put her arms around his shoulders. "Has that changed?"

"Before I answer your question, I think you should ask another one. You haven't asked me how long I'm staying this time."

"I don't want to know that. I'm enjoying the blessing of having you here right now."

"Ask me."

"Why? The party—"

"Please, Sarah, ask me."

Though she had to fight to push each word out, she tried to keep her voice light as she asked, "How long are you going to be here for this time, Toby?"

He took her hands again and laced his fingers through hers. "For the rest of my life."

"What?" She was sure she'd heard him wrong.

"Your boss has offered me a job. He advanced me enough money to purchase a few acres along Harmony Creek. I plan to build a house and become a member of the *Leit* here."

"You do?" This had to be a dream. The sweetest dream she'd ever had. "J.J.—"

"Is happy because he knows I'll be here to train the horses he breeds, and he'll have Summerhays Stables as a customer for years to come." He drew her to him. Letting her hands go, he slipped his arm around her waist. "Sarah, how can I leave you after you've taught me how important it is to be connected to others and to God?" His fingers swept along her cheek again, sending tingles zipping through her. "How can I leave the one I love? We hadn't even reached the main road before I knew I had to return here to ask you to be my wife."

"You've been gone for three months."

"I had to follow your advice." He brushed a strand of hair back toward her *kapp*. "You told me before I left that I needed to forgive my *daed*. You were half right. I needed to forgive him *and* forgive myself. It took me two months to find out where my parents were living." He shook his head. "Believe it or not, they've found a settlement that suits them. It's not like any plain settlement I've ever seen because there's constant debate about everything, but they love it. When I saw how happy they were, forgiveness came easily."

She folded his hand between hers and squeezed it. "The Lord has blessed you."

"He's blessed all of us. When I finally listened to my *daed*, I discovered he'd been looking for a place where he thought my *mamm* and I would be at home. Somehow, he found it for us." His grin widened. "The day I was ready to leave my parents' house, Summerhays called with a job offer, and I knew God approved of my plan. Will you marry me this Christmas, Sarah? You've made Summerhays and his wife realize they want to be a real family, and you've made me realize I want you and me to be a family, too."

She couldn't answer because four young voices were shouting, "Toby! It's Toby!"

The Summerhays *kinder* poured into the room and rushed to throw their arms around him. Sarah stepped back to give them space. She laughed when they all talked at once, asking questions, telling him about what they'd been doing, urging him to try the cookies they'd baked for the party.

Toby gently peeled Ethan and Mia from his legs and set them back a step. He patted the older two on the shoulders before saying, "I've told you a bunch of times that you need to listen and give Sarah a chance to answer before you ask more questions." The *kinder* looked puzzled, until he added, "Let's start by having her answer *my* question. Will you be my Christmas bride, Sarah?"

Excited squeals came from the youngsters, but Sarah looked only at Toby.

"Ja," she said, unable to stop the tears tumbling out of her eyes again. *"Ja,* I want to be your wife. I want us to be a family." She laughed. "You'll be my Amish Christmas groom in every meaning of the word."

"Finally! Someone got it right and knows I'm not a cowboy." He gave her the grin that caressed her heart, the smile she knew he shared with nobody else.

"I don't care what you call yourself as long as you're mine. *Frelicher Grischtdaag,* Toby."

He wished her a Merry Christmas, too, before his laughter warmed her lips as he claimed them in a kiss that thrilled her to the tips of her toes.

Shouts of more congratulations drew them apart, and Sarah saw her brothers leading the cheers. She leaned her head on Toby's shoulder, knowing her most precious dreams were coming true.

* * * * *

AN AMISH
HOLIDAY WEDDING

Carrie Lighte

For those who are strong enough
to share their vulnerabilities.

With continued thanks to my agent, Pam Hopkins,
and my editor, Shana Asaro.

And he said unto me, My grace is sufficient for thee: for my strength is made perfect in weakness. Most gladly therefore will I rather glory in my infirmities, that the power of Christ may rest upon me.

—*2 Corinthians* 12:9

Chapter One

Faith Yoder secured her shawl tightly around her shoulders, climbed onto the front seat of the bicycle built for two and began pedaling toward Main Street. It wasn't quite five o'clock in the morning and her brothers hadn't yet risen to do the milking. Her headlight cast a weak glow, barely illuminating the empty lane in front of her. The rest of Willow Creek, Pennsylvania, was still asleep and the November moon was her only companion.

Or almost her only companion. As she made a wide turn onto the primary stretch of road leading into town, she spied a lone figure lumbering beneath the streetlamp a few yards ahead of her.

"Watch out!" she warned as her downhill momentum propelled her closer.

The man lifted his head but didn't move from her path, so she quickly swerved onto the shoulder to avoid hitting him. Her front wheel wobbled off the road and into the shallow ditch, causing her to lose her balance.

"My *oier*!" she shouted and jumped clear of the heavy bicycle, which clattered on its side. The cargo she'd been carrying in a crate strapped onto the backseat—two dozen eggs—smashed against the pavement. "My *oier* are ruined and now my cupcakes will be, too!"

"You ought to be as concerned about hitting pedestrians as you are about making cupcakes," the man replied in *Pennsilfaanisch Deitsch* as he hobbled to where she was searching the ground for any unbroken eggs.

"I *didn't* hit you, so you can quit that limping," she contended and peered at him under the dim circle of light cast by the streetlamp.

Although the young man's hair was mostly hidden by his hat, a few dark brown curls sprang from beneath the brim. He wore no beard, which meant he'd never been married. He was average height, but his shoulders seemed unusually broad beneath his wool coat. She didn't recognize him as being from Willow Creek. Most Amish women in their district wouldn't have argued with a stranger on a deserted road in the wee hours of the morning, but Faith Yoder wasn't most Amish women. Having grown up with six brothers, she knew how to hold her own.

"If you're so worried about getting hit," she continued, "you could exercise common sense and walk on the side of the road, not in the middle of the lane."

The man seemed at a temporary loss for words. He gave her a once-over before replying, "It seems strange you're lecturing me on common sense, when you're the one riding a tandem bicycle pell-mell through the pitch-dark with a basket of *oier* strapped to the backseat. You might consider getting a headlamp."

"For one thing, it's not pitch-dark—there's a full moon out. And for another, I *have* a headlamp," Faith retorted, setting her bike upright and extending the kickstand.

But noting the sickly glow waning from the light on

her handlebars, she recognized she probably bore the responsibility for their near-collision. Chagrinned, she added, "It does seem I need to replace my battery. I hadn't noticed. I travel this road so often I probably could make the trip blindfolded. My name is Faith Yoder. What's yours?"

She couldn't tell whether it was a smile or a grimace that flickered across the man's face. "I'm Hunter Schwartz, Ruth Graber's great-nephew."

Hunter Schwartz, of course. Faith had heard Hunter was bringing his mother from their home in Parkersville, Indiana, to care for Ruth. The elderly woman had broken her ankle and severely sprained her wrist after falling from a stepladder in the little cannery she owned across the street from Faith's bakery.

Faith should have recognized Hunter from his childhood visits. If it hadn't been so dark, she undoubtedly would have spotted the cleft in his chin and remembered his earnest brown eyes. Coupled with a valiant personality, his boyish brawniness had caused many of the young *meed* to dream of being courted by him the autumn he was sixteen.

"I'm sorry," Faith apologized. "I didn't recognize you. It's been a long time."

If Faith remembered correctly, the last time he'd been in Willow Creek was the year his great-uncle died. After the funeral, Hunter stayed for several months to fix Ruth's roof and help with other household repairs. It was during harvest season, when many of the *leit*, or Amish people in the district, were tending their crops, and Hunter frequently helped out on the Yoders' farm, as well as attended singings and other social events with Faith's brothers. The following year, he'd gotten a full-time job in Indiana working for the *Englisch*, who limited his holiday breaks. From then on, Ruth said it made more sense for her to visit Hunter's family in Indiana than for them to travel to Willow Creek, and he hadn't been back since.

"*Jah*, about eight years," he answered. "I didn't recognize you either. You've, er, you've really grown."

She'd really grown? Faith knew what that meant, and she smoothed her skirt over her stomach. There was no denying she'd put on weight since she was a scrawny, flat-as-a-washboard tomboy, but she rather appreciated the womanly curves she once wondered if she'd ever develop. Well, she mostly appreciated them, anyway. She'd lost all but fifteen of the pounds she'd gained after Lawrence Miller broke off their courtship. Now she was down to the weight she was while she and Lawrence were courting. She didn't consider herself fat, but she wasn't thin by any standard. Still, she thought it was impolite for Hunter to draw attention to her size; he used to be so well mannered. But, reminding herself vanity was a sin, she shrugged off his observation.

"I suppose it was my fault I nearly ran into you. I'm grateful it's only my *oier* and not your legs that are cracked," she conceded amicably.

Hunter again looked taken aback, almost as if she'd insulted him instead of apologized. He paused before saying, "I'm sorry about your *oier*, too, but at least they were only intended for dessert instead of for breakfast. Most people can do without cupcakes, but not without a meal."

Now Faith couldn't deny feeling insulted. Who did Hunter think he was, assuming she was making the cupcakes as a mere indulgence for herself, just because she was a bit…a bit *round*?

"For your information, I own a bakery in town and the *oier* were for cupcakes I need to make for an *Englisch* customer," she sputtered as she mounted her bike. "The customer's *daed* is turning seventy-five and this special birthday treat is as important to their family as your breakfast apparently is to you, so I'd better be on my way to remedy the situation. *Mach's gut*, Hunter. Enjoy your morning meal."

Without another word, she sped away as quickly as she could pedal.

Hunter rubbed his jaw, watching Faith disappear into the dark. His bewilderment about her hasty departure temporarily distracted him from the pain coursing through his lower back and legs. Had his jest about her bike riding offended her? Or was it that she expected him to have known she was a business owner? If anything, he figured *he* should have been insulted by *her* remarks. Was she trying to be funny, chastising him not to limp? And what about her remark about being grateful his legs weren't cracked? Considering his physical condition, that was nothing short of cruel.

But as he trudged back toward his aunt's home, Hunter realized that however unnerving Faith's comments were, she must have made them in complete ignorance. His aunt undoubtedly told the *leit* in Willow Creek about the accident that took his father's life, but she wouldn't have necessarily told them about Hunter's ongoing recovery from his own injuries, especially since he concealed his pain from everyone, even his family members. Besides, from what Hunter recalled, Faith Yoder simply didn't have a cruel bone in her body. She was tough, yes. Outspoken, definitely. But Hunter remembered that as a young girl, she went out of her way to demonstrate compassion and generosity, especially toward anyone who was mistreated, ill or otherwise suffering.

Granted, Faith was no longer a young girl. It had been too dark to get more than a glimpse of her, but he'd noticed the sharp angles of her girlish face had been replaced with a becoming, feminine softness. Gone was the rash of freckles splashed across her nose; her skin appeared as lustrous and unblemished as the moon. Hunter wouldn't have believed the same scrappy girl he'd known from his youth had blossomed into the stately young woman he encountered on the road that morning if she hadn't told him her name: Faith Yoder. Yoder—that meant she was still unmarried, although Hunter assumed she was being courted, perhaps was even betrothed.

Imagining Faith's suitors reminded him of Justine, the woman he'd walked out with in Indiana. She was devastated when Hunter ended their relationship after his accident a little more than a year ago. It pained him to cause her heartache, but breaking up was in her best interest: Hunter wouldn't seriously court a woman he didn't intend to marry, and he wouldn't marry a woman if he couldn't be a good provider for their family. After all, the accident cost him his job at the *Englisch* RV factory and it had severely limited his mobility. At the time Hunter broke up with Justine, there was no telling whether he'd even be able to walk again.

Eventually, Justine accepted another man's offer of courtship, and now she'd be getting married in two weeks. It was exactly what Hunter prayed would happen for her, but he was still relieved he wouldn't be in Indiana to attend her wedding. While he no longer cared for Justine the way he once did, witnessing her getting married would have emphasized how much his life had changed since they were courting. Shivering, he forced thoughts of the past from his mind.

The frosty air intensified the ache clenching his lower spine. He stopped and waited for it to pass. The long van ride from Parkersville had wreaked havoc on his body. Walking into town didn't help much, but it was better than lying in bed, waiting for the minutes to pass and the pain to subside.

"Guder mariye," he greeted his mother when he returned, startled to see her out of bed. For years, her rheumatoid arthritis manifested itself in periods of extreme fatigue and sore, swollen joints, and ever since Hunter's father died, her flare-ups were more frequent and intense. "You're up early."

"Jah, and your *Ant* Ruth is awake, too," his mother replied. "I'm fixing her something to eat. She was asking after you, since she was asleep when we arrived last night. Would you keep her company while I make breakfast?"

Hunter tentatively approached the parlor where his aunt was reclining on the sofa with her leg propped on a stool. Her skin was pale and she wore a white cast on her foot, as well as a sling on her arm, but her eyes were lively.

"There he is, my favorite nephew!" she squealed.

Despite his pain, Hunter chuckled at their old joke; he was Ruth's *only* nephew. After giving her a careful embrace, he asked, "How are you feeling, *Ant* Ruth?"

"I'm madder than a wet hen!" she exclaimed. "You probably know better than anyone how frustrating it is to be confined to bed when you're used to being out and about."

Hunter clenched his jaw. "That I do."

"But it's worth it if it means I get to see you and your *mamm's* faces again," Ruth said, her voice softening. "I wish I could see your *daed's* face again, too."

Hunter shared the same wish. The last time he'd seen his father's face was the evening of the accident, some fifteen months ago. They were returning home from work when a truck driver lost his brakes, sideswiped their buggy and rammed into the wall of an overpass, where he perished in the fiery crash. Hunter and his father were trapped beneath their mangled, overturned buggy, unable to help him or themselves.

"Hunter, if *Gott* spares your life, promise you'll take *gut* care of your *mamm*," his father pleaded while he lay dying. After Hunter agreed, his father whispered, "Two of my greatest blessings in this lifetime were being a husband to your *mamm* and a *daed* to you. I couldn't have asked the Lord for a better wife or *suh*."

"Nor I for a better *daed*," Hunter echoed before passing out. By the time he was cognizant enough to speak again, Hunter learned he was in the hospital and his father had already been buried for three days.

Remembering, Hunter shuddered and shifted in his chair. To his relief, his aunt changed the subject.

"Mmm, that smells good. What is your *mamm* making for breakfast?"

"*Oier*, I think," Hunter guessed. Then he launched into a narrative of his roadside encounter with Faith.

"Ach!" Ruth exclaimed. "What a fiasco! You must collect *oier* from the henhouse and deliver them to Faith after breakfast. She'll need them to fill her customers' orders."

"I'm the last person she wants to see again today," Hunter protested.

More to the point, he didn't want to see *her* again today. In fact, he didn't wish to see—or to be seen—by anyone in Willow Creek just yet. The questions about his circumstances would come soon enough; he'd rather field them after he recovered from the tiresome journey.

"Nonsense! Take the buggy if you'd like, but it's the right thing to do, even if Faith was at fault. She'll be so glad to see you coming she might even treat you to one of her *appenditlich* cream-filled doughnuts. The trip will be worth your while."

"Okay," Hunter agreed. He knew better than to argue with his aunt once she'd made up her mind, but he'd made up his mind, too. He'd drop the eggs off, but he wasn't going to hang around Faith's bakery eating doughnuts, no matter how delicious Ruth claimed they were.

Of all days to have an egg mishap, Faith was dismayed it happened on a Saturday, the busiest day of the week and the same day she had a special order to fill. When she arrived at the bakery, she surveyed the glass display case, taking inventory.

The honey bars would stay moist through Monday. There were plenty of fresh whoopee pies and molasses cookies, but she'd have to move the cinnamon rolls to the day-old shelf. She had intended to start a few batches of her renowned cream-filled doughnuts before the bakery opened at seven, but now she wouldn't have enough eggs. When her only employee, Pearl Hostetler, arrived, she'd ask her to whisk over to the mercantile, which didn't open until eight thirty, to purchase more. Meanwhile, the egg shortage would put them behind schedule on all their baking for the day.

Faith sighed. First things first. She set about mixing yeast with hot water. Although she preferred baking more elaborate goodies, several of her *Englisch* customers depended on her for homemade bread. Every purchase counted if she was going to meet her financial goal by the first of the year, which was only a month and a half away.

That was the deadline the *Englisch* landlord required for the down payment on next year's lease. In addition to the small storefront and kitchen, Faith would also rent the one-room apartment above the shop, since the current tenant was moving out. He was the third resident to leave in four years, and with each turnover, there had been a three- or four-month delay before a new resident moved in. Disgruntled by the gap in revenue, the landlord was adamant that from now on, the apartment and building space were to be a package deal. Faith either had to rent both or lose the bakery to Seth Helmuth, who wanted to set up a leather shop in the prime location downstairs and use the upstairs apartment for storage and supplies. But Faith had first dibs, and although the down payment amount was more than she had saved, she was arduously working to earn the total sum.

"Won't you be lonely, living all by yourself?" Pearl asked when she discovered Faith would be moving into the apartment.

Living alone wasn't something most Amish women voluntarily chose to do, and as someone who dearly missed her three children who moved out of state, Pearl couldn't fathom why the opportunity might appeal to Faith.

"I won't have time to be lonely," Faith responded. "I'll

wake up and *kumme* right down here, where I'll have the privilege of working with you and visiting our neighbors and serving our customers. I'll spend the better part of Sundays and holidays with my family and with the church. The only difference is I won't have to ride my brothers' old hand-me-down tandem bicycle to get here each day."

Faith's sister-in-law Henrietta was even more dismayed about Faith's decision.

"You can't allow her to separate herself from the family like this," she once told Faith's oldest brother, Reuben.

"The *Ordnung* doesn't forbid it, so neither do I," Reuben replied. "Faith is a thoughtful person. I trust she prayed about this decision and is aware of the challenges."

As the eldest son, Reuben became the head of the family when their *daed* died five years earlier, since their *mamm* had passed away five years before then. Reuben and Henrietta lived in the large Yoder farmhouse with their three young sons, Faith and four of her five other brothers. The fifth brother, Noah, lived with his wife, Lovina, and their children in a small adjoining *daadi haus*. Faith knew she'd always have a place and purpose within her family, but given how cramped their dwelling was, she couldn't understand why Henrietta objected to her moving.

"If you live alone, you'll appear uncooperative or proud. You've already got one significant reason a man wouldn't wish to marry you—do you want to make it even more difficult to find a mate?" her sister-in-law asked her.

While Faith knew Henrietta had her best interests at heart, her words stung. The "significant reason" a man wouldn't wish to marry her was Faith's most intimate secret, something only family members knew. Well, only family members and Lawrence Miller. Faith felt compelled to confide in her former suitor after he asked her to marry him two years ago.

She vigorously kneaded a lump of dough as she recalled the afternoon she disclosed her secret to him. She'd been so nervous she hadn't eaten for two days, and when she finally worked up the courage to tell him, she was uncharacteristically tearful.

"There's a possibility I might not be able to bear *kinner*," she confessed, chewing her lip to keep herself from weeping.

The color drained from Lawrence's long, thin face as he slowly shook his head. That's what Faith remembered most clearly—his shaking his head without saying a word.

She was too modest to explain that the year she turned seventeen, she had surgery to remove dozens of cysts from her ovaries. The cysts were benign, but the doctor warned the surgery caused scarring that could result in infertility. At the time, her relief over not having the kind of cancer that claimed her mother's life outweighed any concern Faith had about not bearing children. She hadn't fully appreciated the repercussions of the surgery until she and Lawrence began walking out and planning a future together.

"I know how upsetting this must be to hear," she consoled him. "But if it turns out I can't become, well, you know… We might consider adopting—"

She may as well have suggested flying an *Englisch* rocket to the moon to retrieve a child there for how preposterous Lawrence claimed her idea was. Adoption took too much time, he said, and it was too costly to adopt one child, much less the six or eight he was hoping to have.

"The doctor said there's a *possibility* I won't be able to have *kinner*," Faith emphasized in between the sobs she no longer tried to stifle. "It's only a *possibility*."

"I'm sorry, Faith, but that's not good enough for me," he said.

She knew he meant *she* wasn't good enough for him. She was damaged. Scarred. Less than a woman. She understood then that she'd probably never marry—at least, not until she was much older, or unless a widower with children of his own sought to court her. And since she wouldn't marry, there was no sense courting, either. But Faith didn't mind because it meant she'd never have to tell any man her secret ever again. The rejection and the shame of disclosing her condition were more than she could bear a second time.

She clapped the flour from her hands as if to banish the memory of Lawrence from her mind. Regardless of what Henrietta or anyone else said, she didn't need a *mate* to take care of her. With God's grace, she'd take care of herself just fine. As for living alone, she was looking forward to it.

For the moment, she had six dozen lemon cupcakes with lemon buttercream frosting to prepare for the *Englischer* who'd pick them up at eleven o'clock. She started mixing the ingredients, using every egg that wasn't required for the egg wash for the bread. She'd have to forgo making doughnuts until later, but her customers would just have to settle for something else.

We don't always get what we want, she thought as she mixed the batter into a smooth, creamy texture. *But we can make the most of the options we have.*

Which was exactly what she intended to do herself. No matter what anyone thought about her decision to live alone, Faith was determined not to lose the bakery. A few cracked eggs or critical remarks weren't going to keep her from accomplishing her goal. Nor was a future without a husband going to keep her from being happy.

During breakfast, Hunter's aunt asked if he'd assist her with a significant undertaking.

"Of course I'll help you, *Ant* Ruth. That's why I'm here. I'm happy to make house repairs and tend to the yard and stable. Do you need me to take you to your doctor's appointments, as well?"

"*Jah,* I have appointments coming up soon. But what I really need you to do is oversee my shop. It's been closed for the past week, and Thanksgiving and *Grischtdaag* are just around the bend. They're my busiest seasons."

Hunter took a large bite of biscuit so his mouth was too full to respond. His uncle owned a furniture restoration business, with his main workshop at home and a smaller storefront in town. After he died, Ruth converted the space in town into a cannery, where she sold jams, relishes, fruits and chow chow. Hunter knew nothing about canning, and he didn't particularly care to learn.

As if reading his mind, Ruth explained, "You wouldn't be expected to do the canning. I've put up plenty of jars for now, and harvest season is over. If the shelves run low, your *mamm* has agreed to help with the canning, although she'll have to use store-bought produce for the ingredients, which is what I sometimes do in the winter."

"You want me to serve customers?" Hunter questioned. "I wouldn't be able to distinguish pickled beets from raspberry preserves!"

"*Neh*. My employee, Ivy Sutter, waits on customers. She knows everything there is to know about the products. But she has a special way of learning, so when she's ringing up purchases, she needs supervision—and protection. She's such an innocent *maedel*. Our regular customers are fine people, *Englisch* and Amish alike, but I'm concerned some of the tourists might take advantage or make demands."

Hunter set down his fork. He was familiar with his aunt's compassion for anyone who struggled with a difference of ability or who didn't fit in as well as others did. But Ruth was gifted; she had a way with people. He didn't. At least, he didn't anymore. Most days, his pain was so intense it took all of his resolve not to snarl at his own mother. How would he tolerate demanding customers or keep his patience with a girl who had learning difficulties?

"You wouldn't just be supervising Ivy. You'd also restock the shelves and keep the books. Of course, I'd pay you fairly," Ruth concluded.

"He wouldn't think of accepting payment, would you, Hunter?" his mother, Iris, interjected.

Hunter's ears felt inflamed. He knew it was a sin to be prideful, but his aunt's offer of a salary wounded his ego—primarily because he was in such desperate need of an income. It had been so long since he'd had full-time employment, he forgot what it felt like to receive an honest day's wage. Since his accident, he'd taken as many odd jobs as he could get, but they were few and far in between. The *leit* in his district helped with a significant portion of his hospital bills, but his rehabilitation was ongoing. In fact, he'd prematurely quit physical therapy because he knew they could no longer afford the sessions *and* pay for his mother's medical costs. He didn't want to keep imposing on the church, especially since others' needs seemed greater than his own.

Most humiliating of all, right before they left for Willow Creek, he'd received a notice from the bank stating they were on the brink of losing the house if they were delinquent with another mortgage payment. To the Amish, making a payment late was considered almost akin to stealing, since it denied the payee their fair due on time. While the payments were very small, Hunter still had difficulty scraping together enough to cover the mortgage. He shielded his mother from their financial woes, but he was so overwhelmed he was tempted to accept a lawyer's offer to sue the trucking company that employed the driver who hit them. Thankfully, the temptation left him almost as soon as it struck: it was unthinkable for the Amish to engage in a lawsuit for financial gain.

Swallowing the last of his coffee, Hunter decided although he might not be able to provide for a wife and he was floundering in caring for his mother, the least he could do was manage his aunt's shop without accepting a cent for it. He'd always had an interest in bookkeeping; perhaps the experience would afford him new skills he could use in Indiana.

"We're family and we're here to help, *Ant* Ruth," he finally stated. "Provided there's absolutely no more talk of payment, I'll be glad to oversee your cannery."

Yet as he hitched his horse to the post in town, he was anything but glad. Rather, his legs were so sore and stiff they felt like two planks nailed to his hips. He tottered down Main Street with a basket of eggs, hoping he didn't appear as conspicuous as he felt.

Stopping beneath the simply carved sign that read Yoder's Bakery, Hunter noticed a smaller cardboard sign propped in the window. "Early morning delivery person URGENTLY needed. November 27–December 24. Willow Creek to Piney Hill. Inquire within," it said. He wondered how "early" was early. Could he make the deliveries and still return to Willow Creek in time to open the cannery? Would Faith even consider him for the job, given their interaction that morning?

Hunter squinted through the spotless glass window. The bakery contained five or six small tables with chairs. Beyond the cozy dining space was a pastry case and behind that Faith was stacking bread on a shelf. Hunter noticed what had been too dim to see earlier: the fiery red hair of her youth had faded to a richer, subdued shade of auburn.

"Do you see something in there you think you'd like?" a woman behind him asked. "Everything we make is excellent."

Embarrassed, Hunter turned and stuttered, "You— you work there?"

"I do. My name is Pearl Hostetler. But wait—aren't you Hunter, Ruth's nephew?" the tall, thin, silver-haired woman asked.

"I am," he answered sheepishly. "It's *gut* to see you again."

"It's *wunderbaar* to see you, Hunter," Pearl said, placing her hand on his arm. "Ruth told me about your *daed*. I was very sorry to hear what happened."

"Denki." He coughed, surprised by the emotion Pearl's sincere sympathy elicited. He extended the basket of eggs. "I brought these for Faith. Hers broke this morning when she was cycling into town. Also, I'm… I'm interested in hearing more about the delivery job."

Hunter hoped Pearl would simply receive the basket and provide him details about the job, but she pushed the door open and announced, "Look who's here, Faith. Hunter brought you *oier* and he wants to be your delivery-man, as well!"

Noticing Faith's eyes narrow, Hunter didn't wish to appear too eager. He clarified, "I'd like to hear more about the job, that is."

"It's pretty straightforward," Faith replied, brushing her hands against her apron. "I need someone unfailingly dependable to deliver my baked goods to an *Englisch* booth at the Piney Hill Festival between seven and seven thirty every morning, Monday through Saturday. The festival begins in less than two weeks, on the day after Thanksgiving, and runs until the day before *Grischtdaag*. The delivery person would have to commit for the duration of the festival in order to make it worth my while to rent booth space."

Mentally calculating the distance between the bakery and Piney Hill, Hunter was certain he could complete the deliveries, return the horse and buggy to his aunt's home and walk to town with a good fifteen minutes to spare before the cannery opened at nine o'clock. And when Pearl blurted out the sum he'd earn for each delivery, Hunter was confident the arrangement was an answer to his prayers.

Looking Faith in the eye, he said, "Beginning Monday, I'll be managing Ruth's shop from nine until five o'clock, but I'd be available in the early morning to make deliveries for the duration of the festival."

Faith nodded slowly. "*Jah*, I'd appreciate that. The job is yours," she confirmed. She paused as a mischievous grin crossed her face. "But I do hope you're more careful about where you steer than you are about where you walk. My sales are very important to me."

"Your sales will be fine, provided you bake better than you bike," Hunter retorted, giving her an equally rascally smirk before setting the eggs on a table and exiting the store.

As he stepped into the brightening day, he realized Ruth was right: the trip had been worth his while. Being a part-time deliveryman for Faith Yoder might not have been his first choice for employment, but it was a steady, paying job, and that was all that mattered to him.

Chapter Two

After the door closed behind Hunter, Pearl dramatically clasped her hands together. "Ach! What a relief that is! I was beginning to think we weren't going to be able to sell our goods at the festival."

Hosted by a neighboring town right off the main interstate, the Piney Hill Christmas Festival was an enormous, commercial *Englisch* endeavor attracting thousands of passersby shopping for Christmas. Part of its appeal was the "Christmas Kingdom"—an elaborate prefabricated "Santa's Workshop" where children could have their photos taken with Santa. The bishop didn't prohibit the Amish *leit* from selling their goods at the festival, as long as they only rented space at booths hosted by the *Englisch* and didn't staff the booths themselves.

"Jah," Faith said, tentatively optimistic. "Although there's no guarantee we'll sell enough at the festival to make the down payment, without it, we wouldn't have stood a chance."

"It's a *gut* thing Hunter is in town again, both for Ruth and for us," Pearl gushed, hanging her shawl on a peg inside the hall leading to the kitchen. "Hasn't he grown into a fine, strapping young man?"

Although Hunter's mature physique hadn't escaped Faith's notice, she didn't know quite what to make of his personality. He definitely seemed more personable just now than he'd been on the road earlier that morning, and bringing her eggs was a nice gesture, but that might have been at Ruth's urging. Before Faith could respond, the phone rang and Pearl grabbed the receiver. "Yoder's Bakery, how may I help you?"

Landlines and electricity weren't allowed in Amish homes, but the *Ordnung* permitted them to be used for business purposes in their district, provided the buildings were owned by the *Englisch*. The bakery utilized both electricity and a phone, but neither service would be continued in the overhead apartment once the current tenant moved out, making it permissible for Faith to live there.

After hanging up, Pearl waved a slip of paper. "Another pie order for Thanksgiving! Two apple and one sawdust. If this keeps up, you'll have to start turning down orders."

"Not if I want to keep the bakery, I won't. I'll bake every night until midnight if I have to."

Although one of her chores growing up included baking for her family, Faith hadn't always enjoyed the responsibility. But while she was recovering from surgery, she began experimenting with dessert recipes. She soon discovered that even among the Amish she possessed an unusual talent for making goodies, and she reveled in the process of creating savory treats. That autumn, she made cakes for her second-oldest brother Noah's wedding to Lovina that were so scrumptious several guests requested she bake for their special occasions, too. Faith's business was born.

Sharing a kitchen with Henrietta proved to be impractical for both of them, however, so eventually Faith rented her current space. The bakery was the one good thing that resulted from her surgery, and she had no intention of letting it go without doing everything she could to raise the income for the down payment for her lease. So, when an *Englisch* customer called to say he couldn't pick up his large, unpaid order by the time the bakery closed at five, Faith continued to make pies to freeze for Thanksgiving until he showed up. It was six thirty by the time she finally locked the door behind her.

A frosty gust nearly blew her outer bonnet off her head as she pedaled uphill in the dark toward the big farmhouse. She meant to purchase a new battery at the mercantile during her dinner break, but she'd been so busy she didn't stop for an afternoon meal. Ravenous, she hoped her family hadn't worried about her when she missed supper.

"There you are," Henrietta said when Faith entered the kitchen. Her cheek was smudged with flour and she was jostling her youngest son on her hip. Utensils and ingredients were spread in disarray across the table. "Didn't you remember you were going to help make the bread for dinner tomorrow?"

The following day was their Sunday to host church worship services and they would need to serve a light dinner to everyone in attendance. Henrietta usually provided the traditional after-church meal of bread with "church peanut butter," homemade bologna, cheese, pickles and pickled beets. An assortment of desserts were supplied by other women in the district.

"Ach! I forgot," admitted Faith.

"You mustn't put earning money before the needs of the church," Henrietta scolded.

Faith hung her head. She wouldn't have stayed so late waiting for the customer if she'd remembered she promised to help bake bread after supper. Still, the fact that she'd forgotten indicated her priorities were on her business, not on the church.

"I'm sorry," she earnestly apologized. "I'll make the bread as soon as I've had something to eat."

"Something to eat? Your *ant* works in a bakery all day and she expects us to believe she hasn't had anything to eat," Henrietta cooed to the infant, who drooled when she tickled the fold of skin beneath his chin. "Do you believe that? Do you?"

Unsure whether her sister-in-law was joking or not, Faith ignored her comment. She opened the icebox and removed a bowl of chicken casserole to eat cold, along with a serving of homemade applesauce.

"Did I tell you my sister is visiting for Thanksgiving?" Henrietta asked while Faith devoured her supper. "My *mamm* and *daed* can't make the long journey, but I haven't seen Willa for so long that I pleaded with her to *kumme* anyway. She'll have to travel alone, which is difficult for her. She's not as…*strong-minded* as you are, but she misses me, too, so she's willing to make the effort. It will be *wunderbaar* to have another woman in the house, someone I can talk to."

Maybe she was overly tired, but Henrietta's comments nettled Faith and she had to work to temper her response. "That's nice. I'm sure we'll make room for her somewhere."

Then she washed, dried and put away her dish and

utensils before rolling up her sleeves to prepare the dough. It would be midnight before she finished baking after all.

Although Hunter felt his lower back seize up as he lifted Ruth into the buggy on Sunday, he met the challenge without a word of complaint. The Amish only missed church in cases of severe illness or extreme circumstances, and according to Ruth, her injuries weren't going to keep her from worshipping on the Sabbath.

"Do you remember the way to the Yoders' farm?" she asked. "It's their turn to host."

Hunter hadn't forgotten. He'd spent many Sunday afternoons fishing in the creek behind their property with Noah and Mason Yoder when he was a youth. As the horse pulled their buggy over the familiar hills and alongside the pastures and farmlands on the rural end of Willow Creek, he was flooded with remembrances of more carefree times.

After church service, men whose names he'd forgotten but whose faces were etched in his memory affably welcomed Hunter to the men's dinner table. By then, his legs were throbbing from sitting on the cold, hard benches in the drafty barn the Yoders used for a gathering room. He ate even quicker than the other men, who were all aware someone else was waiting for a turn at the table and hurried to vacate their places. Hunter wanted to return to Ruth's home and warm himself in front of the woodstove, but he didn't see his aunt and mother anywhere. Undoubtedly, Ruth was chatting with friends while his mother helped the other women clear tables and clean dishes.

Figuring if he couldn't warm his aching legs, he could at least stretch them, he slipped away from the men conversing in small clusters and awkwardly navigated the uneven terrain leading to the creek a few acres behind the Yoders' house.

He didn't notice until too late that a woman was already there, leaning against a willow, pitching stones sidearm into the current. He couldn't turn around without being rude and he couldn't keep moving without drawing attention to his unsteady gait, so he came to an abrupt standstill.

"*Guder nammidaag*, Hunter," she called when she noticed him, dropping the stones.

It was Faith. Hunter had no option but to continue in her direction and hope she didn't notice his unusual stride. He didn't want her to doubt his abilities and regret hiring him.

"*Guder nammidaag,*" he replied and motioned toward the water. "The creek is shallower than I remember. I suppose everything probably seemed bigger when I was a *kind.*"

"We had a dry summer, so it's been running low," she acknowledged. "Do you really still remember the creek?"

"How could I forget?" Hunter asked as he positioned himself next to her. "The year I was twelve, Noah, Mason and I tried to build a footbridge over it and it collapsed. Don't you remember? You were there, too."

A smile capered from Faith's lips up to her eyes, and for an instant her expression reminded Hunter of the spunky young girl who used to tag along on her brothers' adventures. "You boys sent me across the bridge first to test whether it would hold," she recalled.

Hunter reminisced, "*Jah*, but you were only a little wisp of a thing, so of course it withstood your weight. I don't know what we were thinking, for the three of us boys to join you on it, with none of us knowing how to swim. It was a *gut* thing your *daed* heard our cries and ran to give us his hand."

Now a shadow troubled Faith's countenance. "Sometimes I wish my *daed* would still *kumme* running to give me his hand, even though I'm no longer a *kind* and it's been five years since he died," she lamented.

Hunter hadn't meant to stir up sad memories. "I'm sorry about your *daed*. I have fond memories of him," he said. He was quiet before adding, "My own *daed* died a little over a year ago, so I understand why you miss yours."

"I'm sorry for your loss, too, Hunter," Faith murmured, her hazel eyes welling with empathy. "I should have said as much yesterday. My brothers were especially grieved to hear about the accident. Ruth mentioned you were hurt in it as well, but I'm grateful to see *Gott* answered all our prayers by healing you."

Not wishing to admit he wasn't fully recovered, Hunter blew on his fingers and then changed the subject. "A lot has changed since we were *kinner*. Who would have expected little Faith Yoder would grow up to own a bakery?"

A furrow momentarily creased Faith's brow before she straightened her posture and asked, "And what about you? Do you still work at the RV factory?"

Pushing his hat up, Hunter massaged his forehead. The crick in his spine seemed to be traveling upward, giving him a headache. He didn't want to be dishonest with Faith, but he was concerned if people knew about his job loss, he might become the object of gossip. Or worse, the object of pity.

"I—I—" he stuttered.

His sentence was cut short by Mason calling out, "Faith! Hunter! We've been looking for you!"

Faith's brother traipsed down the hill in their direction, and Lawrence Miller ambled a few paces behind. They were followed by two young women. Hunter sensed the questions he'd been dreading had only just begun.

As she watched her peers approach, Faith felt uncharacteristically peevish.

Ordinarily, she relished the time she spent chatting with the other women during Sabbath dinner cleanup, but today Lawrence's fiancée, Penelope Lapp—an eighteen-year-old deacon's daughter who lived in a neighboring town—was visiting her relatives in Willow Creek. After church, Faith overheard Penelope fawning over Henrietta's infant, claiming she hoped God would bless her with a baby by this time next year.

Although Faith no longer felt any romantic attachment to Lawrence, it distressed her to be reminded of why they'd broken up. She escaped to the creek to gather her composure, only to be discovered by Hunter, who pointed out what a "little wisp of a thing" she used to be and made her sentimental by calling to mind a long-forgotten memory of her departed father.

If all that weren't unsettling enough, now she was going to have to exchange pleasantries with Lawrence!

"Hunter, how *gut* it is to see you," Mason said, clapping him on the back.

Lawrence did the same and Hunter responded in kind.

"Please meet Katie Fisher," Faith's brother said. "She's the schoolteacher here."

"And this is Penelope Lapp," Lawrence stated. "My intended."

"Your intended?" Hunter repeated.

"Don't sound so surprised," Lawrence ribbed him. "I'm twenty-two, almost twenty-three. It's past time for me to marry and start a family."

Faith winced, supposing if it weren't for the time he lost courting her, Lawrence wouldn't feel his marriage and family plans were behind schedule.

"How about you, Hunter?" Penelope asked. "Are you betrothed or walking out with someone?"

"Neh," was all he said.

"Neh? That's a surprise," Lawrence replied. To Penelope, he explained, "Hunter lived here for a while when he was sixteen and he was so sought after, he had his choice of *meed.* He could have courted anyone he wanted."

Faith's irritation was becoming more difficult to suppress—it sounded as if Lawrence were describing horses at an auction, not young women.

"Did you want him to court you, Faith?" Penelope asked.

"I was only thirteen!" Faith exclaimed. "Despite what some people may think, not every *maedel's* sole dream is to get married as soon as she possibly can."

She was appalled by Penelope's nerve. Even if Faith had developed a crush on someone as a schoolgirl, it wasn't something she'd discuss, especially not in front of male acquaintances. Courtships and romance among the Amish tended to be private matters.

"He didn't court or even favor anyone, if I recall," Lawrence said. "He claimed he didn't believe in courting unless he intended to marry, and since he was only sixteen and lived in Indiana, there was no point in walking out with anyone here. He was probably the only person who actually attended our singings just for the singing."

Penelope sniggled but Katie asserted, "*I* attended sing-ings in my district primarily for the singing when I was a youth. There's nothing wrong with that."

Faith smiled at the stout, dark-haired woman. She always appreciated Katie's forthright manner, and she was glad Mason was walking out with her. When Faith glanced at Hunter, she noticed he was shifting his weight from foot to foot, as if embarrassed by the conversation. She couldn't blame him and she quickly switched topics.

"Speaking of youth, Hunter and I were just talking about how you boys used to spend time down here at the creek," she said to Mason. "Do you remember the footbridge?"

"*Jah*, of course." Mason regaled the others with the anecdote about their footbridge disaster and subsequent submersion in the creek.

"After your *daed* pulled us out, he promised if you fin-ished the fieldwork early the following week, he'd help us build a sturdier bridge," Hunter recalled.

"*Jah*, and you were so excited that after working all day for Ruth, you'd come and help us every evening in the fields and on Saturday, as well," Mason reminisced, shaking his head. "My *daed* frequently commented about what a strong, dedicated worker you were. I often had to ask *Gott* to forgive my envy."

"He's still strong—look at those shoulders," Lawrence observed, lightly punching Hunter's arm.

Faith wasn't certain if she imagined it, but Hunter's face seemed to go gray. Was it modesty or the cold wind that caused him to set his jaw like that? Although as a boy, he was as congenial as could be, there was some-thing stilted about his posture now that gave him an air of aloofness. Ordinarily, Faith would have been put off by an unsociable demeanor, but she sensed Hunter was uncomfortable with the attention, and she wanted to spare him further uneasiness.

"The bridge is still standing," she informed Hunter. "This past summer I brought my nephew down to the water so he could cross it."

Hunter visibly relaxed his shoulders. "I'm not surprised," he said, looking directly at Faith as he smiled. "Your *daed* made sure it was durable."

"I'd like to see it," Penelope suggested. "Why don't the men lead the way?"

Faith had never taken Lawrence to the bridge before, and she didn't want him visiting it now. The bridge belonged to another part of her life; it belonged to her dad and brothers and nephews—and even to Hunter. But not to Lawrence. "I really ought to return to the house—" she started to say.

"There's no need to hurry back," insisted Penelope. "If you're hungry, there will still be leftovers in another hour. And it's not as if you need to dash to the evening singing to meet a suitor, is it?"

Faith huffed. She never mentioned wanting to eat, and she didn't appreciate Penelope's digging for information about whether she was being courted. "Actually, my concern is that I ought to be helping clean up."

"But who knows when I'll be back here again?" Penelope sounded like a wheedling child. "Please, Faith?"

"Alright," Faith agreed, "*kumme* along." She had no idea why it was so important to Penelope to see the footbridge, but she gave in since the young woman was a guest in their district. As a member of the host family, it was up to Faith to be especially hospitable to her. But that didn't mean she was going to let the men take the lead.

* * *

Although Faith courteously accommodated Penelope's request, as she pivoted toward the woods Hunter noticed the spark in her eyes. What put it there? Why did she suddenly say she needed to get back to the house? Was it really that she wanted to help clean up, or did Faith have a suitor waiting after church for her? Hunter didn't know why the possibility caused him to experience a twinge of disappointment now, when only yesterday he assumed she was being courted. But perhaps that wasn't the reason she wanted to leave at all. Maybe Faith was simply tiring of Penelope's intrusive inquiries.

Hunter sure was. He gladly would have returned to the house, too, but the only thing he wanted to do less than hike along the creek was to explain why he didn't want to hike along the creek. He intended to avoid discussing his injuries as long as he could. After all, what would Lawrence say once he knew Hunter developed such broad shoulders from months of turning the wheels of a wheelchair and hoisting himself along the parallel bars at the clinic? Would Mason think Hunter was less of a hard worker when he found out he'd lost his job because he wasn't mobile enough to meet the assembly quota at the RV factory? Would it suddenly dawn on all of them why he was no longer "sought after" as a bachelor? What might Faith—not just as his employer, but as a woman near his age—think of him then?

It wasn't that Hunter believed any of them would be unsympathetic if they found out about his injuries; it was that he didn't want their sympathy in the first place. He worked too hard at recovering to have to answer personal questions about his condition from the likes of Penelope Lapp. So he bit his lip and tried to match his stride to

Mason's and Katie's, while Faith marched up ahead and Penelope and Lawrence lagged behind.

"How long will you be visiting Willow Creek?" Katie questioned conversationally.

"Until my *ant's* leg heals, probably sometime after the first of the year. I'm managing her store until she's better." Hunter pushed a branch out of his way, holding it to the side so it wouldn't spring back and hit Penelope.

"What do you do for employment at home?" Penelope questioned.

"He works in an RV factory, isn't that right?" Lawrence replied before Hunter had a chance to answer. "You must have accrued a lot of time off to take such a long leave. That's one *gut* thing about working for the *Englisch*. It's not like a farmer's work, which is never done."

While Hunter contemplated how best to respond, Penelope swatted at Lawrence with the end of her shawl. "I've heard it said that it's a farmer's *wife's* work that is never done," she taunted.

"That, too," Lawrence allowed.

"Business owners don't exactly sit around twiddling their thumbs, and Katie has her hands full as a schoolteacher, too," Faith countered over her shoulder. Hunter chortled inwardly in appreciation of her feisty tone. She was never one to let her brothers claim their work was more important or difficult than anyone else's, including hers, when they were kids.

"*Jah*, that's probably true," Penelope concurred. "Oh! Speaking of business owners, I almost forgot. Lawrence and I want you to make the cakes for our wedding, don't we, Lawrence?"

"*Jah*, if she's willing."

"Of course I'm willing, but please give me your exact

order ten days in advance. I know Lawrence prefers everything to be just so, and I wouldn't want to disappoint him," Faith said without slowing or turning to face them. Did Hunter detect a note of sarcasm in her reply?

"I will," Penelope agreed happily. "Hunter, you must attend our wedding, too. All of the *leit* from Lawrence's church are invited. We'll match you up with a—"

"There's the bridge," Faith interrupted, and Hunter was thankful she'd saved him from embarrassment once again. She scampered down the rocky embankment, and the others followed.

Each step seemed to jar Hunter's hip bones against their sockets as he descended the slope. The small bridge was weathered and a few boards were missing, but it rose in a functional arc above the shallow current, just as he'd remembered.

"It's as good as new," Mason jested, confidently crossing it to the other side. He held out his hand for Katie to join him.

Katie stalled reluctantly. "I don't know... I might be too heavy for a *kinner's* bridge."

"Don't you trust my workmanship?" Mason teased, so she darted across the planks.

Penelope took her turn, and then Lawrence stepped onto the structure. "You call this durable?" he gibed, stomping on the bridge with the heel of his boot. "This board here feels a little loose."

After Lawrence crossed, Hunter waited for Faith, who seemed to be dillydallying. "Ladies first," he uttered patiently.

Faith hesitated before placing one foot onto the bridge. As she lifted her back foot from the shore, the waterlogged board beneath her front foot gave way.

From the parallel embankment, Katie shrieked, "Help her!"

It happened so suddenly and his joints were so stiff, Hunter wasn't able to spring forward quickly enough to prevent Faith from falling. Her front leg wedged through the crack into the creek while her upper torso lurched forward onto the bridge.

Mason and Lawrence raced down the opposite bank while Hunter bolted into the icy current from his side of the water. With one foot dangling in the creek, Faith was using her dry, bent leg and her arms to try to crawl onto the bridge.

"Are you hurt?" Mason asked.

"I'm *stuck*!" she yelped, red-faced. "Stop pulling me! You're making it worse."

"I've got her," Hunter said authoritatively. "I'll lift her up so you can free her leg. Be careful. Here, Faith, lean back against me."

From behind, he gently wrapped his arms around her waist and clasped her to his chest until Lawrence and Mason eased her leg from between the planks. Then he carried her to the embankment. Her stocking was torn and her leg was scraped from her ankle to her knee, but it didn't appear to be seriously injured.

Kneeling before her, Hunter hesitated. He feared his legs would lock up on him, but he offered, "If it hurts your ankle to walk on it, I can carry you back to the house."

"Neh," she snapped and what seemed like a look of disgust clouded her face. He didn't blame her; he might as well have pushed her into the creek for as slowly as he'd moved to prevent her from falling in.

Then she quietly added, "*Denki*, but my foot is fine. It's just very cold, so I'm going to hurry up ahead."

Katie, who had waded over to be sure Faith was alright, said, "My feet are wet and cold, too, so I'll go with you." She linked her arm through Faith's for support and they scuttled away.

Stranded on the opposite bank without a bridge to cross, Penelope called, "What about me? Lawrence, help!" until Lawrence waded across the water, hefted her to his shoulder as easily as a sack of grain and waded back, setting her down next to Mason and Hunter.

The four of them walked in silence the rest of the way, too chilled to speak. In fact, until Katie mentioned her feet were wet, Hunter hadn't realized his legs were, too. The icy water had made them so numb that for once he wasn't aware they'd ever been hurt at all. Wishing the same could be said of his self-esteem, Hunter kept his chin tucked to his chest as he tramped against the wind.

Chapter Three

On Sunday night, Faith rose so many times to don her prayer *kapp* and kneel beside her bed that she feared she'd wake her two nephews, ages three and five, who slept on the other side of the divider in the tiny room she shared with them. Each time she finished praying, she was certain she'd thought her final uncharitable thought, but another one would come to mind as soon as she slid back under the quilt and she'd have to ask the Lord to forgive her all over again.

Much of her resentment was directed at Lawrence, whom she blamed for her clumsy plunge into the creek. If he hadn't deliberately trampled over the bridge like a big ox, the board wouldn't have broken when it was her turn to cross. She was equally piqued by Penelope's constant chatter and references to her upcoming wedding. Faith understood the young woman was barely eighteen, but it seemed she could have exercised a bit more discretion.

Yet oddly, it was Hunter's conduct that ruffled her most. Rationally, she knew he was being helpful, but she was utterly mortified when he wrapped his arms around her midsection and held her above the water. Not to mention how embarrassed she was by the pained expression on his face right before he offered to carry her home. He couldn't have appeared more daunted if he'd volunteered to shoulder a dairy cow!

She admitted she was overweight, but she wasn't *that* overweight. Wasn't Hunter supposed to possess extraordinary strength, anyway? Wasn't that what Mason and Lawrence claimed? She remembered his youthful vitality, too, just like she remembered how popular he was. But what good did either of those qualities do him now, if he couldn't be gracious enough to overlook the fact she was no longer "a little wisp of a thing"? Not that she wanted his assistance, but he didn't have to pull such a face when he offered it—especially in front of Lawrence and his skinny fiancée, Penelope.

Faith socked her pillow. With the exception of the afternoon she confided her secret to Lawrence, she'd never felt so unfeminine and humiliated as she'd felt that afternoon. By the time she drifted to sleep, she wasn't certain whether her leg ached from falling through the bridge or from kneeling so long, praying for God to forgive her pride and anger.

When she awoke on Monday, her indignation had faded, but as she bicycled through the dark, her leg burned with each painful rotation of the pedals. Feeling cranky, she hoped she'd have a few minutes alone before Pearl arrived. Usually, the older woman didn't come in until seven thirty or eight, but this week she planned to work longer hours to help fill the Thanksgiving pie orders.

Faith sighed. Thanksgiving was ten days away and they were behind schedule as it was. They'd received so many orders that Faith resorted to limiting the number of fresh-baked pies she'd sell during the half week before the holiday. Instead, she offered customers the option of buying unbaked, frozen pies, which they could pick up anytime. Many *Englischers* said they'd be glad to experience the fragrant aroma of "homemade" pies baking in their ovens. Some brought in their own pie plates, and Faith inferred they might intend to take credit for making the pies themselves, but she didn't mind one bit; each order brought her closer to making her down payment.

But exactly how much closer was she? The surge in orders was generating more income, but since she was also spending more on ingredients and paying Pearl for extended hours, Faith wasn't sure how the figures would balance out. Bookkeeping wasn't her strength, but she planned to review her financial records as soon as things slowed down in the bakery.

"Guder mariye," Pearl cheerfully greeted Faith. "You're limping! What happened to your leg? Were you romping through the woods with those darling nephews of yours again? You dote on them. You'll make a fine mother someday—"

"It's nothing," Faith cut in. She was edgy enough without being reminded she probably *wouldn't* make a fine mother someday. "You're here even earlier than I am. Did you start a pot of *kaffi*?"

"I just put it on."

They took turns making and rolling pie dough and peeling and slicing apples until it was time to flip the sign on the door to Open.

"Guess who's up bright and early this morning?" Pearl chirped, returning from the task. "Hunter Schwartz. I spotted him in the shop."

Her cheeks burning at the mention of Hunter's name, Faith only mumbled, "Hmm."

"The cannery doesn't open until nine. He must be an especially hard worker."

First Pearl called him a fine, strapping young man and now she was praising his industriousness. Faith knew the older woman well enough to suspect her comments were a prelude to matchmaking.

"Jah," Faith carefully concurred. "Diligence was always one of Hunter's admirable attributes, even when we were *kinner*." Then, so Pearl wouldn't read any personal interest into Faith's admission, she added, "That's one of the reasons I didn't hesitate to hire him."

"We should extend a personal invitation for him to join us for his afternoon meal, the way Ivy and Ruth always do. You could go over there before the customers start arriving and—"

Now Faith felt positive Pearl was laying the groundwork for a match between her and Hunter. *"Neh!"* she refused more adamantly than she intended.

Pearl put her hand to her throat as if wounded. "Oh," she apologized meekly. "I just thought it would be a neighborly thing to do."

Faith realized she may have misinterpreted Pearl's intentions and regretted her decision hurt Pearl's feelings, but she didn't back down. "It's a lovely thought, Pearl. But we're so busy filling orders I don't foresee myself taking proper dinner breaks. It wouldn't be polite for me to personally invite him and then not join all of you once he got here."

"Neh, of course not, I understand," Pearl said. "Work comes first."

"I didn't mean that," Faith clarified. "I only meant…"

The bell jangled on the door and one of the *Englisch* regulars stopped in for his morning coffee and honey bar. Faith was relieved she didn't have to confess the real reasons she couldn't possibly sit down and eat dinner with Hunter Schwartz. For one thing, even though he was already well aware of the size of her waist, she didn't want him to know how much she ate and judge her for it. For another, there was something about seeing him again as an adult that made her doubt she could swallow two bites in front of him. The feeling wasn't merely the awkwardness over broken eggs or broken bridges, nor was it necessarily an unpleasant sensation, but it was unsettling all the same. Once Faith became accustomed to working with him, perhaps she'd feel different. For now, she hoped she wouldn't see much of Hunter until after Thanksgiving, when he began making deliveries. Perhaps by then, she'd even lose a couple of pounds.

Hunter wiped his palms against his trousers. On Saturday he'd mopped the floor, and he'd come into the cannery early this morning to restock the shelves so that everything was exactly where it should be. Rather, everything except one very important person: Ivy. It was ten minutes before nine o'clock. The shop opened at nine on weekdays, and Ivy was nowhere to be seen.

Hunter was afraid this might happen. Ivy lived alone with her grandfather, Mervin Sutter, who introduced Ivy to Hunter and Iris after church on Sunday. The blonde, petite, sixteen-year-old girl wouldn't look Hunter in the eye as she mumbled a barely audible greeting. He attributed her shyness to his own appearance, assuming she was intimidated because he was twice her size. Also, his pants were dripping from walking into the creek and he was shaking with cold. To her, he probably looked like a crazed bear, which was a bit how he felt at that particular moment.

Glancing through the window toward the bakery, he wondered how Faith's leg was this morning. He knew from experience pain had a way of getting worse as the day wore on. As he uttered a quick prayer this wouldn't be the case for Faith, he caught sight of her approaching a table toward the front of her shop. She disposed of a napkin and paper cup and scrubbed the table in swift circles with a cloth. To his surprise, when she was done she lifted her hand in acknowledgment. Pleased she seemed to have put his shortcomings during yesterday's incident behind her, he waved back.

Then he realized she wasn't waving to him, but to Ivy, who was passing on the sidewalk in front of the cannery. She pulled the door open just as the clock began to chime on the hour.

"Ruth Graber turns the sign to Open at nine o'clock," Ivy stated in a monotone.

Hunter was startled speechless by her greeting. Then he recalled Ruth advising him that habits were very important to Ivy and he mustn't disrupt her routine.

"Of course, *denki* for the reminder, Ivy," he said as he flipped the sign on the door.

For the rest of the morning, Ivy didn't say a word unless asked. But she led the customers to any item they requested and she could quote the jars' contents and prices by heart. However, Hunter quickly discovered that while her recitation skills were excellent, Ivy had no ability to add or multiply figures. So, he used the cash register to create receipts while she bagged the customers' purchases.

Virtually all of the customers were *Englischers*, but at midmorning, a slightly built, bespectacled Amish man, Joseph Schrock, paid a visit to introduce himself. Joseph's father, Daniel Schrock, owned Schrock's Shop, which featured Amish-made crafts and goods that were especially appealing to tourists, and the store turned a healthy profit.

"It's *gut* to meet another businessman," Joseph said. "Sometimes I catch grief because I'm not a carpenter or a farmer, but I knew from the time I was a *kind* I had a head for figures, not a body for a farm. *Gott* gives us all different talents, right?"

"*Jah*," Hunter agreed, although he wasn't sure if Joseph's comment made him feel better or worse about not being able to do the physical labor he'd been accustomed to doing. What if his physical strength was his only God-given gift? What if he didn't have a "head for figures"?

He didn't have time to dwell on the thought, though, because customers were lining up. Soon, Ivy declared, "It's quarter to one. Ruth Graber and I take our dinner break with Faith Yoder and Pearl Hostetler at one o'clock. Ruth Graber turns the sign to Closed."

Hunter didn't mind if Ivy went to Faith's bakery for her dinner break, but he had no intention of going with her. During the working day on Main Street, his association with Faith was strictly professional, not social. "You've done such a *gut* job teaching me how to serve customers, Ivy, that I'll keep the shop open and stay here while you take your break."

The girl's face puckered in confusion. "You won't eat with us?"

"I'll eat my dinner now in the back room. If any customers *kumme* in and you need help, call me. I'll be done before one o'clock," Hunter assured her.

In the sterile back room where Ruth did her canning, Hunter leaned against a stool. Standing all morning caused his hips and lower spine to burn with pain, but if he'd been sitting all morning, he would have claimed the same discomfort. The fact was, there was little that didn't cause his back and legs to hurt and even less that helped them to feel better.

He listened for customers arriving as he downed his cold mincemeat pie. After church, Henrietta Yoder sent a pie home with them, saying Faith made the pie especially for Ruth the evening before, once she finished baking bread for the church meal. Hunter, his aunt and his mother enjoyed it for supper, and he was pleased there were leftovers he could bring to work for dinner. If the rest of Faith's baking was as good as her pie, Hunter figured it was no wonder her business was flourishing.

He returned to the main room with four minutes to spare. The door was left open and Ivy was gone.

"Ach!" he said aloud. "She must have gone to Faith's already."

Yet it troubled him that she'd left the door ajar. Also, she was so time-conscious that it seemed unlikely she would have left before the clock chimed. However reluctant he was to face Faith again after his ineptness at the creek, Hunter wouldn't be satisfied until he made certain Ivy was at the bakery. He put on his coat and hat and crossed the street.

"Guder nammidaag!" Pearl exclaimed when he stepped inside, where a tantalizing aroma filled the air. "Faith, look who's joining us for his dinner break."

"Oh?" Faith's neutral response was difficult to interpret as she bent to slide a tray of apple fry pies into the display case.

"Actually, I already ate my dinner," Hunter explained. "I'm here to check on Ivy. She left without letting me know she was going."

Faith abruptly popped up from behind the counter, her eyes wide. "Ivy's not here. She never steps foot in the door until the clock strikes. How long has she been missing?"

"Missing? I don't think she's *missing*," Hunter faltered as a wave of panic washed over him. "She's just not at the shop, that's all."

Noticing Hunter's ashen complexion, Faith felt almost as much concern for him as she did for Ivy.

"Don't worry, we'll find her," Faith promised. "When exactly was she last in the store?"

Hunter stammered, "She—she was just there fifteen minutes ago. It was quarter to one. I told her I'd eat my dinner in the back room and when I was finished she could *kumme* here to take her dinner break with you."

Faith immediately knew what the problem was, but she didn't have time to explain it to Hunter. She glanced at Pearl, who was already tying her winter bonnet beneath her chin.

"I'll check the other Main Street shops for her, but meanwhile you'd better get to the pond," Pearl advised. "She has a fifteen-minute head start."

Grabbing her shawl, Faith asked Hunter if he'd brought his buggy into town.

"*Neh*. I walked."

"Follow me, then," she urged and led him through the

kitchen and out the back door. She wheeled her tandem bicycle away from the wall it was leaning against.

"You can take the backseat, I'll steer," she instructed. Although the pond was situated right down the hill from his aunt's house, Hunter was so dazed Faith wasn't sure he'd remember where to turn off the main road.

"We're going to ride the bike?" Hunter asked. He seemed to be moving in slow motion and Faith wondered what was wrong with him. Was he in shock?

"*Jah*, now hop on," Faith ordered, hoping her no-nonsense attitude would bring him to his senses. "I'll tell you more as we ride, but for now I need you to pedal as hard as you can."

They wobbled a bit as they started down the secondary road running parallel to busy Main Street, but after three or four rotations, Faith felt the bicycle surge forward and suddenly they were sailing. She immediately recognized Hunter's reputation for stamina was well earned: the heavy bike never glided so briskly when Faith rode it alone. If she weren't so distraught about Ivy, she might have enjoyed the rush of nippy November air against her cheeks as they cruised along together.

"Where are we going?" Hunter shouted.

"Wheeler's Bridge," Faith spoke loudly over her shoulder.

The covered bridge spanned the far end of Willow Creek, which wound its way through much of the farmland in the area, including the Yoders' property. As a small, single-lane structure, the bridge was mostly used by Amish buggies or by tourists taking photos. It was situated just before the point where the current pooled into a deep and sizable pond.

Faith noticed an immediate lag in their speed as

Hunter gasped. "Do you think Ivy might have jumped off the bridge?"

"*Neh, neh!* Of course not. Ach, I'm so sorry, I should have explained." Faith panted. She felt terrible to have alarmed him, but she was winded from talking and pedaling. "When Ivy gets upset, she goes to the pond and hides under the bridge. No one knows why. Usually, she crouches on the embankment underneath it, where she's relatively safe. Our fear is she might slip and fall into the water. Like most Amish in Willow Creek, she can't swim."

The bike jerked forward as Hunter rapidly increased his pedaling again.

Touched by his unspoken concern, Faith promised, "It's going to be alright, Hunter."

"I shouldn't have let her out of my sight," he lamented. "There weren't any customers in the store. They were the ones I thought I had to watch. I never thought Ivy would leave."

"I know it's upsetting, but it's not your fault," Faith tried to comfort him as they rounded the final bend. "It happens so often Pearl gave her the nickname Wandering Ivy."

"Look! Under there!" Hunter whooped. "I see bright blue. It's her dress. Steer right, Faith, right!"

"I'm steering, I'm steering!" Faith declared, giddy with relief as she angled the handlebars to the right.

It didn't take long to coax Ivy from beneath the bridge. For one thing, the girl had neglected to put on her shawl before leaving, and the air was bitterly cold. For another, Faith promised they'd share a cream-filled doughnut when they returned, warning Ivy they'd have to hurry back before the sweets were sold out.

"Hunter Schwartz didn't want to eat dinner with Faith Yoder," Ivy mumbled as Faith took off her own shawl and wound it around Ivy's shoulders.

"That's okay," Faith patiently explained. "Men don't always like to eat dinner with women, especially if they aren't well acquainted with them. Maybe Hunter will join us one day for a special occasion after he gets to know us better. And when Ruth returns to the shop, she'll eat with us again. Until then, you may *kumme* to the bakery by yourself for your dinner break."

This compromise seemed to be acceptable to Ivy, who nodded and repeated the phrase, "Men don't always like to eat dinner with women."

"Here," Hunter said to Faith. He slipped off his coat and placed it over her shoulders. It was still warm from his body, and as she snuggled it tightly around her, she felt as if she'd received an affectionate embrace. *Such a silly thought!* she told herself. *It's no different from me letting Ivy use my shawl.*

Since Ivy didn't know how to ride a bicycle and it seemed unwise for Faith to leave her alone with Hunter since she'd just been so upset by him, the three of them sauntered back to town together. With Faith limping, Hunter pushing the bicycle and Ivy stopping every five yards to adjust her borrowed shawl, it took them over an hour to return. But at least Ivy was happy: there was one—and only one—cream-filled doughnut left in the display case.

"Denki," Faith mouthed to Pearl, who undoubtedly saved the doughnut, knowing Faith would have used it as leverage to bring Ivy back. They'd been down this road before.

Faith sighed as she heard the clock strike three. She'd

have to stay at the bakery past supper time again if she was going to catch up with the baking, and Henrietta undoubtedly would have something to say about her tardiness. Still, Faith had missed dinner and she was so hungry that the apprehension she felt about eating in front of Hunter was all but forgotten.

When he came in from stowing her bike in the back, she asked, "Would you like a hot cup of *kaffi*? A little dessert after our long walk, perhaps?"

"That's kind of you to offer, but I've got to get back to the shop," he said. "I've been away from it too long. Who knows how many sales I already lost?"

As if that's my fault! Faith bristled inwardly, noticing he was standing in that wooden manner of his again, as if on guard against her friendliness, and the tenderness she'd felt toward him on their bike ride vanished.

"Well, don't let me keep you," she replied, lifting his coat from her shoulders. "And don't forget to take this."

I hardly need a man's coat wrapped around me anyway, she thought. *The ovens in my bakery will keep me plenty warm.*

Faith turned on her heel and disappeared into the kitchen before Hunter had the opportunity to thank her for her help. He stood by the table where Ivy was eating her doughnut, awkwardly holding his hat in front of him, unsure whether to wait until she finished or to leave without her.

"If you'd like, I'll see to it Ivy returns when she's finished," Pearl suggested.

"I'd appreciate that," Hunter said. He glanced toward the kitchen, wondering if Faith might reappear. When she didn't, he requested, "Would you please tell Faith I said *denki* for—"

He was going to say, *for helping me find Ivy,* but the young girl seemed to be absorbing his every word as she licked chocolate from the top of her treat. He didn't want to offend her by drawing attention to the fact she'd run away.

"Please tell her I said *denki* for the bicycle ride. I appreciated it that she knew where to—er, that she showed me the pond," he finished, and Pearl winked at him above Ivy's head.

Although initially the bicycle ride caused his back to knot up, the combination of pedaling and then slowly walking from the pond caused Hunter to feel more limber than he had since before he quit going to physical therapy. However, while his bodily aches lessened, his mental unease intensified. What should he tell Ivy's grandfather when he arrived to pick her up? How would he explain to Ruth sales were already down because he'd temporarily lost her employee and had to close the shop in the middle of the day? Some help he was turning out to be. His aunt would have done better to keep the shop closed— that way, she wouldn't have to pay Ivy's salary.

But his worries about what to tell Ivy's grandfather proved needless: when the clock struck five, Ivy put on her shawl and announced, "Mervin Sutter waits for me at the hitching post behind the mercantile at five o'clock." Then she walked out the door.

He wished it would be as easy to avoid telling his aunt about Ivy's escapade, but he knew Ruth would be waiting to hear how things went. He reconciled the cash with the receipt tape, checking his figures twice, and locked the money in the back room. At a minimum, he wanted to assure Ruth he'd efficiently managed the bookkeeping.

He dimmed the lights and pushed his arm through the sleeve of his coat. He hadn't noticed earlier, but the wool absorbed the smell of whatever ingredients Faith was using—cinnamon? nutmeg?—before she'd worn it this afternoon. Pausing to savor the fragrance, he noticed her storefront was closed, but a light glowed from the hall leading to the back kitchen.

He wondered if he should pop in and thank her in person for her help that afternoon. He certainly appreciated how calm and focused she'd been. Her patient kindness, both to him and then to Ivy, hadn't escaped his attention, either. He found it hard to believe someone like Faith wasn't walking out with a suitor, as Penelope implied. Perhaps because Faith was so dedicated to her business, she didn't have time for socializing? Or was it because the men in Willow Creek weren't acceptable to her? What qualities did she prefer in a suitor?

The clock struck on the half hour, jolting Hunter from his thoughts—he didn't know how his mind wandered to the subject of courting. He decided not to disrupt Faith since he'd already taken her away from her responsibilities once today. As the person who'd be making her deliveries, he wanted her to be confident he was efficient. Instead, he trekked home, glad for the cover of darkness. His spine had begun to tighten again and he walked so crookedly he feared if anyone saw him, they might assume he'd had too much to drink—something he never did.

"Hunter, *kumme* tell us all about your first day," his aunt beckoned from the parlor before he'd even latched the kitchen door behind him.

"I will, *Ant* Ruth, as soon as I tend to the stable," he stalled. "I came in to retrieve a pair of gloves first."

"If Ivy Sutter can walk from Main Street to Wheeler's Bridge without a shawl, I hardly think you need a pair of gloves to pitch hay," his aunt joshed.

Hunter poked his head into the room where his aunt and mother were giggling behind their hands like two schoolgirls.

"You heard?" he asked, his ears aflame.

"We *saw*," his mother replied, pointing to the large window, which in daylight afforded a view of the bridge and pond.

"I'm sorry, *Ant* Ruth," Hunter began. "I can explain—"

"No need to explain," his aunt protested. "I'm used to Ivy's ways and I can guess what happened."

Hunter hung his head. "But you trusted me to supervise Ivy and I failed. I wouldn't blame you if you didn't want me to—"

"You didn't fail," Ruth lectured, bending forward over her cast and pointing her finger. "You encountered a setback. That's not failure—it's life."

Hunter nodded solemnly and his aunt leaned back against the cushions again.

"The important thing is, when the challenge arose, you managed it," Ruth emphasized. "Of course, we noticed you had a little help. Faith Yoder is a very special woman. It's confounding that she's not walking out with anyone."

So, Faith wasn't being courted? Startled by the twitch of pleasure in his ribs, Hunter tempered his response. "She's a decent cyclist," he stated blandly.

"A decent cyclist?" Ruth snorted. "You and Faith sped so fast on that double bicycle, your *mamm* and I thought we'd seen a couple of wild geese flying by, didn't we, Iris?"

"*Jah*, the two of you made quite some pair!" His mother laughed exuberantly for the first time in a very long time.

In spite of his doubts he'd ever make a pair with any woman, especially not Faith Yoder, Hunter joined his aunt and mother in hearty merriment, laughing louder than both of them combined.

Chapter Four

"You've gone as white as flour," Pearl commented after Faith hung up the phone on Friday shortly before noon. "Whatever is the matter?"

"That was Marianne Palmer, checking on the cupcake order for her daughter's engagement party this afternoon," Faith muttered, shaking her head in disbelief.

Pearl beamed and asked, "Did you tell her how beautiful they look? It's a *gut* thing we're allowed to take liberties with how we decorate our confections for *Englisch* customers, because I've never seen anything so fancy."

Pearl was right. The blush-pink frosting rosettes framed with white lacy ruffles was by far the daintiest, most complex design Faith had attempted for such a large order. Staying at the bakery until nine o'clock on Thursday night and arriving earlier than usual the next morning paid off: the three hundred cupcakes looked almost too pretty to eat. There was only one problem.

"I told her they're ready to be picked up," Faith answered, "but she said I promised I'd deliver them."

"You did?"

"*Neh*, of course I didn't," Faith adamantly objected.

On rare occasions, she employed one of her younger brothers to make local deliveries using their courting buggies or even the tandem bicycle if needed. But the boys worked erratic schedules during nonharvest months, both on their farm and off, and she couldn't count on them having free time in advance. She never would have committed to delivering such a large, important order to the Palmers, who lived on the other side of Willow Creek.

Pearl harrumphed. "Then she'll just have to pick them up herself."

Faith and Pearl strived to delight their customers, but Marianne had a habit of taking advantage and she could be uncompromising about her demands.

"She can't—she was calling on her way to pick up her daughter at the airport. Her husband is at home without a car, since their son is collecting the daughter's fiancé separately. The party starts at two o'clock and it's supposed to be a big surprise."

"Oh dear, I wish I could offer you my buggy, but as you know, my husband's fetching me at noon to accompany him to his doctor's appointment," Pearl apologized. "If you hurry home and retrieve your family's buggy, you should be able to make the delivery in time."

"I can't," moaned Faith. "Henrietta is using the buggy to fetch her sister from the van depot. I don't want to pedal all that way only to discover none of the other boys are home, either. I have no choice. I'll have to call a taxi."

"Ach!" Pearl's hands flew to her cheeks. "The nearest taxi will have to drive all the way from Lancaster, with the meter running. Won't that cost more than we'll earn from the cupcakes?"

"Probably, but I can't risk a dissatisfied customer, especially not such a loyal one. We fill our biggest orders for her."

"My Wayne will take you when he arrives," Pearl volunteered. "He'll be only too happy to cancel his appointment."

Faith squeezed her friend's arm, moved by her generosity. But as the business owner, this was her problem to solve, not Pearl's.

"You'll do no such thing. It's far more important for you to help your husband take care of his health than it is for me to save a few dollars. It will all work out. But I'd better let Ivy know no one will be here for dinner today, lest she finds the bakery empty and runs away again."

"I'll call the taxi while you go tell her," Pearl proposed.

Before she reached the stoop, Faith spied Hunter through the window of the cannery. Leaning against a stool behind the cash register, he was poring over an open ledger with a serious expression on his face. It seemed he often wore a serious expression lately, quite unlike when they were younger. What was it that caused him to frown so frequently?

Yet when Faith tugged the door open, Hunter's head snapped upward and his eyes twinkled with a zest she remembered from when they were teens. It was no wonder the *meed* had been so enamored of him. At that age, girls were often taken in by any measure of attention paid to them, and Hunter's ebullient gaze made it seem as if there was no one else in the world he'd rather be speaking to.

"*Guder nammidaag*, Faith," he said, rising. "What a pleasure to have you visit the shop. How may I help you?"

In her frazzled state, Faith was so moved by his kind tone that she was momentarily at a loss for words. How many times had she asked her customers, *How may I help you?* Hearing Hunter direct the question toward her in such a genuine manner made her forget how irritated she'd been at him the last time they parted.

"*Guder nammidaag*, Hunter. I actually came to see Ivy."

Hunter's shoulders drooped. "Mervin stopped by this morning to tell me Ivy is home sick with a cold. She won't be in tomorrow, either."

"I suppose that's what happens when she flees to the creek without a shawl," Faith said, shaking her head. Then she divulged the reason she wanted to speak to her.

"A taxi from Lancaster? That will cost a fortune!" Hunter exclaimed when he heard Faith's plan. "I took the buggy into town this morning. I'll deliver the cupcakes, but since I don't know where your customer lives, you'll have to accompany me."

"*Neh*, Hunter, that's very kind, but Pearl already called the cab company."

"Then she should call them back and cancel while I'm hitching my horse. I'll meet you in back of the bakery and we'll load the carriage there," Hunter instructed, removing the cash box from the register.

"*Neh*," Faith protested again. She was an independent woman, accustomed to addressing her business dilemmas on her own. She didn't need a man to rescue her. "I can't ask you to do that. You've got your shop to mind."

"You didn't ask—I offered. As for minding Ruth's shop, I won't close the store to take a dinner break, and I can keep it open as late as needed this evening. Besides, Ruth would want me to help. Let me stow this box and we can be on our way."

Faith opened her mouth to object a third time, but there was something so sure-minded about the look in Hunter's eyes that when he returned from the back room, she accepted his offer of assistance without further hesitation and followed him straight out the door.

As Hunter yielded off the battered side roads onto the main highway leading to the commercialized end of Willow Creek, Faith complimented his skills.

"You handle your horse expertly. If one of my brothers were making this delivery, I'd worry the cupcakes would be upside-down cakes by the time he arrived!"

Hunter didn't confide he'd perfected his technique while he was recovering from his accident, when even the smallest variation in pavement or jerking of the horse's gait could ignite his body with unspeakable pain.

Instead, he said, "*Denki*, that means a lot to me, especially coming from someone who routinely transports *oier* on the back of a tandem bicycle."

"If you think that's impressive, you should see the tricks I can do on my unicycle," Faith quipped. They erupted with laughter and then the two of them fell into easy conversation.

Although severe back pain had kept him awake most of the previous night, causing him to take the buggy into town that morning, Hunter hardly noticed the lingering knot in his muscles as the horse carried them toward the Palmers' house. If he wasn't mistaken, Faith also appeared more carefree, giggling at his jokes and making some of her own, until eventually they pulled up at their destination: an enormous, newly constructed home situated on an elaborately manicured lawn at the end of a private lane.

"They must have a lot of *kinner*," Hunter commented nonchalantly.

"*Neh*, just two. One son and one daughter."

"That's a shame," Hunter said, thinking aloud as he brought the carriage to a halt.

"A shame? What's so shameful about that?" Faith asked in an exasperated whisper. "They're *Englisch*, not Amish. Not every family has half a dozen *kinner*."

"I only meant that they have such a large dwelling. It seems a waste of resources when there are only four people living in it," he explained.

"Well, please keep your voice down so they don't hear you," she hissed.

Hunter didn't know what to make of Faith's sudden annoyance. He hadn't intended to distress her, nor to insult her customers. Following her to the large entryway with a tray of boxed cupcakes in his arms, he attributed the abrupt shift in her mood to nervousness: from what Faith told him, Marianne Palmer was a bit intimidating.

However, Marianne's husband, James, couldn't have been more congenial. After introducing them to two young women dressed in black-and-white uniforms, James said, "Sharon and Isabella will take the trays into the kitchen. While you're unloading the rest of the order, I'll get the checkbook. I know it's around here somewhere."

Several minutes later, James reentered the foyer just as Faith and Hunter were carrying the last of the cargo into the house.

"Here's a pad of paper, Faith," James said. "If you'll itemize a receipt, it will keep me from getting in trouble with my better half, since she's keeping track of the wedding-related expenditures. Why don't you have a seat? You look as if you could use a rest."

He pulled out an antique, elaborately carved armless walnut chair beside an equally impressive walnut desk.

"Thank you," Faith said in *Englisch*, moving toward it.

"Neh!" Hunter interjected, causing Faith to hop back. "You shouldn't sit in that chair. You might crack it."

"She might crack it?" James questioned. "That chair is made of walnut. It's a very sturdy wood."

"The wood is solid, *jah*. But look at this here," Hunter said, pointing to a barely noticeable line in the middle of the seat. "That's a hairline crack. The wood might be fine for years, or someone could sit on it at just the right angle and it would split in half."

"I never noticed that," James mused. "This chair is one of my wife's prized possessions, an heirloom from her grandmother. She'd be crushed if anything happened to it."

"I could fix it for you," Hunter offered. "My *onkel* was a master furniture restorer, and I have access to his tools and workshop. Your wife is right—it is a handsome piece. But if it's going to be used for functional purposes, it ought to be safe."

James knitted his brows. "You won't damage the original design of the chair?"

"I'd have to remove the seat in order to repair it. I'd match the epoxy to the original shade of the chair and you won't even be able to find the crack again. There'd be absolutely no damage to the design of the chair. Your wife runs a greater risk of damaging it by allowing people to sit on it in its current state. If someone puts their full weight on it—"

"Here you go, James," Faith interjected, holding out a sheet of paper. Hunter discerned by her brusque interruption she was eager to cut the discussion short so they could get back on the road, and he let the conversation drop.

After scanning the receipt, James signed a check with a flourish and tore it from his checkbook.

"Thank you, Faith. I anticipate your cupcakes will be the talk of the party," he said. Then he turned to Hunter. "I'd appreciate it if you'd fix the chair as a surprise of sorts for Marianne, and now is the perfect time to do it. My wife will be too caught up in the party to realize it's missing."

"It will be my privilege," Hunter replied.

He really meant it, too; he was itching to get his hands on a carpentry project again, even a small one. Besides, by offering to repair the chair for Faith's *Englisch* customer, he hoped to prove to her he didn't intend any disrespect to the Palmer family with his earlier remarks about their house. After agreeing on a fee, giving James his contact info and arranging a date for him to pick up the piece of furniture, Hunter hoisted the chair to his shoulder with one hand and opened the door for Faith with the other. He felt more adroit and upbeat than he had since before his accident.

Faith couldn't even look at Hunter strutting down the walk beside her like a rooster. It was disgraceful enough that he'd witnessed her splinter an entire footbridge in front of her Amish peers. But to have him point out to her *Englisch* customers that their chair wouldn't hold her weight—that was too great an indignity to bear! She took her seat in the buggy and fixed her gaze straight ahead. Hoping her cheeks didn't appear as blazing as they felt, she tried to distract herself by counting the rhythmic *clip-clop* of the horse's hooves against the pavement.

After traveling a mile in silence, Hunter said, "So, you mentioned your sister-in-law's sister is visiting for Thanksgiving?"

"Correct," Faith uttered. Her cheeks still smarted.

"That's nice. What's her name?"

"Willa. I'll introduce you if you'd like." Faith couldn't believe Hunter was adding insult to injury by expressing interest in her sister-in-law's sister.

"Are you alright? You seem upset."

"Upset? Why would I be upset? Just because you completely embarrassed me in front of my customer, why is that any reason to be upset?" Faith blurted out.

"Embarrassed you?" Hunter looked as surprised as he sounded. "Faith, James couldn't have heard what I said about the house and even if he did—"

"It's not what you said about the house," Faith broke in, folding her arms across her chest. How could he be so dense? "It's what you said about the chair."

Hunter threw his free hand up in the air. "I honestly don't know how expressing concern about the condition of the Palmers' chair caused you any embarrassment, but I assure you, my intention was to do them—and you—a service."

He sounded so perplexed that Faith realized he truly didn't know how insulting it was that he publicly called attention to the crushing effects of her size. She had no intention of reliving the humiliation by detailing the nature of his offense.

"Never mind," she said, waving her hand. "It doesn't matter."

"It matters to me," Hunter persisted. "I wasn't being critical of their furnishings, if that's what you think, but

if you believe James received my gesture as an insult,
I'll apologize."

Noticing how a shadow seemed to creep over Hunter's profile, Faith suddenly questioned whether she was
overreacting. After all, it wasn't Hunter's fault she was
on the chubby side. And she would have been a lot more
embarrassed if she'd actually broken the chair—at least
he'd prevented that from happening. Faith shivered as
she recognized once again Hunter was only being helpful and she'd rewarded him with a temperamental display of her own wounded pride.

What had gotten into her to act in such a way? If one
of her brothers had offered to fix her customer's chair,
she would have been grateful, not indignant. She had no
right to lash out at Hunter as she'd done.

"*Neh*, I'm the one who needs to apologize to you,
Hunter," she said in a small voice. "You showed the Palmers a kindness, just as you've shown me one by helping
me make the delivery. I should have been more appreciative of your efforts. I'm sorry."

Hunter shrugged and mumbled, "It's alright."

Faith tried to think of something to ask to break the
discomfiting silence that followed, but she came up blank
until Hunter pulled to a stop behind the bakery.

"I'll let you off here," he indicated.

"Oh, okay," she said, although she wouldn't have
minded walking back with him from the hitching post
lot. "*Denki* for your help, Hunter."

"You're welcome," he duly responded and clicked for
his horse to walk on.

Faith stood outside the back entry, her key poised to
unlock the door, but she hesitated before going in. She
felt completely deflated. The ride to the Palmers' house

had been an unexpected resolution to her delivery issue, and she'd reveled in exchanging chitchat with Hunter. But on the return trip, she felt as if someone had doused them both with a bucket of ice water—and that some-one was her.

She knew she couldn't fully blame her outburst on the pressures of running a business, but right then, her heart weighed like a brick within her and she wished she didn't have to enter the bakery. She wished she could run to the creek, like Ivy, or return home and help Henrietta fold laundry and mind the children. Feeling weary and alone, she prayed, *Please, Lord, give me the strength to serve my customers well. But more importantly, help me to serve You well. Forgive me for my prideful attitude and help Hunter to forgive me, too.*

It wasn't until she'd hung up her shawl and was about to wash her hands that Faith realized she was still clutch-ing the check from James. She unfurled it and gasped at the amount. He'd given her far too much. She'd have to call and notify him of his mistake. But then she squinted to read the memo line: "cupcakes & delivery fee & well-deserved tip for both" it said in tiny print. She tapped her heels against the floorboards—she could keep it!

Well, most of it. She'd give Hunter the delivery fee, of course. She'd also give him the entire tip to demonstrate just how appreciative she really was. She wouldn't even wait to deposit the check—she removed his portion from her cash box and slipped it into an envelope, and then dashed across the street.

She burst through the door and nearly exclaimed, "Hunter, guess what!" before realizing he was helping a customer retrieve a jar from a shelf.

"Let me get that for you," he said to the diminutive

Amish woman who was standing on her tiptoes beside him, her fingers wiggling to reach a large jar of corn relish. "I wouldn't want it to crash down on your head."

"Denki." She giggled, accepting his aid. "Your arms are much longer and stronger than mine."

Faith forced a cough and they both turned at once.

"Faith!" the young woman exclaimed. Her high-pitched voice was familiar, but Faith couldn't place her slender figure and delicate facial features until the woman teased, "Don't you recognize me? I'd recognize you any day. You look as healthy as ever. It's me, Willa, Henrietta's sister."

"Jah, of course. *Wilkom,* Willa," Faith responded haltingly. As she enfolded the young woman's tiny frame in an embrace, she couldn't help but notice how bony she'd become. "What are you doing here?"

Willa tee-heed. "I'm visiting for Thanksgiving. Didn't Henrietta tell you?"

Faith didn't know if Willa was acting kittenish for Hunter's benefit or if she really didn't understand the question. *"Neh,* I mean what are you doing in the cannery? We've put up plenty of corn relish at home."

"Really?" Willa asked innocently. "Henrietta directed me here to purchase a jar. She had items to buy at the mercantile, so we divided the errands to make them go faster. Besides, my sister knew that after being in the van for so long, I'd appreciate the opportunity to walk around and meet the *leit* of Willow Creek."

You mean the bachelors *of Willow Creek,* Faith thought as Willa fanned her eyelashes. The arrangement smacked of Henrietta's matchmaking schemes; it was obvious Henrietta sent Willa to the cannery to meet Hunter. From Henrietta's numerous remarks, Faith knew her sister-in-law wanted Willa to find a spouse as much as she wanted Faith to find one. But there was one significant difference: Willa keenly desired to get married, whereas Faith positively did not. Especially not if it meant sharing her secret again.

Regardless, it riled Faith that Henrietta decided Willa was a more worthy candidate for Hunter's affections than Faith was, presumably because Willa was likely able to bear children. Faith was so irked to be reminded of her own physical inadequacies she couldn't drum up a single word of civility. Standing opposite the thin young woman, she sucked in her stomach and tried to remember why she'd come into the cannery in the first place.

Hunter shuffled impatiently. He'd hoped to wolf down a few bites of his dinner before the Friday afternoon tourists began streaming in, but he wouldn't have time if Faith and Willa didn't leave soon.

"If you aren't sure whether you need corn relish, I'll set it aside for you," he suggested to Willa. "Faith can pick up the jar whenever you run low, right?"

"*Gut* idea," Faith piped up, "but before I go, may I speak with you for a moment in private, Hunter?"

He scrunched his eyebrows together. "*Jah*, alright."

When Willa looked at them askance, Faith explained, "It's about a business matter," and motioned for Hunter to follow her into the back room, where she presented him a white envelope.

"What's this?"

"It's the delivery fee for taking me to the Palmers' house," she declared, her face aglow. "Plus a tip!"

"A delivery fee? A *tip*?" Hunter repeated, deeply offended.

"*Jah*, although we don't accept tips in the bakery, sometimes the customers give us a gratuity with their large orders, which is what Mr. Palmer did today," Faith expounded, as if he didn't know what she'd meant by a tip.

Hunter stood with his mouth agape before shoving the envelope back into Faith's hand. The offer of payment for something he'd done as a…a *friend* was an affront.

"I don't want your money," he stated definitively. "And I certainly don't need a *gratuity*. I'm not your employee. Not yet, anyway."

"But Hunter, you took me all the way to the other side of Willow Creek in the middle of your working day," Faith protested. "If one of my brothers had made the delivery, I would have paid him and he would have accepted it. I don't understand—it's just a practical matter of business."

"That's what everything is to you, isn't it, Faith? Just a practical matter of business?" Hunter spouted. "Okay, then, fair is fair. I ought to have compensated *you* for taking time away from your business to find Ivy with me on Monday."

"That's entirely different and you know it," Faith countered, blinking rapidly.

Her face looked as crimson as Hunter's face felt and her shoulders sagged in apparent dejection, but it wasn't his fault her feelings were hurt. She'd brought it upon herself by being prideful, and not allowing him to help her without turning it into a financial transaction. That may have been the *Englisch* way, but it wasn't the Amish way. It wasn't the *neighborly* way.

Just then the bells on the door jangled. "Excuse me, I have customers of my own to serve now," Hunter said, grateful for the opportunity to distance himself. He stepped past Faith into the storefront, where he discovered Henrietta Yoder whispering with Willa near a display of preserves. Initially they didn't notice his presence, so he allowed them to browse while he gathered his thoughts.

Eventually, he cleared his throat. "*Guder nammidaag*, Henrietta. There was some question about whether you need relish or not. Have you made up your mind? I can ring it up for you, or if you'd prefer, I'll return it to the shelf."

"*Jah*, we'll take it, please," Henrietta replied as Faith drifted into the room. "There you are, Faith! Willa and I stopped at the bakery earlier and the store was locked. She was concerned something awful must have happened in order for you to close down your business early on a Friday."

"*Neh*," Faith answered feebly. "I had an order to deliver."

"Didn't I tell you!" Henrietta trumpeted, turning to Willa. "Didn't I say the only reason Faith would close her business in the middle of the day would be to serve another customer?"

Hunter noticed Faith's eyes flash as she responded, "That's not entirely true. We close the bakery every day for our dinner break—"

"Speaking of dinner breaks—" Henrietta snapped her fingers, as if just remembering "—I wanted to invite your *ant* and *mamm* and you to our house for Thanksgiving dinner, Hunter. I understand Ruth's abilities are limited, and rather than have your *mamm* prepare such a big meal for the three of you, we'd like you to be our guests."

Ordinarily, Hunter might have treasured celebrating

Thanksgiving with the Yoder family, but after today's thorny interaction with Faith, he couldn't imagine feeling comfortable spending the better part of a day at their house.

"Denki," he replied noncommittally as he placed the relish in Henrietta's canvas bag. "I'll extend your invitation to my *ant* and *mamm.*"

"Perfect!" Henrietta remarked. "We'll check back to confirm you're coming."

"I know some special games we can play in the evening," Willa suggested. "The more the merrier, I always say."

To Hunter's relief, Faith diverted their attention. *"Kumme,* Willa and Henrietta, let's continue making plans in the bakery over a mug of hot chocolate and a treat."

"None for me. I've lost weight, but I still have to control my appetite." Willa ran her hands down her hips. "I only have to look at a slice of pie and I gain three pounds."

"Then you'd better close your eyes while I eat mine," Hunter heard Faith retort as she ambled toward the door.

He didn't notice she'd left empty-handed. It wasn't until hours later when he was locking the cash box in the back room that he saw the white envelope sitting on the counter. Faith must have used his pen to inscribe a message across it:

Hunter, you earned this fair and square, so I hope you'll accept it. However, I'd rather take the money back than let go of a friendship I've had since childhood.—Faith.

He exhaled loudly. He had accused Faith of being too prideful to accept his help, but wasn't he being just as arrogant to decline the delivery fee? He peeked at the contents of the envelope. The money would definitely come in handy and he was grateful for it, but it didn't put a grin on his face the way Faith's repartee had done all the way to the Palmers' house. She was right: their friendship—yes, *friendship*—was more important than a quibble over money. Yet he couldn't quite bring himself to accept the payment, so he left it lying on the counter.

He locked the door and trod to the lot where he hitched his horse that afternoon. It took a moment for his eyes to make sense of the odd shape in the back of the buggy. When he comprehended it was the Palmers' chair, he wryly clucked his tongue. If it weren't for Faith's business, he wouldn't have any job at all, much less two. Hunter realized the furniture wasn't the only thing he needed to restore: his relationship with Faith could use repair, as well.

He clumped back toward the bakery to thank Faith and apologize for his cloddish behavior in rejecting the money. But when he reached the bakery door, there wasn't a single light on, not even in the back room.

She probably had to get home to help host Henrietta's sappy sister, he concluded. *I'll have to talk to Faith tomorrow.* Then he hurried home, eager to tell his aunt and mother they'd all been invited to the Yoders' house for Thanksgiving dinner.

Chapter Five

After setting up a narrow cot for Willa in Faith's half of the room, the young women whispered so as not to wake their small nephews on the other side of the divider.

"I know it's forward of me to ask," Willa said as she sprawled lengthwise on her bed, "but are you and Hunter walking out?"

"Of course not," Faith replied. "What would cause you to ask such a question?"

"There was a hint of tension between the two of you at the cannery this afternoon," Willa commented. "To be honest, you both wore the kind of wounded expressions people who are secretly courting wear when they've quarreled."

Although inwardly impressed by how astute Willa was to have observed the friction between Hunter and her, Faith felt no need to elaborate on the nature of their discussion.

"I assure you, we're definitely not courting," she said as she reclined and tugged the quilt to her chin. "Hunter and I are... We're business associates."

Earlier in the day, she would have referred to Hunter

as a friend, but when he didn't respond to her note that afternoon, she began to question whether he held her in the same regard. She cringed to recall how expectantly she'd waited for him to visit her at the bakery, where she envisioned their making amends over a piece of dessert, or how her insides joggled each time a customer approached her doorstep.

When Hunter didn't arrive during business hours, Faith convinced herself it was because he couldn't come until the cannery was closed. She dared to hope that after locking up the shop, he might offer her a ride home, and they'd talk then. As the clock struck five, she busied herself with fastidiously wiping down tables and restocking the napkin dispensers in the storefront, so as not to appear as if she was purposely loitering until he arrived. When she finally peeked up from her chores, she noticed the cannery was dark. Hunter must have slipped out of his store without her noticing. Crestfallen, she couldn't get out the door and onto her bicycle fast enough.

"I know at least three couples in Indiana who worked together before they started courting," Willa prattled in a hushed tone. "Working with each other can be a *gut* way to gauge compatibility."

Although she agreed with Willa's general theory, Faith dismissed it in regard to Hunter and herself. "Be that as it may, I won't spend much time working with Hunter. He's only in town temporarily."

"You never know what might develop to make him stay," Willa insinuated. "Consider me, for example. I've just *kumme* for a visit, too, but if I found a purpose for lingering, such as the prospect of getting married and starting a family, I would."

Faith allowed Willa's reference to hang in the air without responding to it, although her mind was reeling. Willa might stay in Willow Creek? Was Henrietta designing to match Willa with Hunter as an incentive to extend her visit? Faith's thoughts took on a momentum of their own, and she tossed and turned while Willa drifted into a sound slumber.

Faith desperately wanted to turn her flashlight back on and read until she was drowsy, but she feared she'd rouse her guest or one of the children. She comforted herself with the knowledge that it wouldn't be long until she could read all night whenever she desired, provided she earned enough for the down payment on the apartment and bakery lease.

She mentally tried to calculate her earnings for the week, minus expenses and Pearl's salary, but she needed a pencil and paper to capture all the figures. Eventually, she gave up and her thoughts looped around to Willa's observation about the discord between Faith and Hunter. Faith was beginning to wonder if she'd further offended him with her note. Did he think she was overbearing? Perhaps he needed a little time to move beyond their squabble? She hoped so; otherwise, Thanksgiving dinner would feel like a long, awkward occasion instead of the worshipful and celebratory feast it was meant to be.

Slowly exhaling, she rested her hands on her stomach. She wondered how Willa lost so much weight since she'd seen her last. A prick of envy stabbed Faith's heart, and out of nowhere, she imagined Willa and Hunter walking out together. As absurd as the inkling was, she pictured their getting married, having six or eight children and building a house that wasn't "a waste of resources." Wasn't that what all men wanted, a large brood of children and a skinny wife who walked around with a baby on each hip, saying, "the more the merrier"? The very thought caused tears to stream down Faith's cheeks and into her ears. She rolled onto her side so Willa wouldn't hear her sniffing.

After a few minutes, she blotted her eyes with the end of her pillowcase. She was being ridiculous, contriving these outlandish scenarios. Besides, whoever Hunter and Willa walked out with or married was none of Faith's concern. Unlike Willa, Faith didn't need a husband—especially not one as bullheaded as Hunter—to make her feel as if she had purpose in Willow Creek. Faith had customers to serve and a financial deadline to meet, and what she really needed was a good night's rest so her emotions wouldn't get the best of her again.

Indeed, the next morning as she careened into town on her bike, she felt entirely refreshed. Saturday was always a bustling day in the bakery, and the Saturday before Thanksgiving promised to be their busiest day yet. She was always energized by her customers' appreciation and good cheer, particularly around the holidays, when she enjoyed meeting people whose travels took them through Willow Creek.

Between working the counter, answering the phone and baking new treats, Faith and Pearl barely had a moment to speak to each other until it was time for dinner.

"Since Ivy will be out sick again today, perhaps we should work through our dinner break this afternoon?" Pearl suggested.

Faith replaced an empty tray of sticky buns with a full one. Although she was tempted to take Pearl up on the offer, Faith knew it would be counterproductive to skip their dinner break. Henrietta could imply what she would, but Faith wasn't so driven to make a sale that she'd deny Pearl and herself a much-needed rest.

"*Neh*, we deserve to put our feet up for a bit. Besides, I want to hear how your husband's appointment went yesterday."

They changed the sign on the door to Closed, lowered the lights and retrieved their lunchboxes from the back room before bowing their heads to say grace. As they ate, Faith apprised Pearl of the outcome of the Palmer delivery, and Pearl reported the doctor said her husband's blood pressure reading was out of the danger zone.

"Praise *Gott*!" Faith's voice reverberated in the empty room.

"I only wish Ruth Graber's health was improving, too," Pearl remarked.

Faith wrinkled her forehead. "I thought her recovery was progressing nicely."

"Well, we stopped at her place last evening and she said the doctor had paid her a house call. He was concerned about the results of blood tests he'd done when she went to the emergency room. So, although her bones are healing nicely, she's been advised to get more rest. From what I gather, she isn't supposed to go out and about in the buggy, either. Something about her lungs and the cold weather…"

"What a shame. If I know Ruth, she must feel cooped in. Just yesterday Henrietta invited her to our house for Thanksgiving. I guess that means she won't be able to *kumme*."

"Ach! Where's my head? They mentioned that to me last night. I was supposed to convey the message Hunter will be the only one attending. Iris doesn't want to leave Ruth alone, but she insisted Hunter should go by himself."

Faith was nonplussed. Did Hunter truly wish to spend Thanksgiving with the Yoder family, or had he been put on the spot and felt obligated to accept the invitation?

"Ruth and Iris are going to spend Thanksgiving alone?" Having dined with Ruth nearly every day for the past two years, Faith was aware of how much pleasure the older woman derived from eating together. She supposed Ruth had to eat alone so often at home that she prized the chance to gather around the table with others. It was a shame she'd miss celebrating Thanksgiving at the Yoder farm.

"It doesn't seem fair, does it? Since my *kinner* aren't coming to visit until *Grischtdaag*, and Wayne and I will be alone, too, I considered offering to go to Ruth's, but I couldn't invite myself, could I?"

"*Neh*… But what if you and I were to cook dinner here at the bakery and bring it to Ruth and Iris? That wouldn't be the same as inviting ourselves to be their guests. Perhaps we could ask Ivy and her *groossdaadi* to join us, too?"

"Ruth would love that!" Pearl joyfully waved her spoon. "But only if it's okay with Henrietta that you won't be home to help with your family's dinner preparations."

"Willa will be there to take my place—she can give Henrietta and Lovina a hand with whatever needs to be done," Faith reasoned earnestly. "Besides, both Ruth and Iris's husbands are deceased, and *Gott's* Word instructs us to honor widows. Henrietta can't argue with that."

And this way, Faith rationalized to herself, *Willa can have Hunter all to herself, which is whom I assume she really meant when she said, "the more the merrier."* As for Hunter, Faith reckoned he'd barely notice her absence anyway.

* * *

Hunter racked his brain for a way to show Faith he was sorry for his lack of humility the day before, but even apologizing for being prideful sounded, well, prideful. He finally decided he'd pay her a visit at the bakery and let her know he was looking forward to spending Thanksgiving with her and her family. Perhaps he'd order a few of the apple fry pies he'd heard so much about and bring them home to his aunt and mother. But every time he attempted to lock the cannery, another customer entered. He didn't want to turn away business, so he resigned himself to waiting until after closing time.

When the hour came, he noted the crowd of customers still milling about in Faith's storefront, so he meandered to the mercantile, where he was inspired to purchase a packet of batteries for her bicycle headlamp. Exultant at having found the perfect token to give Faith when he expressed his regret, Hunter charged out the door, nearly barreling into Joseph Schrock, his wife, Amity, and Amity's visiting parents. Hunter refrained from tapping his foot as introductions were made and details about holiday plans were exchanged. Finally, the group bid him a joyous Thanksgiving, but it was too late: Faith's bakery was empty and its lights were off. Hunter slid the batteries beneath the breast of his jacket and trudged home.

After serving customers by himself all day, he had a new appreciation for Ivy's assiduousness. His muscles burned, and he was relieved the next day was an "off Sunday," meaning the *leit* didn't congregate for church. Rather, they held private worship services in their own homes. After Sunday dinner, he was so exhausted he excused himself for a brief nap but ended up sleeping right through another visit from Pearl and Wayne.

"Isn't that kind?" his aunt was remarking to his mother in the parlor when he got up.

"Indeed," his mother replied. To Hunter, she explained, "Pearl and Faith offered to prepare Thanksgiving dinner for your *ant* and me. They planned to make it at the bakery and deliver it to us, but we thought it would be better to cook it here, where I can help. Faith will make the pies in her bakery in the morning, so as to be out of Henrietta's way. Ivy and Mervin Sutter are also invited."

"Faith won't be eating at her own home?" Hunter asked.

"Uh-oh, do I detect a note of disappointment?" Ruth teased. "We thought you'd enjoy dining with your young male friends for a change, but if it's Faith's company you're interested in keeping, tell Henrietta you've changed your mind and you'll be staying here with us."

"*Neh*, it's…it's not that—" Hunter stammered. "I'm surprised she wouldn't want to be with her family, that's all."

Yet he couldn't deny a sense of disappointment that Faith wouldn't be present at her family's celebration. He also couldn't help but wonder if she was deliberately avoiding him. Not that he would have blamed her—she probably wondered why he still hadn't acknowledged her note.

He decided he'd visit her at the first opportunity, but Monday and Tuesday were so busy at the cannery, he didn't have a moment to pull himself away from the shop. Before he knew it, it was four fifty-five on Wednesday afternoon.

"On Thursday I'm eating Thanksgiving dinner at Ruth Graber's house," Ivy announced, just as she'd announced on Monday and Tuesday afternoons.

"That's right, Ivy." Hunter smiled.

"Faith Yoder is making dessert," Ivy informed him.

"Her pies are bound to be *appenditlich*. I hope I have treats that taste as *gut* as at Henrietta's house."

"*Neh*, you're eating at Ruth Graber's house with Faith Yoder."

Hunter cocked his head to the side. He didn't want to upset Ivy by contradicting her, but she was so particular about details that he wondered why she thought he was eating at Ruth's.

"You mean after dinner, I'll come back to Ruth's house for leftover dessert, right?" he asked.

"*Neh*, you're eating Thanksgiving dinner at Ruth Graber's house. One thirty on Thursday."

Hunter pressed her for clarification. "Ivy, who told you that?"

"Willa Gingerich from Indiana."

The conversation was confusing, even for him, but he shouldn't have been surprised Ivy kept everyone's names straight. She seldom erred with memorizing names or numbers.

"Well, that's almost right, but not quite," Hunter explained. "Willa Gingerich from Indiana invited me to eat at Henrietta Yoder's house."

"*Jah*. Willa Gingerich from Indiana invited Hunter Schwartz to eat dinner at Henrietta Yoder's house," Ivy repeated, and Hunter breathed a sigh of relief. She had the story straight.

Then she added, "I told Willa Gingerich *neh*. Hunter Schwartz is eating dinner at Ruth Graber's house with Faith Yoder. One thirty on Thursday. Thanksgiving Day, a special occasion."

Recalling how Faith told Ivy that he might eat with

them on a special occasion, Hunter's mouth fell open. "When, Ivy? When did you tell this to Willa?"

"Three thirty. Willa Gingerich purchased one jar of sweet mustard. Four dollars. Exact change."

Three thirty *today*? Hunter must have stepped out to use the washroom at the very moment Willa stopped in for the mustard. Henrietta's sister was probably nattering on to Ivy about Thanksgiving dinner and that's when the misunderstanding arose. Hunter was so flabbergasted he couldn't speak.

"Mervin Sutter waits for me at the hitching post behind the mercantile at five o'clock," Ivy stated as the clock tolled, leaving Hunter alone to shake his head in silence.

Now what was he going to do? If he sprinted to the bakery to explain the situation to Faith and tell her he was still planning to go to the farm, it would look as if he was going out of his way not to keep company with her on Thanksgiving. But if he let the misunderstanding rest, the Yoder family might assume he changed his plans just to be with Faith.

Hunter had met *meed* like Willa who would conclude he was interested in Faith romantically. Not that courting Faith wouldn't have appealed to him under different circumstances, but Hunter knew he was in no condition, physically or financially, to be anyone's suitor. No, he had to explain; he just hoped with the recent friction between Faith and him, she'd see the humorous side of the situation.

But the laugh appeared to be on Hunter, because by the time he locked his shop and started across the street, the bakery was already deserted. Adjusting his hat to protect his ears from the cold, Hunter supposed there were far worse things than spending Thanksgiving at Ruth's house with Faith. He only hoped Faith felt the same way about spending the holiday with him.

Faith figured by closing her shop half an hour early on Wednesday and returning home to make the pies and rolls for her family's Thanksgiving dinner, she'd demonstrate she really did value the time she spent with Henrietta and Willa. But after everyone finished eating supper and the women were left alone to clear and clean the dishes, Faith could hardly get a word out of the two sisters.

Finally, she commented, "It's so quiet I can hear the clock ticking in the parlor. Are you upset with me because I'm not going to be home for Thanksgiving dinner?"

"*Neh*, not at all," Henrietta claimed. "We'll miss having you here, but I think it's *wunderbaar* you're showing hospitality to Ruth and Pearl, and Ivy and her *grooss-daadi*."

"You forgot to mention Hunter and his *mamm*." Willa sulked, circling the bottom of a bowl with a dish towel.

"*Jah*, I'll be celebrating the holiday with Hunter's *mamm*, but not with Hunter—he'll be eating with you," Faith corrected her.

Henrietta winked at Faith. "It's alright, you don't have to pretend you're not courting. Ivy told Willa today Hunter wants to have dinner with you instead of coming here. Don't worry, your secret is safe with us."

Faith suspended a dirty pot above the dishwater, too stunned to move. She didn't know for certain what Ivy told Willa, but she didn't have to know: based on her knowledge of Ivy's communication skills, Faith could guess the gist of what transpired.

"I'm afraid Ivy was speaking out of turn," she explained. "She didn't know what she was talking about."

"*Neh*, Ivy was very clear about what she was saying." Willa pouted. "I only wish you'd been more honest about your interest in Hunter before I got my hopes up."

"Willa!" Henrietta intervened with a sternness that surprised Faith. "You know how discreet most Amish couples are about their courtships. Faith has done nothing wrong by keeping her relationship private. Besides, you can have your pick of suitors at home—Hunter may be Faith's only option here in Willow Creek. Now if you'll excuse me, I need to put the boys to bed, fold the laundry and then finish the cleaning I didn't get to do this afternoon."

Abashed, Faith plunged the pot into the soapy water. The nerve of her sister-in-law to insist Faith and Hunter were courting, when Faith specifically denied it! And didn't Henrietta understand how hurtful it was to hear her announce Faith's courtship options were limited, whereas Willa's were limitless? Ironically, Faith knew if she pointed out her sister-in-law's insensitivity, Henrietta's own feelings would be hurt, since she truly believed she was standing up for Faith. Instead of responding aloud, Faith nearly scoured a hole right through the copper-bottomed pot.

Eventually, to Faith's chagrin, Willa acquiesced. "I suppose Henrietta has a point. I'm sorry, Faith—I was being selfish. Now, would you like my help making the pies?"

"Definitely not!" Faith barked. Then, recognizing how cross she sounded, she forced a joke. "You said you gain weight just looking at pies, so I wouldn't want to tempt you. I think that's what happens to me—one minute I'm measuring ingredients, the next minute, I've eaten a third of a pie!"

"You're blessed to have found a suitor who doesn't mind that you're carrying a few extra pounds."

Faith held her tongue as she retrieved a bowl of eggs from the icebox. *Please*, Gott, *help me turn the other cheek*, she silently prayed.

"I *haven't* found a suitor," she iterated. "But you've done very well to lose so much weight, Willa. Are you following a special meal plan?"

"Neh." The normally talkative Willa went silent as she tugged a cupboard door open, shielding her face. After stacking the dry plates inside, she closed the door and confided, "I just lost my appetite for a while about a year ago."

Faith could tell by the way Willa wouldn't meet her eyes that she was embarrassed by whatever triggered her weight loss. "I didn't mean to pry," she said. "You don't have to talk about it."

"It's alright," Willa responded, draping the damp dishcloth over the rack to dry. Lowering her voice, she confided, "You see, I started losing weight because my suitor said I was getting too fat."

"Really?" Faith was appalled. "He actually told you that?"

"Not in so many words, *neh*, but one time he was embracing me and he whispered, 'my plump, darling heifer,' into my ear and then he sort of laughed."

"Willa! He didn't!" Faith yelped, and then quickly cupped her hand over her mouth. In a quieter tone, she admitted, "I would have been livid!"

Willa shrugged. "I was more hurt than angry, especially since I hadn't ever allowed him to hug me before then because I was self-conscious about my size. He said he meant it as a term of endearment and that I was being overly sensitive. It was true, I *was* overweight, so I tried not to let it bother me when he kept calling me that, but I felt so... I don't know, *unwomanly* somehow. I completely lost my appetite. If you can believe it, I became so depressed, I had to force myself to eat!" Her face was beet red as she half laughed, half choked at the memory.

Faith understood how devastating it was to be vulnerable with a suitor, only to have him respond in a crushing manner. "I'm so sorry his comment affected you like that, Willa."

"Does Hunter make critical remarks about your weight?"

Faith blew air through her lips. Was there any sense trying to convince Willa that Hunter wasn't courting her? Faith decided just to answer Willa's question.

"*Neh*, Hunter never says anything critical about my weight," she replied, suddenly realizing he never directly *said* anything about her weight at all. Was it possible the awkward feelings she had about her size in Hunter's presence actually originated in Faith's own mind and she wrongly attributed them to him? Could it be she jumped to other conclusions about him that were inaccurate, too? Perhaps she'd been too quick to assume his lack of communication lately meant he didn't care about their friendship—was it possible he'd just been too busy to respond to her note?

"I don't think I'd continue to walk out with a suitor who put me down," Faith continued, "even if his comments were supposedly truthful or affectionate or made in jest."

"Neither would I," Willa said, smugness curling her

mouth. "But it took me a while to get to that point. Once my confidence returned, I told him I'd rather walk barefoot through a field of cow pies than walk out with him any longer because he had no idea how to treat a lady!"

The two young women clutched each other's arms as they giggled. When they straightened, Faith wiped her eyes with the corner of her apron and suggested she'd be pleased if Willa would roll the pie crusts while Faith measured the fillings. Their four hands made light work of the process, and when Henrietta rejoined them hours later, they were sliding the final pies into the oven.

"Mmm," Willa said, closing her eyes and breathing in. "The aroma is my favorite part of baking."

"Leftovers are my favorite part of baking," Henrietta remarked. "There's enough here so I won't have to bake again for days."

"*Eating* is my favorite part of baking," Faith admitted, accidentally dropping an empty pie tin, which clattered raucously against the floor.

When the men rushed into the kitchen to see what the commotion was about, they found the three women doubled over in laughter.

"Are you alright?" Mason asked.

"We're fine," Faith said. "*Kumme*, everyone grab a fork. It's neither too late for pie nor too early to give thanks."

The way Faith saw it, she was doubly blessed, and she wasn't going to wait until Thanksgiving to express her gratitude to God. As she sliced into the warm golden crust, she silently prayed. *Lord*, denki *for this time with my family tonight and for the fellowship I'll have with my friends at Ruth's house tomorrow.*

* * *

That evening, when Hunter told his aunt and mother what Ivy communicated to Willa, Ruth raised an eyebrow at Iris.

"Our Ivy is more insightful than folks give her credit for," Ruth said.

"What's that supposed to mean?" Hunter heard the defensiveness in his own voice.

"It means we'll be glad to set a place for you at the table tomorrow," his mother responded, giving her son's arm a squeeze.

"This works out better anyway," Ruth declared. "I was going to ask Wayne to pick up Faith and her pies from the bakery in time for our devotions before dinner, but this way, Hunter can get her."

Hunter knew it was useless to resist Ruth's overt matchmaking attempts, and besides, he welcomed the opportunity to clear the air with Faith in private. He'd already set off for town the next day when he realized he'd forgotten the batteries he purchased for her, but he didn't want to draw attention to his gift by returning home, so he rode on. Since Main Street was virtually deserted, Hunter pulled up in front of the bakery and rapped on the glass pane of the door.

Faith quickly appeared, gliding into the square of sunshine to unlock the door. She was wearing a verdant green dress that accentuated the green flecks in her hazel eyes, and her hair glinted in the light.

"Happy Thanksgiving, Hunter," she greeted him, grinning mischievously. "I assume you're here to court me?"

Hunter faltered backward and nearly tumbled down the stairs.

"Ach! Be careful." Faith giggled as he regained his balance. "I was kidding! I heard what Ivy told Willa, and if your *ant* and *mamm* are anything like my sister-in-law, we've both been hearing the same farfetched insinuations about our relationship. I thought by making light of it, I'd put your mind at ease. Don't worry, I know we consider ourselves to be business associates."

"Business associates, that we are," Hunter confirmed. He cleared his throat and added, "But we're friends, too, right?"

Faith's eyes twinkled as she gave him a single, decisive nod. "Since childhood."

Hunter's shoulders relaxed. "Actually, I was trying to think of a way I could put *your* mind at ease," he confessed. "Not just about Ivy's mix-up, but about my behavior the other day. I tried several times to apologize, but I kept missing you. I'm sorry for not accepting the delivery fee. Sometimes I can be as stubborn as a mule."

Faith tittered. "That makes two of us. Now, speaking of deliveries, could you please give me a hand with the trays in the back room?"

They secured the dinner rolls and pies in the back of the buggy and took their seats in front. Because their tradition was to fast on Thanksgiving morning, the smell made Hunter's mouth water. "I'm tempted to dig into those pies this very instant," he said. "What kind are you holding on your lap?"

"I hate to disappoint you, but it's not a pie. It's a pumpkin roll," Faith teased.

"With pecans on top?"

"Of course."

"Mmm," he moaned, licking his lips. "That's how Justine always made them."

"Who's Justine?"

Hunter was so hungry he hadn't realized he'd spoken aloud. "Er, she was someone I courted, but it was a while ago," he answered vaguely before redirecting the conversation. "How many pumpkin rolls did you sell before the holiday?"

"I'm not sure I remember off the top of my head," Faith said with a sigh. "In fact, I'm not sure I've even logged the amount. Paperwork is not my specialty, I'm afraid."

"As long as you're turning a profit, I suppose that's what matters."

"*Jah*, I suppose," Faith replied.

"But?" Hunter pushed, sensing she had more to say.

"But I'm not sure I *am* turning a profit. To be honest, my books are riddled with errors. I keep trying to balance the figures, but I must be doing something wrong. I wouldn't be so worried if I didn't have to put a down payment on the lease by the first of the year, for both the bakery and the apartment upstairs. I'm not sure I'm going to make it, but I hardly have a moment to stop and assess the numbers."

As Faith spoke, her voice began to tremble, and Hunter briefly felt an impulse to wrap his arm around her shoulder.

"Trust me," he said in a quiet voice, "I understand what a burden it can be to carry a financial pressure alone."

Faith turned toward him, sheepishly rolling her eyes. "Listen to me, complaining about finances on a holiday! I'm sorry, Hunter. My sister-in-law is right—my priorities aren't where they should be. She says I am too focused on my business."

"You needn't apologize," Hunter argued. "If you'll

allow me, I'll look over your books for you. But there is one condition."

Faith's face brightened. "Of course, what is it?"

Hunter delivered his condition carefully but firmly, "You mustn't offer me payment. This is something I want to do for you as…as your friend."

"But if it interrupts your working day—"

"It won't. Tomorrow morning is my first round of deliveries. I'll arrive early to review your accounting. How does five thirty sound?"

"That would be *wunderbaar*, Hunter," Faith acknowledged. "But the very least I can do is make you breakfast."

"Agreed." Hunter nodded. "Would you like me to bring my own *oier*, or can you transport some yourself?"

"I'll transport them myself," she said with a nudge to his arm. "But if I should wobble into a ditch, we'll have to eat them scrambled."

Even as he was laughing, it occurred to Hunter that Ruth was right: Ivy was more insightful than people gave her credit for. That day, he was so thankful to be among his family and friends, he hardly noticed the pain in his lower back, hip and legs. And when he bit into the pumpkin roll Faith served, every memory of Justine and the past vanished. All he could taste was the goodness of the here and now on his lips.

Chapter Six

As Faith unlocked the back door to the bakery at four thirty on Friday morning, she felt her stomach rumble. After Thanksgiving dinner and dessert at Ruth's, followed by a round of leftovers when Hunter brought her back to her own house and stayed for supper, and then more dessert while they played games with her family, Faith didn't think she'd be hungry again for days.

She decided it must be the morning air stirring her appetite. Shivering, she turned up the heat in the bakery. As unseasonably cold as the temperature was, she was grateful it hadn't snowed yet, which would mean she'd have to walk instead of ride her bike to the bakery. She hoped the inclement weather would hold off until after Christmas, when she'd be settled into her apartment and wouldn't have to worry about trekking into town in frigid conditions.

Once the room warmed, she began preparing the bread dough to rise before turning her attention to the display shelf. In her haste to get home early on Wednesday evening, she neglected to wrap several trays of goodies. They'd gone dry and most of them would have to be moved to the day-old shelf. She also marked down the price of two pies that hadn't sold. How was she going to make a profit if she was so careless with her products? She sighed and focused on mixing the ingredients for molasses gingerbread cookies, which she'd come in especially early to make to send with Hunter to the Piney Hill festival.

She was concentrating so hard on what she was doing, an hour later she didn't notice Hunter standing inside the back entrance until he cleared his throat.

"*Guder mariye*, Faith," he spoke softly, sweeping his hat from his head. Her eyes traveled from his thick, curly hair, down the masculine lines of his cheekbones, and lingered on the distinctive cleft in his chin.

"*Guder mariye,*" she replied, embarrassed she'd been staring. "You startled me."

"The door was unlocked, so when you didn't hear me knocking, I came in," he explained, his brows crimped together. "If you don't mind my saying so, you really should bolt the door when you're here alone."

"As you'll soon discover from my ledger, there's not much to steal," Faith joshed, "unless someone wants day-old bread, in which case, they're welcome to it."

"It's not your money I'm worried about," Hunter responded, the frown lines in his forehead deepening. "A woman working alone in the early morning hours—"

Faith flattened a lump of cookie dough with the rolling pin. While she was touched by Hunter's concern, his advice was unnecessary. She was strong. She knew how to take care of herself. She'd better; after all, she was going to be doing it for the rest of her life.

"*Denki* for your concern, but I doubt anyone in their right mind would trouble a sturdy Amish woman wielding one of these!" she said as she waved the rolling pin. She was half kidding. The Amish practiced nonviolence and she couldn't imagine ever physically striking another person, but that was her point: she doubted she'd ever need to. "Besides, I usually do lock the door, but I must have forgotten. Please, take off your coat. Would you like breakfast now or after you've finished reviewing my finances?"

"After I've finished. I'm not hungry yet. I confess, when I returned from your house last evening, I devoured another slice of pumpkin roll."

"Really? That must have been your third piece!"

"My fourth," he confessed. "What can I say? I know a *gut* thing when I have it."

Faith felt her cheeks go rosy. "I'm glad you enjoyed it. Now, I'll put on a pot of *kaffi*. Would you like to work at that little desk over in the corner, or would you prefer to work at a table in the storefront?"

"I'll work at this desk," he replied. "If you turn the lights on in the storefront, someone might think the bakery is open."

Although she hardly spoke to Hunter except to answer questions he had about her calculations, Faith enjoyed his presence nearby as she baked. There was something cozy about being in the same room with him while working on separate tasks that felt different from when she baked with Pearl. About an hour before the bakery was scheduled to open, she heard a persistent knocking on the front door.

"Early bird customers," she explained to Hunter. "Usually, we'd make them wait, but as you can probably tell from my books, I need all the business I can get. I'll be right back."

Through the glass pane she saw three young *Englisch* men wearing jackets with a nearby college's insignia on them, huddled on the front step. Two of them appeared to be holding up the third, and Faith raced to the door, concerned he was injured.

She was so flustered that she spoke in *Deitsch* instead of *Englisch*. "Is he hurt?"

The young man who was being propped up raised his head and jeered in a slurred voice, "I must be worse off than I thought because I didn't understand a word she just said."

He and the boy on his right both howled, but the man on his left apologized, "I'm very sorry, miss, but could we purchase a cup of coffee and some bagels? He really needs to get some food into his system."

Faith hesitated. The young man reeked of alcohol. Had he been drinking all night or had he just begun? She was aware of how dangerous the effects of alcohol consumption could be.

"Jah," she said, allowing them entrance to the bakery, "but I don't sell bagels, so you'll have to make another selection. How do you take your *kaffi*?"

"Kaffi," snorted the drunk man. "Did you hear the way she said *coffee*?" He staggered as his friends eased him into a chair, before adding, "I take it piping hot and extra sweet, just like you."

Although her hands were trembling, Faith spooned sugar into the cup and secured the lid. In the most authoritative voice she could muster, she stated to the other two men, "You may have this complimentary cup of *kaffi*, along with a few honey bars to counter the effects of the alcohol, but I don't want you to stay in the bakery. Please take your friend and leave."

"You can't kick us out!" the drunk man bellowed. "I'll complain to your manager. What's his name?"

"My name is Faith and *I'm* the manager. This is my bakery and I want you to leave," Faith repeated, placing her hands on her hips and glaring at him. "Now, please."

The drunken man slapped his thigh. "Look—her face is turning as red as her hair!"

Faith's throat burned. She was torn between wanting the floor to swallow her up and wanting to give the man a verbal chewing out he wouldn't soon forget.

Hunter stepped into the storefront and said in a deep, commanding voice, "Faith asked you to leave, so you need to get going. This instant."

"Who's going to make me, farm boy?" the young man ridiculed. He wobbled upon rising from the chair.

Hunter had wrangled calves that were more robust than this college kid and he advanced forward, but his Amish beliefs prohibited him from physically assisting the boy out the door.

"Shut up, Bill," the smaller of the two other men ordered, grabbing his friend's arm and steering him toward the door, nervously eyeing Hunter over his shoulder. "We're going."

The third student stepped forward to take the cardboard tray of coffee and goodies Faith had prepared. "I'm very sorry, miss, sir," he said and scampered toward the exit.

Crossing the room to relock the door behind the unwelcome patrons, Hunter noticed the last one to leave placed a crumpled wad of bills on the far tabletop. He picked it up.

"I assume this is supposed to make up for their coarse behavior," he said incredulously.

But when he turned around, he realized Faith had retreated into the kitchen. He spotted her at the sink, washing her hands.

"Why did you do that?" she asked. Her head was angled so he couldn't read her expression, but her tone was one of resentment.

Hunter was dumbfounded. "Do what?"

"You're here to reconcile my accounting, not to interfere with my interactions with my customers."

"Are you joking?" Hunter brayed. "Faith, that man was drunk. He was harassing you. You don't know what might have happened if I hadn't told them to leave."

Faith vigorously scrubbed her fingernails with a brush beneath a torrent of water that was so hot steam was rising from her skin.

"I know how big your muscles are, Hunter, and how much you pride yourself on your physical strength, but *Gott* would have protected me. Besides, I'm a strong woman. I can look after myself."

Pride in his physical strength? Faith had no idea just how weak Hunter felt! That very morning it had taken him five minutes to put on his trousers because his hips and legs were so tight he could hardly lift his feet from the floor.

But since he wasn't about to confide that in her, he spat out the words, "You're not as strong as you think you are, Faith. You're just f—"

He was about to tell her she was just foolish, but remembering what *Gott's* Word said about calling anyone a fool, he held his tongue.

"I'm just *what*, Hunter?" Faith challenged. Now she

was scrubbing the skin in between her fingers. "I'm not strong, I'm just *fat*, right? Go ahead—you're not the first to think it and you won't be the last!"

"What? *Neh*," Hunter protested. He didn't know why on earth Faith would imagine that was what he was thinking. "I was going to say you're just *foolhardy*. You may believe you're strong enough to overcome someone who wishes to do you harm, but you don't know what some men can be like. When they're around a becoming woman like you, they exhibit barnyard behavior—"

Faith's sobs interrupted what he was going to say. Her torso shook with the intensity of them, but she didn't stop cleansing her hands and she kept her face averted. As Hunter watched her quaking profile, he realized she wasn't really mad at him. She was upset by what had just transpired and she was trying to wash the incident away.

He gingerly walked to her side and turned off the water. Picking up a dish towel, he reached for her hand. She allowed him to lift her arm, but she wouldn't look him in the eye. Very carefully, he patted her palms and fingers dry and gently placed her hand by her side. Then he reached for her other hand and dried that one, too. Finally, she lifted her chin upward and sighed. He handed her the cloth so she could wipe the tears from her cheeks and dab the skin beneath her eyes.

She blinked her long, reddish lashes twice before directly meeting his gaze. "*Denki*, Hunter. For everything."

He knew she was thanking him for guarding her as well as comforting her, and the appreciation and admiration in her eyes reminded him of how he used to feel when Justine complimented his abilities, only better, because he never thought he'd feel that capable again. He humbly replied, "I'm glad I can help."

"I'll get started making breakfast now," she stated practically.

"I'd like that. We can discuss my findings while we're eating, and then I'll be on my way to Piney Hill."

After Faith served them each a plate heaped with breakfast scrapple, orange slices and toast made from freshly baked bread, Hunter said grace.

"*Gott*, we thank You for Your provision in this meal as well as for Your protection in our lives. Please help us to forgive those who trespass against us, just as Christ has forgiven us our trespasses."

"Amen!" Faith confirmed loudly. Then, a few bites into their meal, she asked the question he'd been dreading. "So, will I have enough money to make the down payment by the first of the year?"

Faith could tell Hunter was stalling by the deliberate way he was chewing his food. She knew the answer wasn't good, and she braced herself for his response. She had already cried in front of him once this morning. She appreciated how tender and respectful he'd been in response to her outburst, but she wouldn't allow herself to break down again.

"Well, based on your records and your projections for the rest of the season," he hesitated, "it looks as if you may fall a bit short of your goal."

"How short?"

"Twelve to eighteen hundred dollars."

"Twelve to eighteen hundred dollars!" Faith yipped. "The landlord won't renew the lease if I'm even *two* hundred dollars short! My future depends on the bakery—I can't lose it, I just can't!"

Hunter narrowed his eyes. "I know it's not the answer

you wanted to hear, Faith, but I had to be honest with you about my calculations. There still may be ways to meet your goal, but if not, I'm certain *Gott* has a plan for your future, whether or not you keep the bakery."

Faith kept her eyes from overflowing by focusing on separating a triangle of orange from its rind. Hunter had no idea why it was so important for her to keep her business, and she would never tell him. But, as upset as she was, she recognized the ultimate truth in what he was saying: her future depended on God, not on the bakery itself.

"You're right," she agreed solemnly. "I believe *Gott* has a plan for my future, even though I may not know what that is yet. I only know for now, He has provided me this bakery, which I treasure. I still have several weeks to meet my financial goal, so, with *Gott's* help, I'd like to do everything I can to make the down payment."

Hunter rubbed his chin. "Alright, let's discuss ways you might do that."

As they ate their breakfast and Faith bagged up the goodies for the festival, they volleyed ideas about how she could increase her revenue. Having worked for an *Englisch* company, Hunter was more familiar with practices that appealed to *Englischers*, and he brought a fresh approach to their brainstorming session.

"Have you considered keeping the bakery open later?"

"Ordinarily, I might," Faith said. "But my concern is Henrietta doesn't think I spend enough time with my family as it is. Who knows what she'd say if I came home later than I already do?"

As soon as she spoke, Faith felt a stitch of guilt. She hadn't meant to air her sister-in-law's grievance, but it was so easy to be open with Hunter that the words just slipped out. She quickly added, "To be fair, she has a point. On occasion I wish I could spend more time at home, too. Regardless, I don't think my in-store bakery sales would be significant enough to justify extended hours. I earn the most money on large orders my regular *Englisch* customers place for holidays and other special celebrations. I wish I could increase those sales."

Hunter scratched his chin. "Well, *Grischtdaag* and New Year's Eve are coming up, and *Englischers* are known to throw big parties, both at home and at work, with lots of food," he said. "What do you do to advertise to the *Englisch* community?"

"I've requested if *Englisch* customers enjoy my goods and services they'd spread the word to their friends in neighboring towns, but I'm afraid…" Realizing it would be immodest to complete her thought, Faith allowed her sentence to trail off.

Hunter pushed her to finish it. "You're afraid what?" he asked. Faith noticed that about him: he was genuinely interested in her opinions, especially those she was most hesitant to express.

"It's puffed up of me to say, but I'm afraid some of them, like Marianne Palmer, might not want to 'share' me—those are her words, not mine. I don't know if I could actually count on them to tell others about the bakery."

"Well, I think you should keep asking customers to tell others about your shop," Hunter advised. "But meanwhile, look at that box you're holding."

Faith glanced at the plain white cardboard box. What was wrong with it? She shrugged in confusion.

"You don't have your business name, hours and phone number on it," Hunter explained. "The *Ordnung* for Willow Creek doesn't prohibit including that information on your packaging, does it?"

"*Neh*, provided it's simple, not ornamental, and it doesn't contain any graven images," Faith confirmed. "I considered having boxes and bags printed for the bakery, but I discovered it was more costly than I anticipated. I'm not sure it would be worth the investment, especially when every penny counts."

"Hmm… Labels are cheap. Could you affix labels to your boxes and bags? There's a printing shop on the other side—"

"Of Willow Creek! I know the place," Faith exclaimed. "That's a fantastic plan, Hunter."

His eyes were alight as he replied, "I'll go right past the printer when I make the delivery to Piney Hill. If you jot down your information, I can take it to the printer this morning."

"Really? You'd do that for me?" Faith meant to express her gratitude, but she realized her choice of words might make Hunter think she was playing coy, so she quickly elaborated, "I mean, I'd really appreciate it."

Hunter grinned. "We're business partners, aren't we? Your success is my success and mine is yours. Speaking of which, I'd better get on the road to the festival."

Faith was so absorbed in their conversation she hadn't realized how late it was getting. "Of course. I'll finish packaging these while you bring your buggy around to the back."

After helping Hunter carefully load the backseat of the buggy, Faith watched him pull down the lane. *Business partners.* The words carried a different meaning from *business associates*, and Faith liked the idea of partnering with Hunter to meet her goal. She might never have the support of a husband, but at least for the moment she had a kind man to encourage her and give her a hand when she needed his help. And, she had to admit, she secretly felt complimented that this kind man happened to have referred to her as a "becoming woman," too.

As his horse galloped toward Piney Hill, Hunter's mood was buoyant, knowing he was helping Faith try to meet her financial obligations while simultaneously meeting his own. He recalled how her countenance shone while they discussed ways to increase revenue, and it was a boost to his confidence that she clearly valued his input. Grateful he could apply the accounting skills he was learning at the cannery to Faith's books, Hunter hoped the experience might allow him to earn a living in Indiana doing something other than the manual labor he'd been accustomed to performing.

Of course, he wasn't yet financially independent by any means: his aunt supplied all of his and his mother's meals and sundries. Ruth insisted, claiming she was beholden to them for looking after *her*. That's why when Hunter first informed his aunt and mother he was going to run Faith's morning deliveries, he didn't care if they exchanged knowing glances. He preferred for them to imagine he was taking on the extra responsibility because he fancied Faith than to realize it was because he'd come perilously close to losing the house in Indiana.

But that danger was behind him for the time being. According to his calculations, with the money he'd earn from the deliveries, plus the fee James Palmer would pay when he picked up the finished chair on Monday, Hunter not only would be able to pay the outstanding house and medical bills, he might have enough left over to purchase a small Christmas gift for his aunt and mother. His breath formed steam in the frosty morning air as he called out to God, "*Denki*, Lord, for Your plentiful blessings!"

He made good time getting to the festival, and the printing shop had just opened when he pulled into the parking lot on his return trip. The manager offered to print the labels within half an hour, but Hunter didn't want to risk returning late to the cannery, so he agreed to pick them up the following morning.

After returning from Piney Hill, Hunter brought the horse and buggy home and then walked back into town. If his hips and legs felt clunky, the sensation was negligible compared with the feelings of competence and optimism carrying him down Main Street and into the cannery.

Maybe it's not so unreasonable to believe I'll be able to support a wife and family one day soon, he allowed himself to think as he gazed out the window while waiting for Ivy to arrive. Spotting Faith's quick, energetic movements in the storefront of her bakery, he again pondered why she wasn't being courted. Faith was so clever, persevering and vivacious. She was someone who seemed to really love to laugh…most of the time. What was the secret burden she hid beneath her quick smile? Hunter had no idea, but whatever it was, he doubted it was the reason she wasn't being courted. More likely, she had no interest in marriage because she was consumed with her business. Didn't she say the bakery was her future?

Ivy passed by the cannery window and lifted her hand toward the bakery storefront, startling Hunter from his thoughts. Flipping the door sign, he greeted her when she came in.

"Hunter Schwartz had Thanksgiving dinner with Faith Yoder on Thursday at Ruth Graber's house. One thirty,"

Ivy stated as she turned a jar of preserves so its label was aligned with the others.

"*Jah*, that's right. You were there, too, with your *groossdaadi*," Hunter acknowledged. "I enjoyed myself very much, did you?"

"*Jah*, I enjoyed myself very much," she repeated. "A special occasion."

Hunter barely had time to grin back at the winsome young girl before the first of a long stream of customers entered the shop. Sales didn't slow down until right before Hunter closed the store at five o'clock. As he meandered home, he noticed snowflakes that were so light they appeared to be floating upward instead of falling down. He'd felt his legs and hips growing tighter throughout the day, but the store was bustling and he hadn't wanted to retreat to the back room to stretch. Now, the cold air worked its way into his joints, and with each footfall he imagined his legs cracking like ice. Once home, he declined supper, opting for a hot bath. He was asleep within minutes of lying down, and it seemed within minutes of sleeping, it was time for him to rise again.

Although his back was still stiff and the short buggy ride into town the next morning seemed to rattle his bones, all discomfort was forgotten when Faith unlocked the back door for him. Her smile was a sunrise as she extended a steaming mug of coffee.

"*Guder mariye*, Hunter."

"*Guder mariye*," he echoed, his fingers momentarily encircling hers as he accepted the hot drink. "I'm glad to see you secured the door today."

"*Jah*, I might be as stubborn as a mule, but may it never be said I'm *foolhardy*." The glimmer in her eyes told him she was jesting at her own expense. There was something fetching about her ability to be lighthearted so early in the morning that lifted Hunter's disposition, too. "Would you like a muffin with your *kaffi*?" she asked.

"*Denki*, I'd appreciate that." Having skipped supper the night before, he was ravenous. "But I'll have to eat it in the buggy. I want to allow time to stop at the printer's on the way back and pick up your labels."

When he arrived at the festival booth, the *Englisch* vendor greeted him enthusiastically. "I'm glad to see you brought more items today," she said. "Your goodies sold out by eleven in the morning yesterday. I had several people stop by in the evening who said they'd eaten the cookies during the day at work and wanted to purchase some for their families. Faith ought to increase the volume even more than what I see here. My booth closes at six thirty, but there's a big rush between about four and six o'clock, when people are getting out of work. You could make a second delivery for the late-afternoon shoppers, say, around three thirty? People are always drawn to goodies still warm from the oven."

Hunter couldn't have been more pleased. "That's an interesting proposal. I'll talk to Faith about it."

By the time he picked up the labels, returned home, stabled the horse and walked back to town, Hunter had come up with a plan for how he could make an afternoon delivery in addition to his morning run. But since it was already four minutes before nine o'clock, he decided he'd propose his strategy to Faith during her dinner break.

So, while Pearl and Ivy ate their meals at a table in the front of the bakery, Hunter quietly repeated the vendor's suggestion to Faith in the back room. "If you'd like me to make a second daily delivery, I figured out how to make it work. Ivy and Pearl could switch places in the afternoon. That way, Pearl would be available to help you with the extra baking for most of the day, but I wouldn't have to leave Ivy unattended to make an afternoon delivery."

"I don't know…" Faith wrung her hands.

"If you're hesitant about working with Ivy, you needn't be. She's very diligent. I realize she doesn't like making changes, but she's so fond of you I think she'd flourish here. And I can't imagine Pearl objecting." Hunter had to pause to catch his breath. "I truly believe this will put you in a much better position to make your down payment."

"Well, then, let's do it!" Faith exclaimed loudly, smiling so broadly her ears wiggled. "Of course, we'll have to ask Pearl and Ivy first."

"Ask us what?" Pearl called from the other room.

Faith and Hunter charged into the storefront, both speaking so excitedly they kept interrupting each other as they asked Pearl and Ivy to participate in their plan.

"I think it's a splendid idea," Pearl said. "What do you think, Ivy?"

"I'll work in Faith Yoder's bakery from three o'clock until five o'clock," Ivy agreed. "A splendid idea."

Hunter felt like hugging the girl. Instead, he silently thanked the Lord for how smoothly the plan was coming together. When he told Ruth about it, she was thrilled, too.

"I've been concerned Ivy isn't being challenged enough in the cannery. A change will do her good. But it's a waste of time for you to return home to fetch the buggy twice a day. It would be better to hitch the horse in town. You can take breaks to feed and water him there."

"Are you sure?" Hunter asked. His frame was already aching from a single jaunt into town and he imagined it would only worsen when he began doubling his trips.

"I'm sure. It's not as if your *mamm* and I need the buggy ourselves," Ruth said. "I hope this plan pays off. I know how much Faith's bakery means to her."

Indeed, the first week of delivering baked goods twice daily to the festival proved even more lucrative than Hunter expected, benefiting them both, and Ivy adapted quickly to her new afternoon role at the bakery. All around, Hunter's new partnership with Faith was what the *Englisch* referred to as a win-win situation. Or, as he preferred to think of it, an answer to prayer.

Chapter Seven

Faith yawned as she locked the front door to the bakery after Ivy left for the evening on Monday. For a week, Faith had been arriving ninety minutes earlier to keep up with baking for the in-store sales and her customers' special orders, as well as for the festival. She figured Henrietta couldn't fault her for not spending more time with her family in the morning, since everyone was still sleeping when she left for the bakery anyway. She tried to get home in time to help prepare supper, but there were some evenings, like tonight, when she had to stay late to clean the pans and utensils she didn't have time to wash during the day.

She was rinsing the trays when someone rapped on the pane of the front door. A woman dressed in hospital scrubs cupped her hands against the glass and peered in, while a second woman continued knocking.

"Oh, thank you!" the first woman, a blonde, exclaimed when Faith opened the door. "We were afraid we missed you."

Faith regretted turning away customers, even after hours, but her shelves were nearly bare. "I'm sorry, but the bakery is actually closed and I'm sold out of almost everything," she said.

"I'm not surprised," the blonde replied. "We purchased one of your sticky bun wreaths at the festival on our way to work today, and it was so fantastic we wanted to come by on our way home to see what else you make. We'd like to place a large order for brunch on Friday."

"Yeah," the other woman added, "your husband suggested we give you a call, but we wanted to sample a few items before deciding what to get."

"My husband?" Faith echoed. "I don't have a husband."

The first woman replied, "The man making deliveries isn't your husband? Sorry, he raved so much about you I just assumed you were newlyweds."

Faith felt as if her skin burst into flame. Waving her hand dismissively, she said, "Ah, well, you know how men enjoy food. They're very complimentary when it comes to a woman's baking."

"It wasn't just your baking he complimented," the woman insisted. "What was it he said when he was giving us directions, Rita?"

The other woman sighed theatrically. "He said there may be several businesses with the name 'Yoder's' in Lancaster County, but we'd know we were in the right shop if the owner had hair the color of ground cinnamon and a *wunderbaar* laugh."

Faith's knees felt wiggly. Did Hunter really say that? She invited the women inside and served them samples of the freshest items still in stock. After helping them decide what to order for their party and sending them off with a complimentary loaf of bread that would have wound up in her brothers' bellies, she returned to her dishwashing task.

Denki, Lord, that everything seems to be working out, Faith prayed as she slid a tray into the rack to dry. Her cookies, breads and pastries were selling out daily at the festival. Meanwhile, Pearl and Ivy had adjusted well to the changes; Pearl claimed she preferred the relatively slower afternoons in the cannery, whereas Ivy was flourishing in her new role at the bakery.

What especially gladdened Faith was seeing Hunter's face first thing in the morning. No matter how early the hour or biting the air, he always wore a dashing grin and he was appreciative of the coffee she prepared for him to take on his deliveries. One morning she even convinced him to sit down for a breakfast of French toast topped with pecans, since she knew how much he liked them. Other than Pearl, she'd never had someone express such an active interest in the success of her business, and she wanted him to know she appreciated his support. It didn't hurt that she thoroughly enjoyed his company, either.

When Faith finished washing the dishes, she double-checked the storefront and back room for any last-minute tidying. The following day was Tuesday, December 8, and the bakery and cannery would be closed so she, Pearl, Ivy and Hunter could attend Penelope and Lawrence's wedding in Penelope's hometown. The occasion would begin with a three-hour service in the morning, followed by meals and socializing lasting until nine or ten o'clock at night. It was an Amish tradition for businesses—and even schools—to shut down so all the *leit* could attend the weddings of couples in their districts, which were held on Tuesdays or Thursdays during November and December. Confident nothing was left undone, Faith locked the shop and made it home just in time for supper.

"Are you certain you want to charge Penelope for the wedding cakes?" Henrietta asked Faith later that evening while hemming a seam in her son's trousers.

Ever since Willa left, Henrietta seemed more focused on Faith's work at the bakery. She was continually asking Faith about her orders and making suggestions about what Christmas goodies the customers might enjoy. Faith appreciated her interest, but Henrietta couldn't seem to understand that some traditional Amish items, such as skillet pear ginger pie, weren't in demand enough to be worth preparing them.

"Why shouldn't I charge Penelope for the cakes? She's a customer like anyone else."

While Amish weddings often included homemade pies, cakes and goodies prepared by family members and friends, it wasn't unusual for the bride to purchase one or more cakes from a professional baker, too. Although the cakes were plainer than those at most *Englisch* weddings, they were still special-ordered for the occasion.

"*Jah*, but you're friends with the bride and especially the groom," Henrietta argued. "You were walking out with Lawrence, after all."

That's the very reason I shouldn't *bake their cake at no cost*, Faith thought facetiously as she adorned the fireplace mantel with boughs of evergreen and a solitary red candle in the center. Ornate Christmas decorations were prohibited by the *Ordnung*, but simple garnishing was allowed in Amish homes and businesses, and Faith relished creating a festive environment for her family and customers to enjoy at this time of year.

"Reuben is friends with Turner King, but when Reuben's buggy needs repair, Turner doesn't fix it for free," Faith countered, trying to help Henrietta see her decision from a business perspective. "Likewise, Reuben doesn't stock the Masts' pantry with free produce during harvest season simply because you're friends with Colette."

"*Jah*, but Reuben and Turner are men. Their incomes are necessities—they support their families," Henrietta reasoned.

"My income will allow me to keep the bakery and lease a living space for myself," Faith said as calmly as she could.

"But that's not essential. You could always live here. Either way, a few wedding cakes aren't likely to set you back. It seems you could be a little more gracious to your friends, that's all."

"A little more gracious?" Faith sputtered, twirling toward Henrietta. "Do you have any idea how much graciousness it takes to attend the wedding of a man who rejected me because of something that's not even my fault?"

Her sister-in-law peered at Faith over her reading glasses as if she couldn't quite fathom what was causing her to be so distressed. Faith lowered her volume. She didn't want to speak in anger: she wanted Henrietta to understand how she felt and to stop interfering in her business.

"Listen, Henrietta, not only am I closing the bakery to attend Penelope and Lawrence's wedding—which means I'll lose a full day's worth of business during the busiest season of the year—but as a gift to the couple, I gave Penelope a steep discount. She only paid for whatever ingredients I didn't have in stock, such as coconut milk for the special frosting she requested. So please, show *me* a little graciousness. If you can't support me, at least don't lecture me on how to run my business or conduct my friendships. I know you intend to be helpful, but sometimes your comments are actually quite hurtful."

When Henrietta didn't reply, Faith simply bid her good-night and went upstairs to her room. She had never spoken to her sister-in-law so firmly, but she wasn't going to apologize. Not tonight, anyway. Too tired to undress, she unlaced her boots and collapsed into bed, pulling the quilt over her sideways. Covering her head with her arm, she nestled into her pillow and before she knew it, her nephew was jostling her awake.

"*Mamm* said I'm not to bother you, *Ant* Faith," the five-year-old announced in a raspy voice. "You need privacy to get ready for your wedding."

Faith groggily opened her eyes to discover she was nose to nose with the chubby youngster. *"Lappich bu,"* she said, affectionately referring to him as a silly boy as she reached out to touch his ruddy cheek. "It's not *my* wedding we're going to."

"Why not?" He tipped his head and squinted. "Don't you want to have a wedding?"

His innocent curiosity caught her off guard, and she tried to distract him by tossing aside the quilt and shifting to a sitting position.

"Not today I don't," she answered succinctly.

"But when you get married, you get your own special cake."

The boy's sentiment caused Faith to burst out in laughter. *"Jah,* that's true, Andy, but when you get married, you're also pleased to share your special cake with your wedding guests. You'll see—today you'll get a slice."

"I will?" His enormous eyes seemed to grow even larger.

"There you are, Andrew," Henrietta called as she peeked around the divider. "*Kumme*, let your *ant* get dressed while I comb your hair."

"*Guder mariye*, Henrietta," Faith said as she rose, hoping there was no lingering tension between them. "I must have been more tired than I realized. I rarely sleep past sunrise."

"*Jah*, it's half-past the hour. We'll be leaving in five minutes."

"Five minutes!" Faith shrieked. "I only have five minutes to get ready?"

Henrietta flinched as if she'd been hurt. "I thought you were waiting to get up and get ready until we were all out of your way and you could have the washroom to yourself. I was trying not to interfere. I assumed Hunter would be picking you up shortly after we left."

Although she believed Henrietta had her best intentions at heart, Faith was too dismayed about being late to mince words. "I don't know how many times I have to tell you I'm not romantically involved with Hunter Schwartz," Faith said with an emphasis she hoped was convincing, "And he is not picking me up, so I'll need to go with you and Reuben and the *kinner*."

She grabbed a pair of stockings from her drawer, whisked her clean dress from the closet and then hurried down the hall to the washroom to try to make herself appear more presentable on the outside than she felt on the inside.

Hunter shifted on the long, hard bench. He felt as fidgety as a child, but he couldn't sit still; the knot of pain in his lower back and hips was radiating downward, causing his left foot to tingle. He'd noticed his discomfort grew progressively worse ever since he began the afternoon deliveries, and he regretted making the long journey to Penelope's house on the one day he could have had a respite from traveling in the buggy. But Ruth had come down with a bad cold and she insisted he attend to extend her good wishes to the young couple. His mother stayed behind, too.

If there was one consolation, it was that the wedding allowed Hunter the opportunity to socialize with Faith. Over the past week, he'd enjoyed bantering with her first thing in the morning before he headed to Piney Hill, or lingering over a treat in the back room of the bakery before he left for the festival in the afternoon. But their visits were always briefer than he would have preferred and their conversations were usually focused on their businesses. He was hoping the late-afternoon wedding festivities would include the kind of fun and games he'd engaged in with Faith and her brothers when he took her home after Thanksgiving dinner.

By the time the three-hour service ended, Hunter could barely pull himself to his feet. He picked up the wooden bench and stiffly hobbled toward where the men were stacking them so a second group could carry them to the bench wagon. If this were a regular worship service, they'd flip and stack the benches to create tables for the *leit* to gather around to eat dinner. But since it was a wedding, the guests would eat in shifts at special tables the men were setting up in a U shape around the gathering room.

Hunter hoped no one noticed how haltingly he moved, and as soon as the men's work was finished, he slipped outside to pace around the yard, hoping to loosen his muscles before it was his turn to sit down to eat. The wind was raw, and he rubbed his hands together. On his third loop around the perimeter, a small child came bounding across the yard.

"Andy!" he heard a female beckon remotely. "Andy, you stop wherever you are right now. This isn't a game. We're not playing tag!"

The child giggled and continued to run pell-mell toward where Hunter was standing. Despite the ache in his lower body, Hunter bent over and adroitly scooped the boy up, somersaulting him into a sitting position on his right shoulder. A moment later, Faith appeared from around the side of the large house. Her shawl was askew and her cheeks were aflame, whether from the cold or from emotion, Hunter didn't know.

"Is this the runaway you're looking for?" he asked as he flipped Andy upside down and set him back on his feet.

"*Jah*, this is my nephew Andy," she panted. "Andy, say hello to Hunter."

Andy looked up in awe at Hunter. "You're even stronger than my *daed*!" he declared.

Chuckling, Hunter replied, "I'm not sure about that. But what I do know is if you keep eating all of the meat and vegetables your *mamm* serves you, you'll grow to be big and strong like your *daed*, too."

"I always clean my plate," Andy happily informed him. "Especially today. Today we get to have wedding cake after dinner."

"I'm looking forward to that," Hunter commented. "I heard your *ant* Faith made it, and everything she bakes is *appenditlich*."

"*Jah*, but it's not her wedding cake. It's for Penelope and Lawrence. They have to share," Andy carefully explained. "Ant Faith doesn't want to get married. She told *mamm* she's not 'mantically interested in—"

"Look!" Faith interrupted, taking Andy by the hand. "Here comes your *daed*. He's been searching for you."

As Reuben approached the trio, Andy ducked behind Faith's skirt.

"There's no use hiding, Andy," Reuben scolded. "You've already been disobedient, running away like you did. I'm afraid there will be no wedding cake for you."

The boy's eyes immediately welled but he nodded sadly, as if to accept his punishment.

"He gave us a fright when we couldn't find him, it's true," Faith intervened. "But I don't think he meant to. I think he was stretching his legs after sitting so still through the entire service. I'm sure he won't run away again, will you, Andy?"

"No, never," Andy agreed. "I'm sorry I gave you a fright, *Daed*."

Reuben paused before tousling the boy's hair. "You're forgiven, *suh*. I suppose your running about like that made you extra hungry, so you may have a piece of wedding cake after all. *Kumme*, let's go back inside."

Faith and Andy led the way, with Hunter and Reuben following. As they walked toward the house, Reuben confided, "One of the challenges of being a *daed* is knowing when to show grace and when to stand firm for the *kinner's* sake."

"It seems today you've made the right decision," Hunter responded.

"The doubts linger," Reuben replied. "If you have *kin-*

ner one day, you'll know what I mean. Being a *daed* is difficult work."

Hunter thought of the grace and forgiveness his father had shown him throughout his life. Considering his own behavior, especially during his *Rumspringa* years, he knew it must not have always been easy for his father, and suddenly a great loneliness washed over him.

"Being a *daed* is definitely a weighty responsibility," he affirmed. Then, remembering what his father said to him right before he died, he added, "But I'm told it's one of life's greatest blessings."

"No doubt about that," Reuben agreed.

Faith felt like crying. It wasn't that she had any abiding heartache because Lawrence rejected her and married Penelope. Nor was it because, halfway through the sermon, Faith realized in her haste to get ready, she'd grabbed her baking apron instead of a clean one to wear over her dress. As disheveled as she felt, that wasn't nearly enough to reduce her to tears, either. Nor did she cry out when Andy accidentally hopped on her big toe with the heel of his boot right before he took off across the lawn.

No, it was Hunter's statement about fatherhood being a blessing unlike any other that crushed her spirit. Until she heard him make that comment, Faith hadn't realized the extent of her affection for him. Without fully being aware of it, she must have allowed Henrietta's fanciful imaginings about their walking out together go to her head, because lately Faith had been entertaining notions that perhaps, just perhaps, her relationship with Hunter might develop from that of business partners and friends into a more personal connection.

But what sense was there in daydreaming about a romance with Hunter when he hadn't given the slightest indication he was interested in courting her? As she'd explained to Willa, Hunter was only in Willow Creek temporarily until Ruth's fractures healed. Even if Willa was right and Hunter developed a reason to settle in Pennsylvania permanently, Faith couldn't consider him as a suitor, knowing what she did about her health condition. Hunter made it clear long ago that he wouldn't court anyone he didn't intend to marry. And now, Hunter made it clear he wanted children, too. Why wouldn't he want them? It was only natural; Faith couldn't fault him for that. But neither could she continue to kid herself: Hunter was helping her save her business and that was all. She needed to squelch her unrealistic romantic yearnings.

But that was easier said than done when she was surrounded by people extolling the virtues of marriage. She was as sociable and courteous as she could be, but after several hours her cheeks ached from plastering a smile across her face. Seeking to leave with Henrietta and Reuben when they took the boys home, she poked her head into the kitchen in search of her sister-in-law.

"Faith, those cakes you made are as scrumptious as they are beautiful," Doris Plank gushed. "You have a real talent."

"Denki," Faith replied, relieved that everyone seemed to be enjoying her confections.

"Don't you worry, your turn will come soon enough," Doris continued. "Look at me—I was well into my thirties when I married, and now here I am with a *bobbel* in my arms! You've got plenty of time, doesn't she, Collette?"

"Jah," replied Collette Mast, one of Henrietta's friends. "Your sister-in-law frets about your future, but

I tell her anyone who can bake like you do will make an excellent wife."

Mortified that Henrietta had been discussing her fears about Faith's lack of suitors with Collette Mast, Faith quickly excused herself and walked outside toward the barn where the other single people were gathering before the second meal. It was an Amish tradition for the bride and groom or another married couple to pair young male guests with young female guests. The couples were expected to sit together and converse during the informal supper that occurred in the early evening. As she wove through the crowd, Faith spotted Mason speaking with Katie Fisher, so she asked him if he'd seen Reuben, Henrietta and the children.

"They already left," Mason told her. "Henrietta suggested you might like to stay and socialize, since you've been working such long hours. I told her you could ride with Katie and me if no one else offers to take you home. But Penelope's already started the matchmaking, so perhaps she'll pair you with someone who has a courting buggy."

Faith rubbed her forehead in disgrace. Her brother's halfhearted offer of transportation home was embarrassing enough, but now she'd also have to endure the humiliation of Lawrence's bride matching her with a man she deemed suitable? Faith silently considered walking to the nearest phone shanty and calling a cab. It would almost be worth the expense.

"What your brother means to say is any man would be privileged to give you a ride home, Faith," Katie tactfully clarified, elbowing Mason. "But if not, we'd *wilkom* your company."

As it turned out, Penelope paired Faith with Hunter,

the one man she was specifically trying to avoid. They took seats opposite one another at the far end of the table. The room was filled with noisy chatter, so when Hunter spoke, Faith had to ask him to repeat himself.

Rather than raising the volume of his voice, he leaned forward to be heard.

"I said you look a bit drawn. Have you been eating enough?"

No one had ever asked her that question before, and she couldn't tell if he was joking.

"I haven't *stopped* eating," she said, gesturing to the plate piled with macaroni and cheese, fried sweet potatoes and chicken.

"There sure are plenty of tasty dishes to choose from," Hunter remarked. "And I heard everyone praising the wedding cake you made."

"Almost everyone—Andy was disappointed. He complained it wasn't nearly as *gut* as one of my peanut butter sheet cakes." Faith giggled, relaxing a little. "I told him when he's old enough to marry, that's what kind I'll make for him."

Hunter flashed a broad smile. "You have a special way with *kinner*."

Faith had heard this compliment before, and it was often followed by a remark about how she'd make a terrific mother someday. Because motherhood was most definitely not a topic she cared to discuss with Hunter, she simply shrugged and said, "He's my nephew, so I'm used to handling his behaviors."

"Neh," Hunter protested. "It's not just with your nephew. It was also with Ivy at the bridge. You were so nurturing and calm—"

Growing more defensive, Faith snapped, "Ivy's a

young woman, not a *kind*. I knew what to say to her because the situation happened many times before, not because of any inherent maternal instinct on my part."

As she straightened her posture, she realized she'd been leaning so far forward that a glob of macaroni and cheese had gotten stuck to the front of her cape. Inwardly and outwardly, she couldn't have felt any less attractive than she did at that moment.

Hunter swallowed. He hadn't meant to insult Ivy; he only meant to pay Faith a compliment. She was usually so good-humored and easy to talk to, yet as he watched her bowing her head to wipe the front of her cape with a napkin, he realized she was in pain. It wasn't necessarily physical pain that disturbed her, but she was undeniably deeply troubled. He recognized the symptoms. After all, how many times had he forced himself to put on a good face—or at least go through the motions of what was expected of him—when inwardly, he was grimacing in agony?

After a brief silence, he apologized. "I'm sorry. I know Ivy isn't a *kind*, and I don't think I've ever treated her like one. I have nothing but respect for her diligence and gratitude for her skills. I'd be lost without her at the cannery. I only meant you seem to know the right thing to say at the right time to keep a situation from growing worse."

Faith placed her napkin beside her plate. "You needn't apologize, Hunter," she said. "Once again, I'm the one who ought to be sorry. I'm afraid I'm not much of a supper companion. If you'll excuse me, I need some air."

After hurriedly sopping up the last of his gravy with his bread crust, Hunter followed Faith outdoors. He passed several young couples exchanging sweet nothings in hushed tones near the side of the house. If he knew Faith, she'd seclude herself on the farthest end of the property, much like she'd done at the creek at her house the Sunday the Yoders hosted church. Squinting, he carefully picked his way across the property.

"You haven't got on a shawl," he said when he spied her leaning against a willow tree.

"You aren't wearing a coat," she countered.

"I'm too full to be cold."

Her laughter sounded the way the stars looked in the night sky: clear and bright. "That doesn't make any sense," she scoffed lightly.

"It doesn't make any sense to leave the table before dessert is served, either, but here you are," he replied.

"I'll hardly starve."

"But you'll miss the best part of the meal," Hunter objected. When his comment elicited only a shrug from Faith, he realized he was being dense. "Ach! I understand. You didn't want to be paired with me."

"Neh," she said. "I mean, it's not that I didn't want to be paired with you, Hunter. It's that I didn't want to be paired with anyone. I wanted to go home hours ago, which I know seems like an ungracious thing to say, but I just feel... I feel so..."

"You feel so what?" He noticed she had a tendency to withhold her thoughts, but he hoped she was becoming more comfortable expressing herself to him. Trying to draw her out, he teased, "You're not coming down with something, are you?"

"Neh, it's not that." Faith strolled a few yards from the tree, keeping her back turned toward Hunter as she continued to explain. "I used to walk out with Lawrence until...until he decided he didn't want to marry me. It was

a very difficult time, but now I wish him and Penelope all the best, I truly do… I just wish I didn't have to wish it all day long, if that makes sense."

Because he recalled how relieved he was not to be present in Indiana to attend Justine's wedding, Hunter understood perfectly. For the life of him, though, he couldn't imagine why Lawrence would choose a girl like Penelope over a woman like Faith. Hunter thought about little Andy saying Faith didn't want to marry. Was her heartache over Lawrence what made her decide she was no longer interested in marriage to any man?

"I can't say I blame you for wanting to leave," he admitted. "If you wouldn't object to being paired with me for the journey home, I'm happy to take you now."

"Really?" Faith questioned. "You're sure you're ready to go, too?"

"I'm sure," Hunter replied.

Faith's company was the only reason he'd stayed so late, and now that he knew she preferred to leave, there was no sense in his sticking around, either. He'd much rather share three minutes of genuine, joyful interaction with Faith at the bakery than three hours of contrived, cheerless courtship at a social event—even if he was the one who specifically requested Penelope match him with Faith in the first place.

Chapter Eight

As grateful as Faith was to Hunter for helping her depart the celebration prematurely, she was simultaneously dismayed at herself for divulging the reason she wanted to escape. *What a* bobblemoul *I am*, she thought, *blabbering on about Lawrence like that*. Hunter characteristically was an attentive and nonjudgmental listener, but he wasn't Faith's confidant, and she was mortified that she disclosed such personal feelings. If she wasn't more careful, who knows what else she'd share in a moment of emotional distress? She resolved to keep her mouth shut on the way home, but as it happened, Hunter barely uttered a word, either.

Because she accepted a ride with him instead of returning home with Mason after the wedding, Faith knew there'd be no convincing her sister-in-law she wasn't walking out with Hunter, so she decided she wouldn't try. When she entered her room, she simply greeted Henrietta, who was tucking the boys in for the night.

"I'm tired. I think I'll go to bed now, too," she whispered. *"Gut nacht."*

Yet instead of sleeping, she interlaced her fingers behind her head and stared at the ceiling.

"*Ant* Faith," her nephew whispered from the other side of the divider, interrupting her thoughts. "Are you awake?"

"*Jah*, what is it, Andy?"

"*Mamm* says soon you're going to leave us to go live in the bakery."

"*Jah*, in an apartment above the bakery."

"Don't you like living with us anymore?"

"Of course I do. But when I move to the apartment above the bakery, your *daed* can take the divider down and you and your brother will have lots more space."

"I don't want lots more space." Andrew sniffed. "I want you to stay here with us."

Faith squeezed her eyes tightly, and two tears dribbled down each side of her face. "I will visit every Sunday, and you may visit me above the bakery, too."

"Will your compartment smell like peanut butter sheet cake?"

Faith giggled. "*Jah*, I suppose my *apart*ment will smell like peanut butter sheet cake if that's what I've made in the bakery. When you visit, we'll eat a piece of whatever I baked that day, okay?"

"I would like that, *Ant* Faith. *Gut nacht*," the boy whispered sleepily.

"*Gut nacht.*"

As Faith stretched on her bed, she was filled with self-doubt. Maybe her sister-in-law was right: it wasn't essential for her to move or even for her to earn a salary—Henrietta probably would have been more appreciative of Faith's help at home, in the garden and around the farm than she was of the financial contributions Faith made toward their household expenses.

Faith asked herself why she was striving so hard for something that wasn't considered a necessity. She already knew the answer: she liked being a business owner, she liked serving her customers and she liked baking. There was nothing she was better at doing or relished doing more.

In fact, for the first time since Lawrence broke up with her, Faith realized how relieved she was that she hadn't end up marrying him after all. She'd been a farmer's daughter her entire youth. She'd had a wonderful childhood and learned many useful skills, but she didn't necessarily want to be a farmer's wife—or a farmer's sister, for that matter—and spend the rest of her life on a farm. Was it so wrong to want to do something different, since she had a choice?

She wished Henrietta and other women in her district understood that just because she was a single woman didn't mean her business was a mere hobby to distract her until she got married. Granted, virtually all Amish women quit working full-time once they had children, so she could see why some people assumed the bakery was only a passing interest, but Henrietta knew better. She knew Faith might never marry or have children. Faith resented that her sister-in-law didn't seem to accept that Faith's life was following a course that was different from Henrietta's.

Faith shifted onto her side, cocooning herself in the quilt. Even Hunter's observation, "you have a special way with *kinner*," seemed fraught with the underlying expectation she would eventually nurture children of her own. Or was she reading too much into his praise? Had seeing Lawrence again influenced her perception, causing her to feel as if she couldn't quite measure up to anyone's standards? She didn't know what to think anymore.

All that was certain was she had three weeks to meet her financial goal and she wasn't going to let anything stop her from doing her best to raise the money she needed. Slipping an arm from beneath her covers, she pulled her battery-operated alarm clock from her nightstand, set it to three thirty and placed it beside her on the pillow. Three thirty was a ridiculously early hour to rise, but how else could she keep up with the orders and in-shop sales? She couldn't risk falling behind, not with her deadline only weeks away.

The next morning there was a thin sheet of ice on the road, and twice the bicycle almost skidded out from under her, but she pedaled as quickly as she could. On the way, she determined she had set a poor precedent by chatting with Hunter each morning and afternoon. By doing so, she had allowed herself to imagine a flirtation existed between them. Further, those precious minutes were better spent kneading dough, mixing ingredients or otherwise preparing the bakery to receive customers. She also decided she and Pearl needn't be so chatty: they could increase their productivity if they spent less time jabbering and more time baking.

As efficient as Ivy was at boxing the customers' selections for them, Faith still had to be present to ring up their purchases, which disrupted her afternoon baking. Recalling that Hunter told her Ruth thought Ivy needed more challenges, Faith wondered if she could assign Ivy some light baking responsibilities. She expected since Ivy was excellent with numbers, she'd have no problem with measurements and following the sequence of a recipe, once she committed it to memory. It was worth a try.

By the time she arrived at the bakery, Faith was trembling with cold and excitement. The wedding was behind her: this was a new day and a fresh opportunity to apply herself to the undertaking that would bring her far greater contentment than if she had married Lawrence. She was certain of it.

A week after the wedding, Hunter crept up the back steps to the bakery, pausing before he rapped on the door. After each delivery, his legs, hips and back ached with an intensity he hadn't experienced since immediately following the accident. The night before, he'd suffered through a particularly sleepless night, and his left leg was buzzing with pain.

"*Guder mariye*, Pearl," he said when the elder woman opened the door. "I didn't expect to see you here already."

"Faith asked me to arrive early. She wants—I mean, *we* want—to increase the festival sales even more," Pearl explained, wiping the back of her hand across her brow.

"If you don't mind my saying so, Pearl, you look as if you could use a cup of *kaffi*," Hunter hinted. "I know I could."

Faith bustled into the room from the storefront. "I thought I heard you gabbing with someone," she said to Pearl. "*Guder mariye*, Hunter."

"We were hardly gabbing," Pearl replied, clearly bristling. "We were just commenting about how we need a cup of *kaffi*. I'll put a pot on."

"But that will take—"

"It will only take a few minutes," Pearl interrupted. "And while it's brewing, I'll wrap the last of the gingerbread cookies—rather, the gingerbread *men* for Hunter to take with him."

Ever since the wedding, Hunter sensed Faith was rushing him out the door. Gone was her customary smile and garrulous greeting. Instead, she barely glanced up long enough to load his arms with stacks of boxed goodies. At first, he wondered if he'd done something to offend her, but now that he observed how blunt she was being with Pearl, he realized it was more likely she was tense about her looming financial deadline. Realizing Faith was trying to be as efficient as possible, Hunter suddenly wished he hadn't indicated he wanted coffee. He would have preferred getting on the road to staying in the high-tension environment, especially when he was already on edge from his physical condition.

"Pearl thinks I shouldn't have changed the gingerbread cookies' shapes from circles into gingerbread men," Faith explained, rapidly tying a clear plastic bag with a bright red ribbon. She held it up, displaying its contents: half a dozen gingerbread men, each with white frosting squiggles on their arms and legs, three red dots for buttons, a green bow tie and a smiley face with two eyes. "Although the *Ordnung* doesn't forbid them, Pearl thinks they look like graven images."

"That's not what I said," Pearl clarified. "I said I wouldn't want the *Englisch* to *think* they look like graven images and accuse us of hypocrisy just to sell cookies, since they know we don't allow our *kinner* to own dolls with faces."

Feeling as if his lower back were being prodded with a burning poker, Hunter shifted his stance. "Either way, I'm sure they taste the same," he said diplomatically.

"That's just it—they don't taste the same," Pearl contended. "The round ones are softer. The flatter ginger-bread men go brittle enough to crack your teeth in a day."

"Ha!" scoffed Faith. "She's exaggerating. Besides, we make these fresh every morning. It's not our business if the customers keep them in their cupboards for a week. Don't you think the cookies will sell better if they look a bit more festive, Hunter?"

"Er," he stammered. This argument was between Pearl and Faith and he didn't want to give his opinion on the topic, but since Faith pressed him, he answered, "They've sold out nearly every day as they were, so…"

"That's exactly what I said!" Pearl tossed her hands in the air.

"*Jah*, but this way, we'll sell even more of them, which is why I've doubled the amount I'm sending with you, Hunter. They're bigger, so I'm increasing the price, too," Faith reasoned. "But you'll have to be extra careful trans-porting them, so their arms and legs don't break off."

"Yet another reason the round cookies are more prac-tical," Pearl mumbled as she handed Hunter his coffee.

"*Denki,*" he quietly thanked her.

"Here, let me carry some of these boxes to the buggy," Faith offered, hinting he should be on his way.

"*Neh*, I'll make a couple trips. I don't want to take you away from your baking." Hunter winced as he took a few steps toward the boxes.

"I'll help you," Pearl insisted, and the look on her face indicated neither Faith nor Hunter should challenge her offer.

When they were outside, Pearl questioned whether he was feeling alright. "Your posture seems a little…a little crooked," she noticed.

"I must have slept funny last night," he said.

"You'd better turn in early tonight, then," Pearl lectured kindly. "I'm only now experiencing how imperative it is to get a *gut* night's rest. I'm afraid I'm in a miserable mood without it—and so is our friend Faith."

Despite how uncharacteristically gruff Faith had been, Hunter defended her. "She does seem high-strung, but I imagine she's preoccupied with making the lease down payment."

In the light cast by the open bakery door, Hunter noticed Pearl was arching her eyebrow curiously at him. "That's probably true," she said. "She's blessed to have a young man like you to support her."

I'd do almost anything for Faith. The thought instantly flitted through Hunter's mind, but he couldn't let Pearl assume his support was based on anything other than a business partnership.

"I know she feels blessed to have such a loyal friend and staff member as you, too," he replied. "As for me, I'm glad to have the extra work and she pays me well, but I'd better get going before she changes her mind."

"Be careful," Pearl cautioned. "The roads are slick, and the *Englisch* aren't always aware of the black ice."

Hunter nodded. "I'll see you in the afternoon."

By the time Ivy and Pearl switched stores at three o'clock, Pearl's energy seemed to have returned. Hunter's, however, was flagging. The pain in his back was so exacting it took all of his stamina simply to place one foot in front of the other to limp down Main Street to the hitching post to retrieve his horse and buggy.

"Hunter!" Faith cheered when he shuffled through the back entrance. "Guess what? Marianne Palmer is having an impromptu neighborhood party and she's asked me to bake pear cake and plum pudding. She's also purchasing six dozen of the gingerbread men for all the *kinner*!"

"That's *wunderbaar*," he acknowledged.

"*Jah*, but there's one little catch. The party is tonight and she asked if we could deliver the goodies to her house since she has to do some last-minute decorating and her husband is out of town. I told her I'd check with you first. After you return from the festival, could you make a second delivery of the cakes? You'd receive double pay, of course."

Hunter's back was causing him such agony that the extra salary held little appeal; all he wanted was to get home and soak in a hot bath. But when he saw the hopeful look in Faith's sparkling eyes, he couldn't say no.

"*Jah*, I'll stop in for Marianne's goods when I get back from Piney Hill," he promised.

Faith didn't tell Hunter she'd already prepared the cakes and begun steaming the puddings for Marianne. It was a risk, but Faith knew she could count on Hunter. She figured if he couldn't make the delivery for some reason, she'd negotiate another arrangement, since she speculated if Marianne was pressed, the woman would find a way to pick up her items in person. If Marianne refused, Faith would have had no choice but to add them to the display case for other customers to buy. But thanks to Hunter's dependability, it hadn't come to that.

With Marianne's order tended to, Faith slid an applesauce cake into the oven. Then, while Ivy helped the steady stream of customers make selections and boxed their goodies for them, Faith devoted herself to ringing up their purchases. After half an hour or so, there was enough of a lull for Faith to lay out the ingredients for Ivy to begin making gingerbread cookies. Since Ivy struggled with manual dexterity, Faith would have to assist when it came time to use the cookie cutter, but Faith figured it would be helpful if Ivy got a start on the dough. She had just finished reviewing the instructions with her when the bell on the front door jangled.

"*Guder nammidaag*, Faith," Isaac Miller greeted her. "I don't see any bread on the shelves, which means you must be holding some for me in the back."

As a widowed man with three small children, Isaac was one of the few Amish customers who depended on Faith's bakery for his bread supply. He stopped in at the end of the day on Tuesdays, Thursdays and Saturdays to purchase two or three loaves of bread. If Faith or Pearl noticed they were running low or Isaac was later than usual, they set a couple of loaves aside for him. But today had been so busy and Faith was distracted by Marianne's last-minute order.

"Ach! I'm sorry, Isaac," she apologized. "I got so caught up in my *Grischtdaag* orders, I entirely forgot."

"Your *Grischtdaag* orders?" Isaac repeated blankly.

Faith was embarrassed, knowing how weak her excuse sounded to an Amish man with three hungry children to feed.

"I'm sorry, Isaac. Let me at least wrap some gingerbread cookies for the *kinner*—no charge," she offered.

"*Neh.* I'd prefer they didn't have sweets today, since I'll have to stop at the *Englisch* grocery store for bread and that has enough sugar in it to last them a week."

"Oh, okay," Faith uttered. "See you on Saturday, then."

Isaac lifted his hand in a halfhearted wave. No sooner had the door shut behind him than Ivy's piercing wail sounded from the kitchen, followed by a terrible racket.

The puddings! Faith panicked.

But no, Ivy was standing near the open oven, not by the pudding molds. At her feet, the large applesauce cake Faith had been baking was overturned, and a dishcloth lay next to the crumbly mess. Tears streamed down the girl's face as the timer on the back of the oven buzzed loudly.

Faith gasped. "Ivy, are you alright? What happened?"

Ivy pulled away, hiding her hand behind her back.

"Did you burn yourself? Let me have a look," Faith insisted.

The girl slowly opened her fist, allowing Faith to examine her skin.

"It doesn't look that bad." Faith sighed. "Let's run it under cold water, shall we?"

"I did it the way you did it," Ivy sobbed. "When I took the cake out of the oven, I used the dish cloth so I wouldn't burn myself."

"But Ivy, that cloth was wet. You can't use a wet cloth to retrieve a pan from the oven. That's why you burned your hand," Faith explained, a hint of exasperation in her voice.

"I'm sorry!" Ivy howled louder.

Faith pressed her lips together and counted to five. "It's okay, Ivy. You didn't know. It's not your fault. Please stop crying."

She wrapped her arms around her petite friend and hummed a hymn they'd sung together at Thanksgiving. Soon the young woman's sobs turned into sniffles. Finally, Ivy raised her head from Faith's shoulder and stated, "I need to add one-half of a cup of molasses next."

"Okay, Ivy. You finish mixing the cookie ingredients while I sweep up the cake," Faith instructed.

As she bent to clean the floor, Faith mentally calcu-
lated how much money the wasted cake would have gar-
nered in sales. She was immediately ashamed of herself,
and her hands trembled as she lifted the dustbin. As re-
grettable as it was the cake had gone to ruin, she was
relieved no harm had come to Ivy. Faith hadn't realized
how closely Ivy watched her. From now on, she'd have
to remember to use pot holders and avoid other short-
cuts she took as an experienced baker. And she'd have to
limit Ivy's responsibilities to helping customers, even if
it meant Faith might fall behind with the baking.

When Ivy left for the evening, Faith sent half a dozen
warm gingerbread men cookies with her, saying, "Your
groossdaadi will be very impressed you made these."

By that time, Faith had placed another applesauce
cake in the oven and was carefully crating the plum pudding and pear cakes for Hunter to deliver to the Palmers' house. Usually he was back long before five, and
she wondered what was keeping him. The day had been
trying enough with Pearl's complaints and Ivy's mishap;
the last thing she wanted was for Hunter to be late with
the Palmer delivery.

"There you are!" she exclaimed when he knocked on
the door several minutes later. "I was beginning to worry
you'd changed your mind and decided to head home for
the night instead."

"I gave you my word, so here I am," Hunter replied
curtly. "Are these the boxes?"

"Jah," Faith acknowledged. She had only been joking,
but judging from Hunter's austere demeanor, she sensed
she'd offended him. Trying to make up for it, she offered,
"Would you like a cup of *kaffi* before you get back in the
buggy? I have some sweet rolls—"

"*Neh*, the roads are icy and I've seen several *Englisch* cars spin out. Rush hour is peaking and I want to make this delivery and get home as soon as I can," he said as he lifted a crate.

"Alright, well, you must be very careful," Faith advised as she held the door for him.

"Don't worry, I have a system for stacking these," Hunter said. "Nothing will get ruined or broken along the way."

Faith had been referring to his safety, not to her baked goods, but he was in too much of a hurry for her to elaborate. After he departed, she tarried on the back doorstep, allowing the sleet to pelt her upturned face as she wondered what Henrietta was fixing for supper that night. Ducking into the bakery, she buttered a roll and poured herself a cup of lukewarm coffee before washing the trays and wrapping the baked goods for the next day.

It was nearly seven o'clock by the time Faith began bicycling toward home. Because she'd never replaced it, the battery in her headlamp was completely depleted and the moon was obscured by clouds. The road was so slick she had to keep dismounting to push the heavy bike along the slipperiest stretches of pavement. Faith knew her sister-in-law would have an opinion about her tardiness, but she didn't want to jeopardize her safety by taking unnecessary chances. Ivy's burn, however slight, served to warn Faith against reckless behavior.

She'd just pushed her bicycle over the crest of a hill when she heard a horse whinnying and shifting its hooves restlessly against the hard pavement. Faith spied the flashers and headlights of a buggy halted on the opposite side of the road, but she didn't see anyone in the front seat. She dropped her bike and darted toward the carriage, thumping on its exterior frame with her gloved hand. "Hello? Hello? Is someone in there?" she questioned.

"Jah," a man groaned. "I'm in the backseat."

Faith's stomach dropped and her legs went squishy. Although the man's voice was distorted by pain, Faith recognized it immediately. "Hunter!" she cried. "It's me, Faith!"

Hunter felt the buggy shift slightly as Faith climbed inside, and the minor movement caused his lower spine to vibrate with pain.

"Please," he pleaded, "Don't jostle me. I'm… I'm injured."

"Where does it hurt? Tell me what happened!" she pleaded. Her voice was above him now, and although he couldn't see her features in the dim light, her tone conveyed both authority and alarm.

Hunter was in too much misery to detail how, on the return trip from Marianne Palmer's, he thought he heard something slide off the seat behind him. Concerned he'd forgotten to bring one of Faith's boxes into the house, he stopped the horse, set the parking brake and reached into the back of the carriage. When he initially failed to locate anything amiss, he stretched farther, triggering a spasm in the small of his back that was so acute he lost his balance and toppled over the seat, knocking the back of his head when he landed faceup on the floor. Wedged there for at least fifteen minutes, he was writhing in agony when Faith happened upon him.

Light-headed, he could only utter, "My back. I fell and hurt my back. I can't feel my leg."

"Are you bleeding?"

"Neh. Just in pain."

Hunter could barely make sense of Faith's movements overhead as she bit the tip of her glove and pulled her fingers free. Pressing her bare hand to the side of his face, she murmured, "Cold and clammy." Then she unwound her shawl and spread it over his chest, tucking it in behind his shoulders.

"Don't worry," she consoled him. "I'm going to run to the phone shanty and call an ambulance. I'll be right back."

"*Neh!*" Hunter roared as another wave of pain coursed through his spine. "No ambulance. Too expensive."

"Hunter, don't be *lecherich*!" Faith argued, calling him ridiculous. "You need medical help and you need it now. There's a medical center in Highland Springs—"

Hunter used his free hand to grab her wrist. "No ambulance," he insisted. "You take me. In this weather, it's safer with a horse and buggy. You take me."

"But Hunter—"

"It's quicker. You take me," he demanded, too afflicted to waste his breath with niceties.

"Okay, let go of my arm and I'll take you," she agreed.

"*Denki*, Faith," he said, and after he released her wrist, he broke out in feverish hilarity. "If you think I'm bad off, wait until you see the gingerbread men I landed on."

"Hush now," Faith instructed over her shoulder before calling for the horse to giddyap.

The buggy lurched forward unevenly, sending another jolt of pain through Hunter's body, and he gasped before passing out. When he came to, he could hear pellets of sleet riveting the roof of the buggy as Faith recited the twenty-third Psalm. In his delirium, he thought he might be dying and he worried about who would take care of his mother now—not that he'd done a very good job of fulfilling his father's final request. Remembering his dad's tortured expression as they lay side by side after the accident, Hunter began to sob.

"It's okay, we're almost there," Faith promised from the front seat. "Be strong for a few minutes longer, Hunter. You're going to be alright."

Hardly able to catch his breath, Hunter felt anything but strong, yet just as the pain escalated to a point he thought was beyond what he could endure, Faith announced, "We're here! *Denki*, Lord, *denki*. You made it, Hunter, we're here."

Though his eyes were closed, Hunter sensed the light brightening around him and he heard someone say, "This area is for ambulances only. You have to move your buggy immediately, miss."

"Not until you help my friend," Faith replied. "He's in the back. His leg is numb and I think he might have bumped his head. He's been in and out of consciousness all the way from Willow Creek. You must help him."

The buggy shifted as someone climbed aboard. Hunter squinted to see two men peering down at him.

"What's your name, son? Can you tell us your name?"

"Hunter Schwartz," he answered, tasting blood. In his torment he must have bitten the inside of his cheek.

"Hunter, we're going to get you out of here, but we have to stabilize your neck and back first, so we're going to secure you on a board that will help us carry you. It might be uncomfortable. Can you tell us what happened?"

"I was hit by a truck," he muttered feebly. He meant to convey it was his previous injury that was plaguing him, but he couldn't form the sentence.

"A truck hit you?" the man repeated. "Were you walking or in your buggy when it hit you?"

"Neh, neh." His head felt so fuzzy.

"Hunter? Hunter, stay with me," the man urged him. "How were you injured?"

"My *daed* died," he groaned, trying to make them understand. "Someone has to let my *mamm* know I'm here. If I'm late returning home, she'll worry that…"

But he passed out again before he could finish expressing the dreadful thought.

Chapter Nine

"Was there a fatality at the accident scene?" the medic asked as the men lifted the board Hunter was strapped to onto a gurney.

"What?" At the word *fatality*, Faith's heart pummeled her ribs even harder than it had during the harrowing journey to the hospital. "What accident scene?"

"Hunter said he was hit by a truck and his dad died."

"He was injured and his *daed* was killed when a truck struck their buggy, *jah*," Faith answered, following the men as they wheeled the gurney through the automatic doors of the emergency room entrance. "But that happened over a year ago. He must be confused—could it be from knocking his head?"

The two men met each other's eyes without answering her. "Is he on any meds?" one of them asked. "Any painkillers, herbal remedies, anything like that?"

"Why would he already be on painkillers? He just got here."

A nurse intercepted Faith by her shoulders as the medics briskly rolled the stretcher through another set of doors. "I'm afraid you can't go with them. The doctors will take good care of your friend."

"But I need to make sure he—"

"Look, hon, you're dripping wet," the nurse pointed out. "I'm going to get a thermal blanket for you to wrap yourself in and this young man is going to head outside to hitch your horse, right Tyler?"

A man wearing blue cotton scrubs smiled broadly at her. "If your mare is like my grandpa's, she won't like the sound of the ambulances, so I'll find a quiet, dry place to settle her, okay?"

"Jah," Faith agreed distractedly. Thinking aloud, she added, "I should… I should call the phone shanty. Or maybe Joseph Schrock is still at his shop. He usually stays late on Tuesday nights to do his accounting. I should call him so he can tell Hunter's *mamm* Hunter is here in the hospital."

"That's a good idea," the nurse said kindly, leading Faith to a room containing a small sofa, a row of chairs and an end table with a phone. "I'll be right back with the blanket."

"Denki," Faith automatically replied in *Deitsch.*

She dialed Joseph's number, praying, "Please, *Gott,* let him be there," as the phone rang one, two and then three times.

On the fourth ring Joseph picked up and Faith rushed her words so quickly he interrupted her, asking, "Who is this?"

A second time she explained Hunter's predicament. "I don't know what's wrong with him yet, but the nurse said he's in *gut* hands with the doctors, and we know he's in *Gott's* hands, so he's bound to be alright."

Even as Faith spoke, the phone quivered in her grasp.

With the exception of when her *mamm* had been in childbirth with her youngest brother, she'd never heard anyone cry out in pain as Hunter had done during their traumatic trip to the medical center. The only thing more disturbing than Hunter's wails puncturing the night air was when he'd fallen silent in the back of the buggy.

"I'll bring Iris to the hospital straightaway," Joseph suggested.

"Would you send someone to my house in the meantime, to let them know I'm alright?" she asked.

"Of course. I'm sure your absence has them very worried."

Faith wasn't as certain. She'd been working late recently; perhaps Henrietta would assume she was still filling orders at the bakery. Suddenly, Faith missed her family so much that she couldn't wait to kiss her nephews' pudgy cheeks and listen to her brothers' animated joshing at the supper table. More than anyone, Faith missed Henrietta, and she longed to confide to her sister-in-law about her grueling journey into Highland Springs.

While Faith didn't know exactly how Hunter had been injured, she surmised he never would have gotten hurt if she hadn't requested him to make a second delivery just to placate Marianne Palmer. As Faith sat in the deserted waiting room, she realized she not only had been pushing herself too hard lately, but she'd been pushing Pearl, Ivy and Hunter, too. She was filled with such regret that she would have begun blubbering on the spot if the nurse hadn't opened the door to deliver the blanket and a cup of hot tea.

"I'll let you know how Hunter is as soon as I hear from the doctors," she promised.

Despite the thermal blanket and warm drink, Faith

couldn't shake the chill that permeated her to the core. Shivering, she recalled the alarmed expressions on the medics' faces when she said Hunter was confused. Did they fear he had a concussion? Then she thought about how Hunter had said he couldn't feel his legs—didn't that indicate paralysis? What if his condition was permanent? What if he couldn't walk again? She'd never forgive herself. *Please, Lord, make Hunter well*, she prayed.

Over an hour later, her head was still bowed in prayer when Hunter's mother and Joseph Schrock entered the room. Faith leaped to her feet to embrace Iris, whose eyes were red-rimmed.

"We saw the nurse on the way in," Iris explained. "She told us Hunter is resting comfortably and we can visit him in a few minutes. *Denki* for bringing him here, Faith. Who knows what might have happened if you hadn't come along the road when you did?"

Still feeling guilty about Hunter's injuries, Faith was relieved when Reuben and Mason strode into the room and she didn't have to reply.

"Faith!" they exclaimed in unison and took turns enveloping her in bear hugs.

"Mason found your bike on the side of the road," Reuben explained. "We didn't know what to think, and Henrietta was frantic. When we went to town to look for you, we crossed paths with Joseph, who was heading to Ruth's house to bring Iris the news. Henrietta stayed behind to assist and comfort Ruth, but I think Ruth might be the one comforting Henrietta instead."

As Reuben finished speaking, the nurse pushed the door ajar. "We're keeping Hunter overnight for observation," she said. "The doctor will explain everything, but

Hunter is medicated and he needs to sleep, so we have to limit his visitors."

"May I stay the night?" Iris inquired.

"Of course," the nurse said. "But wouldn't you be more rested if you—"

"I'll stay the night," Iris repeated firmly.

"I'd like to stay with you," Faith offered. "If you don't mind."

"I'd appreciate that."

The men quickly made arrangements to take Ruth's buggy to her house and to return in the morning to transport Iris and Hunter home. Joseph promised he'd also stop at Pearl's house and ask her to mind the bakery for Faith the following morning.

"Tell her not to worry about doing any extra baking," Faith requested. "And please ask her to intercept Ivy from the cannery at nine o'clock sharp, otherwise the poor girl will become distraught."

"I'll be sure to pass along the message," Joseph agreed. "If there's anything else I can do to help with the bakery or the cannery, let me know."

"*Denki*, Joseph," Faith said, and then she turned to embrace her brothers. "I appreciate the two of you coming all this way, too. Please tell Henrietta I promise there will be no more late nights for me."

"You did well, Faith," Reuben whispered into her ear, giving her shoulder a squeeze. "You're a brave woman."

But when Faith opened the door to Hunter's room and glimpsed his ashen complexion against the backdrop of needles, wires and monitors, she felt as timid as a child.

Hunter couldn't lift his eyelids. The nurse informed him he might become drowsy from the medication, but he didn't expect to feel this wiped out. As his muscles re-laxed, he began to breathe easier, relieved of the anguish he'd endured for the past several hours.

"Hello, I'm Dr. Henderson," the physician at the end of his bed said to whomever just entered the room.

"I'm Iris Schwartz, Hunter's *mamm*," his mother replied. "And this is Faith."

Aha, so Faith must have notified his mother and aunt about his fall. While he was grateful his mother was aware he was alright, he wished Iris and Faith wouldn't see him in this state. To his increasing embarrassment, the doctor began providing the two women an explicit summary of Hunter's condition. Hunter tried to pro-test, but his thoughts were too addled and his mouth was too dry to speak. The doctor used words like *muscle inflammation*, *steroids* and *neuropathy*. Although he couldn't make sense of everything the physician was saying, Hunter understood the gist of it to mean his con-dition was due to his original accident. His lack of ongo-ing physical therapy combined with muscle overuse had caused his condition to worsen progressively.

"Reaching over the seat like he did was the straw that broke the camel's back, so to speak," the doctor said. Then he emphasized, "*Not* that Hunter's back is broken—that's the good news. Sometimes when we see symptoms like these, it's because a broken bone is exerting pres-sure on the nerves. But his X-rays look great. And other than an egg-sized bump on the back of his skull, I don't think there's any reason to be concerned about his head injury, either."

"So he'll be able to walk again?" Faith's voice was quavering.

"Absolutely," the doctor asserted. "In fact, the trick

will be to keep him from walking too far too soon. He needs to learn to pace himself."

After the doctor left, Hunter had to strain to hear Faith tell his mother, "I didn't know how badly he'd been hurt in the crash. I knew he lost his *daed*—your husband— in an accident, but I didn't realize Hunter sustained any permanent injuries."

My injuries are not *permanent!* Hunter felt like shouting.

"That's because he didn't want anyone to know," Iris confided. Hunter silently willed her to stop talking, but she continued. "My big, strong *suh*. He must have been in pain for so long, yet he never let on. I should have known. I'm his mother. I should have known my *kind* was in pain."

From the sound of his mother's sniffling, Hunter realized she was crying, and inwardly it made him cringe. Ordinarily, he might have regretted causing her such distress, but right now he only felt humiliated by her doting sentiments.

"It's not your fault, Iris," Faith argued. "If it's anyone's fault, it's mine. I asked him to make a second evening delivery. You heard what the doctor said about the straw that broke the camel's back. If it weren't for me—"

"Quiet!" Hunter finally managed to gasp. "You two are disrupting my sleep."

"Hunter, you're awake!" his mother declared, and suddenly she was brushing his curls from his forehead.

"I am now." He grimaced, his eyes still shut. "It's hard to sleep with you two clucking over me like worried hens."

"I'm sorry," Faith apologized. "I can go back to the waiting room."

"*Gut* idea, and take my *mamm* with you," he said.

At least he that's what he thought he said; maybe he only imagined saying it, or perhaps it was a dream. When he woke, he could hear the patter of sleet against the window and what he guessed was his mother's rhythmic breathing as she slept in a chair nearby. He fluttered his eyelids open, trying to adjust to the faint fluorescent light.

"Can I get you something?" Faith whispered, quickly appearing at his side.

His mouth was too dry to speak, so he shook his head.

Faith lowered a bent straw to his lips so he could sip the water she offered.

"Are you in pain?" she asked, her mouth so close to his ear he could feel her warm breath on his cheek.

"*Neh,*" he answered falsely and shut his eyes so he wouldn't have to face her concerned, pitying expression.

When he woke again, it was morning and his hips were burning with pain. As he tried to adopt a more comfortable position, he was appalled to notice the lower half of his white, atrophied leg had been exposed from the knee down as he slept. Flipping the flimsy blanket over it, he moaned from the small exertion.

Startled awake, his mother sat upright. "Hunter, dear, how do you feel?" she asked.

"His mouth is probably dry. He might need a sip of water before he can answer," Faith suggested, rushing to his bed with a cup and straw.

"I'm fine. Stop talking about me like I'm not here," Hunter barked in a scratchy voice.

Both women looked taken aback, which irritated him all the more, but before he could say anything else, there was a rapid knock on the door.

"*Kumme* in," his mother called.

A new, younger doctor introduced himself and asked Hunter how he was feeling this morning.

"Fair," Hunter responded grimly.

"I'm surprised you're doing that well," the doctor commented, as he perused Hunter's chart. "But, with physical therapy, I have every confidence you'll regain your full strength. It's going to take time and you'll have to limit certain activities, especially riding in your buggy or sitting and standing for long periods. And it's vital that you continue the regimen until you've completed your course of PT."

After the doctor left, Hunter scoffed, "He only wants me to go to more physical therapy because that's how the *Englisch* clinicians make their money."

"Hunter," his mother argued, "if physical therapy keeps you from being bedridden again, it's worth every penny."

Hunter was mortified his mother disclosed he'd previously been confined to bed.

"I don't want to discuss this in front of *her*," he said, motioning toward Faith with a jerk of his thumb. "The last thing I need is all of Main Street knowing my private business, whether it's about my health or our finances."

Faith's face immediately blotched with color. "*Neh*, of course not. I promise not to say a word to anyone and I'll give you two your privacy now. My brothers will be here shortly to take me to the bakery. When they arrive, I'll have them stop in to make arrangements for bringing you both home once you're discharged, too, if that's alright?"

Hunter turned his face and closed his eyes, but his mother answered, "*Jah*, we would appreciate that. *Denki*, Faith, for everything you've done."

* * *

Wrapped in the fresh, dry shawl Lovina sent for her, Faith was quiet as she journeyed in Mason's buggy to Willow Creek. The temperature had risen, melting the ice, and the wet roads glittered in the morning sunshine. As they flew past the same landmarks Faith had felt as if she'd never reach the night before, she fretted over Hunter's parting words.

Understanding that pain could bring out the worst in people and recalling how miserable she'd been after her own surgery, Faith tried to dismiss his sentiment and tone. But it stung that he wouldn't even look at her or say her name. Perhaps Hunter decided she was responsible for his hospitalization. She couldn't blame him if he did. Despite Iris's insistence Faith wasn't at fault, Faith was having a difficult time letting go of her guilt. She shouldn't have asked him to travel to Marianne Palmer's house in inclement weather.

But how could she have known making deliveries would exact such a toll on his physical health? He never mentioned his previous injuries or indicated any kind of struggle. It was only in retrospect Faith realized the source of Hunter's awkward posture and somber expression: he was suffering.

The last thing Faith intended to do was add to his hardship by giving information about his condition to anyone else. So, she made up her mind that when the *leit* asked her questions about his health—and they *would* ask, because they truly cared for each other—she'd refer them to him. She'd guard his secret as fiercely as if it were her own, and eventually he'd understand how trustworthy she was.

"It's out of the way, but could we stop at Ruth's?" Faith

asked as they neared Main Street. "I'd like to update her and say hello to Henrietta before going to the bakery."

Mason waited in the buggy while Faith went inside, where the two women were sipping tea in the kitchen.

"Faith!" Henrietta exclaimed, flinging her arms around her sister-in-law. Faith hugged her back.

Then, with characteristic candor, Henrietta pulled away and said, "I hope Hunter is doing better than you are. You look exhausted."

"As soon as I have a cup of *kaffi*, I'll be wide awake. As for Hunter, I believe he'll be home this afternoon, so he can tell you himself how he feels. I stopped to see if there's anything either of you needs before I go to work."

"That was thoughtful," Henrietta remarked. "But we're as snug as can be. Don't tell Lovina this, since she's at home watching my *kinner* as well as her own, but once we were assured you and Hunter were alright, it was very peaceful spending the night here. I didn't anticipate how much I'll enjoy visiting you at your apartment when you move, Faith."

Ruth added, "*Jah*, but unlike me, Faith will have plenty of delicious treats on hand to offer you, such as apple fry pies. We've had to make do with sweet bread and honey."

Now that Hunter can't deliver my goodies to Piney Hill, I doubt I'll be moving into the apartment or even making delicious treats much longer, Faith thought. But she forced herself to smile. Before leaving, Faith told Henrietta she'd be home for supper, since Mason had brought her bicycle with them for her return trip.

Just as she expected, when she arrived at the bakery Pearl peppered Faith with questions about Hunter.

"Whatever happened to our dear boy?" she asked before Faith crossed the threshold of the back entrance. "I knew something was wrong, but when I asked him he told me he was fine. What did the doctors say is the matter with him?"

Again, Faith felt overwhelmed by guilt. If she hadn't been so preoccupied with her own financial worries, might she have noticed Hunter was in no condition to go to the Palmers' house?

"I don't know the correct terms for his condition, Pearl," Faith answered truthfully. "But when he's out of the hospital, you can ask him. Meanwhile, Ruth said the cannery should remain closed."

At that, Ivy emerged from the storefront. "Hunter Schwartz is in the hospital. The cannery sign says Closed. I will work here until the cannery sign says Open," she stated definitively.

Pearl raised an eyebrow at Faith. "It would allow one of us to dedicate ourselves to baking," the older woman suggested.

It would also cost Faith more money in salaries. But now that she likely wasn't going to meet her financial goal anyway, what did it really matter if she paid Ivy for a few extra hours? Faith knew Ivy would be at a loss without a daily routine to follow, just like she was the week the cannery was closed after Ruth's fall. Besides, Ivy provided a beneficial service to holiday shoppers: with her help in the storefront, the line would continue to move quickly.

"We'd welcome your help until Hunter reopens the cannery, Ivy," Faith said. "But no more baking for you—I don't want you to burn yourself again. And it's very important you don't tell customers or anyone else that Hunter went to the hospital."

"No more baking," Ivy agreed, before returning to

the storefront. "And I won't tell anyone Hunter Schwartz went to the hospital."

"As for you and me," Faith said to Pearl, "how about if I focus on filling orders, if you don't mind managing the register for Ivy?"

"Of course. When it's slow, I'll give you a hand in the back."

"*Neh*, when it's slow, you can take a break. You deserve one. I'll keep up with the orders the best as I can, but if we have to turn some away, then we'll do that. It's not worth…not worth an accident or any tension between us, Pearl," Faith replied, her voice warbling.

Pearl waved her hand, saying, "It's okay."

"*Neh*, it's not okay. My behavior to you recently has been unacceptable. You're not just an employee here, you're my friend and I'm very sorry I acted so demanding after everything you've done to support me."

"It's okay," Pearl repeated. "I understand why you've been so tense. I'm sorry, too, for carrying on as I did. Sometimes I can be a bit stuck in my ways."

"*Neh*, you were right. The gingerbread men *are* crunchier than the round cookies and they break far too easily." Remembering how Hunter joked about landing on the box of gingerbread men in the backseat of the buggy, and imagining his pain, Faith burst into tears.

Pearl handed her a handkerchief and then patted her back. "There, there. You must have had a terrible fright. But Hunter's alright now. You'll see. Everything's going to be just fine."

Everything was going to be just fine? Knowing what she did about Hunter's injuries, the last words he'd spoken to her, the status of their deliveries and the uncertainty of her future, Faith thought Pearl's words sounded like a hollow promise, but she lifted her head and dried her tears.

"Enough of my sniveling," she announced. "I should get to work—but first I think I'll have a cream-filled doughnut. I'm famished."

"I don't need your help," Hunter snapped. "I need my privacy."

The nurse scowled but said nothing. Hunter knew she probably thought because he was an Amish man, he was too modest to have a female nurse help him with his morning routine, and it was true, he was. But it was more than mere modesty that kept him from accepting her assistance—it was independence. He didn't need help with his clothes, nor did he need to drink from a straw, like a baby from a bottle. What he needed was to have the room to himself so he could get ready to go home.

However, once the nurse vacated the room, Hunter became heady as he tried to stand. He sat back down and waited for the room to stop spinning so he could put on the clean clothes Mason Yoder had brought him. Unable to bend at his waist, he decided to forgo wearing socks altogether. But as he attempted to wiggle his foot into his boot, his lower back was seized by a cramp that was so excruciating he stumbled forward. The male nurse, Tyler, burst through the door and caught him just in time. He assisted Hunter with his socks as well as his boots, and then briefly left, returning a minute later with a wheelchair and a cane.

"This is your new best friend for the next several weeks," he quipped, displaying the dark wooden stick with rubber padding on the handle and tip. "You'll need to lean on it whenever you walk. Unless, of course, you're out with your girlfriend, in which case, you've got the perfect excuse to hold her hand."

It annoyed Hunter how brazen the *Englisch* were about discussing personal relationships. "I don't have a girlfriend," he snapped. *And if I ever had a chance of courting Faith, it's gone now.*

"Faith isn't your girlfriend? Oh, man, that's too bad," Tyler replied, shaking his head. "She was so concerned about you I assumed you two were a couple. Anyway, here you go, it's all yours."

When Tyler pushed the stick toward him, Hunter shook his head and muttered, "Canes are for old men."

Tyler shrugged. "It's up to you if you take it or not. But I guarantee if you don't, you're going to fall and end up more miserable than you are right now."

Hunter eyed the young, brawny *Englisch* man who appeared to be the picture of health. "What would you know about falling?" he challenged. "Or about being miserable?"

"Plenty. I broke my leg in a motorcycle accident when I was eighteen," Tyler said. "But I was like you—too stubborn for my own good. Afterward, I refused to use a cane and one day I wiped out on a crack in a concrete sidewalk. A sidewalk! I ended up in traction."

Glowering, Hunter snatched the cane from Tyler's outstretched hand. Leveraging his weight against it, he transitioned from the bed to the wheelchair, and then the nurse wheeled him to the front entrance while his mother followed behind.

"What's this?" Hunter asked when a taxi pulled to the curb in front of them. "Where's our buggy? Faith brought me here in our buggy."

"One of the Yoder brothers took it home for us. The

weather was bad overnight and the horse needed to be fed and sheltered. The hospital arranged for your transportation home because they wanted you to be comfortable. It's all paid for, too," his mother explained. "Wasn't that generous?"

"We don't need charity from the *Englisch*," Hunter snapped. "It's bad enough we have to take it from the Amish *leit*."

As if apologizing for a temperamental child's behavior, Hunter's mother whispered to Tyler, "I'm so sorry. I don't know what's gotten into him."

"I do," Tyler said, directing his encouragement at Hunter. "But it will pass, trust me."

Ignoring him, Hunter used the arms of the wheelchair to push himself into a standing position. "Ach!" he hollered in anguish and frustration as he teetered.

Tyler dived forward to steady him. "Remember your new best friend," he reproached, placing the cane across Hunter's knees once he was safely situated in the backseat. "You need to lean on this everywhere you go. Unless you wise up and ask a pretty redhead to hold your hand."

Tyler closed the door and then he escorted Hunter's mother to the other side of the vehicle, and Iris slid into the seat next to her son. Because traveling by car made his mother nervous, Hunter usually tried to distract her with small talk, but today he was too physically and emotionally depleted to do anything other than stare out the window.

As they sped along the Pennsylvania countryside, Hunter was reminded of the van trip that brought them to Willow Creek a month ago. Suddenly he realized he was back to square one in regard to his finances—and maybe he was even worse off than before he began working for Faith. His earnings from the deliveries wouldn't cover the cost of his hospital stay, and he was more annoyed than comforted by his suspicion Ruth would insist on contributing to his bills. Hunter had journeyed to Willow Creek specifically to assist her; instead, he was becoming a burden. Not only was he failing to keep his aunt's cannery running smoothly, but he was failing to support himself and his mother, and he was failing to help Faith support herself, too. If he didn't get back on his feet again soon and accomplish what he'd set out to do, those failures would be more painful to him than his injuries ever were.

Chapter Ten

By Saturday afternoon, Faith was worried. She hadn't heard a word about Hunter's condition since she'd left the hospital. She stopped in at Schrock's Shop on Friday because she knew Joseph had gone to see Hunter on Thursday, but all Joseph said was Hunter was asleep when he visited. Torn between wanting to respect Hunter's privacy and wanting to offer support, Faith decided she'd wait until Monday, and if she hadn't heard anything by then, she'd visit Ruth's household with some treats.

Saturday evening was the first opportunity she had to examine her bookkeeping to assess whether she could still meet her financial goal. After putting the supper dishes away, she opened her ledger at the kitchen table. Hunter had organized her accounts so fastidiously that Faith had no trouble working out the figures now. She marveled that she'd actually profited more in the past several weeks than in the previous several months combined. However, she estimated she was still at least $600 short of making the down payment on the lease. She calculated she could net up to $250 before the year's end, but even that would be a stretch, especially now that she wasn't baking for the festival and she had Ivy's full-time salary to pay.

Faith crossed her arms on top of the paperwork and buried her head in them. The future she planned was gone. It was time for her to give up. She had to accept that owning a business apparently wasn't God's will for her.

"Faith?" Henrietta asked. Faith hadn't heard her come in. "What's wrong?"

"I can't do it." She sniffed and raised her head. "I can't make the lease down payment. I have until January 1 to close the bakery, move my things out and tell Pearl she doesn't have a job anymore."

"But you've literally worn yourself to the bone trying to accomplish your goal. Look at your dress," Henrietta said, pinching the excess fabric where it hung loosely around Faith's waist. "You've worked too hard to lose your business."

"Apparently, I didn't work hard enough."

"Sometimes, hard work isn't what you need—what you need is graciousness." Henrietta announced, "That's why Noah and I decided we want to give you a loan of up to five hundred dollars."

"What?" Faith was incredulous. "But I thought you didn't want me to move away from the farm!"

"I don't," admitted Henrietta. "Because I'll miss you. Don't you know that? I have a special bond with you that I don't share with anyone else, not with Lovina, not even with Willa. But I can't allow my selfish desires to interfere with *Gott's* plan for your life."

Touched by her sister-in-law's generosity, Faith swallowed, suppressing a sob. "Henrietta, I don't know what to say."

"Say you'll accept the loan. And promise me I'll be the first person you have over for tea."

"I promise." Faith giggled, throwing her arms around her sister-in-law's shoulders. "Just don't tell Andy—he thinks he's coming over for peanut butter sheet cake the first day I move in."

As she lay in bed that night, Faith imagined how euphoric Pearl would be to hear about the loan. Ivy would be glad, as well. But the person Faith was most eager to tell was Hunter. Were it not for his partnership, she never would have come so close to meeting her goal. She fell asleep picturing his smile when she told him the great news.

The next morning she woke to her nephews' jubilant cheers: overnight Willow Creek had been transformed by a glittering snowfall. The little boys' wonderment and the scintillating landscape enhanced Faith's joy about the loan and her anticipation about seeing Hunter again.

"*Ant* Faith," Andy beckoned. "*Daed* said he'd take us sledding by Wheeler's Bridge. Will you *kumme*, too?"

Faith couldn't resist. "*Jah*, of course. I'll ask your *daed* if we can stop to see if the Miller *kinner* want to join us, too. I brought something home from the bakery I was planning to give them anyway."

Isaac Miller was delighted to accept the two loaves of bread and jar of preserves Faith brought him by way of apology, and his children were even happier to join Faith's nephews sledding on the big hill.

"I'll stand at the bottom to make sure the *kinner* don't veer toward the pond," Reuben informed her. "The surface is frozen, but with the snow cover, I can't assess how thick the ice is underneath. I wouldn't want them to fall through."

Faith remained at the top of the hill, aligning the children on their sleds before giving them running pushes. She whooped and clapped as they careened down the long, gradual descent, shrieking and shouting all the way to the bottom.

"I don't know who's having more fun, you or the *kinner*," a soft voice said behind her.

"Iris, hello!" Faith trilled. "I've been thinking of you and Ruth, and praying for Hunter. How is he?"

"He's doing better physically," Iris said. "But I'm afraid his mood is no better than what you experienced at the hospital."

Faith loosened her scarf around her mouth. "I was in the hospital once," she confided. "And for about a week after I was discharged, I was so dismal I think everyone in my family wanted to send me back."

Iris laughed. "*Jah*, I figured since I couldn't tell him to go take a walk, I'd take one myself."

"May I visit him?" Faith asked. "I have news that might cheer him up."

Iris's face clouded over. "I don't know if that would be a *gut* idea right now," she said.

Faith didn't wish to exacerbate Iris's stress. "I understand. How about if I send a quick note? Henrietta keeps a pen and paper in the buggy. I'll walk back that way with you."

Faith signaled Reuben at the bottom of the hill, where the children were lobbing snowballs at him. "I'll be right back," she called. He gave her a thumbs-up signal before scooping a heap of snow to toss in the children's direction.

Iris smiled. "Hunter always enjoyed his exploits with your brothers when he was little. He'd come home and announce that when he became a *daed*, he was going to have at least six *kinner*. He thought it was great the Yoder boys had so many brothers."

Ignoring the barb of resentment she felt whenever the subject of large families came up, Faith drolly replied, "Spoken like someone who never had to wait his turn for the washroom."

"Or keep the floors clean with six boys tromping through the house!" Iris declared, and the two women didn't stop laughing until they reached the buggy.

Hunter, Faith wrote on a small square of paper she ripped from the bottom of Henrietta's grocery list, *I pray you are doing better each day. I look forward to seeing you when you're ready for company. Meanwhile, I have exciting news I couldn't wait to share: Reuben and Henrietta are providing me a loan—I get to keep the bakery!* Deciding she couldn't adequately express her appreciation for Hunter's help on the tiny scrap of paper, Faith concluded by simply signing her name. She'd thank him in person later.

As she watched Iris trudge through the snow to Ruth's house, it occurred to Faith that Hunter's mother probably wanted to have more children as much as Hunter wanted to have a sibling. *We don't always get what we want*, Faith reminded herself, just as she'd done the morning she hired Hunter. Back then, what she desired more than anything was to keep her bakery. And now, because of God's abundant blessing, through hard work and help from Pearl, Hunter and her family, Faith's business was secure. She had gotten exactly what she wanted, and she was grateful.

So then, what was this yearning still gnawing at her

heart? And why, as she plodded back toward the children, did she suddenly feel more like weeping than laughing?

Because the snowfall made the ground especially slippery, Hunter secluded himself in his room for most of Sunday afternoon. He was practicing walking without a cane when Ruth called to him, so he picked up the stick again and toddled into the parlor.

Back from her stroll, his mother was warming her hands by the stove. "There's something your *ant* and I want to discuss with you," she said. "Do you need help sitting down?"

"*Neh*, I can manage." Hunter eased his body onto the sofa with the aid of his cane. "I've grown accustomed to using this stick. I think if I stand on a milking stool, I can maneuver myself into the buggy, so I should be able to go to town tomorrow to reopen the cannery."

"That's what I want to discuss," Ruth replied. "To be candid, I've decided not to renew the lease on the cannery next year, and since you're still recovering and we haven't continued to put up jars for the holiday season, there's no sense reopening the shop. Instead, I'll talk to Faith about stocking a few items on a shelf in her bakery. Now that her business is booming, I anticipate she'll be glad to keep Ivy on permanently, provided she's able to make her down payment."

If Hunter hadn't already been seated, the magnitude of his aunt's announcement would have knocked him flat. "I don't understand. You've run the cannery for years."

"*Jah*, but the doctor told me it's time to slow down. While I'm not ready to be put out to pasture quite yet, I do have other undertakings I'd like to focus on at home and in our community."

Hunter narrowed his eyes. It wasn't like Ruth to take an *Englischer's* advice, even if he was a doctor. Why hadn't she consulted Hunter about the decision? Then he realized *he* was the reason she was closing shop. She probably thought he'd fallen so far behind on the sales it wasn't worth the effort to catch up. "I'm sorry, *Ant* Ruth. I know I've disappointed you," Hunter apologized. "But if you give me another chance—"

Ruth cut him off. "How have you disappointed me? By injuring yourself because you were working so hard? If I had compensated you, as I should have insisted on doing, you never would have taken a second job," she railed. "*You* disappointed *me*? Ha! You've seen my books. You know the business is doing fine. You, however, are *not* doing fine. Anyone can see that."

"*Neh*, really, I'm—"

"Hush up and listen to your old *ant*, because there's something else I need to tell you," she warned, pointing a finger at Hunter. "Since I already set aside the down payment for next year's lease, I want you and your *mamm* to have it. It will cover any outstanding bills you have in Parkersville, and it should help with your physical therapy costs, too."

Hunter grimaced and adjusted his posture. "*Denki*, that's very generous of you, *Ant* Ruth, but it isn't necessary."

Before his aunt could reply, Iris firmly stated, "*Suh*, I believe it *is* necessary. I appreciate that you've tried to protect me from worrying about our mortgage payments, but I'm aware the bills must be stacking up. Ruth and I discussed the matter earlier and I believe we should gratefully accept her gift to us. As far as the cannery goes, it's up to Ruth to determine what to do with her business, and I know you'll respect whatever she decides."

Hunter's shoulders stiffened and he clamped his jaw shut. So, the two of them had made up their minds without so much as considering his opinion first. He felt so disregarded he could hardly look at them. "I should tend to the animals," he said flatly.

"Ach! I forgot," his mother remarked as he was pulling himself to his feet. "I saw Faith by Wheeler's Bridge when I went for my walk. She asked me to give you this." She handed him a folded square of paper.

Faith. Of course! She probably wanted to know when he could resume making deliveries. As Hunter shambled toward the stable, he was struck with a plan. The doctor didn't *prohibit* him from riding in the buggy; he just advised him to limit the length of his journeys. Hunter figured without the cannery to manage, he could take his time running Faith's deliveries, stopping to stretch his muscles along the way. Perhaps he could even make a few additional deliveries to local customers.

As he hobbled toward the stable, Hunter's mood brightened. There was still a way to help Faith meet her goal. There was still time to prove that Ruth's gift wasn't necessary, and that Hunter could take care of his mother, just as his father trusted him to do. And there was still hope that maybe he'd be able to support a wife and family of his own one day, too.

When he reached the outer building, Hunter unfolded the piece of paper. The dusky light glowed enough for him to read Faith's message. After his behavior in the hospital, Hunter wouldn't have been surprised if she wanted to keep her distance, so he smiled to read she was eager to see him again. But his optimism plummeted with her words; *Reuben and Henrietta are providing me a loan.* Apparently, his services were no longer required.

First his aunt and mother, and now Faith had lost confidence in his abilities. Even though he hadn't given up on helping them, they'd given up on him. And why wouldn't they? He disappointed them when they needed him most. He felt so hurt, angry and ashamed that he whacked his cane against a post—once, twice, three times before it split in half—rendering it just as broken and useless as he was.

Although Faith didn't receive a visit from Hunter on Monday as she had hoped, early Tuesday morning, she heard someone drumming the back door. "Hunter!" she exclaimed as she unbolted the lock.

"*Neh*, it's me, Joseph Schrock."

Faith wiped the back of her hand against her brow to conceal her embarrassment. "*Guder mariye*, Joseph. Please *kumme* in. I'll pour you a cup of *kaffi*."

"*Denki*, but I can't stay. I came to town early this morning to prepare for the rush of *Englisch* holiday shoppers. Last night Amity and I paid a visit to Ruth Graber's household, and I was asked to give you this."

Faith was so eager to read the note Joseph presented her she didn't even inquire about Hunter's condition. When Joseph departed, she tore open the envelope.

Dear Faith, the message read. Faith recognized the flowery penmanship as Ruth's, and her smile wilted; she'd assumed the note was from Hunter. *I have something important concerning the cannery I'd like to speak with you about. If you could call on me at your convenience, I'd appreciate it.* Ruth ended the note by asking

Faith to extend her greetings to Pearl, Ivy, and Faith's family.

What could Ruth have to tell her about the cannery? Faith wondered if the news was related to Hunter's injuries, and she fretted his condition had worsened. Perhaps that was why he hadn't responded to Faith's note? Now that Ruth invited her to stop by, Faith wouldn't have to wait any longer to find out how Hunter was faring. If only she had known she'd be visiting, Faith would have brought from home the small "get well and thank you" gift she'd gotten for him: a reflective vest to keep him safe on his early morning walks as he recovered.

Shortly before one o'clock, Faith told Pearl and Ivy she wouldn't be dining with them during their break.

"If you're working through dinner, so will I," Pearl offered.

"*Neh*, I'm not working—I'm riding my bicycle to Ruth's house. She loves my apple fry pies and I want to deliver some while they're still warm."

Pearls lips curled. "He—I mean *she* will appreciate them. Please give my *gut* wishes to Hunter while you're there, too. Don't hurry back. We'll take care of everything here, won't we, Ivy?"

"*Jah*, we'll turn the sign to Open at one thirty," Ivy agreed, "so Faith Yoder can visit Hunter Schwartz at Ruth Graber's house."

Faith laughed; although she'd been summoned to Ruth's house by Ruth herself, there was no sense denying that seeing Hunter was her ulterior motive for taking a midday jaunt.

"Oh, Faith, you know those are my favorite!" Ruth applauded when she discovered Faith brought apple fry pies. "Iris will put a kettle on while you warm yourself by the stove. Your cheeks are bright—it must be very cold out there."

"*Jah*, it's freezing," Faith admitted, glancing toward the hallway. If Hunter was in the house, she couldn't hear him.

While Iris was fixing a tray, Faith inquired after Ruth's health. It was then Ruth disclosed she didn't intend to reopen the cannery. Faith readily agreed to sell certain remaining jarred goods in her bakery, and she was delighted to accept Ivy as a permanent employee.

"I want you to do what's best for your well-being, Ruth, but our dinner breaks won't be the same without you," Faith lamented.

"Oh, you won't be rid of me—I plan to join you fine women for dinner as often as possible," Ruth promised as she handed Faith the key to the cannery and a list of goods to sell.

"Has Hunter tried your apple fry pies?" Iris questioned when she returned with a tray of teacups. "He loves your baking."

"Why don't you beckon him?" Ruth suggested. "I believe he's out by the stable."

"Of course." Faith grinned and donned her shawl, scarf and gloves.

She approached the building just as Hunter tottered out of it, balancing against what looked like a walking stick whittled from a tree limb. She didn't know if he was scowling from pain or merely squinting against the sunlight, but she was so tickled to see him she rushed in his direction.

"*Guder nammidaag*, Hunter," she said. "It's *wunderbaar* to see you out and about!"

"Were you expecting me to be bedridden?" he asked.

There was a hardness about his mouth and jaw that indicated he wasn't jesting.

"*Neh*. I only meant I'm happy to see you. I've been praying for you and wondering how you're feeling."

Hunter frowned. "What are you doing here in the middle of the day?" he asked without addressing her concern.

"Ruth needed to talk to me, and I wanted to bring her some apple fry pies. We're about to have them with tea."

"You'd better get back inside, then."

Although his dismissal hurt, Faith thought perhaps she hadn't made it clear he was invited, too. "Would you like to join us?" she asked.

"*Neh,*" was his succinct reply.

Faith felt buffaloed by his bluntness. Was he upset with her? Was that why he wasn't conversing or acknowledging the big news in her note? After working so hard to help her accomplish her goal, Faith thought Hunter would have been pleased she was getting a loan. Did he feel slighted that she hadn't expressed more appreciation?

"Alright, but I can't leave without saying *denki* for all your help recently. I don't know what I would have done without—"

Hunter didn't allow her to complete her sentiment. "Running deliveries was my job and you already paid me for my service. There's no need to say *denki* again."

Faith's mouth dropped open. He was making it clear he no longer considered her to be a friend; he considered her to be an employer—a former employer, at that. Maybe even a stranger, given the distant look in his eyes. Faith was crushed. "Oh, okay, then," she uttered. "*Mach's gut*, Hunter."

She swiveled toward the house and was halfway across the yard when she dashed back to where he loitered at the threshold of the stable. Like the bakery, their relationship meant too much to Faith to let it go without doing everything she could to save it.

Peering into his dark, impassive eyes, Faith implored, "I'm so sorry I pushed you to make a second trip to the Palmers' house during the ice storm. If you hadn't helped me with that last-minute delivery, you wouldn't have strained your back. I don't blame you for being angry with me. If you'll let me, I'll do anything I can to help you as you recover. I just hope in time you'll forgive me."

Hunter's expression remained as unyielding as the frozen ground beneath their feet. "I understand the bakery is the center of your life, Faith, but neither you nor it is responsible for my injuries, so there's nothing for me to forgive. As for my recovery, I don't need or want your help."

His caustic remarks made Faith's eyes smart, but she managed to hold back her tears. She suspected Hunter's indifference and self-sufficiency were a facade to conceal how wounded he felt. She should know; she had often acted that way herself. Perhaps by inviting Hunter into her secret sorrow, she could draw him out of his.

"I appreciate that struggling with a health issue can be a lonely, frightening experience," she began.

"What would you know about my struggles?" Hunter jeered, balancing his weight to thrust his walking stick under Faith's nose. "What would you know about walking down the street using one of these? Or about losing your job because you can't move half as fast as you used to?"

Although he noticed Faith's face blanch and her eyes fill, Hunter couldn't seem to stop himself from haranguing her. "How often do you lie in bed counting every second until your muscle spasms subside? Did you ever hesitate to hold a *bobbel* because you're afraid your back might seize up and you'll drop him? And speaking of *bobblin*, when was the last time someone laced your boots for you, as if you were a pitiful little *kind*?"

Faith wiped a tear from her cheek. "I am so sorry that you've been—that you *are*—suffering. It's true, I don't know what your pain feels like. But I do know what it feels like to have a body that isn't capable…that isn't exactly as I wish it would be."

"Ha!" Hunter roared, glaring down at her. "Being a couple of pounds overweight isn't anything like having chronic back, hip and leg pain. All you have to do is go on a diet for a few days. I have months, maybe years, of physical therapy to endure. Expenses aside, do you have any idea how exacting that's going to be? So don't you dare whine about your weight to me!"

Faith gasped, momentarily recoiling. Then she thrust her hands onto her hips, stepped forward and bore into him with her eyes as she retorted, "For your information, I wasn't referring to my weight, but *denki* for pointing out I should go on a diet. I'll start by forgoing the apple fry pies I brought. Please tell your *ant* and your *mamm* I'm sorry I had to leave, but something ruined my appetite."

Agape, Hunter watched Faith storm to where she'd leaned her bicycle against a tree. Before getting on, she whirled around and shouted, "If you want people to stop treating you like a pitiful little *kind*, then you ought to start acting like a man, Hunter Schwartz!"

Hunter was so peeved he might have broken his walking stick just as he'd broken his cane if he hadn't caught a glimpse of his mother in the picture window. The two women inside undoubtedly watched—and possibly heard—his altercation with Faith as it unfolded, and they were probably shaking their heads about it now. He didn't care. His words may have seemed unkind but they weren't untrue, and it was a relief to have admitted how he felt.

He pulled open the door to the stable and went inside where they couldn't see him walking without his stick. Navigating the interior from post to post, he seethed over Faith's departing comment. She might as well have kicked him in the shins for the blow she delivered to his manhood by telling him he was acting like a *kind*. After all he'd done to disguise his pain so he could help her with deliveries! If there was any consolation in Ruth shutting down the cannery, it was that Hunter wouldn't have to return to Main Street. *I don't care if I never see Faith again*, he thought. *I can't return to Indiana soon enough.*

Around and around he paced until his fuming was interrupted by his mother's voice. "Hunter?" she said from the entryway. "You must be deep in thought—you didn't hear me calling your name."

"Oh," he said noncommittally. He hoped she wasn't going to press him for information about what transpired between Faith and him.

Instead, she perched on a bale of hay, hugged her shawl tightly around her and said, "There's something I wanted to say the other day, but not in front of Ruth. Could you please stop your marching and *kumme* sit for a moment?" His mother patted the hay.

Hunter hadn't realized he was still moving. He gingerly lowered himself into a sitting position on the bale of hay. "What is it you'd like to discuss?" he asked.

"Living here with your *ant* has been a blessing to me. Caring for her has helped me stop focusing on my grief over losing your *daed*. I won't ever stop missing him, but I clearly see now that the Lord still has work for me to do. I believe part of that work is to care for Ruth in her later years. It's what she needs, and it helps ease my loneliness, too."

Hunter gulped, fearing his mother wished to extend their stay in Willow Creek.

"I think you and I are opposites," she said. "You're more like your *daed*. You need to learn to rely more on other people and I need to learn to stop relying on them so much. I've leaned heavily on you since your *daed* died, and it's time I stand on my own two feet again—with more of *Gott's* help and less of yours."

"Neh," Hunter contradicted. "You haven't leaned too hard on me, *Mamm.*"

"Jah, I have. And I couldn't have made it to this point without your help, so I'm very grateful. But you're a young man. You should be thinking about a wife, not about supporting your *mamm*. I know you'll always care for me and help me wherever you are, Hunter. It's what kind of *suh* you are. But I've decided I'm not going back to live in Indiana. There are too many memories of your *daed* there, and Ruth needs me here. I think you should consider selling the house. I know we won't make much of a profit, but whatever we make, half of it is yours to do with what you choose. If you want to return to Parkersville permanently, you may. If you'd prefer to stay in Willow Creek, Ruth has already said you are *wilkom* to live with us."

"But *Mamm*—"

His mother squeezed his hand with her gloved fingers. *"But* nothing. The only thing worse than being in pain myself is watching my *kind* suffer. You didn't have a choice about whether you suffered physical pain from the accident. But you do have a choice about whether you continue to suffer unnecessary emotional pain. It's up to you."

"What do you mean?"

"I think you know, *suh*," she replied. "I've witnessed how deeply you and Faith cherish each other."

Even in the frigid air, Hunter's ears burned. He opened his mouth to tell his mother she couldn't be more mistaken, but the words that came out were, "I'm… I'm hungry. Are there any apple fry pies left?"

Chapter Eleven

"Faith!" Pearl exclaimed when Faith returned to the bakery. "Your face is so... Are you alright?"

"It's probably wind burn," Faith mumbled, avoiding her friend's eyes as she hung up her shawl. She couldn't disclose that she'd wept so hard on the way back from Ruth's house she had to dismount her bike three times because her lungs ached from inhaling deep, sobbing gasps of the arctic air.

"Even so, you ought to take the afternoon off," Pearl urged. "You don't want to get sick right before *Grischtdaag*. I'll stay here until the last customers collect their orders. Truly, it's not a hardship, especially since I'm taking the day off tomorrow to meet our *kinner* at the van depot."

It didn't take much to persuade Faith to go home early: her eyes were nearly swollen shut, her stomach ached and she couldn't imagine being attentive enough to ring up a purchase or follow a recipe. Feeling as if there were an ox cart hitched to her bicycle, Faith slowly trundled along the winding roads leading to the farm.

"What's wrong?" Henrietta asked when Faith traipsed into the kitchen. "You look terrible."

"I *feel* terrible," Faith replied.

"Go straight upstairs and gather fresh bedclothes while I put on a kettle for tea and draw a bath for you," Henrietta ordered, and Faith complied.

But when she reached her room, Faith was so chilled and the bed looked so inviting she burrowed under her quilt and didn't stir again until nearly five o'clock the next morning. Her first thought upon waking was of the conversation she'd had with Hunter, and she would have begun weeping again if she had any tears left to cry.

She felt like a fool. All this time, she thought he was her friend—in fact, she even wondered if he wanted to be more than friends, considering his comments about her hair and her laughter. At the very least, she believed he cared about her and respected her goals as a businesswoman, just as she highly esteemed him and his interests. She assumed he understood how much her relationships meant to her. Come to find out, he saw her as vain and worldly, as someone who was interested only in her appearance and her business.

I'd gladly gain fifty pounds if it meant I could have a bobbel, and I dare say I'd give up the bakery if I had to, too, Faith thought. Hunter had no idea what was important to her, and she was appalled to think she'd been on the cusp of sharing her most intimate secret with him. If his opinion of her was that low before she confided about her condition, what would he think of her once he knew?

She'd be polite to him, but beyond the usual pleasantries, she had nothing more to say to him. Didn't Ruth mention she was getting her cast off next week? Faith hoped Hunter would leave town as soon after that as possible. The past two months had been grueling, but Faith looked forward to starting the new year afresh.

To her surprise, as she was tucking her shawl around her waist, Henrietta approached her in the kitchen. "Your nephews couldn't rouse you for supper last night. I checked on you, but since you didn't have a fever, I let you sleep. How are you today?"

"Better now," Faith said, hoping her sister-in-law wasn't going to try to persuade her to stay home. Pearl was taking the day off to pick up her daughter's family from the van depot, and Ivy couldn't be left on her own.

"I woke Reuben to take you to the bakery. He'll pick you up, too."

Grateful for Henrietta's nurturing gesture, Faith promised her sister-in-law she'd bring home special treats for dessert. She slogged through the morning, and by dinner break, Faith was exhausted. She knew she'd have to tell Ivy about the cannery closing, so in order to get her accustomed to the idea, she presented her with a little gift: a pair of blue oven mitts, Ivy's favorite color.

"Remember, you must never get them wet except to wash them," Faith instructed.

"But you said no more baking."

"I've been thinking about that, and if you'd still like to bake, Pearl and I can give you lessons," Faith said. Then she explained about the changes that were to occur at the cannery.

"Ruth Graber isn't coming back to the shop?" Ivy repeated.

"*Neh*, but she'll come into town to visit," Faith explained. "And she'll invite you to her home and you'll see her at church, too."

"Did Hunter Schwartz tell her I ran away on his first day?"

"Oh, Ivy, Ruth isn't angry with you. She just needs a change in pace. She's getting older and she needs to take care of her health."

"But her leg is mending."

Faith decided to switch tactics. "Ivy, don't you want to continue working with Pearl and me? We really need your help."

"I dropped your applesauce cake."

"That's alright. I made another applesauce cake."

The timer went off in the back room. Sighing, Faith rose to check on the rolls. She wondered if she'd made a mistake by telling Ivy today instead of waiting until after *Grischtdaag*. She didn't want to spoil the holiday for the young girl. Her own holiday already felt ruined by her rift with Hunter.

"Listen, Ivy, I have an idea," Faith said when she came back into the storefront.

The room was empty.

Wearily, Faith glanced toward the coat pegs in the hall. At least Ivy remembered to take her shawl. Grabbing her own garment, Faith turned the ovens off and locked the front entrance before exiting through the back door. Until that moment, she'd forgotten her bike was at home, so she fled for the pond on foot. By that time, Ivy had taken a significant lead and Faith lost sight of her.

For an instant, her thoughts turned to the day she and Hunter pedaled down the same lane, and her lips twitched at the memory before she blotted it from her mind. *I'd better get used to solving problems on my own again*, she thought. *Or at least, solving them without any help from Hunter Schwartz.*

* * *

After spending a sleepless night of ruminating on his mother's words, "I've witnessed how deeply you and Faith cherish each other," Hunter's concentration was lagging. He had just finished refreshing the horse's water when his balance was thrown off by a small dip in the floor. Spreading his arms, he tried to steady himself, but he floundered backward against a stack of baled hay. It knocked the wind out of him and pain coursed through his hips and back, but his landing was less damaging than it could have been. As Hunter lay supine, trying to catch his breath, Proverbs 16:18 came to mind: "Pride goeth before destruction, and an haughty spirit before a fall."

The truth of Scripture seared Hunter's conscience, and he finally acknowledged he'd have many more falls, both literally and figuratively, if he continued to act in such an arrogant manner. Furthermore, his pride wouldn't just destroy his own body and future; it would damage his relationships, as well. Hunter knew he had a long list of people to apologize to, including his aunt and mother, Joseph, the staff at the hospital and Faith. Especially Faith. But first he needed to ask the Lord's forgiveness.

Please Gott, *forgive my disdainful attitude and with Your grace, help me to change*, he prayed, and then propped himself up on his elbows. Was that a car door he heard nearby? The doctor paid Ruth a visit the day before—was he back again? As Hunter pulled himself upright, James Palmer appeared in the entryway.

"Hello, Hunter," he said. "I hope you don't mind me paying you an unexpected visit. I looked for you at the cannery, but it was closed. A man named Joseph told me I could find you here."

"Wilkom," Hunter replied. "What can I do for you?"

"I'm wondering if you might be able to refinish more furniture for me," James requested. "You did a terrific job on the chair and my wife was thrilled. We've been storing an antique dining table and chair set in our attic for years. I'd like to have the furniture redone as a Christmas gift for Marianne. Obviously, I don't expect you to finish them—or even begin them—in the next two days, but if I have your word you'll start them soon, I can wrap a big bow around one of the chairs and set it in the dining room on Christmas morning as a symbol of what's to come. Marianne will be delighted."

She's not the only one! Hunter thought, amazed. Here was a provision to his financial needs he hadn't had to strive for one bit: the Lord literally delivered it to his doorstep.

"I'd be glad to," he said, without hesitating to consider the project would extend his time in Willow Creek.

After James left, Hunter hobbled to the house as quickly as his makeshift cane enabled him. Expressing sincere regret for his recent surliness, he promised his aunt and mother they'd see a changed man from now on. Then he told them about the restoration project.

Ruth beamed. "Your *onkel* would have been pleased you're using his workshop."

"And your *daed* would have been pleased, too," his mother said. "He was always proud of your skills at the factory and of your handiwork, but he thought you were especially good with numbers, too. I think he always imagined you'd run your own business one day."

"Who knows, maybe he might yet," Ruth suggested with a wink.

Hunter ambled back outdoors to look at the supplies in his uncle's workshop. Recalling how happy Faith was to tell him about her order from Marianne Palmer the day of the accident, Hunter wished he could share his good news with her. As much as she may have wrongly blamed herself for his accident, Hunter wanted Faith to know it was actually her customer who played a role in God's provision for him.

He was so lost in thoughts of her he imagined her calling, "Please come back. I need to talk to you. Please."

Then he realized, he *was* hearing her voice. He exited the workshop and surveyed the landscape. Down the hill at the pond, he spied Ivy ducking into her usual hiding place beneath the bridge. Perhaps the ground there was especially muddy or slick, but a moment later, she re-emerged and sauntered across the snow- and ice-covered pond as nonchalantly as if across a field.

"Ivy!" Faith hollered from a distance behind. "Stop right there! You're walking on the pond! The ice isn't strong enough to hold you!"

Hunter darted into the stable, grabbed a rope and started for the pond just as a tremendous crack reverberated through the air like a gunshot, paralyzing Ivy in place.

"I'm coming, Ivy. Stay right there," Faith commanded.

Loping down the hill, Hunter trained his gaze on both of them as Faith shuffled toward where Ivy was standing. When Faith was within a few feet of the girl, she tossed one end of her scarf toward her.

"Hold on to that, Ivy," she instructed, her voice carried by the crisp winter air.

Ivy whimpered as the end of the scarf fell at her feet. When she crouched to lift it, the ice shifted again. Apparently startled by the sound, Ivy bolted past Faith back to solid ground, leaving the scarf behind. Faith cautiously rotated toward the embankment, leaning from side to side, as if trying to establish her balance. But the ice cracked a third time and down she plunged, the water closing over her head. Hunter didn't so much run as hurtle himself forward.

"Kick!" he remembered the *Englisch* swimming instructor urging him the summer Mason, Noah, Hunter and Faith fell into the creek. After the accident, their fathers enrolled the children in a special swimming clinic for Amish kids. Although the Amish rarely swam recreationally, after the footbridge mishap, their parents wanted the children to know what to do if they ever found themselves submerged. *Pretend you're a frog and kick*, Hunter willed Faith as he reached the edge of the pond.

She must have remembered the instructor's directive, too, because suddenly she surfaced and took an enormous gasp of air before bobbing back under. As Hunter looped the rope around a nearby tree and began inching toward where she'd fallen in, Faith surfaced again, thrashing at the water. This time, she stayed afloat and Hunter could hear her breathing was fast and furious. Knowing her hyperventilation would subside within a minute as her body adjusted to the cold, he tossed the rope toward her, but it was too light and fell short. Faith continued to tread water until her breathing normalized, and then she flung her arms over the ice and pushed her torso upward, but the edge broke off and she nearly went under again.

"Hold on, Faith, I'm almost there," he shouted as he worked the end of the rope into a bulbous knot.

A second time she tried to lift herself but Hunter could tell the ice was too slippery and she couldn't heave her lower body from the water. Her arms wobbled, and she disappeared again. Hunter crept precariously close to the fractured ice, praying for the Lord to save her. When she came up again, he adroitly lobbed the rope straight to her. "Grab the rope, Faith, and wrap it around your wrist!" he coached.

Faith clumsily grasped the knobby end and managed to stretch her upper body over the ice as she wound the rope twice around her wrist.

"*Gut*, that's *gut*! Now, on the count of three, you're going to kick as hard as you can so your legs rise behind you, like a swimmer's," Hunter commanded. "You need to make yourself flat and straight so I can pull you forward. Ready? One…two…three!"

As Faith vigorously thwacked her legs against the water, Hunter heaved with all of his might until Faith's body jerked forward, out of the water and atop the solid ice. Hand over hand, he reeled her closer and closer until she lay not a yard from him and he swept her into his arms. By the time they reached the shore, her teeth were chattering so hard she couldn't speak.

As Hunter lurched toward his house, he didn't register his own pain or the cold, nor could he fully process the words Ivy was screaming—all he noticed was Faith's bluish pallor. He held her body close to his to try to subdue her shaking.

His mother and aunt must have heard the shouting and seen what had happened, because they were ready with blankets and dry clothes. Ruth directed him to lay Faith on the bed in her room and for Ivy to put on a pot of tea. Then the women shooed him from the room.

As he headed outside to get more wood for the stove, Hunter beseeched the Lord, using the simple petition he often uttered in regard to his own health, "Please, *Gott*, make Faith well again."

* * *

Drifting in and out of lucidity, Faith had the impression she was sinking—not into water, but into sleep—and she felt unable to fight the enticing pull of its gravity.

"She's dry now, but we can't let her doze off," Iris was saying. "Let's get her back on her feet."

Even with Iris and Ivy supporting her, it took all of Faith's strength to rise from the bed. She was fatigued when the day began, and her icy dunking drained the rest of her energy. She could barely move under the weight of the quilt wrapped around her shoulders. The three slowly made their way to the parlor, where Iris and Ivy settled her into a rocking chair positioned near the woodstove. Ruth placed her hand over Faith's forehead.

"That tea was enough to warm you but not enough to give you energy. You need sustenance," Ruth decided, doddering toward the kitchen. "I've heated some soup. Ivy, *kumme* give me a hand."

"I don't know if I could lift a spoon," Faith mumbled, but the words felt funny in her mouth.

"Let's warm your toes," Hunter's mother said. Cupping Faith's foot by the ankle, Iris slowly guided it onto a stool in front of the fire. Then she did the same with the other foot.

"Whatever will I do if I'm sick when I live alone? How will I manage?" Faith tried to say, but the words were barely audible. She was so sleepy.

Ruth gave her a gentle nudge and handed her a mug without any spoon. Faith's hands trembled as she lifted the piping liquid to her mouth and blew on it. "It's *gut*," she said after her first swallow. She hadn't realized how hungry she was.

She was slurping the last noodle from her second serving when Hunter tentatively stepped into the parlor as if unsure whether he was allowed to enter. His arms were full of firewood. "I thought I should stoke the stove," he proposed.

"If I get any warmer, I'll start to sweat!" For some reason, the notion amused her, and she giggled.

"I think she's still... She's still thawing out," Faith heard Iris comment to Ruth.

"Jah," Ruth confirmed. "She'll be back to herself in another hour or so."

"I'll go wring out her clothes," Iris replied.

"Gut idea. *Kumme,* Ivy, you ought to have some soup, too," Ruth instructed. "Hunter, keep an eye on Faith for a minute, will you?"

Hunter unloaded the wood into the bin beside the stove and then clapped the debris off his sleeves before turning toward Faith. He scrutinized her, rubbing his thumb against the cleft in his chin. "Are you feeling better?" he asked.

"Jah," Faith answered. Vaguely recalling her last conversation with him, she wondered if thanking him for coming to her aid on the ice would be well received. Would he brush her off, the way he'd done when she tried to thank him for helping her keep her business? Regardless, she figured saving her life merited an expression of gratitude. *"Denki* for rescuing me, Hunter," she said simply but ardently.

Hunter's voice was tremulous and his countenance astonished as he confessed, "I'm so relieved the Lord gave me strength to pull you out. I wasn't sure I could."

Fearing he'd further injured himself from the effort, she replied, "I'm sorry if carrying me put a strain on your back."

Hunter frowned. "*Neh*, I didn't mean that. I meant—"

"Excuse me," Iris interrupted as she bustled in with Faith's clothes and a wooden drying rack. "I need to hang these in front of the fire. Hunter, would you take Ivy back to town? She feels terrible about what happened and she wants to be helpful, so she's volunteered to tidy the bakery before closing it for the night. If you leave now, she can finish by the time Mervin arrives to pick her up. When you return here, perhaps Faith will be warm enough for you to take her home."

Hunter promptly agreed, although he lingered where he was standing, as if there was something else he wanted to say. But when Ivy entered the room a moment later, he simply remarked, "I'll go bring the buggy around," and exited the house.

Wrapping her shawl around her, Ivy announced, "I'll make sure the goodies stay extra fresh overnight."

Faith smiled benignly. "*Denki*, Ivy."

"I won't eat anything, not even a cream-filled doughnut," she promised solemnly. "You don't have to worry about that."

Her expression was so earnest that Faith couldn't allow herself to laugh. Aware her young friend felt guilty about Faith's icy plunge and was doing her best to make up for it, Faith said, "I trust you, Ivy. But since the cream-filled doughnuts don't keep well overnight, I'd appreciate it if you'd take them home to share with your *groossdaadi*."

Ivy's eyes went wide. "Really?"

"It would be a big help to me if you would."

"Oh, I will, Faith," Ivy said, nodding fervently.

After she left, Faith leaned back in the chair and closed her eyes. How cozy it was to be bundled in a quilt, her insides warm from sipping homemade soup, and her mind at ease because her friends were tending to the bakery on her behalf.

"You're not dropping off on us, are you?" Ruth asked, limping to the sofa.

"*Neh*, I was thinking about how blessed I am to have such *gut* friends," Faith explained. Then, for the umpteenth time, she reminded herself she didn't need a man in her life. She had her friends as well as her family, and she was going to be fine, just fine—wasn't she?

When Ivy was situated in the buggy beside Hunter, she asked, "Are you angry at me?"

"*Neh*, I'm not angry, Ivy. But you did give us a scare. You have to stop running away when someone hurts your feelings."

Ivy sniveled.

"I know it's not easy," he confessed. "Sometimes when people hurt my feelings, I want to run away, too."

"But you can't because you use a cane, right?"

"I guess that's one of the reasons," Hunter replied, chuckling. "From now on let's both try not to run away when someone hurts our feelings? How about if we tell them, 'You hurt my feelings and I'd like to talk about that'?"

"Okay," Ivy agreed. Then, without missing a beat, she said, "Hunter, you hurt my feelings and I'd like to talk about that."

Hunter smiled again. "I'm sorry I hurt your feelings. What did I do?"

"You don't want me to sell jarred goods anymore. You didn't think I was doing a *gut* job. That's why Ruth Graber is closing her shop."

"I understand it might feel that way, Ivy, but it's not the

truth. My *ant* Ruth closed the cannery because she's getting older and she has to take care of her health. Her decision has nothing to do with your abilities." As he spoke, Hunter realized his assumptions about Ruth's decision were as ridiculous as Ivy's. He added, "Ruth's decision doesn't have anything to do with my abilities, either. In fact, I don't think she ever would have closed the shop if she thought working there was the only thing you or I could do. She would have kept it open to make sure we had employment."

"I have a new job now," Ivy said. "In the bakery. Faith Yoder and Pearl Hostetler will give me baking lessons. Faith bought me blue oven mitts."

"See? You've got so many talents you get to do something else now!" Hunter exclaimed. "But no matter where you are or what you're doing, I hope we'll always be friends."

"We'll always be friends," Ivy repeated.

The two of them decided to keep the shop open for any last-minute sales while Ivy wrapped up the baked goods and Hunter swept the floors. They were halfway through their tasks when Henrietta arrived to pick up Faith, saying she'd sit in the storefront until closing time. Hunter took her aside and told her what had happened at the pond.

"I knew I shouldn't have allowed her to *kumme* to work today!" Henrietta asserted. "She looked absolutely miserable when she arrived home early yesterday, and she slept straight through supper. I should have insisted she get more rest."

As Henrietta departed for Ruth's house, it occurred to Hunter that his spiteful remarks the previous day probably contributed to Faith's malaise. Overcome with regret, he agonized, *I acted like such a* dummkopf. *How can I ever repair our relationship now?*

That night Hunter counted the minutes ticking by— not because he was waiting for his pain to subside, but because he was afraid when he closed his eyes he'd envision the glacial water closing over Faith again. Although he'd responded swiftly and skillfully during the emergency as it occurred, now that he lay in the secluded dark of his room, he reflected on how horrified he'd been at the possibility she'd slip beyond his reach.

To comfort himself, he said aloud, "But she's alright now. She's alright." With the help of God, he'd found the strength to draw Faith to safety, despite his physical challenges. In fact, he had no idea when or where he discarded his walking stick in the process of rescuing Faith. All he knew was that when he recognized she was in danger, the only thing that mattered was gathering her into his arms.

Hunter suddenly realized there was absolutely no weakness, except his own attitude, stopping him from being a husband one day, and he bolted upright in bed. He'd almost lost Faith once already, and he wasn't about to lose her again. Tomorrow he was going to tell her he no longer wanted to be her friend: if she'd have him, he wanted to be her suitor.

Chapter Twelve

Because the dress Faith wore the previous day was rumpled from her accidental dip in the pond, and her other two workday dresses were dirty, she donned her Sunday dress. Then she inched down the stairs half an hour earlier than usual in order to avoid waking her sister-in-law, who most likely would pressure Faith into staying home to rest. Today was too festive of an occasion to miss going to the bakery.

Dear Henrietta, she wrote on a pad of paper. *Please don't worry about me; tonight Ruth and Wayne will give me a ride, since we'll be delivering pies—including several to our household—and I won't be able to ride my bike home*. Denki, *Faith*.

Since it was the twenty-fourth of December, Faith intended to close the storefront at two o'clock, so she, Pearl and Ivy could dedicate themselves to making pies to give to their neighbors on Main Street, as well to other members in need in their community. The three women would bake enough to take home for their own families, too.

Although Faith looked forward to spreading good cheer, she was filled with nostalgia as she coasted down the hill into town. Because the tenant above the bakery was moving out on the twenty-seventh and Faith was free to move in on the twenty-eighth, this would be one of the last times she'd bike to work. While she wouldn't miss traveling in inclement weather, she always enjoyed the solitude of her early morning ride.

The new year would bring other changes, too; namely, who would lease the cannery space now? Faith's thoughts darted to Hunter. What would he be doing, come January? Two days ago, she couldn't wait for him to leave, but this morning she was surprised by how thoughts of his departure added to her wistfulness. She wished time would stand still a little longer.

"It smells like it's going to snow," Pearl said when she arrived a couple of hours later.

"Jah," Faith agreed loudly as Pearl walked into the hallway to hang her shawl. "My nephews will be thrilled if we have a white *Grischtdaag*. They were disappointed the first snowfall is already nearly gone."

"Faith!" Pearl called from the storefront. "Why did you use so much plastic wrap on these treats?"

"What?" Faith asked, carrying in a fresh tray of sticky bun wreathes. She surveyed the display case for the first time that morning. Then it dawned on her. "Ivy covered those trays last night. I guess she wanted to make sure they stayed fresh."

"Covered them? She *swaddled* them!"

"Neh—they're mummified!"

The women were gripped with laughter. After they composed themselves, Faith recounted the story of her unexpected swim in the pond.

"Didn't I say it was a *gut* thing such a fine, strapping

man was in town again?" Pearl asked when Faith described how Hunter reeled her ashore.

"That's what you said alright," Faith responded ambiguously, belying the surge of conflicting emotions she felt about Hunter.

Turning the discussion to Pearl's visiting children, Faith tore the plastic from a tray in order to prepare complimentary samples for the customers to nibble on as they sipped free spiced cider, coffee or hot chocolate, a holiday tradition at the bakery.

At midmorning, Faith was surprised to see Hunter emerge from a taxi idling in front of the bakery. Her stomach fluttered, and she would have disappeared into the kitchen to avoid him, but Ivy was in the washroom and Pearl was running a personal errand at the mercantile. Faith's pulse pit-a-patted as Hunter entered the bakery, adroitly maneuvering his cane in rhythm with his footsteps.

"Guder mariye," she said while polishing the countertop.

"Guder mariye," he replied. His eyes were lustrous and a huge grin adorned his face. "How are you feeling?"

"Fine, *denki*. What can I do for you?"

"I need three sticky bun wreathes, please."

"Three?" Faith questioned skeptically.

"Jah," Hunter answered. "I'm accompanying Ruth to the hospital to get her cast off. I was rude to the hospital staff after my injury, so I wanted to bring them a token of apology. I couldn't think of anything better than something you baked."

Hunter seemed to be carrying himself with a new confidence, and his ruddy cheeks created a striking contrast with his dark hair. To be honest, his presence took her breath away, and when he complimented her, she felt her resolve to keep him at a distance melting away, like icing on a warm cake. She couldn't allow that to happen. She'd be cordial, yes, but she wasn't going to let him pretend they hadn't fallen out—even if he *did* save her life. It was fine and good he was apologizing to the hospital staff, but that didn't change things between the two of them.

"I see," she said crisply, and turned boxing the treats.

"Ah, there you are," Faith said when Ivy walked into the room a moment later. "Please assist Hunter if he needs to purchase anything else. I hear the timer going off." Before leaving, she added, "I hope all goes well for Ruth at the hospital. *Mach's gut*, Hunter."

After pulling the bread from the oven, Faith raced into the washroom and splashed water on her face as her heart boomed in her ears. Ruth's cast was coming off, which meant Hunter likely would leave even sooner than expected. *It won't be soon enough*, Faith thought— not because she wanted him gone, but because she was beginning to hope he'd stay.

Hunter sat beside his aunt in the taxi and balanced the boxes on his knees. Faith disappeared before he asked if he could take her home that evening in order to speak with her in private. Although she looked especially lovely and she stated she was fine, there was something about her manner that suggested she was preoccupied. Either that, or she wasn't nearly as pleased to see him as he'd been to see her. Not that she should have been, considering their last full conversation. *Perhaps it's best if I show up unannounced at the end of the day*, he mused. *That way, Faith won't have time to think of an excuse to decline a ride.*

Twisting his head toward Ruth, he cleared his throat. "*Ant* Ruth," he began in *Deitsch* so the driver wouldn't understand him. "I want to apologize for how ungracious I was the other day when you offered my *mamm* and me such a generous gift. I've had a prideful attitude lately, and I'm sorry."

Ruth chortled. "*Jah*, you've been a bit of a bear. But I understand. After my accident, I felt pretty low, too. And the lower I felt, the more puffed up I became, not wanting to admit my weakness. That's why I didn't notify you and your *mamm* about my accident right away. I thought I'd be fine on my own. I didn't want to admit my own limitations."

Hunter nodded. His aunt had hit the nail on the head.

"But it's when we're weak *Gott* is strong," Ruth reminded him. "You're like me. Sometimes you've got to stop trying to do everything by yourself and start relying more on *Gott's* grace and on those who are in the position to help you. And that means accepting the money I set aside for the lease."

"But how can I accept such a big gift, knowing I might not be able to repay it?"

"It's a *gift*, Hunter, not a debt. It's like…like *Gott's* grace to us. We can't repay grace, we can only receive it. And the way we receive it is with humility and a grateful heart."

Hunter nodded again. Then he placed his hand over his aunt's and said, "*Denki*. I appreciate your gift, but with the exception of my recent hospital bills, I've managed to stay on top of our expenses from Indiana. So, if it's alright with you, I'd like to use your gift for the lease after all. That is, I'd like to keep the building space and use it to set up a furniture restoration shop."

"Wunderbaar!" Ruth whooped.

Hunter's apologies to the hospital staff were also well received, with several nurses cheering when he announced he brought goodies.

"So where's your 'new best friend'?" Tyler chided with his mouth half-full. "That stick isn't the one we sent you home with."

"Neh, this is the Amish version," Hunter joshed, embarrassed about breaking the first one. "I made it. See how I can hold on to it here, or prop it beneath my arm, like so…"

Tyler's eyes widened. "Nice work, but I still think you'd do better holding hands with a successful, pretty woman who can bake like this." He held up the last of his treat for emphasis before popping it in his mouth.

"Er, actually…" Hunter began. Ordinarily, he wouldn't confide in an *Englisch* acquaintance, but Tyler had been so encouraging that Hunter wanted to share his good news. "Actually, when she gets done with work, I'm asking if I can court her."

"On Christmas Eve? Nice touch, very romantic!" Tyler said, bumping Hunter's shoulder with his fist. Then someone urged him into a patient's room and he was gone.

Ruth was so giddy to have her ankle free of its cast she chatted all the way home, but Hunter could barely concentrate. His most difficult apology lay before him. Would Faith hear him out? Would she accept his offer of courtship? Would she even accept his offer of a ride home?

He spent the afternoon working on the single chair James Palmer left with him as a sample of the furniture set, and then, an hour before hitching the horse, Hunter shaved again and put on a fresh shirt.

"It's so *gut* to see you! How well you appear!" Pearl exclaimed when she unlocked the front door. "How are you feeling?"

Pearl had such a genuine way of inquiring about his well-being that Hunter's nervousness temporarily vanished. "I'm much better, *denki*," he said. "You must be well, too, now that your *kinner* are home for a visit?"

Their easygoing conversation was interrupted when Faith emerged from the back room with several boxes stacked in her arms. She couldn't see around them, but when she set them down them on the counter, she looked surprised.

"Oh, hello again, Hunter," she said. Over the course of the day, her hair had loosened within its clip, and her skin had a pleasant, arresting glow.

Hunter wiped his palms on his trousers. "Hello again, Faith," he managed to reply.

"There's Wayne's buggy outside," Pearl said as she donned her shawl. "Since I'm eager to get home to my family, Hunter mentioned he'd give you a ride instead, okay? We'll drop the last pies off at Isaac Miller's house, so all you'll have to deliver are the pies going to your own family."

Faith almost imperceptibly cringed, but she politely agreed. They helped Pearl with her pies and then loaded Hunter's backseat with pies for the Yoder family and one for Ruth's household, as well. By the time he was seated side by side with Faith, Hunter's mouth was so dry he didn't know if he could say the words he'd been so desperate to express.

Hunter directed the horse toward Faith's home, clearing his throat so many times she was about to search her satchel for a lozenge when he announced, "I'm glad you accepted a ride, Faith, because there's something important I want to discuss with you."

Faith interwove her gloved fingers on her lap to steady her hands. Why was she so nervous? "*Jah*, what is it?"

"It's that I'm sorry. Very sorry. For what I said the day you came to Ruth's house with the fry pies." Hunter's voice was guttural and his words came out in spurts. "I said things that were unkind. And misdirected. I said hurtful things. I'm sorry and I hope you'll forgive me."

"There's nothing to forgive," she answered, echoing the words and impervious tone he'd used when she apologized to him for contributing to his injuries. "You were only telling the truth, and you were right. I don't know anything about the extent of your health issues. In some ways, I have made the bakery the center of my life. And my struggles are small compared with yours."

"*Neh!*" Hunter exclaimed. "Those things weren't true expressions of how I felt. I said them because I was in pain. Not just physical pain, either. I was… I was scared, Faith. When you found out about my previous injuries, I felt weak. Exposed. I assumed you thought of me as… as less than a man. And I felt if I hadn't failed you, you wouldn't have had to get a loan. So I lashed out. My behavior was deplorable."

Stirred by Hunter's brave admission and how similar his fears were to her own, Faith had to lick her lips before softly replying, "I understand, Hunter. *Denki* for explaining. I accept your apology."

As her eyes adjusted to the evening light, she could see the grin crinkling his face as he turned toward her, and his voice was filled with relief. "You have no idea how much your forgiveness means to me," he said. "There's something else I want to discuss. How about if we stop here?"

Curious, Faith agreed. Hunter guided the horse until they'd reversed direction on the side of the road and were overlooking Main Street in the valley below. The landscape twinkled with Christmas lights and candles in houses owned by *Englischers* and the Amish, and as if on cue, snowflakes began powdering the landscape. "How pretty!" Faith raved. "I love Willow Creek, don't you?"

"I like it so much I've decided to stay permanently," Hunter replied.

Faith peered at him. "But what will you—"

"*Ant* Ruth has given me the gift of a year's lease on the cannery, which I'm going to convert into a furniture restoration shop. It was your customer, James Palmer, who gave me the idea when he commissioned me to work on another set of antique furniture. I'll probably perform most of the tasks in my *onkel's* old workshop, but I'll need a prominent location in town to attract *Englisch* customers."

"Wow, your own business— I'm so happy for you!"

"*Denki.* If it weren't for accompanying you on that first delivery to the Palmers' house when I offered to fix their chair, I probably never would have had the opportunity."

Faith was every bit as pleased as Hunter was. Adjusting her scarf to better inhale the snappy night air, she silently marveled that the Lord had used her weight—or at least, a fractured chair seat—to help Hunter. *It's not the first time the Lord has used my brokenness as a blessing*, she thought, remembering how her business was born as a result of her surgery. "I'm glad we'll be neighbors on Main Street again," she said.

"Mmm-hmm," Hunter murmured. He was quiet for a pause, and when he spoke again, his voice was raspy. "Actually, I've been reflecting on how well we worked together as business partners—before I started acting like such a *dummkopf*, that is—and I'd like to continue to, er, be paired with you, but not as your business partner or as your neighbor on Main Street. I'd like it to be a more personal partnership. What I'm trying to say, Faith, is that I'd like to court you."

Faith's heart leaped in her chest and just as quickly sank to her feet. This was simultaneously the most wonderful and terrible moment of her past year. She couldn't accept Hunter's offer, nor could she make herself refuse it. Stunned, she sat wordlessly watching as steam puffed from the horse's nostrils in front of them.

When she didn't reply, Hunter said, "I don't take courting lightly, if that's your hesitation. My stance is the same now as when I was sixteen—I wouldn't ask to court you if I didn't think we have a possibility of marrying someday."

"I understand," Faith answered soberly. "Which is why I can't accept your offer of courtship."

"What? Why not?"

The impulse to share her secret was so overwhelming it frightened her. It made her feel, in Hunter's own words, weak and exposed. True, Hunter was very respectful and understanding when she opened up to him about her business concerns and her breakup with Lawrence. Not to mention how compassionately he responded to her breakdown after the incident with the drunken student. There was no doubt he'd witnessed sides of her she wouldn't ordinarily reveal, and she'd grown to trust him to keep her secrets, which was why she had even considered telling him about her health issue the other day. But that was different.

That was before he asked if he could be her suitor. She couldn't risk being that vulnerable now. She couldn't bear to watch his mouth drop open as he struggled to think of a way to rescind his offer. Getting over Lawrence's rejection was difficult enough, but what helped was that Faith rarely saw him after their breakup. She was sure to cross paths with Hunter on a daily basis now that he was opening a shop across the street from her. No, she just couldn't bear the shame. Not again.

"As fond as I am of you and as valuable as your friendship is to me, you and I wouldn't be compatible as a courting couple, Hunter. Our...our shortcomings would end up disappointing each other at some point in the future."

Hunter removed his hat and rubbed his forehead before saying, "I can't promise I'll never disappoint you in the future, Faith. I don't think anyone can promise that to another person because only the Lord is unfailing. But I'll do my best. And if I hurt your feelings or let you down, I pledge to work out our misunderstandings with an attitude of respect and forgiveness."

"We *have* worked out misunderstandings within our friendship with mutual respect. But as you mentioned, courtship leads to marriage and marriage...marriage is an entirely different kind of relationship."

"Which is why we wouldn't rush into it. We'd take our time courting so we could be certain we were ready."

"Time isn't going to make a difference."

"So you're saying you never want to get married at all?"

"I do, but—"

"But not to me." Hunter finished the sentence for her.

"*Neh*, you don't understand." Faith choked out the words as tears streamed down her cheeks. *It's exactly the opposite. If you knew the reason, you'd realize* you *are the one who doesn't want to marry* me.

Faith was right; Hunter didn't understand. Why was she turning him down? What did she mean they wouldn't be compatible as husband and wife? They already proved how well they worked together. Their conversations were easy and genuine, and they enjoyed many good laughs. How could he have been so wrong in thinking Faith shared the same degree of connection to him that he'd felt toward her? Why did she say they'd end up disappointing each other?

"Is it that you don't think I'd make a good provider because of my injuries?" he persisted. "I don't blame you for thinking that. I've thought that myself. But one thing I've learned since coming to Willow Creek is my future is in the Lord's hands, not mine, no matter how hard I work. So, I'll continue to do my best and leave the rest up to Him."

"*Neh*, that's not it." Faith wiped her eyes with the end of her scarf. "Please, Hunter, take me home."

Ignoring her request, he dropped his voice an octave as he asked, "Is it that you don't think I'm strong enough, or manly enough?"

Straightening her posture, Faith snapped, "Of course I think you're manly and strong! Who else could have tugged me ashore so quickly I barely got my stockings wet yesterday? But physical strength is hardly what makes a man a man—it's his character that defines him. I've seen your strength of character, Hunter. I've witnessed how you've been in pain, yet you've fought to overcome obstacles and to help others along the way, especially your family. Especially *me*. The Lord couldn't have blessed me with your friendship at a more crucial time."

Hunter smacked his knees. "That's exactly how I feel about you, too! I believe the Lord intends for us to be each other's helpmate—and not only when we've fallen over a buggy seat or plunged into an icy pond, or even as neighbors on Main Street or *leit* within the same church district. I believe we have a future together as husband and wife."

Faith wouldn't look at him. Shaking her head, she whispered, "I'm sorry but the answer is *neh*."

"You've told me *neh*, but you still haven't told me why."

"I can't."

"You're not being fair," Hunter argued. "You've seen me at my most vulnerable, you've heard me crying like a *bobbel*, yet you refuse to be vulnerable in return. You've accused me of false pride, yet you're being false, too. You're hiding something beneath that *wunderbaar* smile of yours. Please tell me, Faith."

"I want to go home now," she demanded, reaching for the reins, but Hunter held them to the side. This was one conversation that was too important to allow her to disappear before it was finished.

"Talk to me, Faith. Please?" he implored.

Although she shook her head, Hunter sensed she was on the verge of telling him what was troubling her.

"You almost drowned yesterday," he prodded gently. "I risked my life to save you, and I'd do it again in a heartbeat. But now it's your turn to take a risk on my behalf.

Don't I deserve that much? Don't I deserve to know why you won't walk out with me?"

"It's me. It's that I'm not… I can't…"

Hunter reached over and squeezed her hand. "Please tell me," he urged.

Faith pulled her arm away and covered her face. "I might not be able to have *kinner* and you want to have lots of them," she wailed. "I had surgery when I was seventeen and I—I—"

Sobs racked her body and she didn't finish her sentence. There was no need; Hunter understood. He slid closer, enveloped her against his chest and rocked back and forth until her shuddering subsided and she'd caught her breath. Then he dabbed the tears from her cheeks and cupped her face in his hands so he could gaze directly into her eyes. "Do you want to have *kinner* when you get married?" he inquired softly.

Faith pulled back, as if stumped by the question. "That's sort of a moot consideration, since I don't really allow myself to think about getting married anymore. But ideally, *jah*, if I were married I'd like to start a family. However, we don't always get what we want. Sometimes the Lord has other plans for us."

"That's true," Hunter agreed. "Although sometimes, the Lord gives us our heart's desires, just not in the manner we had planned." He took a deep breath before asking, "Would you ever consider adoption?"

"*Jah*, absolutely. But it's expensive, time-consuming, and—"

"And worth every penny, every second and every teardrop put into the process," Hunter interjected. "At least, that's what my parents told me."

"You were adopted?"

"Jah."

Faith clutched her stomach and bent forward. At first, Hunter thought she had burst into tears again, but then he realized she was laughing, and he laughed along with her until their joy seemed to echo across the valley.

When they quieted, she looked directly at him and said, "Now I'm positive you're *Gott's* gift to me."

Despite the cold, Hunter's insides melted. "I have no doubt you're His gift to me, too."

"And just in time for *Grischtdaag*," she quipped, playfully nudging his arm.

"Does that mean we're walking out now?"

"Are you sure you want to?"

Instead of answering aloud, Hunter leaned closer, placed his hand on the nape of her neck and gently drew her mouth to his. Her lips were plump and velvety, and she smelled faintly of cinnamon.

When they pulled away, Faith opened her eyes halfway and peered at him from beneath her lashes. "I'm sure, too," she said. Then she turned and rested her head against his shoulder.

They sat side by side in silence, admiring the view, until Faith finally suggested, "I suppose we'd better go deliver these pies to my family before they freeze."

"Alright," Hunter reluctantly conceded. This moment had been so long in coming he hated for it to end.

When he reached the Yoders' farm, he said, "I'd like to see you tomorrow. Perhaps I can bring you home from work again?"

"Neh, I don't think that's a *gut* idea," Faith replied.

Hunter was confounded. Was she joking? He decided to tease her, too. "You don't need to ride solo on a bicycle built for two anymore, Faith—you have me now."

She covered her mouth with her hand and giggled. "*Denki*, but I won't be riding my bike anywhere tomorrow—it's *Grischtdaag*!"

"So it is," Hunter sheepishly admitted. Apparently, kissing Faith not only turned his heart inside out, but it turned his brain upside down, and he'd lost all sense of time.

"You're *wilkom* to visit anytime the following day," Faith suggested. The Amish *leit* in their district celebrated Christmas by fasting and worshipping at home with their families and then feasting together in the late afternoon. December 26 was traditionally reserved for visiting friends and extended family, exchanging small gifts and eating treats.

"I'll see you bright and early on the twenty-sixth, then," Hunter promised.

While he enjoyed reading Scripture, singing carols and devouring the meal Ruth was thrilled to be mobile enough to prepare, Hunter was relieved when twilight finally arrived. But once in bed, he tossed and turned. Thoughts of Faith kept him awake. Instead of counting the ticking of the clock, he counted his heartbeats until he'd see her again. It did no good; he still couldn't sleep. He lay awake until almost dawn, and then donned his clothes, grabbed his flashlight and tiptoed outdoors. It had snowed off and on since Christmas Eve, and his footsteps crunched loudly as he made his way toward the stable.

After quietly hitching the horse, he directed it toward the Yoders' house. At the bottom of a big hill, he stopped the buggy, set the brake and cautiously lowered himself onto the ground to trek partway up the incline. His muscles were sore and tight, but after fifteen minutes, he finished his trek and continued in the buggy to Faith's house.

"Hunter!" Faith whispered when she opened the kitchen door. "What are you doing here? The sun isn't even up yet!"

"I said I'd be here bright and early, didn't I? Please, grab your shawl and *kumme* with me. There's something I need to show you."

Faith pursed her lips and shook her head, but she put on her shawl and followed him out the door. Once they were on the road, she asked, "What would you have done if I hadn't been awake?"

"You're a baker. You're always up at this hour," Hunter replied smugly, causing Faith to giggle.

When they reached the bottom of the hill, and he reversed the buggy so they were facing the incline, she asked, "What is it you want to show me? It's too dark to see anything."

"Be patient. You'll find out."

"If I had known we were going to sit out here, I would have brought *kaffi*," she complained good-naturedly. "And a sticky bun."

"*Jah*, I'm hungry enough to eat an entire wreath of them myself."

Faith lifted her hands to her cheeks. "Ach! Speaking of wreaths, I forgot to say *Frehlicher Grischtdaag*!"

"*Frehlicher Grischtdaag*," he echoed as the sun began peeking over the horizon, tinting the snow with a soft orange hue. "There's something else I forgot to say. It might seem premature, but we've been through so much together already and it's something I need to, er, to spell out plainly, so there's no question about it."

Faith tipped her head. "*Jah?*"

Hunter gestured toward the incline on the hill in front of them, where he'd etched the words *I love you, Faith Yoder* in the snow with his boots. When she read it, her face blossomed with pink and she gave him a sideways squeeze.

"I love you, too, Hunter," she declared and nuzzled his cheek.

"Your nose is like an ice cube," he said, chuckling.

"*Jah*, but this cold spell is almost over. It's supposed to get to forty degrees today," Faith replied, sighing. "Which means your message will melt."

"That's alright. I'd rather say the words directly to you than inscribe them in the snow."

"Uh-oh! Did it hurt your legs to tromp about writing that?"

"*Neh*, not really. It's just I prefer whispering 'I love you' because then I'm close enough to do this," Hunter explained softly as he pressed his lips to hers.

She allowed him to kiss her twice before she teased, "*Kumme*, let's go have breakfast. I've been told most people can't do without their morning meal."

"Actually, I was kind of hoping for a treat, maybe a cupcake or…didn't you mention something about sticky buns?" Hunter gibed. As Faith giggled, Hunter picked up the reins with one hand and encircled her waist with the other. The sun had just risen, but it was already one of the happiest days of his life.

Epilogue

When Faith and Hunter were married one week before Christmas the following year, Faith made their wedding cakes: peanut butter sheet cake for the *kinner*, at Andy's request, and pumpkin spice with cream cheese frosting and shaved pecans—in tiers, not rolled—because pumpkin rolls were Hunter's favorite.

"I can't decide between them, so please cut me a sliver of both," Ruth requested after most of the wedding guests had left and the women were in the kitchen, putting away leftovers and doing dishes.

"That sounds *gut*," Iris said. "But I'll serve it—Faith is about to leave."

"That's okay. Hunter is still hitching the buggy," Faith replied. "There's always time for cake!"

"It doesn't appear you've been eating dessert at all lately," Willa commented. "Is that how you lost so much weight?"

"*Neh*, I still have my share of treats, but this past year I've done more biking than usual."

"Even though you don't have to ride to town anymore?"

"*Jah*. You see, when Hunter first returned to Willow Creek, I nearly ran into him on my bicycle built for two. It was still dark, and he blamed me for not having a headlamp. I blamed him for walking in the middle of the lane. Last *Grischtdaag*, we gave each other funny little gifts. I received batteries for my headlamp from him, and he got a reflective vest from me," Faith explained.

Willa wrinkled her forehead. "But how did that help you lose weight?"

"Well, we decided we couldn't let our presents go to waste, so for the past year, we've been biking together after work as often as the weather allows. With my headlamp and Hunter's vest, drivers can clearly see us from the front or behind. Anyway, Hunter's doctor says cycling has been beneficial for his hips, and I guess it's been beneficial for my hips, too!" Faith said.

"Of course, all of this cycling happened *after* she finally admitted they were courting," Henrietta teased. "She tried to keep it a secret, but I knew right away."

Before Faith could deny it, Iris exclaimed, "So did we, right, Ruth?" Ruth's mouth was too full to reply, but she nodded vehemently.

"*Jah*, anyone could see they were smitten with each other," Willa claimed.

"Hunter Schwartz loves Faith Yoder," Ivy chimed in, and the room filled with peals of laughter.

Standing in the entryway, Hunter cleared his throat and grinned. "You're absolutely right, Ivy," he said. "But now that we're married, Faith's name is Faith Schwartz."

Faith's heart thumped to hear him call her that. "I suppose it's time for me to say goodbye," she said to her friends.

One by one, they embraced her. When it was Henrietta's turn, her sister-in-law held on to her extra long. "I'm going to miss visiting you."

"What do you mean?" Faith asked. "You'll still *kumme* see me, won't you?"

"If I'm still *wilkom*. Things change once a woman becomes a wife."

"Perhaps, but I still very much need—and *want*—close relationships with all my female friends and relatives. Especially you, Henrietta," Faith insisted.

Henrietta beamed and hugged Faith again before ushering her and Hunter out the door. Once they were situated in the buggy, he tucked a wool blanket about Faith's lap.

"Denki," she said. Linking hands with him, she leaned her head against his shoulder as they traveled toward town. Just before they turned onto Main Street, she jerked to an upright position.

"Oh, *neh*," she fretted aloud. "In my excitement about our wedding, I forgot to replenish the wood box. We'll freeze!"

Hunter threw his head back and laughed. "Hauling wood upstairs will be my chore from now on, Faith. You're not responsible for doing everything anymore. You've got me."

"I've got you," Faith repeated, resting her head again.

Once inside the apartment, she lit an oil lamp while Hunter started a fire. Turning from the stove, he noticed she was shivering. "You're cold," he said. *"Kumme* here."

As he enveloped her in his arms, she suggested, "One *gut* thing about living in such a tiny apartment is it heats up very quickly."

"Is that a *gut* thing? I rather prefer cuddling for warmth."

Faith tittered. "I have to warn you, it can get pretty hot

up here in the summer, especially with the ovens going in the bakery below."

"If the Lord keeps blessing our shops with success as He's done this past year, by the summer I'll be able to build a house of our own. Something bigger."

"Bigger?" Faith questioned. "I thought you believed big houses were a waste of resources."

"Only if they're excessive. Besides, our house won't be huge. Its size will be practical for both of us and perhaps someday for our *kinner*," he said, pausing to kiss the tip of her nose. "Maybe we can even build it on a plot of land near the creek."

"Oh, I'd like that!" She kissed him back on the lips.

Then he cautioned, "Of course, we'll have to enroll the *kinner* in swimming lessons, so they'll know what to do if they fall into the water by accident."

It made Faith's heart swell to hear him speaking as if their babies had already been adopted or born. "I'm not worried. With the grace of *Gott*, I trust you to keep them safe," she mumbled dreamily, and nestled deeper into her husband's muscular, loving embrace.

* * * * *

SPECIAL EXCERPT FROM

After returning to his Amish community after losing his job in the Englisch world, Aaron King isn't sure if he wants to stay. But the more time he spends training a horse with childhood friend Sally Stoltzfus, the more he begins to believe this is exactly where he belongs.

Read on for a sneak preview of
The Promised Amish Bride *by Marta Perry,*
available February 2019 from Love Inspired!

"Komm now, Aaron. I thought you might be ready to keep your promise to me."

"Promise?" He looked at her blankly.

"You can't have forgotten. You promised you'd wait until I grew up and then you'd marry me."

He stared at her, appalled for what seemed like forever until he saw the laughter in her eyes. "Sally Stoltzfus, you've turned into a threat to my sanity. What are you trying to do, scare me to death?"

She gave a gurgle of laughter. "You looked a little bored with the picnic. I thought I'd wake you up."

"Not bored," he said quickly. "Just…trying to find my way. So you don't expect me to marry you. Anything else I can do that's not so permanent?"

"As a matter of fact, there is. I want you to help me train Star."

So that was it. He frowned, trying to think of a way to refuse that wouldn't hurt her feelings.

"You saw what Star is like," she went on without waiting for an answer. "I've got to get him trained, and soon. And everyone knows that you're the best there is with horses."

"I don't think everyone believes any such thing," he retorted. "They don't know me well enough anymore."

She waved that away. "You've been working with horses

LIEXP0119

while you were gone. And Zeb always says you were born with the gift."

"Onkel Zeb might be a little bit prejudiced," he said, trying to organize his thoughts. There was no real reason he couldn't help her out, except that it seemed like a commitment, and he didn't intend to tie himself anywhere, not now.

"You can't deny that Star needs help, can you?" Her laughing gaze invited him to share her memory of the previous day.

"He needs help all right, but I don't quite see the point. Can't you use the family buggy when you need it?" He suspected that if he didn't come up with a good reason, he'd find himself working with that flighty gelding.

Her face grew serious suddenly. "As long as I do that, I'm depending on someone else. I want to make my own decisions about when and where I'm going. I'd like to be a bit independent, at least in that. I thought you were the one person who might understand."

That hit him right where he lived. He did understand— that was the trouble. He understood too well, and it made him vulnerable where Sally was concerned. He fumbled for words. "I'd like to help. But I don't know how long I'll be here and—"

"That doesn't matter." Seeing her face change was like watching the sun come out. "I'll take whatever time you can spare. Denke, Aaron. I'm wonderful glad."

He started to say that his words hadn't been a yes, but before he could, Sally had grabbed his hand and every thought flew right out of his head.

It was just like her catching hold of Onkel Zeb's arm, he tried to tell himself. But it didn't work. When she touched him, something seemed to light between them like a spark arcing from one terminal to another. He felt it right down to his toes, and he knew in that instant that he was in trouble.

Don't miss
The Promised Amish Bride *by Marta Perry,*
available February 2019 wherever
Love Inspired® books and ebooks are sold.

www.LoveInspired.com

Looking for inspiration in tales
of hope, faith and heartfelt romance?

Check out **Love Inspired**® and
Love Inspired® **Suspense** books!

New books available every month!

CONNECT WITH US AT:

Facebook.com/groups/HarlequinConnection

 Facebook.com/HarlequinBooks

Twitter.com/HarlequinBooks

 Instagram.com/HarlequinBooks

Pinterest.com/HarlequinBooks

ReaderService.com

Love Inspired®

LIGENRE2018R2

SPECIAL EXCERPT FROM

LOVE INSPIRED SUSPENSE
INSPIRATIONAL ROMANCE

Danger has caught up with Ashley Willis, and she'll have to trust the local deputy in order to stay one step ahead of a killer who wants her dead.

Read on for a sneak preview of
Secret Mountain Hideout *by Terri Reed,*
available January 2020 from Love Inspired Suspense.

It couldn't be.

Ice filled Ashley Willis's veins despite the spring sunshine streaming through the living room windows of the Bristle Township home in Colorado where she rented a bedroom.

Disbelief cemented her feet to the floor, her gaze riveted to the horrific images on the television screen.

Flames shot out of the two-story building she'd hoped never to see again. Its once bright red awnings were now singed black and the magnificent stained glass windows depicting the image of an angry bull were no more.

She knew that place intimately.

The same place that haunted her nightmares.

The newscaster's words assaulted her. She grabbed on to the back of the faded floral couch for support.

"In a fiery inferno, the posh Burbank restaurant The Matador was consumed by a raging fire in the wee hours of the morning. Firefighters are working diligently to douse the flames. So far there have been no fatalities. However, there has been one critical injury."

LISEXP1219

Ashley's heart thumped painfully in her chest, reminding her to breathe. Concern for her friend Gregor, the man who had safely spirited her away from the Los Angeles area one frightening night a year and a half ago when she'd witnessed her boss, Maksim Sokolov, kill a man, thrummed through her. She had to know what happened. She had to know if Gregor was the one injured.

She had to know if this had anything to do with her.

"Mrs. Marsh," Ashley called out. "Would you mind if I use your cell phone?"

Her landlady, a widow in her mideighties, appeared in the archway between the living room and kitchen. Her hot-pink tracksuit hung on her stooped shoulders, but it was her bright smile that always tugged at Ashley's heart. The woman was a spitfire, with her blue-gray hair and her kind green eyes behind thick spectacles.

"Of course, dear. It's in my purse." She pointed to the black satchel on the dining room table. "Though you know, as I keep saying, you should get your own cell phone. It's not safe for a young lady to be walking around without any means of calling for help."

They had been over this ground before. Ashley didn't want anything attached to her name.

Or rather, her assumed identity—Jane Thompson.

Don't miss
Secret Mountain Hideout *by Terri Reed,*
available January 2020 wherever
Love Inspired Suspense books and ebooks are sold.

LoveInspired.com

LISEXP1219

LOVE INSPIRED

INSPIRATIONAL ROMANCE

UPLIFTING STORIES OF FAITH, FORGIVENESS AND HOPE.

Join our social communities to connect with other readers who share your love!

Sign up for the Love Inspired newsletter at **LoveInspired.com** to be the first to find out about upcoming titles, special promotions and exclusive content.
